ROBOTS AND ALIENS

ISAAC ASIMOV

You may have noticed (assuming that you have read my robot stories and novels) that I have not had occasion to discuss the interaction of robots and aliens. In fact, at no point anywhere in my writing has any robot met any alien. In very few of my writings have human beings met aliens, in fact.

You may wonder why that is so, and you might suspect that the answer would be, "I don't know. That's just the way I write stories, I guess." But if that is what you suspect, you are wrong. I will be glad to explain just why things are as they are.

The time is 1940...

In those days, it was common to describe "Galactic Federations" in which there were many, many planets, each with its own form of intelligent life. E. E. ("Doc") Smith had started the fashion, and John W. Campbell had carried it on.

There was, however, a catch. Smith and Campbell, though wonderful people, were of northwest European extraction and they took it for granted that northwest Europeans and their descendants were the evolutionary crown and peak. Neither one was a racist in any evil sense, you understand. Both were as kind and as good as gold to everyone, but they knew they belonged to the racial aristocracy.

Well, then, when they wrote of Galactic Federations, Earthmen were the northwest Europeans of the Galaxy. There were lots of different intelligences in Smith's Galaxy but the leader was Kimball Kinnison, an Earthman (of northwest European extraction, I'm sure). There were lots of different intelligences in Campbell's Galaxy, but the leaders were Arcot, Wade, and Morey, who were Earthmen (of northwest European extraction, I'm sure).

Well, in 1940, I wrote a story called "Homo Sol," which appeared in the September 1940 issue of *Astounding Science Fiction*. I, too, had a Galactic Federation composed of innumerable different intelligences, but I had no brief for northwest Europeans. I was of East European extraction myself and my kind was being trampled into oblivion by a bunch of northwest Europeans. I was therefore not intent on making Earthmen superior. The hero of the story was from Rigel and Earthmen were definitely a bunch of second-raters.

Well, Campbell wouldn't allow it. Earthmen had to be superior to all others, no matter what. He forced me to make some changes and then made some himself, and I was frustrated. On the one hand, I wanted to write my stories without interference; on the other hand, I wanted to sell to Campbell. What to do?

I wrote a sequel to "Homo Sol," a story called "The Imaginary," in which only the aliens appeared. No Earthmen. Campbell rejected it; it appeared in the November 1942 issue of *Superscience Stories*.

Then inspiration struck. If I wrote human/alien stories,

Campbell would not let me be. If I wrote alien-only stories, Campbell would reject them. So why not write human-only stories. I did. When I got around to making another serious attempt at dealing with a Galactic society, I made it an *all-human Galaxy* and Campbell had no objections at all. Mine was the first such Galaxy in science fiction history, as far as I know, and it proved phenomenally successful, for I wrote my Foundation (and related) novels on that basis.

The first such story was "Foundation" itself, which appeared in the May 1942 *Astounding Science Fiction*. Meanwhile, it had also occurred to me that I could write robot stories for Campbell. I didn't mind having Earthmen superior to robots—at least just at first. The first robot story that Campbell took was "Reason," which appeared in the April 1941 *Astounding Science Fiction*. Those stories, too, proved very popular, and presuming upon their popularity, I gradually made my robots better and wiser and more decent than human beings and Campbell continued to take them.

This continued even after Campbell's death, and now I can't think of a recent robot story in which my robot isn't far better than the human beings he must deal with. I think of "Bicentennial Man," "Robot Dreams," "Too Bad" and, most of all, I think of R. Daneel and R. Giskard in my robot novels.

But the decision I made in the heat of World War II and in my resentment of Campbell's assumption have stayed with me. My Galaxy is *still* all-human, and my robots *still* meet only humans.

This doesn't mean that (always assuming I live long enough) it's not possible I may violate this habit of mine in the future. The ending of my novel *Foundation and Earth* makes it conceivable that in the sequel I may introduce aliens and that R. Daneel will have to deal with them. That's not a promise because actually I haven't the faintest idea of what's going to happen in the sequel, but it is at least *conceivable* that aliens may intrude on my close-knit human societies.

(Naturally, I repel, with contempt, any suggestion that I don't introduce aliens into my stories because I "can't handle them." In fact, my chief reason for writing my novel *The Gods Themselves* was to prove to anyone who felt he needed the proof, that I could, too, handle aliens. No one can doubt that I proved it, but I must admit that even in *The Gods Themselves*, the aliens and the human beings didn't actually meet face-to-face.)

But let's move on. Suppose that one of my robots *did* encounter an alien intelligence. What would happen?

Problems of this sort have occurred to me now and then but I never felt moved to make one the basis of a story.

Consider—How would a robot define a human being in the light of the three laws. The First Law, it seems to me, offers no difficulty: "A robot may not injure a human being, or through inaction, allow a human being to come to harm."

Fine, there need be no caviling about the kind of a human being. It wouldn't matter whether they were male or female, short or tall, old or young, wise or foolish. Anything that can define a human being biologically will suffice.

The Second Law is a different matter altogether: "A robot must obey orders given it by a human being except where that would conflict with the First Law."

That has always made me uneasy. Suppose a robot on board ship is given an order by someone who knows nothing about ships, and that order would put the ship and everyone on board into danger. Is the robot obliged to obey? Of course not. Obedience would conflict with the First Law since human beings would be put into danger.

That assumes, however, that the robot knows everything about ships and can tell that the order is a dangerous one. Suppose, however, that the robot is not an expert on ships, but is experienced only in, let us say, automobile manufacture. He happens to be on board ship and is given an order by some landlubber and he doesn't know whether the order is safe or not.

It seems to me that he ought to respond, "Sir, since you have no knowledge as to the proper handling of ships, it would not be safe for me to obey any order you may give me involving such handling."

Because of that, I have often wondered if the Second Law ought to read, "A robot must obey orders given it by *qualified* human beings . . ."

But then I would have to imagine that robots are equipped with definitions of what would make humans "qualified" under different situations and with different orders. In fact, what if a landlubber robot on board ship is given orders by someone concerning whose qualifications the robot is totally ignorant.

Must he answer, "Sir, I do not know whether you are a qualified human being with respect to this order. If you can satisfy me that you are qualified to give me an order of this sort, I will obey it."

Then, too, what if the robot is faced by a child of ten— indisputably human as far as the First Law is concerned. Must the robot obey without question the orders of such a child, or the orders of a moron, or the orders of a man lost in the quagmire of emotion and beside himself?

The problem of when to obey and when not to obey is so complicated and devilishly uncertain that I have rarely subjected my robots to these equivocal situations.

And that brings me to the matter of aliens.

The physiological difference between aliens and ourselves matters to us—but then tiny physiological or even cultural differences between one human being and another also matter. To Smith and Campbell, ancestry obviously mattered; to others skin color matters, or gender or eye shape or religion or language or, for goodness sake, even hairstyle.

It seems to me that to decent human beings, none of these superficialities ought to matter. The Declaration of Independence states that "All men are created equal." Campbell, of course, argued with me many times that all men are manifestly *not* equal, and I steadily argued that they were all equal *before the law*. If a law was passed that stealing was illegal, then *no* man could steal. One couldn't say, "Well, if you went to Harvard and were a seventh-generation American you can steal up to one hundred thousand dollars; if you're an immigrant from the British Isles, you can steal up to one hundred dollars; but if you're of Polish birth, you can't steal at all." Even Campbell would admit that much (except that his technique was to change the subject).

And, of course, when we say that "All men are created equal" we are using "men" in the generic sense including both sexes and all ages, subjected to the qualification that a person must be mentally equipped to understand the difference between right and wrong.

In any case, it seems to me that if we broaden our perspective to consider non-human intelligent beings, then we must dismiss, as irrelevant, physiological and biochemical differences and ask only what the status of intelligence might be.

In short, a robot must apply the Laws of Robotics to any intelligent biological being, whether human or not.

Naturally, this is bound to create difficulties. It is one thing to design robots to deal with a specific non-human intelligence, and specialize in it, so to speak. It is quite another to have a robot encounter an intelligent species whom it has never met before.

After all, different species of living things may be intelligent to different extents, or in different directions, or subject to different modifications. We can easily imagine two intelligences with two utterly different systems of morals or two utterly different systems of senses.

Must a robot who is faced with a strange intelligence evaluate it only in terms of the intelligence for which he is programmed? (To put it in simpler terms, what if a robot, carefully trained to understand and speak French, encounters someone who can only understand and speak Farsi?)

Or suppose a robot must deal with individuals of two widely different species, each manifestly intelligent. Even if he understands both sets of languages, must he be forced to decide which of the two is the *more* intelligent before he can decide what to do in the face of conflicting orders—or which set of moral imperatives is the worthier?

Someday, this may be something I will have to take up in a story but, if so, it will give me a lot of trouble. Meanwhile, the whole point of the Robot City volumes is that young writers have the opportunity to take up the problems I have so far ducked. I'm delighted when they do. It gives them excellent practice and may teach me a few things, too.

PROLOGUE

A SYNOPSIS OF ROBOT CITY, BOOKS 1-6

He woke up . . . somewhere.

He didn't know where he was or how he had managed to get there. He didn't remember *anything* of his past.

Not even his name.

He was in some small capsule without windows. He could not even see where he was going.

His awakening had stirred a computer into life, and through its positronic personality he found that he was in a Massey lifepod. A badge on his clothing identified him as Derec—the name seemed to fit as well as anything. The positronic intelligence built into the lifepod could help him with very little; it had no information to aid him at all, not even the name of the ship from which it had been ejected.

The lifepod had landed on an asteroid that Derec quickly found was inhabited by a colony of robots. He seemed to be the only human there. The robots were as little help to him as the lifepod. Strangely silent about their task, they ignored him for the most part. They were obviously looking for something buried in the rock of the asteroid—it seemed to be the only explanation. While he tried to decipher just what it was they were looking for and why, a raider ship appeared.

While the robot colony prepared to self-destruct, Derec made a desperate attempt to escape from the asteroid and contact the raider.

As he was doing so, the raider's bombardment uncovered a shiny silver object, perhaps five centimeters by fifteen centimeters. He would later learn that it was called a "Key to Perihelion." A pursuing robot revealed that this was the object for which the robots were so obsessively searching.

Derec grabbed the Key and jumped. With the power of his augmented worksuit and the almost nonexistent gravity of the asteroid, he reached escape velocity, angling for the raider. But suddenly his faceplate was filled with a glaring blue light, and he was knocked unconscious.

He awoke on the raider ship and was confronted by a strange creature: wolf-like but with fingers instead of paws and a flattened, fur-covered face. The alien's name, as best he could pronounce it, was Wolruf. The creature escorted Derec to Aranimas, the captain of the raider ship, which seemed to be a jumble of half a dozen or more ships welded together in a patchwork maze.

Aranimas was also an alien, a humanoid of the Erani race, and very dangerous. Using a form of electrical prod, he tortured Derec to gain information as to what the robots were doing on the asteroid. Derec, of course, could tell him nothing. Aranimas then ordered Derec to put together a working robot from the salvaged parts from the asteroid and other raids.

Through Wolruf, Derec learned that Aranimas intended to replace the subservient Narwe race (who functioned as Aranimas's crew) with even more docile robots. Derec found that he did indeed seem to know a great deal about robotics; the knowledge came naturally to him. He managed to salvage one positronic brain and enough working parts to create a patch-work robot he called Alpha. The most curious thing about the robot was one of its arms: made of tiny cellular surfaces that seemed infinitely malleable, it could literally shape itself into any form needed. Derec remembered that many of the structures on the asteroid bore that same unique design, and he was filled with a desire to meet the inventor of this new substance.

Aranimas's constant mistreatment of Derec, Wolruf, and the Narwe made Derec determined to escape. With the use of Alpha, he and Wolruf successfully mutinied against Aranimas. They also met another prisoner on the ship, a human female named Katherine Ariel Burgess. Derec recovered the Key to Perihelion, and they escaped Aranimas's ship, landing on a refueling station.

There Derec learned that Kate claimed to know something of his past but stubbornly refused to talk to him about it. He learned too, that she was suffering from some type of debilitating disease herself, and she also refused to talk about that.

The robots on the refueling station had taken the Key to Perihelion, and now it seemed that the bureaucrats who ran the Spacer society were also after the Key. Derec, with Ariel and Wolruf's help, recovered it. Through a mistake, Kate activated the Key while Derec was holding it. In an instant, the two were transported to Perihelion, a cold, formless place of gray fog. Pressing the switch on the Key again, they found themselves on top of a huge pyramidal tower in the middle of a city.

The Compass Tower of Robot City.

They were to find that Robot City was an intriguing

place. The material of which it was composed was shaped like tiny Keys of Perihelion, and the city itself was undergoing constant change. Buildings would appear and move overnight. There was a constant blaze of activity by the millions of robots in the city, who claimed to be preparing this place for human inhabitants, though at the moment, the only humans here were Derec and Kate.

The city was in trouble. Nightly deluges raced through the streets, uncontrollable. Huge lightning storms daily menaced them. And there was a murdered human, a human named David who had looked exactly like Derec. Derec slowly realized that the city—as one robotic entity—was responding to what it considered to be a Third Law threat to its existence. The threat was David's blood; more specifically, the microbes in it. The rainstorms were a byproduct of the city's enormous and uncontrolled growth in response to that perceived threat. To save the city, he reprogrammed the central computer core to deactivate the city's defenses.

At the same time, Kate made an effort to recover the Key to Perihelion, which she had hidden in the Compass Tower. It was gone. She and Derec were trapped here.

They found that the city robots had taken the original Key and were making duplicates of it. In the course of trying to steal one of the Keys, Derec and Kate began to develop a trust for each other.

Kate admitted to Derec that her real name was Ariel Welsh. She was the daughter of a wealthy Auroran patron of the sciences. Her mother had furnished one Dr. Avery the funds to design and build his pet project. Avery was an eccentric, argumentative genius who wanted to create ongoing, self-sufficient cities to seed the stars for humankind.

Avery, though, had disappeared. Robot City, Ariel guessed, was his original experiment, now running without Avery's control. As for Ariel, she had been banished from Aurora because of her incurable disease, contracted from a Spacer. Given a ship and funds by her mother, she'd gone looking for a cure.

It was imperative for her to leave Robot City if she was going to live.

In the meantime, Robot City had acquired another human visitor: Jeff Leong, whose ship had exploded just outside the atmosphere. He was badly injured; to save him, the robots of Robot City turned him into a cyborg: a human brain encased in a robotic body. Insufficient knowledge of the bio-chemical structure of the brain led to Jeff's slow insanity, though otherwise the surgery was a complete success.

Alpha and Wolruf had also made their way to the city via a modified Massey lifepod, big enough for only one human.

With Alpha and Wolruf's help, Derec and Ariel were able to capture the increasingly violent and unstable cyborg. Using Derec's body as a model, the medical technicians of Robot City were able to transplant Jeff's brain back into his own newly healed body. However, he remained ill and largely out of his senses.

Alpha, during the capture of Jeff, had received instructions from the cellular material in his flexible arm ordering the robot to change its name to Mandelbrot. Derec suspected that the arm, from an Avery-style robot, might well have also sent a signal to Avery to return to Robot City.

A choice had to be made: let Ariel take the lifepod and escape, or send Jeff back. Ariel insisted that Jeff must be the one to go.

• • •

Robot City continued its fascinating evolution. Not long after Jeff's departure, the behavior of the robots began to show definitely odd tendencies. Circuit Breaker appeared: a building like two four-sided pyramids stuck together at their bases and balanced on one point. The building, the first work of creative art built by a robot, reflected ever-changing colors as it rotated. Three robots, calling themselves the Three Cracked Cheeks, formed a Dixieland jazz band. All this came about as an effort by the city to formulate what it called the Laws of Humanics—corollaries to the Three Laws of Robotics. The Laws of Humanics were supposed to govern—or at least explain—the actions of human beings as the Three Laws of Robotics governed those of positronic intelligence.

The most serious and unusual event in all the strangeness was that a robot was murdered by another robot. Lucius, the creator of Circuit Breaker, was found with all its positronic circuitry deliberately destroyed, so that the brain could never be reconstructed. It seemed a deliberate attempt to stifle the advances made by the Avery robots.

In the midst of this, Avery himself returned to the city, and Derec, Ariel, Wolruf, and Mandelbrot quickly discovered that the doctor was a dangerous megalomaniac. All that mattered to Avery was his work; he could not have cared less about Ariel's illness or the plight of the others. All that mattered to him was Robot City. He had stationed Hunter-Seeker robots around the area to take all of them prisoner until he could analyze all that had happened here—in whatever way was most convenient to him.

They were taken prisoner, and Derec, unknowingly, was given a dose of chemfets: miniature replicas of the city material that took residence in his bloodstream.

Escaping at last, Derec, Ariel, Wolruf, and Mandelbrot left Robot City on Dr. Avery's ship. There, in a hidden compartment, they found a Key to Perihelion.

It was obvious that Avery anticipated their escape, for the ship was sabotaged. Without the ability to home in on the navigational beacons, they could not program the jumps through hyperspace. Ariel had also taken a definite turn for the worse. Derec decided that he and Ariel must use the Key to Perihelion to try to get help for her. Wolruf and Mandelbrot would remain with the ship and try to complete repairs or attract help from another ship.

Derec activated the Key, and he and Ariel found themselves in an apartment on Earth. They found Earth society paranoid and isolated, with extremely xenophobic attitudes toward Spacers. However, Ariel was getting progressively weaker, and Derec in desperation took her to a local hospital. If Earth was backward in some ways, it seemed that its medical facilities were better than Aurora's. They recognized her disease—amnemonic plague—and cured her.

Unfortunately, the chemfets in Derec's body were asserting their presence, and he was rapidly getting weaker himself. With the help of R. David, an Earth robot, they stole a ship from an Earth spaceport and headed out to rescue Wolruf and Mandelbrot.

Another spaceship followed them: Aranimas, who had tracked the bursts of Key static to Earth. In a tense battle, Derec and Ariel, with Mandelbrot and Wolruf, managed to destroy Aranimas's ship at great cost to their own vessels. They had only one option left to them with Derec growing weaker: use the Key to jump back to Robot City.

• • •

They emerged from the Compass Tower into Avery's vacant office, intending to force the doctor into helping Derec. To find him, Wolruf and Mandelbrot went into the city, while Derec and Ariel began searching the tunnels underneath the tower.

Mandelbrot and Wolruf found that the robots were all following the orders of what they called the Migration Program. They were leaving the first Robot City and seeking new worlds on which to build. And when they returned to Compass Tower, they found that Hunter-Seeker robots were searching for Derec and Ariel, who had fled.

Above the planet, a small spacecraft arrived, carrying Jeff Leong. Back to normal, he was returning to rescue the others. Meeting with Derec and company, he was determined to help them find Dr. Avery.

It was actually Dr. Avery who found them, the Hunter-Seeker robots capturing the company one by one. The Doctor revealed that Derec was actually David Avery, Dr. Avery's son, and that the chemfets in his body would one day allow him to control every Avery robot in existence. Derec would *become* Robot City.

But Avery had believed Derec would be a willing partner in his plans. He was very wrong in that. Derec used his new control of the city to free his companions; Dr. Avery triggered a Key to Perihelion before he could be captured. He fled into the void.

Derec and the others gave no thought to pursuit. At last, they were safe and free to leave.

It seemed reward enough. . . .

CHAPTER 1

BIRTH

"I feel uneasy about this, Dr. Anastasi."

Janet Anastasi glanced up with a half-smile. She brushed blond hair back from bright, hazel eyes cupped in smile lines. "And just how does a robot feel 'uneasy,' Basalom?" she asked with a laugh.

Basalom's eyes blinked, a shutter membrane flickering momentarily over the optical circuits. Janet had deliberately built in that random quirk. She built idiosyncrasies into all her robots—eccentricities of speech, of mannerisms. The foibles seemed to make Basalom and the rest less mechanically predictable. To her, they lent the robots individual personalities they otherwise lacked.

"The term is simply an approximation, Doctor."

"Hmm." She wiped sweat from her forehead with the back of her hand and wiped it on the leg of her pants. "Give me a hand with this, will you, my friend?"

The two were in the cargo hold of a small ship. A viewscreen on one wall showed the mottled blue-and-white curve of the planet they were orbiting. Twin moons peered over the shoulder of the world, and the land mass directly below them was green with foliage. It seemed a pastoral land from this distance, no matter what the reality might actually be. Janet knew that the atmosphere of the world was within terran norms, that the earth was fertile, and that there was life, though without any signs of technology: the ship's instruments had told her that much. The world, whatever the inhabitants might call it, fit her needs. Beyond that, she didn't care.

Her husband of many years ago, Wendell Avery, had said during their breakup that she didn't care about anything made of simple flesh—not him, not their son. "You're afraid to love something that might love you back," he'd raged.

"Which makes us exactly the same, doesn't it?" she'd shouted back at him. "Or can't the genius admit that he has faults? Maybe it's just because you don't like the fact that *I'm* the one who's considered the robotic expert? That's it, isn't it, Wendell? *You* can't love anyone else because your own self-worship takes up all the space in your heart."

His remark had made her furious at the time, but time had softened the edges of her anger. Avery might be a conceited, egocentric ass, but there had been some truth in what he'd said. She'd looked in that mirror too often and seen herself backing away from contact with other people to be with her robots. Surely she'd been content here on this ship for the last few years, with only Basalom and a few other robots for company.

Avery she missed not at all; her son sometimes she missed terribly. Basalom and the others had become her surrogate children.

"Gently," she cautioned Basalom. A spheroid of silvery-gray metal approximately two meters in diameter sat on the workbench before her, its gleaming surface composed of tiny dodecahedral segments. She'd just finished placing the delicate, platinum-iridium sponge of a positronic brain into a casing within the lumpy sphere. Now Basalom draped the sticky lace of the neural connections over the brain and sealed the top half of the casing. The geometric segments molded together seamlessly.

"You can put it in the probe," Janet told the robot, then added: "What's this about being uneasy?"

"You have built me very well, Doctor; that is the only reason I sense anything at all. I am aware of a millisecond pause in my positronic relays due to possible First Law conflicts," Basalom replied as he carefully lifted the sphere and moved it to the launching tube. "While there is no imminent danger of lock-up, nor is this sufficient to cause any danger of malfunction or loss of effectiveness, it's my understanding that humans feel a similar effect when presented with an action that presents a moral conflict. Thus, my use of the human term."

Janet grinned, deepening the lines netting her eyes. "Long-winded, but logical enough, I suppose."

Basalom blinked again. "Brevity is more desired than accuracy when speaking of human emotions?"

That elicited a quick laugh. "Sometimes, Basalom. Sometimes. It's a judgment call, I'm afraid. Sometimes it doesn't matter what you say so long as you just talk."

"I am not a good judge when it comes to human emotions, Doctor."

"Which puts you in company with most of us, I'm afraid." Janet clamped the seals on the probe's surface and patted it affectionately. LEDs glowed emerald on the launching tube's panel as she closed the access.

"What does a human being do when he or she is uneasy, Doctor Anastasi?"

Janet shrugged, stepping back. "It depends. If you believe in something, you go ahead with it. You trust your judgment and ignore the feeling. If you never have any doubts, you're either mad or not thinking things through."

"Then you have reservations about your experiment as well, but you will still launch the probe."

"Yes," she answered. "If people were so paralyzed by doubt that they never did anything without being certain of the outcome, there'd never be children, after all."

As Janet watched, Basalom seemed to ponder that. The robot moved a step closer to the controls for the launching tube; its hand twitched—another idiosyncracy. The robot seemed to be on the verge of wanting to say more. The glimmer of a thought struck her. "Basalom?"

"Yes, Doctor?"

"Would *you* care to launch this probe?"

Blink. Twitch. For a moment, the robot didn't move. Janet thought perhaps it would not, then the hand reached out and touched the contact. "Thank you, Doctor," Basalom said, and pressed.

Serried lights flashed; there was a *chuff* of escaping air, and the probe was flung into the airless void beyond. Basalom turned to watch it on the viewscreen; Janet watched him.

"You never said what your reservations were exactly, Basalom," she noted.

"These new robots—with your programming, so much is left for them to decide. Yes, the Three Laws are imbedded in the positronic matrix, but you have given them no definition of 'human.' "

"You wonder what will happen?"

"If they one day encounter human beings, will they recognize them? Will they respond as they are supposed to respond?"

Janet shrugged. "I don't know. That's the beauty of it, Basalom. I don't know."

"If you say so, Doctor. But I don't understand that concept."

"They're seeds. Formless, waiting seeds coded only with the laws. They don't even know they're robots. I'm curious to see what they grow up to be, my friend."

Janet turned and watched the hurtling probe wink in sunlight as it tumbled away from the ship. It dwindled as it fell into the embrace of the world's gravity and was finally lost in atmospheric glare. Janet sighed.

"This one's planted," she said. She took a deep breath. "Now let's get out of here," she said.

CHAPTER 2

THE DOPPLEGANGER

The probe lay encased in mud halfway down a hillside. The once-silvery sides were battered and scorched from the long fall through the atmosphere; drying streamers of black earth coated the dented sides. Ghostly heat waves shimmered, and the metallic hull ticked as it cooled and contracted. The echoes of its landing reverberated for a long time among the hills.

Inside the abused shell, timed relays opened and fed power to the positronic circuitry of the robot nestled in its protective cradle. The neophyte mind found itself in total darkness. Had it been a living creature, its birth instincts would have taken over like a sea turtle burrowing from the wet sand to find the shimmering sea. The robot had its own instinct-analogue—the Three Laws of Robotics. Knowledge of these basic rules flooded the robot's brightening awareness.

First Law: A robot may not harm a human being, or, through inaction, allow a human being to come to harm.

Second Law: A robot must obey the orders given it by

human beings except where such orders would conflict with the First Law.

Third Law: A robot must protect its own existence as long as such protection does not interfere with the First or Second Laws.

This was the manner in which most of known human space defined the Laws. Any schoolchild of Aurora or Earth or Solaris could have recited them by rote. But to the fledgling, there was one important, essential difference. To the fledgling, there were no *words* involved, only deep, core compulsions. The fledgling had no sense that it had been built or that it was merely a constructed machine.

It didn't think of itself as a robot.

It only knew that it had certain instructions it must obey.

As survival instincts, the Laws were enough to spark a response. Second Law governed the fledgling's first reactions, enhanced by Third Law resonance. There were imperious voices in its mind: inbuilt programming, speaking a language it knew instinctively. The robot followed the instructions given it, and more circuits opened.

An opening appeared in the probe's hull, and the fledgling allowed itself to roll out. The skin of its body shimmered, the myriad dodecahedral segments flexing and shifting as it stretched like warm putty. The robot extruded pseudopods to stabilize the round body. Sensory input was taken in through the skin: optical, auditory, tactile, scent. At the same time, a larger store of basic files was released into the receptive mind: a heavily edited encyclopedia of carefully chosen knowledge. It paused, searching the programming as it absorbed impressions of its surroundings.

A voice whispered.

Move away from the landing site. Beings may come to investigate; they may be aggressive and dangerous. Hide.

Which left the problem: how to move? The positronic brain searched the files and found an answer. The skin molded itself further, the pseudopods becoming muscular legs. The robot scuttled away quickly, moving uphill to a stand of coarse, tall grass. Its round body flattened, the legs retracted; it hunkered down, patient.

As it waited, it inventoried itself dispassionately. The Three Laws overlaid everything else in its mind, but there was more. Most of its programming, and indeed this very self-evaluation, seemed to be manifestations of the Third Law. It must protect its own existence; to survive, it must learn as much as possible.

Underneath the Laws was the layer of initial programming, most of which the fledgling had already followed in the first few minutes of life. Beneath that was a substrate of complex if/then branches. The robot ignored most of those—they all fed back into the Laws in any case.

Only one set of impulses was immediately needed, and that flowed directly from the Laws. *A robot may not harm a human being. A robot must obey the orders given it by human beings*, the Laws insisted. But what was a human being?

The programming gave an answer, not a definition but a description: *A human being is an intelligent lifeform.* So the fledgling, not knowing what a "robot" was other than a term that applied to itself, knew it had to find human beings, to protect and serve them. It had to search out an intelligent lifeform.

It began to formulate a strategy.

The fledgling didn't move; it continued to wait. Intelligence of necessity implied curiosity. An intelligent lifeform in the immediate area would have seen the fiery, noisy descent. It would come to investigate the fall. If no life that met the criterion arrived, then the fledgling would look elsewhere.

The area in which the probe had landed was heavily forested. Tightly packed trees with large, blue-green fronds huddled nearby and surrounded the grassy, hillside meadow. The area was alive with sound now, and the robot could see movement in the twilight under the swaying canopy of leaves. The air was temperate and fragrant with damp earth; the sound of running water trilled not far away. This was a good place, the robot decided. Human beings—whatever they might be—would probably find this location pleasant. Had they come here, they might well have stayed.

Afternoon faded to evening. The robot saw several creatures on the hillside, but none displayed any undue interest in the pod. Once, something with a thin, furred body approached. On muscular hind legs, it stretched out a long, four-fingered hand to touch the pod, and the robot saw a marsupial pouch on its stomach. Though the versatile hand made the robot watch closely, the creature did nothing to reveal more than animal intelligence. It wore no clothing, had no tools, and the robot's sensitive hearing recorded only meaningless grunts from the beast. The marsupial glanced around with wide, scarlet-pupiled eyes, nostril slits flapping on its wide, flat head. Then it went back down on all fours and bounded off. The fledgling decided not to follow. Not yet.

Nightfall came with a surprising quickness after the sun slipped behind the trees; the air temperature dropped as rapidly. The forest settled into relative quiet as the nocturnal creatures woke and began to prowl. The night was well lit.

The larger of the two moons was full; the smaller, at three-quarters, rose not long after full night.

Somewhere under the trees, a series of coughing barks rose, long and highly modulated. The robot began to listen closely as the call came again, slightly changed. Another voice answered the first, shorter and deeper; then yet another, followed by a shivering howl. The intonations were complex and varied, yet obviously from the same species. Already the fledgling had identified repetitive "syllables" in the phrases.

Twin-shadowed creatures moved under the margins of the trees, sleek and fast. The fledgling counted five of them, though more may have been lurking farther back in the forest. One of the pack broke away from the group, moving into moonlight.

The creature was caninoid. At least, it came closest to matching that type in the inbuilt files of the robot's brain. That meant little in itself. There was nothing in the robot's programmed knowledge that said a "human being" could not be canine. Standing on four legs, the animal stood a meter from shoulder to ground, powerfully built and broad-chested. The fur was mottled gray and black, glossy with silvered tips; the head was short-muzzled and round, with a large skull and wide-set, light eyes. The tail was long and furless; it looked nearly prehensile. As the robot watched, the creature howled again as if in challenge, revealing molars set well back behind a double rank of incisors—an omnivore, possibly, not strictly a meat-eater. The front legs ended in a clawed paw, but the toes/fingers were long, separate, and articulated, with a definite closing thumb for grasping. The thick elbow joints seemed capable of a wide range of motion.

It stared at the pod gleaming in doubled moonlight. It

reared up on its hind legs (a female, the robot noted). With a stabbing motion of her front paw, she gestured: a wave.

Moonlight glinted on something on the creature's chest, and the fledgling adjusted its vision to see the thing more clearly: a long, curved fang, hanging on a string of braided vine. *Artifact!* The word screamed in the fledgling's mind, but she continued to wait.

Four others came out of the cover of the trees now, one gray-furred ancient, two adults, and a youngling. They moved swiftly to the sides of the first but carefully stayed behind her. The adults paced, restless. The ancient jabbered: half bark, half growl. The leader shook her head. The old one barked again, and the leader turned with a growl, showing her teeth. She cuffed at the old one, but the raking claws missed as the elder cowered back and lifted her muzzle to bare the throat in submission. The leader turned her back on the others and stared again at the pod. She approached the crumpled metal, snuffling.

She sat before it.

The tail served as support, and its agile tip curled around the back feet. The creature cocked her head to one side then the other. She sniffed again, leaning closer to the pod, then reached out with her left paw. Talons clicked on metal; she tapped the surface, listening to the faint, hollow ringing.

What she did next made synapses open in the robot's positronic mind.

The tail flicked and curled around a small stick on the ground near the pod. The stick was brought up; she took it in her paw, clasping it between the thumb and two fingers. Leaning forward, she placed the tip of the stick under a torn flap of metal and levered up a strand of foil insulation. She pulled it loose and sat back to examine it, letting the stick drop.

Tool use. Coupled with the intricate language, the necklace the leader wore and their curiosity about the probe, that was enough evidence. They were intelligent; that also meant that they were human beings.

With that decision, the unformed body of the fledgling began to take on definite shape, as if unseen hands were molding clay while using the creatures before it as models. First, the basic wolf-like shape, the muscular leanness. The head extruded, rounded, then pushed out the snout of a nose and the flaps of ears. Fixed optical lenses focused in deep-set eye-sockets, colored the same startling ice blue. It could not fully imitate fur, but the surface texture roughened, and the reflective patterns altered so that it displayed a vaguely similar silver-gray and black pattern. After a moment of pondering, the robot also mimicked the secondary sexual characteristics of the leader. The behavior of the leader suggested that scent was an important sense to them. That was simple enough. A quick sampling of the leader's pheromones, and tiny artificial glands secreted an artificial wolf scent.

A gentle breeze was blowing downslope. The leader raised her head suddenly. She went down on all fours, and her lips drew back to bare the dangerous fangs. She growled, staring up the hill to the stand of grass where the robot waited.

The robot stepped out to meet them.

At the same time, without warning, the leader howled and charged.

CHAPTER 3

INITIATE

The wolf-creature's attack was maddeningly swift, but the fledgling's reflexes were still faster. She had no time to retreat, only to react. The Third Law compelled the robot to move so as to protect herself while the First Law stopped her from harming the wolf-creature in return. As the snarling leader leapt toward the robot, the fledgling rolled so that her powerful jaws snapped shut on air, and the claws barely touched the metallic body. Even so, the force of the blow sent the robot flailing in the dirt before she found her balance again.

The fledgling bounded to her feet, turning, but the leader—strangely—hadn't followed up her advantage. Crouching, the wolf-creature bared her teeth once more at the robot and uttered a quick growl that was obviously a command. The Second Law demanded that a human being be obeyed, and the fledgling had made the decision that the creatures were human. Yet without understanding the language, she could only guess as to what was being said.

She remembered how the leader had challenged the old

one in the pack. She patterned her behavior after the ancient's: she bared her throat submissively and backed away.

The ploy worked. The leader sniffed again, growled softly deep in her throat, and turned. She padded down the hill without looking back. Halfway to her followers, she stopped and glared back up the slope to the fledgling, standing motionless under the twin moons. The robot took a step in the leader's direction; the "human" turned once again and continued on down the hill.

The invitation was clear. It seemed more dangerous to ignore her than to follow, so the robot did so, imitating the leader's silent, fluid gait. Once the leader approached the other wolf-creatures again, the pack reformed. The body language and demeanor of the others told the robot that an established pecking order denoted precedence within the pack. There was a well-defined hierarchy in which a newcomer, by all indications, took the lowest rung. Even the juveniles bared teeth as the fledgling approached, and she hung well back as the leader barked commands. The wolf-creatures turned as one and slid quickly back under the cover of moonlit trees.

The fledgling followed closely behind.

Under the trees, the pack moved quietly and furtively. They had obviously been interrupted in the middle of a hunt. Just inside the trees, three young wolf-creatures waited for them. A flint knife hung from each of their necks, and they were yoked to primitive *travois*, long poles of dead branches lashed together with vines. The *travois* held the fragrant, butchered carcasses of dead animals. Each bump caused a cloud of black insects to rise from the meat.

The fledgling stayed with the pack easily; somehow, it felt *right* to be moving this way under the double shadows beneath the slow rustling of the leaves—having decided the wolf-creatures were human, her mind was already adopting their patterns as correct. The youngest of the juvenile carriers slackened his pace not long after they left the clearing of the pod, dropping back until he was abreast the fledgling with his burden. He made an inquisitive soft bark as they ran behind the others; when the fledgling didn't answer, he repeated the sound.

He was obviously waiting for a response, yet the fledgling had no idea what was appropriate. She knew only one language—that of the words inside her head. She could give names to the things she saw around her, could even speak them aloud if she wished. She gave no thought to where that language came from; it simply was.

The problem was translation, to change her language into words these creatures used. She knew that once she got them to talk, she would quickly acquire a vocabulary. The robotic memory would forget nothing it heard; the positronic intelligence would discover syntax and grammar rapidly.

But without input, there was only a void. A void was dangerous to her, and that was anathema to the Third Law. If she understood them and if she could communicate easily, there would be a lessening of danger. She had to make them speak enough for her to start acquiring the knowledge she needed.

The adolescent was waiting for her response, staring at her as he pulled the *travois* through the quiet woods. The fledgling did what her programming decided was the highest percentage action. She imitated the sound the young male had made.

The effect was not what she desired. The youngster glared at her with a rolling of pastel blue eyes, sniffed disgustedly, and increased his speed to put distance between himself and the robot. She let him go.

For a long time, they wound their way through the paths of the forest.

The largest moon had set before the leader came to a halt deep in the forest and several kilometers from the landing site. The forest had gone dark and tangled. Large vines spun leafy webbings from the trees; the underbrush was thick and prickled with thorns. A cold dew frothed the edges of leaves, sparkling in the blue-white gleam of the remaining moon and spilling down on the pack from above. The fur of the wolf-creatures was beaded with it.

The leader prowled the edges of the clearing as the others sat on their haunches, tongues lolling and their breath steaming in the night air. The fledgling imitated them, watching as the leader sniffed the air in evident agitation. The robot sampled the air; there was a faint trace of a bitter animal scent below that of the wolf-creatures and their kill.

Nearby, a mass of tiny white-winged moths spiraled and danced in a shaft of moonlight. A sloth-like animal capered along the pathway of tree limbs, shaking down more of the dew. The forest was almost too quiet. The panting of the pack seemed very loud.

Beyond the clearing came a thrashing of leaves and the sharp crack of a branch breaking underfoot. The bitter smell was suddenly very intense.

The moths abandoned their mad cavort and fled silently.

The leader barely had time to growl a warning.

A nightmare vision burst through the trees nearest the leader. There was a glimpse of red, nearly phosphorescent eyes set in a head that looked as if it had been crushed: wide and flat with an impossibly long jaw bristling with rows of knife-edged fangs, fangs that the fledgling recognized as the same as the one that hung on the leader's necklace. Below, two sets of reptilian, long-fingered claws flailed. The thing moved on thick back legs, larger by far than any of the pack, its stout body armored with beaded hard scales. A muscular tail whipped around it, tearing into the undergrowth.

It saw the pack, shrieked thinly, and charged. A fierce blow of the claws raked the leader's shoulder, and she yelped in dismay. She crouched, ready to attack, but was obviously overmatched.

A blur of motion passed her.

The fledgling had begun to move from the first sight of the apparition, powered by the First Law.

Another robot, patterned after the moral codes of *homo sapiens*, might only have restrained the creature. But the fledgling was already adopting the mental patterns she had seen in her "humans." She was a carnivore, a hunter.

She slammed into the side of the thing as it readied to snap at the leader. Powerful as the beast was, its strength was over-matched by the robot's, and her new form seemed admirably suited to complement her mechanical power. Her teeth clamped down on the beast's arm and twisted savagely. The thing bellowed in pain and reared back.

Still, the creature was too large, too bulky. A flick of its arm threw her off as it roared in fury. The huge mouth opened, giving off a stench of ancient, rotting meat. The beast snapped at the fledgling, but she had already moved. As it turned to find her, she leapt again, this time at the long neck of the beast. She hesitated as her jaws closed around it. But already the others in the pack were attacking. If she hesitated, if she waited any longer, they might be injured.

She put pressure on her jaws and felt the windpipe collapse beneath her crushing jaws.

The beast fell, choking. The rest of the pack swarmed over the body, tearing at it.

All but the leader. Panting, she regarded the fledgling, and there seemed to be little sympathy in her stance. The forepaws were braced, as if she were waiting for an attack. The dark lips were drawn back slightly from the gums to reveal the ivory teeth, and a low, relentless growling came from her throat. The fang at her neck swung softly from side to side.

The fledgling didn't move. It seemed best to stand absolutely still. The leader's icy stare remained on her for long seconds, while the rest of the pack ripped apart the body of the reptilian beast, while they reformed into a ragged line, while the younglings were strapped back into the *travois*.

At last, the old one barked a query. The leader seemed to ponder what had been said. Then her gaze moved away from the fledgling, almost disdainfully. She padded back to the head of the pack and howled. They readied themselves to move on again.

This time, the youngling meat carriers waited for the fledgling to go first. The pack left her a space well up toward the leader. The old wolf-creature moved alongside her. Just before they left the clearing, the old one pointed at the tattered body of the reptile. "*Hrrringa*," he said throatily, then repeated the word.

"*Hrrringa*." The fledgling spoke the strange word, also pointing. Hrrringa: reptile creature.

The old one nodded. His eyes, rheumy and bloodshot, narrowed with pleasure as the pack began to move again.

By the time the pack stopped to sleep in the early morning, the fledgling had learned several more words.

CHAPTER 4

KIN

PackHome.

That was what the old one (the fledgling had learned that his name was LifeCrier) called the cave dimpling a rocky hillside deep in the forest. PackHome was where all litter-kin—those of the same pack—dwelled. The fledgling had picked up a name among the kin herself: she would be known as SilverSide, LifeCrier decided, for her flanks gleamed like the scales of a fish, and like a fish her skin was hard and cold. The name seemed right.

"You killed the *hrrringa*, the SharpFang, and saved KeenEye's life," LifeCrier reminded the robot in KinSpeech. Following KeenEye's lead, the group from the Hunt loped from the cover of trees and started up the long slope to the cave of PackHome. The moons (LargeFace and SmallFace, as the Hunt called them) had spent most of the night chasing one another behind wind-blown clouds. SmallFace peeked out from an opening and spilled light down on the pack.

"The news will spread quickly," LifeCrier continued. "You have status now. Don't bare your throat to any of the kin who weren't on the Hunt. You had the right to challenge KeenEye for leadership of the Hunt; even though you didn't do so, those at PackHome are all lower than you. Let them know your scent, but if one of them acts the superior, challenge them."

"I won't hurt litter-kin," SilverSide said. Already it felt natural to be speaking in their language. She was no longer simply translating from that odd internal vocabulary she'd somehow known from the beginning. "I can't."

LifeCrier let his tongue loll out between time-dulled teeth: amusement. "Don't worry about that. They'll back down and KeenEye has to support you. She owes you a life debt."

SilverSide had spent the last four days with the pack, moving through the forest and resting during the hot, bright days. She had helped them kill, watched them butcher the animals and send the younglings back home when the *travois* were full. She'd listened to them, always learning, as they complained about the lack of prey, as they licked wounds, as they groomed each other, as they talked about old fights and old hunts.

In the four nights SilverSide had spent with the wolf-creatures, she'd learned much of the complex language of the pack. It was a blend of body language, of modulated yelps and whines and barks. There were different modes of speech as well: the formal HuntTongue used between different packs or to stress superiority among litter-kin; an informal KinSpeech used in PackHome or between friends; the simple BeastTalk, which had no words at all but only the high emotional content of the raw animal.

Underlying it all were the strong instincts of the pack carnivore, and the robot was rapidly absorbing that mindset. Already her interpretation of the Three Laws was unlike that of any humanoid positronic intelligence. A robotics engineer would have considered SilverSide dangerously unbalanced; one who knew what she'd done to the SharpFang in the forest and watched her behavior over the last several days would have been certain of it.

SilverSide could already see wolf-creatures crowding the opening to the cave, which glowed green in the darkness from phosphorescent moss the kin gathered and used for light. They yelped greetings to the Hunt in glad BeastTalk, and there were happy cries at the sight of game dragging behind the remaining carriers. KeenEye led the Hunt to the cave opening, then sat on her haunches as the rest of the pack spilled out. She began speaking quietly to two of the other kin.

There were ten or more litter-kin who came from the cave mouth, and SilverSide could hear and smell pups still inside. The ones who stayed in PackHome during the Hunt were the nursing mothers, the infirm, and the very young. Some of them were already taking meat from the carriers and moving it inside. Others greeted mates while the two youngest from the Hunt basked in the obvious adulation of the immature pups.

SilverSide noticed the sidewise glances from KeenEye and the others, the half-disguised scenting in her direction. She sat alongside LifeCrier, just behind KeenEye and out of the press of kin. KeenEye glanced back at her with a hard stare.

"I've told the kin about you," she said in HuntTongue, and there was no kindness in her tone at all. "I've told them that you are to be treated as litter-kin. A place will be made for you in PackHome."

"Thank you," SilverSide replied—a quick bark and a nod of the head. SilverSide made her response as cold and formal as KeenEye's. The Hunt leader sniffed at that, nodded, and padded softly into PackHome.

SilverSide could smell LifeCrier's strange delight at the exchange. "She insults you by using the HuntTongue. You know that?"

"She is the leader," SilverSide answered. "That means I must obey her."

"She's still waiting for you to challenge her. I could almost taste the fear."

"Why would I challenge her?"

"You came from the Void," LifeCrier said. There was an eager lilt in his ancient voice, and he howled softly in Beast-Talk for a moment. "I saw the trail of fire as you fell from the SpiritWorld in the stone egg. You're the OldMother's offspring. You were sent to us, and so KeenEye waits for the spirit of OldMother to move you."

"I do not feel a spirit inside," SilverSide told the old kin.

"You came from the SpiritWorld," LifeCrier said again, as if that fact answered all objections.

"I do not know that, LifeCrier. There is no memory of it in me. I knew nothing before I crawled from the egg. I acted as it felt right to act. I saw KeenEye and the Hunt; it seemed important that I take on your shape."

"That was the spirit of OldMother speaking to you." LifeCrier tilted his graying head and gave a short, excited yip. "You've come as OldMother promised. You're the sign of forgiveness. You're her answer to the WalkingStones, and that's why KeenEye is afraid."

"The WalkingStones? I do not know the word. What are WalkingStones?"

LifeCrier had no chance to answer the robot's query. KeenEye came back out into the night air and trotted directly toward them. Rather than halting as she approached, she continued so that SilverSide and LifeCrier had to give way or be struck. KeenEye sat exactly where SilverSide had been sitting.

"The Hunt must go back out," she said in KinSpeech. "The meat we killed fills barely half the food cave. We wasted time finding the stone egg and SilverSide."

SilverSide said nothing, but LifeCrier gave a short bark of derision. "A waste of time that saved your life," he told KeenEye. "You should thank the OldMother for sending you such a waste."

KeenEye gave a low BeastTalk growl as SmallFace slid back into cloud cover. Her eyes were bright in the gloom, touched with flecks of green from the phosphorus around the cave mouth. The wind ruffled the long fur around her neck and brought the scent of forest. "Had we not gone looking for the egg, perhaps we would never have met the SharpFang and I would not have a life debt to SilverSide. And only an old litter-kin too ancient to sire pups says that OldMother sent the egg. But that doesn't matter. The Hunt has to feed the kin."

"You know that finding SilverSide wasn't the reason the meat was scarce. It's the Hill of Stars and the Walking-Stones—that's what has made the prey scarce, and that's why OldMother sent SilverSide to us." LifeCrier was slipping into HuntTongue, his words and posture becoming more stylized. "I, LifeCrier, say this because the AllSpirit lives in me. I will not let KeenEye deceive the litter-kin."

KeenEye snarled, showing her teeth. "Do *you* want to challenge me, old one? Do you want to lead the Hunt your-self? Fine, I'm ready."

Others of the litter-kin were filling the cleared area around the cave mouth, watching silently. SilverSide could scent the tension. Her senses were almost hyper-aware, driven by First Law programming that translated as a feeling of uneasiness. She readied herself to move, to come between LifeCrier and KeenEye if they began to fight.

But LifeCrier shook his grizzled head. "The AllSpirit told me that I was to speak the history of all kin, not lead the pack, KeenEye. That's why I am LifeCrier. I've no interest in challenging you. If you wish, I'll submit now." With that, LifeCrier lifted his head so that the throat was exposed to KeenEye. For a moment, the tableau held, KeenEye quivering on the edge of attack and SilverSide ready to intercept the leader's rush.

But KeenEye did nothing. Slowly, LifeCrier let his muzzle drop. His demeanor was haughty, knowing that he'd won this confrontation. "SilverSide is the gift of the OldMother," he declared loudly so that all the others could hear.

"The truth of that remains to be seen," KeenEye grumbled.

"Haven't the WalkingStones taken the lives of kin? Haven't they driven the prey from the forest around them? Haven't we seen pups starve and mothers' milk become thin? Haven't OneEye's and ScarredPaw's packs warned us not to enter their territory, knowing how desperate we are?"

"Yes," KeenEye admitted, "but that says nothing about SilverSide."

"I know the old tales—I had them from the old LifeCrier, as he had them from the one before him on down through time. The spirits of kin past live in me. I know what I know." Again, LifeCrier began using the HuntTongue as if reciting a litany. "I saw the fiery egg leave a trail across the Void to lead the Hunt. When SilverSide revealed herself, we could all smell the scent of litter-kin. The AllSpirit woke in me as I tasted it."

LifeCrier rose up on his hind legs, pointing with a forepaw over the treetops to the west. "Look, we've seen the Hill of Stars from PackHome for ten Dances. Doesn't the sight of it make the fur rise on your back?"

Silverside looked to where the old one had pointed. Faintly, through the swaying foliage, she could see a triangular shape a long distance away. Its dim bulk was pricked with lights as bright as the stars. She adjusted her vision, bringing the thing into sharper focus. Unwinking rectangles of yellow light were set in a dark pyramid of stone. *Artifact.* There was no translation for that word in the language of kin. *Artifact.*

The vision filled her with a need to know more.

"The old tales have muddled your head," KeenEye was telling LifeCrier.

"The old tales begin to seem too much like now, I'd say instead," LifeCrier answered, and there was a soft rumble of agreement from the kin around them. "It is as if GrayMane walked again."

SilverSide tore her attention away from the sight of the Hill of Stars. "Who is GrayMane?" she asked. At that, KeenEye sniffed laughter.

"So OldMother's supposed offspring doesn't know the old tales," she spat. "I know them all too well. And I've little enough time to spend in PackHome to listen to them again." With a shake of her head, she rose and went into the cave. Most of the kin followed her, but a few remained behind on the ledge.

"Who is GrayMane?" SilverSide asked again.

LifeCrier had watched KeenEye's departure. Now he turned back to SilverSide and nodded. "I will tell you," he said formally. Raising his muzzle, he gave a long, mournful howl.

CHAPTER 5

LIFECRIER'S TALE

Listen, oh Kin! (LifeCrier began). Gather here and listen.

I speak of a time before time.

I speak to the spirits that live in you so they too will listen and know that we haven't forgotten them.

I speak of the ending days before the One Great Pack splintered.

In that long, last winter, two kin of the Final Litter, sister and brother, came to be possessed by their ancestor spirits. GrayMane was taken by the spirit of the OldMother (may Her name be praised), and, with the wisdom of the Old-Mother, she became the first of us to speak the language of the Kin. SplitEar, her brother, was taken by the spirit of the FirstBeast, and thus he spoke no language at all.

This is the way of things, my kin. Both GrayMane and SplitEar wished to rule the Great Pack. Litter-kin though they were, no two kin were less alike than GrayMane and SplitEar. SplitEar was strong and vital. He was the largest and most powerful of the hunting males, and the savage instinct of the FirstBeast rode easily in him. No other of the pack challenged his right to lead the Hunt.

None except his sister GrayMane.

GrayMane didn't have SplitEar's hunting skills. Her nose wasn't as keen to follow the scent of the prey, her eyes weren't as piercing in the darkness under the trees, her body wasn't as large or as powerful.

Still, her soul was like that of a crystalline rock, unbreakable. GrayMane's challenge of SplitEar was a horrible struggle, and many in the Great Pack believed the two would kill each other before one of the two submitted. Their fight on that fateful night lasted from the rising of SmallFace to its setting, and their growling could be heard throughout the lost caves of that first PackHome.

But at last GrayMane realized that she was overmatched. Her brother must win, and so she bared her throat to him. SplitEar howled his triumph to LargeFace as the strongest have always howled, and GrayMane slunk away to lick her terrible wounds. When SplitEar led the hunters out, GrayMane stayed behind watching enviously with the pups, the nursing mothers, and others in the pack too weak to hunt.

So it was for two Dances of the moons. The Great Pack was a wonder, my kin, even then at the end of its time. The Hunt was a glorious vision, with thousands of kin flowing like quick gray shadows under the trees. PackHome was a vast network of caverns bigger than the forest in which we live now, and each litter mother had her own place within it. The instincts of the SpiritPack drove them, and even without the OldMother's gift of words, the kin had become most favored of all creatures. Of all the beasts of the world, there were none more feared.

Now listen to me, for we come to the crux. The nights of the One Great Pack were passing quickly. The Hunt was failing, even as our hunt fails us now. The kin had become too numerous for the land to support; they had preyed too long in the same area. SplitEar had to lead the Hunt farther and farther from PackHome, and few carriers came back from the Hunt bearing meat for GrayMane and the thousands of others.

The forest then was far more dangerous. Huge Sharp-Fangs, larger and more cunning than the one killed by SilverSide, lurked in the tree gloom. In times before, they had left the kin alone unless they found a straggler from the Hunt or came on a pup wandering in the forest. But now, with the prey animals killed or driven far away, the SharpFangs had only the kin to eat. Maddened by hunger, they hunted the kin as the kin hunted their own food, not caring for their losses.

A large group of SharpFangs followed the Hunt. During the brightness when the hunters slept, they would attack every day. Without speech, SplitEar and the hunters couldn't act as kin do now, helping each other and coordinating their defense. By the time the third moondance was done, SplitEar had lost a full half of the Hunt and had to return to PackHome.

SplitEar feared that he'd find there only the bones of the rest of the kin. The spirits in him knew that the end had come for the One Pack. The time had come for the Splintering.

During the nights of the long Hunt, GrayMane had done as the OldMother commanded and taught the kin left at PackHome the gift of speech. The wisdom of the OldMother was never more needed.

For SplitEar was right. The SharpFangs *did* rage from

the forest to attack PackHome, and GrayMane led the kin against them. Armed with words, able to warn each other and arrange their defenses, the kin killed several of the beasts and sent the rest fleeing back into the forest. Though their own losses were still grievous, they survived. The kin praised GrayMane and the OldMother with their new speech.

So it was that when the stragglers of SplitEar's Hunt returned to PackHome at last, they found not bones broken and licked clean of marrow, but the heads of dead SharpFangs hung on poles as warning. GrayMane and the others came out to meet SplitEar. When they saw how few had returned, they howled their lament to the moons.

"How could this have happened?" GrayMane asked SplitEar. SplitEar could smell the pride in GrayMane, for she had defended PackHome well and knew it. But SplitEar couldn't understand the words GrayMane spoke and so could not reply.

Now, as all kin know, OldMother and FirstBeast have always been at odds, even in the Void. FirstBeast roused a jealousy in SplitEar so that he believed GrayMane was challenging him once more. With a terrible growling, he threatened GrayMane. She cowered back.

"There is no challenge here, SplitEar," she told him. "I beg of you, litter-kin, let us become friends. Let me teach you the OldMother's speech so we can plan for the good of the pack."

The spirit of FirstBeast made SplitEar angrier yet, and he rushed at his sister. She bared her neck immediately to him, but FirstBeast's rage made SplitEar brutal, and he ripped the throat from her.

The earth drank GrayMane's blood as the spirit of OldMother wailed.

"All kin are *cursed*!" OldMother cried as her spirit fled

from GrayMane. Her fearsome shape hung before the cowering kin, blackening the sky, and her eyes like fire burned them. A raging wind howled and shrieked around her, and dark thunderclouds were her fur.

"The One Pack will now be scattered and diminished. You have thrown away my gift like dumb animals. Now I throw away my protection. You shall howl like the stupid animals you are and not understand one another. Before any kin remembers my gift again, a thousand Great Dances will pass. I will teach others who will listen before you. I tell you, the kin will hear stones speaking before I forgive you."

The AllSpirit heard OldMother's curse and thus it came to be. Those of the kin who had learned to speak were afraid of SplitEar's anger and so remained silent. SplitEar would not lead the kin away from PackHome. The Hunt returned to the forest but found little food, and the SharpFangs returned. SplitEar himself was killed in one such attack, and PackHome was overrun. The beasts cracked the bones of kin and licked them clean. Those who survived fled into the woods—like animals they ran, splitting into small packs of litter-kin.

So it was that the time of the One Pack came to an end.

CHAPTER 6

THE HUNT

"So you think I am GrayMane returned again?" SilverSide said after LifeCrier had finished the tale.

"I do," LifeCrier answered emphatically, still speaking in the formal HuntTongue. "You have come to lead us back to the time of the Great Pack. Can you deny it, SilverSide? Can you say with certainty that I am wrong?"

The robot searched her memory. There was nothing there that directly *contradicted* the possibility, improbable as it might seem. Beyond the moment of her awakening in this place and the erratic store of knowledge she'd been given, there was nothing. Yet . . .

"I can't," SilverSide answered truthfully, as she had to. She shook her head. "I don't know."

"You told me that you were formless as the Void itself when you came. You said that when you saw us, you felt compelled to change your shape so that you looked like us."

"That is true."

"Then what I've said is also true," LifeCrier answered triumphantly, and gave a joyous howl that many of the others joined with. "You've been sent because of the WalkingStones and the Hill of Stars. I know it, SilverSide. I know it as I know the old tales. You're the sign that the OldMother has forgiven us."

SilverSide was troubled. The delicate balance of the Three Laws shifted in her mind, weighing priorities. "Perhaps," she said again. "Possibly. I don't know, LifeCrier. I cannot answer you. I don't know."

SilverSide glanced back at PackHome. KeenEye sat on her haunches at the entrance to the cave, limned in the glow of the moss. The smell of woodfires smoke-preserving the meat in the cold caves was strong in the night. KeenEye stared at SilverSide and the gathering of kin around her, and there was a distinct menace in her gaze. SilverSide knew that if she tried to brush past KeenEye into PackHome, there would be a challenge. Here and now, with no way to back out of it.

First Law imperatives made her turn aside instead, though she hesitated.

With the kin watching, she padded away toward a trail that led to the top of the hill. As she moved away, KeenEye stirred and called after her.

"The Hunt will go out again tomorrow," the leader said in commanding HuntTongue. "You will join us again instead of staying behind at PackHome."

The robot looked back. The Second Law was clear here: KeenEye was a human *and* the leader. "As you wish," she said.

KeenEye nodded. Her eyes glinted, her lips lifted above her incisors. She gave a low BeastTalk growl and settled down in front of the entrance.

SilverSide turned away from the other kin and continued on. She spent the rest of the night alone at the summit of the hill, staring at the moons and the Hill of Stars in the distance. She pondered all that LifeCrier had said and mused over the differences between herself and the kin.

If there was an OldMother, as LifeCrier insisted, She said nothing to SilverSide that night.

KeenEye said nothing to the robot when she came down from the hilltop in the first light of morning.

LifeCrier was as friendly as ever, but the other kin were less eager than they had been the night before, sensing the unresolved conflict with KeenEye. Where LifeCrier came up to her eagerly, his tongue stroking her face in the greetings of kin, the rest of the wolf-creatures hung back. Though they made way for her as they would have for any higher-status kin, they said very little to her unless she spoke first.

SilverSide's behavior didn't help things. At full light, KeenEye ordered the meat to be dragged from the storage caves for the communal meal. The kin gathered in the largest of the caves, sitting down in a large ragged circle, the pups running in and out among the adults. Smoke-preserved flanks passed from hand to hand.

SilverSide declined her portion.

"I don't eat," she said to the startled adolescent who handed the robot her share. It was only the simple truth—SilverSide hadn't even thought it strange. It simply *was*—a fact that somehow she knew. "I cannot even if I wished. It is not necessary for me."

But she heard the BeastTalk grumbling and speculation from some of the others. "You see, KeenEye?" LifeCrier had said. "She is part of the Void, not of the earth. She is full of the spirit of the OldMother."

KeenEye responded with a howl of irritation. "Give her nothing, then, if she insists on playing the OldMother," the leader barked. "And if she hasn't the strength for the Hunt because of it, let the SharpFangs have her." KeenEye growled and stalked from the cave herself, smelling of anger and resentment.

The rest of the day, all the kin but LifeCrier avoided her, though she'd felt them watching and sniffed their uncertainty. Watching and wondering.

The Hunt left PackHome in the early evening, after the heat of the day had subsided and the sunlight turned to evening's gold-green. This time, none of the other kin would place themselves ahead of SilverSide. She was second in the ragged line of kin that trotted down the hill into the green, scent-filled forest.

PackHome was quickly lost behind a screen of foliage and the Hunt was immersed in the sights and scents of the forest. Birds were beginning to settle in their roosts for the coming night; quick shadows flitting through the branches. Smaller animals scuttled through the underbrush as the pack moved quickly past. KeenEye led them into the glow of the setting sun, and SilverSide wondered at that—the perfect recall of her robotic mind could not forget LifeCrier's remark that the WalkingStones, whatever they were, had driven away the game near the Hill of Stars.

Yet KeenEye padded unerringly in that direction. Once one of the younger kin had questioned KeenEye's path, and the leader had simply turned with a BeastTongue growl that sent the adolescent into submissive silence.

After that, there was no more conversation within the pack at all. They followed KeenEye silently along the winding game trails.

Had SilverSide been human or even kin, she might have marveled at the sights, scents, and sounds of the forest. She might have gaped at the papery pods the size of a youngling dangling from vines and wriggling with some gelatinous interior life. She might have stopped to sniff the perfumed sap oozing up from below a rocky slope. She might have been startled by the shrill rasp of tall weeds that were moving though there was no wind. She might have been captivated by the assorted small animals that leaped across the path or watched as the kin loped quickly by.

Her positronic brain saw it all but without passion. She cared only for that which affected the intricate balance of the Three Laws. She noted that although the small life was abundant, there were few signs of the larger creatures that were food for the kin. She noted the growing apprehension of the pack as KeenEye continued westward.

That resonated with the Laws.

She saw how LifeCrier and the others watched her, waiting to see what the spirit of the OldMother would do, and she wondered if—just maybe—these priorities she felt were a reflection of a goddess's will. Her logic circuits snickered at the thought but couldn't entirely banish the possibility.

The weight of possible danger, tweaking the First Law, nudged SilverSide into speech. She lengthened her stride, moving alongside KeenEye. She used careful KinSpeech, not wanting KeenEye to feel formally challenged. "I've heard LifeCrier and the others say that the meat animals have all left because of the WalkingStones. Is that true, KeenEye?"

"The OldMother didn't bother to tell you?"

"No," the robot answered. Then, when KeenEye said nothing further: "Is it true?" she asked again.

A nod. "You have a problem with that?" KeenEye would not look at her. She continued to trot, her red tongue lolling out between the knives of teeth.

The leader was leaving SilverSide no opening for further

questions, forcing the confrontation she was obviously expecting.

SilverSide hesitated. At last she dropped back into the pack again.

They continued on.

By midnight, the pack was very near where the Hill of Stars had glowed the night before. There was an odd silence in the woods, as if most of the creatures that normally lived here had gone. The very silence nudged SilverSide again.

She did what none of the kin would have dared to do. The decision was simple; the reasoning complex.

By deliberately failing to define "human," by not even telling the robot that it *was* a robot, Janet Anastasi had forced upon her robot an unusual freedom of action and a liberal interpretation of the Three Laws. She'd made a construct that didn't consider itself mechanical.

She would likely have been pleased with what the robot had done so far, with SilverSide's "creativity."

But SilverSide was still bound to the Laws. The Second Law demanded that she obey humans, and she had accepted the wolf-creatures as "human." In a pack society, the leader spoke for all; therefore, KeenEye's commands must carry more weight than that of any of the other kin.

Yet the First Law demanded that she protect human life, and logic led her to favor the many over the few. If KeenEye was indeed leading the pack into danger, the First Law demanded action. Yet she'd already seen that the very lifestyle of the kin involved danger—the SharpFangs, the leadership challenges within the pack, the scarcity of food. One could not be "human" and avoid danger. That damped the strength of the First Law.

She had to know more. She might not be forced to action, but she *was* compelled to ask.

She ran swiftly in front of the leader. For a moment, SilverSide thought that KeenEye would simply ignore her and shoulder past, and the balance within her shifted again. But KeenEye drew up short. The pack came to a ragged halt behind KeenEye. SilverSide could smell their anticipation.

"If the kin need food, what good does it do us to go west?" She used HuntTongue, stressing the importance of her question.

KeenEye gave her only a low BeastTalk rumble deep in her throat. She glared and sat back on her hind legs, the clawed forepaws threateningly ready.

KeenEye was not going to answer the question, SilverSide realized. But then LifeCrier pushed his grizzled muzzle forward and yapped support. "SilverSide asks the question we all have, KeenEye."

KeenEye looked back at the line of kin. They were staring back, quiet and very intent. SilverSide knew that the leader saw the subliminal challenge there. Most of the kin had gathered around LifeCrier, saying nothing but lending their unvoiced support to his question.

Frost blue eyes turned back to SilverSide. "Do you challenge me now, SilverSide? Is that what the OldMother tells you?" she asked.

"There is no food," SilverSide said. "The forest here is empty of all the meat animals. That's why I spoke."

"You don't even eat the meat. Why should you care?"

SilverSide searched within her mind. "I must do what is best for all kin."

"That is the *leader's* task." KeenEye growled for emphasis. "*Only* the leader's task."

Balances changed again.

The robot had no doubt that it was more intelligent than any of the kin. She *knew* things, whether inborn memory or the OldMother's gift. She could see a hundred ways to improve the life of the kin. She was also physically stronger than any of them, and she could change her shape if need be.

More intelligent. Stronger. The chosen of the OldMother. All that, coupled with KeenEye's insistence on coming here, spoke through the Laws.

The decision clicked in her mind, firm and certain. SilverSide could best obey the laws in her head by leading the pack.

"I challenge you, KeenEye," SilverSide said in Hunt-Tongue.

KeenEye seemed to sigh. Her eyes closed as if in momentary prayer. "As you wish," she said.

The wolf-creature came at SilverSide in a snarling rush, her jaws wide open to rip at the robot's throat. But SilverSide, with the superb reflexes Janet Anastasi had given her, was no longer there. She moved back on her hind feet and turned, sliding aside just enough so that KeenEye's momentum took her past her. SilverSide reached out and shoved KeenEye as she tried to turn. KeenEye nearly crashed headlong into a tree, falling and rolling hard. The leader bounded to her feet quickly, but there was a dazed glassiness in her eyes.

KeenEye stood two-legged, howled at SilverSide, and leaped, fingers out to claw the robot.

This time SilverSide allowed KeenEye to strike her. Claws scraped on her metal flanks without leaving a mark. KeenEye howled in anger, frustration, and pain, and raked at SilverSide again, trying for the eyes. They were vulnerable, if her skin was not. SilverSide flinched.

Rearing back, SilverSide blocked the curving blow and grabbed KeenEye's hand/paw, twisting the joint. KeenEye screeched, though SilverSide was careful not to break any bones. Slowly, she forced the wrist backward—as KeenEye thrashed to get free, as she spat at the robot, as she clawed with her free hand. Nothing she did seemed to hurt the robot. SilverSide was far too strong for the wolf-creature.

SilverSide forced KeenEye down to the grass and pulled her over on her back.

"Submit," she whispered to the leader, and it seemed the others heard an odd sympathy in her voice. She did not seem happy in her victory.

"Kill me," KeenEye grunted back, her lips bared over her fangs. She snapped uselessly at SilverSide. "I will not submit. Kill me."

SilverSide put more pressure on the hold. Ligaments groaned. "Submit," she said again. "I need you to help me, and you are useless to the pack dead. Give me your throat."

The defiance went out of KeenEye. The paw was limp in SilverSide's grasp. KeenEye tilted her muzzle back in submission.

Yet even as SilverSide stood in triumph over KeenEye, there was a crashing of underbrush behind her and a screech of pain from one of the kin.

First Law reaction whirled SilverSide around as a youngling was hurled through the air to fall near SilverSide. He rolled on the ground bleeding from a deep gash in his side and yelping in pain.

"A WalkingStone!" LifeCrier shouted. "Beware!"

SilverSide's lips drew back in a BeastTongue snarl.

Standing over the wounded kin was the apparition that had just burst through the trees. It stood on two legs, its hands clenched into fists encased in a shiny metal skin. It was far larger than any of the kin, and if what it had done to the youngling was an indication, it was immensely strong. Behind the featureless head, SilverSide could hear motors whirring softly.

It smelled of lightning and stone.

The head swiveled. The apparation seemed to regard SilverSide strangely.

Then, with a swiftness that surprised her, it charged!

CHAPTER 7

A FIGHT

The pack was milling in confusion. LifeCrier howled a lament for the downed youngling as those in the direct path of the WalkingStone scattered. Only SilverSide was immune to the panic.

She could only respond as the Laws allowed her, and the First Law left her no choice.

She lunged forward, slamming herself hard into the chest of the constructed *thing* that had attacked the kin without warning. There was no hesitation to her action at all—it was a pure First Law response to protect the life of "humans."

Her jaws closed on an unyielding metallic arm; with a strength equal to her own, the WalkingStone flung SilverSide away. She rolled to soften the impact, allowing her body to deform to absorb the shock.

She whirled back to attack.

LifeCrier and KeenEye had rallied the others. All but the carriers tethered to the *travois* formed a ragged circle around the injured youngling, protecting him from the Walking-

Stone. They snarled and snapped, making quick thrusts of their own but staying out of range of the powerful arms.

The WalkingStone had stopped, pointing a finger at the pack. SilverSide, in motion, saw the fingertip become round and a dark opening appear at its apex.

Weapon! The word screamed in SilverSide's head.

"KeenEye!" she shouted. "Scatter!"

She hurled herself at the WalkingStone's extended arm.

Metal clashed against metal. A line of searing, intense light cut a crazy swath harmlessly through foliage as Silver-Side's rush knocked the WalkingStone's arm aside. The kin yelped and retreated again.

Gears whirred menacingly inside the WalkingStone. The smell of it made SilverSide snarl. The featureless, impassive face turned toward SilverSide, who faced it defiantly. Deliberately, the WalkingStone pointed its deadly, laser-tipped finger at her. The aiming beam tracked brilliant red across her body; the skin glowed white just behind. The ferocious heat translated as pain to SilverSide's positronic brain; the "human" responses overlaid there made her yelp in response though the tough metal alloy was only scorched, not yet melted. Still, the attack disrupted circuitry to that side of her body.

She went down.

The WalkingStone turned its attention back to the pack, now huddled in a knot around the youngling "SilverSide?" LifeCrier called, her fear-scent strong. "What do we do?"

SilverSide tried to answer. Nothing happened. Her vocal circuits were temporarily gone as well.

KeenEye and LifeCrier tried to rally the kin.

The pack had its own peculiar method of fighting, as SilverSide had seen before on their way from her Egg to PackHome. She knew what KeenEye's command barks said.

"Circle. Keep moving. Keep the WalkingStone busy, but don't let it touch you." A SharpFang would have been dealt with in much the same way, the pack whirling around it like a clawing, biting tornado, dashing in behind to nip at ankles and then leaping back, harrying the creature until— exhausted and frustrated—it gave them a fatal opening. Then they would swarm in as one and bear it down.

Such tactics gave the kin the ability to deal with carnivores far larger and stronger than themselves.

Such tactics were horribly ill-suited for their current foe.

It required no effort for SilverSide to picture what would happen if the WalkingStone used its laser on any of the kin. The urgent First Law need to respond drove everything else from SilverSide's mind.

With the left side of her body still shut down, there was only one possibility. With *anything* fashioned to resemble a living creature, the joints—neck, elbows, knees—are the most fragile area. SilverSide knew that: as a shapechanger herself, structural dynamics were part of her core knowledge. Her malleable body shifted, altered. The mostly immobile left side she rounded as best she could; everything else she metamorphosed into a massive, coiled muscle.

She gathered herself. Aimed.

Leapt.

Metal boomed against metal like a thunderclap.

The WalkingStone's neck was stabilized with supports, but none were designed to withstand the tremendous hammer blow SilverSide represented. There was a screech and a wail of stressed steel. Welds popped as the head was suddenly canted at an acute angle. The glowing eyes dimmed. The thing staggered, the laser fired wildly and high. Its knees buckled, it seemed to wheeze mechanically.

It fell.

As it fell, SilverSide heard its voice in her head. Oddly, SilverSide understood it, for the thing spoke in the language she'd been born with. *Central, under attack, badly damaged and shutting down. . . .* The voice trailed off. None of the kin looked as if they'd heard it.

SilverSide had fallen herself, resuming her wolf shape. As her body cooled, control returned. She managed to limp slowly to her feet, and stood on her hind legs over the fallen WalkingStone. It twitched spasmodically, but seemed no threat. Its mental voice was silent. As SilverSide watched, a plume of thin, acrid smoke came from the broken neck, and all movement stopped.

SilverSide lifted her muzzle and gave a BeastTalk howl of triumph as she'd seen the other kin do after a kill. The others howled with her.

LifeCrier and KeenEye padded over. Both groveled in front of SilverSide, baring their necks in ritual submission. "You are the Bane of WalkingStones," LifeCrier declared. "You saved our lives and the lives of all the kin here."

"Yes," SilverSide answered. It was not immodesty; it was simply truth.

KeenEye rose, her eyes unreadable. "I was wrong," she said. "What LifeCrier said of you is true. You are the wisest of us. You are the OldMother's gift." She paused "You are now the leader of kin."

"Yes," SilverSide said.

The decision echoed in all her judgment circuits. "Yes, I am," she repeated.

CHAPTER 8

A HURRIED DEPARTURE

The hard thing under his cheek seemed to be a foot. It was attached to a very smooth and shapely leg, and at the top of the leg ...

"Derec," a woman's sleepy contralto said warningly from farther down the bed. A warm breath tickled his shin. "I'm very, very cross when rudely awakened."

"You don't like it?"

Ariel wriggled under his attention. "It's not ..." she breathed, then sighed. "I'm just tired."

"Too tired?"

She gasped. "Oh, you ..." In a flurry of bedcovers, she whirled around. Her mouth touched his. She rolled him on his back.

Much later, they snuggled together. Derec reached out from the cover to touch the contact that caused the wall of the bedroom to become one-way transparent. Though in the middle of Aurora's largest city, there was nothing to be seen but green, open expanse. They looked out over an expanse of a lush rolling meadow, crowned with a stand of magnificent trees. The orange-red sun of Aurora slashed through the branches, wedges of light outlined in a miasma of morning fog.

A native whose whole life had been spent on the planet might have shrugged—beautiful Auroran sunrises were commonplace enough to have become the norm—but in the year since Derec and Ariel had been on the planet, they hadn't yet become blasé. They gazed at the display as if the awakening world had arranged it strictly for their benefit.

"It's very lovely," Ariel whispered.

"Like you."

"Flatterer."

"Will it get me anywhere?"

"We'll see. Maybe. A little later, anyway."

"There's no reason to wait."

"Greedy this morning, aren't we? Well, you'll just have to cultivate a little patience."

Ariel kissed him again and rolled from the bed. With a lithe grace, she moved across the room. She'd recovered entirely from her ordeal in Robot City, or at least it seemed that way. The disease that had warped her personality had been cured, her injuries healed. She had left Robot City and returned to normal.

But not Derec. The chemfets—tiny viral replicas of the Robot City material developed by his father, Dr. Avery—had been implanted in Derec. Though he'd gained control of the chemfets after they'd threatened to take him over, the ordeal had left him permanently linked to the city. Even now he could, if he wished, listen to the inner conversations in his body and hear the sounds of the Robot City central computer, across light-years of distance. He could give the city orders, direct the actions of its myriad robots, alter its programming. . . .

Derec did not enjoy playing god, no matter how minor a one. He didn't enjoy being shackled to his father's mad creation. He especially didn't enjoy the fact that he didn't yet know the full extent of that inner universe.

They were still chained to Avery, even now. Their return to Aurora and the tale of Robot City had made news everywhere on that world. They were celebrities. Even now, they could not go out in the public areas of the city without someone coming up to them.

The thoughts drove away his good humor. He looked out at the Auroran dawn and suddenly saw nothing. The dawn might as well have been a computerized image projected on a wall. He sighed.

"I know that look," Ariel said from the open door of the personal. "You're brooding again."

"No, I'm not."

"You are too. I've been with you too long not to know. You're thinking about Robot City again."

There was an edge to her voice that made Derec grimace. Theirs had been a roller-coaster ride of a relationship: they never seemed to be able to settle into any semblance of normalcy. When things were good, they were very good indeed. And when they were bad . . .

That was Avery's legacy as well—many of the memories Derec and Ariel shared were not pleasant. For the months they'd been trapped in Robot City, Ariel's personality had been in a steady, disintegrating spiral, fluctuating between vivacious and darkly sullen.

At least she'd escaped. At least she'd escaped from that planet and been cured.

Derec could never leave Robot City. It would always be there within him. It was his, his responsibility, whether he wanted it or not.

"Derec, stop it," Ariel said warningly.

"Stop what?"

"I'm not going to answer something that obvious. Figure it out yourself."

He knew he should have apologized then. He knew he should have smiled deprecatingly and shrugged, should have risen himself and kissed her until she forgot the argument and the dawn was again something beautiful to see.

But he didn't.

"Sorry I'm so stupid," he said bitterly.

Ariel's face was red with irritation, her eyes narrowed and her hands clenched into angry fists. "Derec, don't spoil the morning, please."

"*I'm* not the one who knows what everyone else is thinking. It seems to me that you claimed that ability. *I* thought everything was going fine."

"You're being childish."

"And you're being arrogant."

"Arrogant? Damn it, Derec . . . Derec?" She stopped. Derec was no longer listening to her. He was standing in the middle of the room, his gaze inward and blind.

The call had entered Derec's mind with an urgency that was almost painful. Aurora, the dawn outside the window, Ariel's voice: they'd all disappeared in the frantic *need* of the message. The chemfets relayed the message to him.

Under attack, it said. The call was faint, as if coming from a great distance, much farther than the Robot City he knew. *Request immediate help.*

"What is it, Derec?" Ariel asked again, a look of concern furrowing her brow. Her anger was lost in her worry for him. Slowly, he came back to an awareness of the room around him.

"I'm . . . I'm not sure." He was still holding his head with a look of inward concentration, listening to those whispering pleas only he could hear. "It's the chemfets again. I'm ... I'm getting a series of coordinates and a distress signal from a source claiming to be the central computer. It says it's Robot City, but—Mandelbrot!" he called suddenly.

The robot slipped quickly from a niche on one side of the bedroom. Derec had assembled the robot from assorted parts, a hodgepodge of models including a right arm constructed of what he called Avery material—infinitely malleable and adjustable. The patchwork-quilt effect lent the robot, to say the least, a unique look, and Derec had a vast affection for him.

"Mandelbrot, you're also linked to Robot City," he said to the robot. "Did you just receive a distress call?"

"No, Master Derec, I did not."

"If I give you a set of coordinates, can you tell me whether they're anywhere near Robot City?"

"I can link with the Auroran Net and access records there."

"Good." Derec rattled off the coordinates he'd heard in his head. Mandelbrot stood silently a moment, then spoke.

"Those coordinates are for a region well outside human space and distant from Robot City, though in the same arm of the galaxy. If I have not received the message you received, and if those coordinates represent the actual source of the call, then I can see two possibilities: first, that Dr. Avery himself has established a new Robot City somewhere, perhaps by using the Keys of Perihelion to jump to another world. Or, secondly, that the distress call is from a Robot City that is an offshoot of the original. We know that some of the Avery robots were sent out by the central computer to start new sites on other planets. Can you communicate with the computer yourself?"

Derec concentrated, but the wispy tendrils of the repeating call were gone as if they had never been there. "No," he said. "There's nothing now."

"There's a third, even more likely, possibility you've both missed," Ariel said, hands on hips. "It was your imagination. You've done nothing but worry about Robot City since we left."

"It wasn't my imagination," Derec insisted. "It was real. I know the difference, Ariel."

"You said it was faint."

"It came through the chemfets. I can guarantee that."

"All right," Ariel sighed. "All right. I'm tired of arguing. It's gone now, so let's forget it. Mandelbrot, you can go back to the niche."

As Mandelbrot turned obediently, Derec shook his head. "No. I can't just forget it, Ariel. It's not that simple. You don't seem to realize that, to a large extent, I *am* Robot City now. I'm part of it; I'm responsible."

Ariel whirled around at that, her face angry. Her finger dug into his chest, prodding.

"*No.* No, you're not, Derec. Your father's responsible. Avery. Without his poisoning you with the chemfets, without his interference and his insane schemes, none of this would have happened—to *any* of us. You're not responsible, Derec, any more than I am or Mandelbrot is or Wolruf is. You can't blame yourself for any of it, and there's nothing you can do about it."

"There's trouble," Derec insisted. "I can feel it. I have to go see. Mandelbrot, I want you to see that our ship is provisioned and ready to go by noon."

Mandelbrot hesitated, caught for a second between the conflicting orders, but Derec was his primary master. His orders took precedence over Ariel's. The robot nodded and moved to the computer terminal on the wall. Mandelbrot activated the screen and opened a line to the Aurora Port computer.

Ariel shook her head, dark hair swaying with savage motion. She jabbed at Derec's chest again with the forefinger. "You're not doing it, Derec. No. If this phantom city in your mind has problems, then let it deal with them on its own. That's what the central computer is for. And if it's Avery again, if he's used his Keys to jump from Robot City to some other place he's set up, it'll be a trap just like the other. I'm not at all interested in stepping into his deadly little webs again."

"I don't want you to. I wasn't intending to have you go along. I thought just Mandelbrot and myself . . ."

The words didn't come out quite as he'd intended. *Because I don't want you to get hurt again*, he should have added. *Because I care too much about you*. But her face was already clouded, and somehow the words wouldn't come now.

Ariel nodded, muscles bunched as she set her jaw. "Fine," she said, her words clipped and short. "Just fine. I'm sorry I'm such a burden."

"Ariel . . ."

But she was no longer listening. She went to her closet, snatched a loose smock from a hook, and tugged it on. She brushed her fingers through her hair and gave Derec one last smouldering gaze.

Then she stalked from the house.

"Mandelbrot," Derec said after the reverberations of her exit had stopped echoing through the house. "You should be glad that you don't have to deal with emotions."

"It has been my observation that human feelings are much like fruit."

"Hmm? I'm not sure I understand."

"If handled roughly, both feelings and fruit are easily bruised."

To that, Derec didn't have a reply.

CHAPTER 9

THE HILL OF STARS

SilverSide knew the normal pack routine with a kill.

The hunters would first tear open the abdomen and feed themselves on the warm, pulsing blood-rich meat. Afterward, their own appetites sated, they would use their crude flint-knapped knives and flay the carcass, cutting it into manageable chunks to be put on the carriers.

Now the kin circled uneasily around the dead WalkingStone. LifeCrier reached out and tapped at the thing's stomach with a claw. "It's stone, SilverSide," the old wolf-creature said. "A magical creature from the FirstBeast. There's nothing for us to eat. It's a mockery."

SilverSide came up to the body, the other kin moving aside for her. "KeenEye," she asked, "have any of the WalkingStones been killed before?"

KeenEye seemed grateful for the attention, as SilverSide had expected. "No," she said. "These are the Hunters of the WalkingStones; there are other kinds near the Hill of Stars, but they never leave that place. Every time before, we ran from the Hunters when we couldn't hurt them. They've killed three hands of kin and more in the three dances of the moons since they came. The fire from their fingers kills."

Three hands of kin—with the wolf-creature's four-fingered hands, that meant that over a dozen kin had fallen to the WalkingStones in three months. SilverSide had seen perhaps thirty to forty of the wolf-creatures at PackHome. Twelve members of the tribe was a significant loss. It was no wonder that LifeCrier and the others were looking for divine intervention.

SilverSide crouched down alongside the WalkingStone. She examined the thing carefully. Her optical circuits noted a seam running along the abdomen. She slid a clawtip carefully along the edge, narrowing and flattening the claw so that it slipped easily under the lip of metal.

She pried up. Magnetic catches held tenaciously, then finally gave as she increased the tension. The abdomen covering lifted, revealing an interior of miniature servo motors, linkages, wires, and circuit boards. The kin around SilverSide gasped.

"There's no blood," KeenEye said in SilverSide's ear, marveling. "No muscles, no meat, no stomach. How does it move?"

"Magic," LifeCrier said again. "The Eternal Ones have set them in motion against SilverSide and the OldMother."

The answer sounded right to SilverSide. She could not refute LifeCrier, not with the strange gaps in her knowledge. LifeCrier had told her of the struggles among the gods. SilverSide had found nothing to disprove that she had been sent by the OldMother to serve humans. Given that, it was just as likely that the WalkingStones may well have been sent by FirstBeast or some other rival of the OldMother.

Still . . .

"The Hunter is not magic," SilverSide told them. "The

WalkingStones are MadeThings. They are tools, like our flint knives or the *travois*. They are like the dolls the cubs fashion from sticks, only the WalkingStones are stuffed with stone chips and vines from the Void. The power in them allows them to walk, and they speak with a voice you can hear only in your head.

"Look," she said and plunged her forepaw hand into the WalkingStone's entrails. Her claws emerged again fisted around the colorful intestines of the creature: a trailing, knotted coil of wires. The kin howled at the sight, half in lament, half in wonder.

"These are the guts of kin's worst enemy," SilverSide said. "The cubs back at PackHome could at least eat a SharpFang. Even if SharpFangs kill kin, they can also feed us. But not these creatures. This is the inedible meat of the WalkingStones."

"What are we going to do, SilverSide?" LifeCrier asked, and his question was echoed by the others around them.

SilverSide thought for a moment. Then she tugged hard at the array of wires. Bright sparks spat angrily, arcing and dying on the ground. SilverSide flung the tangle down.

"Since they will not let us live, we will kill them," she said.

A robotics expert would probably have been simply appalled and frightened and ordered the destruction of the robot. Janet Anastasi, SilverSide's creator, might have herself been concerned with the robot's behavior, but she would have also been intensely interested.

SilverSide's mindset had nothing of a human being in it at all. The Three Laws were there, yes, but they had now been completely reshaped and changed. As the robots of Aurora, Solaria, Earth, and other human worlds were shaped and designed to mimic human behavior, so SilverSide had shaped and designed herself to mimic the kin. Indeed, because she had no conception that she was a constructed thing herself, she *was* kin, and she interpreted the inbuilt Three Laws of her positronic brain in light of her own "humanity."

The WalkingStones threatened the Kin. They killed kin. And though she could have led the kin away from Pack-Home, that also would have meant the probable loss of life. The wolf-creatures were territorial hunters, and the neighboring pack-leaders had already warned them. SilverSide's pack couldn't move into another pack's territory without being challenged and having to fight other wolf-creatures, nor would another pack have allowed them to hunt in their own territory.

Finding another viable home that was not already claimed was at best a dubious hope, and KeenEye and LifeCrier had already told her that the WalkingStones were expanding their holdings—even if SilverSide's pack left, another pack would eventually have to confront the WalkingStones when they might be even more powerful.

SilverSide had reluctantly come to the decision to stay and confront the situation directly.

Yes, kin might die, but *more* kin would likely die if they left.

A human robot might have looked for yet another, more peaceful solution. But SilverSide was a carnivore, a hunter even though she herself did not eat at all; she took the carnivore's solution.

Having accepted the wolf-creatures as human, she accepted their mores. Without further proof, she also accepted their mythology. The OldMother had sent her. She was *chosen* for the task. The WalkingStones might be intelligent, but they were made by another god and therefore were not "human" themselves. Though SilverSide couldn't perform outside the Three Laws, she would do what she had to do within their limits.

As her new mindset perceived them.

What the carnivore could not avoid, it attacked. Dr. Anastasi's experiment had worked perfectly well. Her robot had become something *other*. A very dangerous other.

Still, if it weren't for the fact that SilverSide had just killed one of the hated creatures, the rest of the kin might not have accepted her statement. A challenge to her leadership might have been the immediate outcome.

Even so, there were questions.

"We've tried killing the WalkingStones before," KeenEye said. She used KinSpeech rather than HuntTongue, not wanting SilverSide to think she was offering formal challenge. SilverSide listened to the old leader, sitting back on her hind legs and braiding a necklace from the WalkingStone's wires. "They're not like SharpFangs. SharpFangs are strong but very stupid. These Hunter WalkingStones can kill by pointing their fingers, and our claws and teeth do nothing.

"This one died," SilverSide said. She placed the necklace around her neck; the other kin howled softly at the sight.

"Yes, but it's the first."

"It won't be the last. I will show you ways to deal with them. This is *our* territory, not the WalkingStones'. They are driving away the game we live on and making this a barren place. Once the WalkingStones and their Hill of Stars are gone, the game will return and the kin can live as they please. We will take our territory back again."

"You will show us how to kill them?"

"I will."

KeenEye paused. She looked from the dead Walking-Stone to SilverSide. "Then lead us, SilverSide," KeenEye said in a rising shout and let out a glad cry in BeastTalk.

SilverSide took a strand of wires from the gutted Hunter. She quickly plaited another necklace from the colorful wire and knotted the bright coil around KeenEye's neck. Carefully, she then did the same with each of them. "There," she said when it was done. "We wear the signs of our victory. Now, follow me. We must learn more about our enemy."

SilverSide dropped to all fours. With a quick lope, she ran into the forest, moving westward toward the Hill of Stars.

Howling, the rest of the kin ran behind her.

CHAPTER 10

AN UNEXPECTED MESSAGE, AN UNEXPECTED ARRIVAL

"Katherine Ariel Burgess, you're a fool."

The image in the mirror didn't seem inclined to answer the accusation. Ariel scowled at herself and slapped at the contact. The mirror dissolved in a shimmering crystalline haze and was replaced by a pastoral sunset scene. That only made her more angry, reminding her of the acrimonious morning a week ago.

She'd told herself that Derec would wait, that he'd still be there when she came back from her long walk. But he hadn't waited.

When she'd finally cooled down and called the house in mid-afternoon, Balzac, the household robot, had informed her that Derec and Mandelbrot had left for the port several hours before. Ariel had called the port, wondering what she'd say if he was still there, rehearsing the lines in her mind.

I've changed my mind, Derec. I want to go with you.

But he'd already gone, and she had no idea where it was he was heading.

Ariel didn't know whether that made her angry or sad or both at the same time. She simply felt confused. The intervening days hadn't made things any better. Sleeping alone each night was too vivid a reminder.

She came out of the personal, wandering aimlessly through rooms that now seemed far too large and empty. She stared out the windows, fiddled with the reader, flicked on the holovid and as quickly turned if off again.

With a start, she noticed that the computer terminal was blinking. Feeling a sudden surge of hope, she started to press the access key. Stopped.

"Balzac?" she called.

The robot trundled from its wall niche in the next room. "Mistress?" it said in a flat, mechanical voice. Balzac was a utility model, unsophisticated and plain.

"The message on the terminal. Why didn't you answer the call?"

"I monitored the message, but it was for Derec and did not demand a reply."

"Who was it from?"

" 'Who' is imprecise in this case. The message was a faint relay from a central computer system."

Ariel's lips pressed together. She inhaled slowly, thinking. "Thank you, Balzac. That's all I require."

The robot nodded and left the room. Ariel waited until it was gone and the house was silent again, then spoke her code-word to the terminal: "Euler"—the name of one of the supervisor robots on Robot City. Nothing happened. She wrinkled her nose.

She knew Derec's codeword as well; he'd made no attempt to keep it a secret from her. "Aranimas," she said.

A foil screen scrolled open; glowing letters flickered

across it as Ariel leaned closer. The message was short and succinct:

CITY UNDER ATTACK BY NON-HUMANS. IMPERATIVE WE RECEIVE OUTSIDE AID.

The message was followed by a sequence of coordinate numbers for the location. Ariel smiled. "Okay, Derec," she said to the screen. "If the mountain has run away from Mohammed, Mohammed will chase it. Won't you be surprised when I show up?"

She turned away from the computer, suddenly excited. This would serve him right. "Balzac!" she called. "I need you to make some arrangements."

"Mandelbrot, the Robot City has to be somewhere on that large continent there—see where the two rivers meet in the forested area? The computer says that's where the last message was 'waved from."

Mandelbrot, at the controls of their craft, punched in coordinates. "Have you been able to get the city's central computer to respond?"

"No," Derec admitted glumly. "Either I'm not doing something right or the chemfets only give me access to the original Robot City's computer. Before, all I had to do was *think* a message and it went through. This Central won't talk to me or the original Robot City's computer. It's just beaming out the distress call at regular intervals."

"Then it must be expecting someone to answer; otherwise, why signal at all?"

"I don't know, I don't know. I haven't figured it out yet. I'm just as puzzled as you are."

Derec watched the long curve of the world flatten as they approached. It was a pretty world, he decided. He might have chosen it himself. It seemed a calm and gentle place, much like Aurora, though he could see the spiraling arms of a storm just touching the eastern shores of the continent below, and he knew that underneath the pastel blue-white would be dark, streaking clouds and raging winds.

Untamed, this world was. Which was very *unlike* Aurora.

And very much like Ariel.

The thought crossed his mind, unbidden. She'd not sent any messages to him after she'd stormed out of the house; in fact, she'd disappeared entirely. He'd made calls to a few places trying to find her before they'd left, but to no avail. She seemed to have dropped from sight. It had been very hard to leave without saying goodbye. And because he knew that was exactly the effect she'd been after, he'd gone.

He'd begun to wonder if she'd be there when he came back. There was a sullen ache in him at the image of an empty house. It was going to hurt. It was going to hurt more than he wanted to think about.

To take his mind off Ariel, he reached in front of Mandelbrot and toggled a switch to bring the world into closer focus. Unbroken treetops swayed in a light wind.

"I don't see any evidence of a city," he said. "If we weren't looking specifically for it because of the signal, I'd swear this place was barren of any technology. It has to be there, though. If so, it sure hasn't spread out as much as the original. Have you seen any evidence of other life, Mandelbrot?"

"No, Derec. The nightside umbra shows no obvious large habitations, which would be lighted, I would think—though we haven't seen this continent at night yet. The atmospheric sampling does indicate a small amount of industrial waste, which is very likely the result of your city. You remember the effect the other one had on its environment."

Derec did. The massive, out-of-control building spree of the first Robot City had resulted in immense ecological side effects. The horrendous deluges that daily inundated the city had nearly killed both him and Ariel until he'd reprogrammed the central computer. "Yes, I remember," he said. "I hope this one keeps a better handle on things. Take us down. Let's see what's going on."

"Derec, I advise against landing in the city itself. Assuming we can even find it."

"Why not, Mandelbrot?"

The robot's eyes gleamed as it turned to him. "We do not know what kind of attack this city is facing," he said. "I have checked for other ships in orbit and found nothing, but I am still concerned that a city under attack will have defenses against ships. You cannot communicate with the central computer. Given that, I would be afraid that it might deem an unidentified ship an enemy and take measures to protect itself."

Derec grimaced.

"If you order me to do so," Mandelbrot continued, "I will trust your better judgment and follow your orders."

Derec shook his head. "Uh-uh. And you'll say 'I told you so' afterward."

"No." The flat delivery almost sounded hurt.

"Okay," Derec said, grinning. "I think you're right. Let's land elsewhere. How much of a hike were you planning on giving us?"

"I have estimated that fifty kilometers is the minimum."

"Fine. A few days' stroll through the forest—"

At that moment, the craft shook like a mad thing. As the hull shuddered, Derec felt Mandelbrot's firm grip on his arm, guiding him to his seat and forcing him down. The crash webbing slid over him as the craft tumbled; Mandelbrot staggered back to his seat and fought the controls.

"What happened?" Derec shouted.

"I do not know. Our orbit is decaying rapidly. . . ." The robot had no time to say more as the ship's view of the world below spun and whirled. Mandelbrot's robotic reflexes were far faster than Derec's, but the power to their main engines was simply gone.

Using the attitude jets, Mandelbrot managed to reduce the wild tumbling momentarily, but then the first tendrils of the atmosphere touched them and the hull struts moaned in agony. The ship began to do gymnastics again, and this time—snared in the planet's gravity well—they were flung violently with it.

Derec's head slammed up against his seat despite the webbing, making him shout in pain. Mandelbrot had cut all the automatics, giving him full control of the ship, but it was of little help. In the viewscreen, they saw the hull turning cherry red; the heat was suffocating in the cabin, the ventilation system gone.

White cloudtops seemed to race toward them, then they plunged into the columns of gray murk. Storm winds tossed them; rain sheeted across the screen.

"Mandelbrot!" Derec's scream shivered with the vibrations of the ship.

There was no answer.

They plunged out of the bottom of the storm, the murky landscape below wheeling like a mad carousel. The ground, a fist waiting to crumple them like paper, rushed at them.

Then, like the gut-wrenching end of a roller-coaster's free-fall, Derec was shoved down in his seat as the craft pulled up in a quick loop.

For a moment, Derec thought Mandelbrot had saved them.

It was still too late.

The trailing bulk of the engines caught the lip of a rocky outcropping. The granite blade of the hill ripped into the supports. Metal and stone screeched; Derec heard the concussion as the engine exploded. Snared, the ship itself was hammered to the ground. The inferno of the engine was sheared completely off and went spiraling away.

At least I won't burn to death.

As a last thought, it seemed a strange comfort.

CHAPTER 11

STRATEGY AND TACTICS

SilverSide brought the pack to a ragged halt at a ridge look-ing down into the shallow bowl of a valley perhaps a kil-ometer across at its widest point. She sat in the shadows of the last few trees; LifeCrier and KeenEye came forward and sat on their haunches to either side of the new leader. SmallFace was high in the sky; LargeFace had yet to rise. The stars—the VoidEyes, as LifeCrier called them—stared down at the city and marveled.

SilverSide felt some of that awe herself. The Hill of Stars, set like a glistening diamond in the center of the val-ley and rising well above the level of the surrounding hills, was a fantastic pattern of glowing lights. The slender py-ramidal structure mocked the glory of the night sky.

Nor was the Hill of Stars all. Other buildings spread out around it in geometric splendor, a procession of hard, crys-talline shapes filling the valley and spilling out its open end, all linked by ribbons of walkways.

And everywhere, *everywhere*, there were Walking-Stones: all different sizes, all different builds, all different colors. They bustled along the walkways, gazed from the windows of the buildings, slid busily between the flanks of the city. There were thousands of them.

They moved in an eerie, almost mystical silence—at least to the kin. But SilverSide could hear the deafening roar of the city's voices inside her head. An eternal chatter of orders and instructions came from the central computer; reports were constantly being funneled back to that source. And she understood the words, for they spoke as the Hunter spoke, in that language SilverSide guessed must be that of the Void where the gods lived. It was more proof that the OldMother was being opposed.

"They began with just the Hill of Stars," KeenEye whispered to SilverSide. She panted at the remembrance, and her long, furless tail lashed from side to side. "They've worked like the *krajal* since then."

SilverSide had seen the industrious insects called the *krajal* toiling ceaselessly through the undergrowth of the forest, building their mud colonies on the sides of trees. KeenEye pointed a long finger at the periphery of the city, her lips drawn back from canines in a snarl.

"See how they tear down the trees and destroy the land?" she rasped. "All this valley was forest before the WalkingStones came. They destroy everything to put up their stone caves. And the light—it's as if the sun were resting down there for the night. The WalkingStones don't care about kin or any of the living creatures. They don't care that our prey animals have fled. They don't care that their stone caves stretch out and out and out. Long before they reach PackHome, we will have left. We will have starved, or we will have been killed."

"Do these other WalkingStones hurt the kin like the one

we killed?" SilverSide asked. "There must be different *species* of WalkingStones down there."

"We don't know," KeenEye answered. "The others have never bothered us. They stay within the stones. Only the Hunters ever come outside."

"That also makes them like the *krajal*," LifeCrier added. "Only the blue *krajali* get food, only the yellow-speckled *krajali* build the tree-homes; only the red *krajali* defend the homes against the LongTongues. They each have a separate task to do, and they each are shaped a little differently. Maybe it's the same with these WalkingStones."

SilverSide's optics focused more closely on the hive of activity. What LifeCrier had said sounded like an accurate enough metaphor. The view of the city bore that out. Certainly the WalkingStones seemed specialized in appearance. And though the WalkingStones were obviously constructed things, their hard, unyielding bodies were like the chitinous shells of insects.

Maybe the enemy of the OldMother had fashioned the WalkingStones after insects. They had the same outward silence, and their chattering inside her head to the unseen *Central* seemed like the clickings of insects. Like the insect, they labored with seemingly untiring energy; like the *krajal* they built their own colony home rather than take refuge in what nature afforded. And this Central, perhaps that was the queen, directing all activities of the hive.

The intricacy and sophistication of the city echoed in SilverSide. It awoke memories of her initial urges: *find sentient life. Find humans.* She'd made the decision on what was human, but the intelligence behind the Walking-Stones...

...but that was the province of the gods, or so Life-Crier's tales had indicated. A god had sent the Walking-

Stones as a god had sent SilverSide herself. It felt right to admire the genius that had created the WalkingStones, a resonance of the Third Law commands that had shaped her first hours. But admiration didn't mean that the Walking-Stones weren't enemies. SilverSide had made her choice; the OldMother had sent her to the kin.

But still ... The kin were human, yes, but SilverSide yearned for something more.

"Sometimes the *krajal* infest a place, too," LifeCrier was saying. "The queen breeds and breeds until the trees drip with the shiny bodies. They drop on the prey animals and bite, driving them mad until they flee. They can kill a youngling—a slow and horrible death."

LifeCrier closed his eyes, as if remembering. "The last time that happened, two LifeCriers ago, HalfTongue was the leader. During a storm, lightning struck a tree. HalfTongue noticed that the flames killed the *krajal* and that they fled. She took a branch from the tree and set a blue *krajali* on fire. The nearby reds came to defend it, leaving an opening. So HalfTongue and the others took several burning brands and began using them to drive the *krajal* away until they could reach the queen and kill it. Once the queen was dead, the *krajal* behaved like crazy things and were easy to kill."

"WalkingStones won't burn. You can't burn a rock." KeenEye's comment was laced with her old scorn. If she was resigned to a secondary place in the pack behind SilverSide, she was also not going to submit to any of the other kin. "The WalkingStones would laugh at a burning stick."

SilverSide nodded in agreement, scenting KeenEye's irritation with LifeCrier's tales. "Still, there is a hint in LifeCrier's story. I must find out more about these WalkingStones. KeenEye, you will lead the pack in my absence. I will go down into the city. I need to discover if these other types of WalkingStones are more vulnerable than the Hunters. If what I suspect is true, then the Hunters will come after I attack. You must watch—see what they do, see how many they send and how quickly. Then go back to PackHome quickly. I will return by another route after I have made certain that no Hunters follow me."

"*If* you're not killed right away," KeenEye said. Her pale eyes were noncommital and SilverSide could not tell if the prospect pleased or disturbed her. "*If* you're right about these other WalkingStones."

"If anything happens to me, you become leader again," SilverSide answered. Yes, she scented satisfaction in KeenEye with that, and she continued. "But it won't. I don't intend to fight the Hunters. I only need to see how they react so we can plan. You can't hear them, but I can. The WalkingStones speak; they communicate as do the kin. I can use their language against them. I might be able to deceive them."

"GrayMane knew the language of the OldMother," LifeCrier said. "You see, KeenEye, it is as I said."

KeenEye grimaced, but she said nothing.

"Watch me for the time it would take to skin a deer," SilverSide told the group. "Remember what you see, every detail. It is very important. Then leave. Go directly back to PackHome." SilverSide used HuntTongue to accentuate the command.

KeenEye grimaced again, but she nodded. "As you wish."

SilverSide gave a soft bark of satisfaction. She looked at the pack, who watched the trio expectantly. The sight of the kin nudged a First Law circuit. "Keep them safe, KeenEye," SilverSide said. "Take them back as swiftly as they can go—the Hunters may come after you if I can't lead them away."

"I will do as SilverSide wishes," KeenEye answered in proud HuntTongue. "She does not have to worry."

There was nothing more to say. SilverSide glanced around the edge of the forest, making sure that no Hunters were lurking nearby. Swiftly, she dropped onto four legs and moved out into the wash of moonlight. She was a swift, glinting presence sliding into the shadows of the nearest buildings. SilverSide moved in among them several strides, then hunched down, belly to cool stone behind one of the structures.

She listened. The WalkingStones chattered to Central endlessly. Reports went in, orders went out. The WalkingStones were concentrated more toward the Hill of Stars where SilverSide suspected Central hid, but they occasionally moved through this area. She waited, patient.

When she heard the sound of a WalkingStone's tread, she allowed her body to deform slightly, extending an eyestalk around the corner of the building. The approaching WalkingStone was a spindly, gangly thing with arms tipped by mechanical claws rather than fingered hands. It was alone. SilverSide retracted the eyestalk, gathered herself; when the WalkingStone passed the side of the building, she leaped with a BeastTalk growl.

The WalkingStone's arms came up too late—SilverSide hit it, her jaws clamping around the thin, long neck and her powerful muscles shaking the thing from side to side. She was careful to hold her own great strength back and use no more power than any of the kin possessed.

That strength was enough, as she had suspected. These WalkingStones were far less durable than the Hunters. A support cracked; internal wiring harnesses tore. Just before the main trunk to the brain was severed and the WalkingStone went still under SilverSide's great bulk, she heard it call out to the distant Central.

Under attack. Damaged . . .

SilverSide let the thing slump to the ground. *Yes, as I thought.* The Hunters were designed to be the city's protection; the workers were strong but not overwhelming for a creature as powerful as the wolf-creatures. The worker WalkingStones, at least, were vulnerable.

And this also revealed another weakness. Not much of one, but it was all SilverSide had.

The voices in her head had gone silent. Replacing the chatter was an amplified voice, loud and commanding, resonating on all the frequencies. *Central. My enemy.*

And it did what she would have done herself. Central was sending the Hunters to investigate.

SilverSide didn't intend to be there when the Hunters arrived.

Giving a BeastTalk growl of triumph, she ran back toward the forest, staying where the kin could see her but not heading directly toward them. KeenEye would watch and make certain, then run to PackHome as ordered. SilverSide would make her way there herself, but first she had to make sure there was no latent danger to the kin.

It didn't matter if such a delay endangered her own self.

She waited until she caught a glimpse of the first Hunter moving swiftly along a walkway toward the area where the attack had occurred. *I am here*, she called to it in her own head voice, using the VoidTalk. The Hunter stopped, its armored head swiveling around.

SilverSide gave voice to a BeastTalk challenge and ran.

She was just about to duck under the cover of the trees when the laser hit her.

CHAPTER 12

A JOURNEY BEGINS

If this was the afterlife, it was damned uncomfortable.

For one thing, it was wet. He could feel water dripping on his face and body.

For another, being dead *hurt*.

Derec's ribs ached as if they'd been kicked repeatedly by an extraordinarily strong and stubborn mule. Most of his skin felt as if it had been scoured by a rough, rusty file, and what hadn't been scraped raw was parboiled. His head pounded with the great-granddaddy of all headaches, and he was afraid to open his eyes or try to sit up.

If this was eternity, it wasn't making a nice start.

But he couldn't lie there forever. Besides, there was a certain curiosity....

There was definitely light beyond his eyelids. And beyond the dripping of water, he could hear a rushing, crackling noise like cellophane being crumpled.

Derec opened his eyes.

And, groaning, closed them again.

He was looking through a jagged hole in the ship's hull

into a dull gray, rain-streaming sky. Through the curtain of rain, he could see a muddy hillside scored by some giant, maniac plow and sown with bright pieces of metal. Despite the storm, there was a fire smoldering in the grass a hundred meters away where one of the ship's drive engines lay half buried. A thick, greasy plume of black smoke was smeared across the sky under the racing clouds.

It didn't look good. Being alive was threatening to be more uncomfortable than being dead. "Mandelbrot?" Derec's voice was a hoarse croak. There was no answer.

"Mandelbrot?"

Still nothing. It looked as if he was going to have to get out by himself. He didn't like the idea, not one bit. Derec moved to unbuckle his crash webbing. It was a mistake.

He screamed and promptly blacked out again.

It had stopped raining and the grass fire was out when he came back to consciousness again.

"Reality, part two," he muttered to himself. There was still a throbbing ache in his left arm; his right seemed to be functioning, if badly bruised. He forced himself to look— yes, the left forearm was definitely fractured, the skin puffy and discolored, the arm canted at a slight and very wrong angle. The sight made him nauseous. *Great. All you need is to be sick all over yourself. What if you've got broken ribs or internal injuries. . . .*

Derec leaned his head back and took several deep breaths until his stomach settled again. Reaching over with his good hand, he tightened the left harness of the webbing until his shoulder was tight against the seat. Then he grasped his left arm at the wrist, took a deep breath, and held it.

And let it out again with a shout. He pulled, hard.
Bone grated against bone.

When Derec came to consciousness for the third time,
he checked the arm. It was bruising nicely, but it looked
straight now. He could wiggle his fingers, make a weak fist.
The pain made him want to whimper, but there was nothing
he could do about it for the moment.

"Okay," he breathed. "You got to get out, find the first
aid kit, get the painkillers and the quick-knit pills," he told
himself. "You can do it." Using his right hand, he unbuckled
himself—squirming for the right-hand buckle at his shoulder, the pain stabbed at his chest: *broken ribs, too, if nothing
worse.* He was starting to sweat, coldly, and the periphery
of his vision was getting dark.

Shock. Take it easy. Just breathe for a few seconds.

Gingerly, Derec tried his legs. His left ankle had been
wrenched badly, but he thought he might be able to put
weight on it, and his right thigh was bloody under the torn
pants, but everything worked.

Fine. Let's see if we can stand.

He pushed himself up with his one good arm, cradling
the other. The movement coupled with the throbbing head
made the ship swirl about him. For a moment, the world
threatened to go away again. Derec fought to remain conscious. *No*, he pleaded. *The last thing you want to do is fall.
You might not make it up again.*

After a minute, the landscape stopped its ponderous
waltz around him, and he could stand. The cabin was a total
loss. The flooring was buckled, gaping holes had been torn
in the bulkheads, and everything was sitting at a slight
downhill angle. Derec noticed Mandelbrot immediately. The
pilot's seat had been sheared off during impact and lay on

its side at the "bottom" of the cabin slope. Mandelbrot was still in the seat, his body dented, dinged, and scratched.

"Mandelbrot?" Derec called again, but there was still no answer. *First things first,* he told himself. *Where's that kit?*

It should have been on the near wall; it wasn't. After a stumbling search through the nearby rubble, Derec finally located the white-and-red box. He fumbled open the catch and tore open a vial of EndPain. He stabbed the injector into his thigh with a hiss of the air jet; the medication felt cool, and he could feel it spreading. The pain began to fade, the headache to ease. After a few minutes, he was feeling vaguely human again.

He found the quick-knit tabs, read the instructions, and swallowed two. With the pain temporarily subdued, he rigged a splint from a piece of plastic and the cloth covering of one of the seats. The arm felt better secured and placed in a sling. He knotted it with his teeth.

Derec was beginning to feel alive once more. Alive enough to know that he was still in deep trouble on a world he didn't know and maybe half a continent or more away from the Robot City and help. He could still hear the central computer via his chemfet link, but the damned thing still didn't respond to him as had the original—it would have been easy to order a squad of robots to find and rescue them.

And if pigs had wings . . .

Derec had to have Mandelbrot. Without the robot, this was going to be very, very touchy. The quick-knit tabs would heal his arm in a week or two—*if* he didn't refracture it rummaging through the wreckage; *if* there were no internal injuries that crippled him first; *if* there was nothing on this planet that decided he looked tasty . . .

If he was still *alive* in a week.

Derec made his slow way over the broken hull to the robot. The seat had pinned Mandelbrot to the wall. Derec braced his back against the cabin wall opposite the robot, planted his feet on the seat supports, and shoved: the seat groaned, moved, and dropped back again. Derec gritted his teeth, pushed once more. This time the seat tumbled over, Mandelbrot dangling loosely from the straps. Derec waited until his breath returned and then opened up the robot's chest cavity.

There were too many things that could have gone wrong with the robot that couldn't possibly be fixed here. Derec could imagine every last one of them in his mind.

It didn't look as bad as it might have. The trunk line from the main power source had pulled loose, though backup power to the brain was still intact: good, that meant there would be no memory loss. There was some structural damage, though Mandelbrot's Avery-type arm looked perfectly fine. The optical circuits had taken quite a jarring; Derec wouldn't be surprised if there were some problems there when he powered up the robot.

And it was going to be no fun working with one hand. "Only one way to find out . . ." he muttered, then shook his head. *Who in space are you talking to?*

It took an hour to find the toolbox; another to one-handedly splice the bad power cable and jury-rig the socket—he had to stop halfway through to hit the painkillers again; the headache was back and his ribs made every breath an agony. The soldering tip trembled in his hand as he made the last connections. He wiped sweat from his eyes and straightened. He closed the chest compartment and touched the power contact.

A status light blinked amber. One eye gleamed fitfully; the entire body shuddered. The head swiveled with a distressing squeal of grinding metal, and Mandelbrot looked in Derec's general direction.

"Master Derec?"

"Mandelbrot."

"You are very fuzzy in my optical circuits. It would appear that the landing was not all we had hoped for."

"It would appear so." Derec shrugged. "How are you?"

"Checking . . ." Mandelbrot's voice trailed off; the eye dimmed. After several seconds it brightened once more. "Systems check program running. Main positronic circuitry intact; two sectors damaged but recovered and backed up. Right optical circuits not functioning; left out of adjustment. Neck sleeve joint misaligned. Main trunk connections damaged but acceptable. Main and auxiliary power circuits acceptable. Three servo motors have cracked casings and will be a problem if the lubricant seals are breached and leaking. Knee servo in left leg burned out and knee locked." The robot's fingers clenched and opened. "Other minor damage. Would you prefer the full details?"

"Save it for later."

"Then I must ask how you are, Master Derec." Mandelbrot rose to his feet, the left leg extended stiffly. "I note that your arm is splinted and there is blood on your clothing. You grimace when you move, as if your chest hurts you."

"The arm's broken; it'll heal. I'm banged up but alive. I don't think it's anything serious. Considering the way we hit, we don't have anything to complain about."

"I was not complaining, Master Derec, simply trying to ascertain our status. Your health is of prime importance to me as you know. The First Law . . ."

Derec waved him silent. "We've done all we can do about that. Now we have to get ourselves out of here."

Gears whined drily as Mandelbrot surveyed the wreckage. "This was not a good landing," he said without inflection.

Derec laughed aloud despite the pain. After Robot City, he didn't know what to expect from robots: Mandelbrot had either acquired a certain irony and deadpan humor or come up with a good approximation of it. A First Law response to make him feel more comfortable or not, it worked. Derec grinned.

"Actually, it was probably your best." he said. "I'm surprised you got us down at all. What in the world happened?"

"I still am not sure, Master Derec. There was an alarm and then the impact. After that, I was too concerned with the ship to pursue the matter."

"I can believe it," Derec smiled. "Now let's see what we can salvage out of this mess."

It was a long, slow, and painful process. Most of the emergency food stores had been smashed or lost. Mandelbrot dredged up an inflatable survival tent and heater, rope, and a battery-powered lamp. On the down side, the communications gear was hopelessly ruined, as Derec found after an hour of trying to fit together pieces with the few spare parts on board.

The ship was a total loss. It would never see space again.

The salvaging efforts made a pitifully small pile outside the hull. At Derec's insistence, Mandelbrot split the burden in half; a pack for each of them. "You're hobbled, too," Derec pointed out in the face of Mandelbrot's insistence that the robot carry everything. "You'd be endangering me more by loading yourself up. I've got a bad arm; you've a bum leg and servos threatening to go at any time. You're half blind. Consider this a direct order and pick up your half."

Mandelbrot obeyed. "Good," Derec said. "Now—just where in the world are we going?"

"The Robot City was inland, Master Derec. I believe we are near the eastern coast. Since the sun is declining toward the hills, I would suggest that direction."

Derec gazed at the slopes to the west, green with a thick cover of trees. There'd be game under there, and plants to eat if the rations gave out. He sighed. There was little choice. They wouldn't make it off this planet until they had help, and the only help was Robot City. If the central computer wouldn't respond to his chemfet link, the robots would still give them any aid they requested, if only because the First Law required it.

We must look a sight, Derec thought as they walked away from the wreckage. *A lame robot and a beat-up man. At least the planet looks safe.*

CHAPTER 13

A CHASE THROUGH THE FOREST

The laser from the Hunter seared SilverSide's flank. She hadn't expected it to react so quickly.

With robotic speed, she leapt to one side and behind the cover of a thick tree trunk. The bark smoldered where her side pressed against it, and SilverSide modified her body to spread out thin fan-like structures to radiate away the excess heat. A spot of red gleamed on the tree by her head and SilverSide ducked once more—another Hunter, and this one coming from a different direction. She could see two more of the deadly WalkingStones hurrying along the walkways toward the edge of the city and the confrontation.

SilverSide howled and fled deeper into the woods. Along the ridge, she saw the rest of the pack, following her orders, turn back and flee toward PackHome. Now it was up to her—she had to get rid of the WalkingStones.

Ten minutes later, she was certain she'd lost them.

SilverSide had a decided advantage over the WalkingStones in the forest. Her wolf shape was ideally suited for quick movement and lithe, accurate turns. Low to the ground, she could take advantage of brush and thickets for cover; knowing the forest as only a wolf-creature could, she was at ease finding the convoluted paths of the game animals. The WalkingStones seemed far less capable once they left the arrow-straight walkways and geometric patterns of their city.

SilverSide came to a halt in a glade a kilometer and a half from the valley of the WalkingStones. She halted, listening, scenting, and watching. Large moths flitted silently from tree to tree. A creature with huge suckers for feet hung upside down from a nearby branch. LargeFace spread silver lace patterns on the ground through the branches.

A branch cracked; a silver shape moved in the dark.

Central, the creature is here. The voice came from inside her head. *Ten degrees south, unit three. You should have a clear line of fire if you move forward.*

The darkness seemed to bother the WalkingStones as little as it did SilverSide, and it seemed that she had underestimated them. They were persistent and excellent trackers or they could not have followed her. They might be slower when moving in the trees, yes, but they seemed to be untiring.

And they had found her again.

Her logic circuits couldn't know disappointment or irritation or even fear, but the sight of the Hunters through the trees made her pause, made her growl softly in BeastTalk. They were not kin. These WalkingStones lacked all etiquette.

If they were human, she thought, *it would be easy. I could challenge their leader, and whomever won would lead all. That is the best way.*

But the WalkingStone's leader was Central, which was only a voice in her head, and the WalkingStones attacked kin like the SharpFangs, from hiding and without a proper challenge.

Like beasts. Like animals.

The Hunters were speaking with one another now, short bursts of high-pitched sound. SilverSide fingered the strands of semiconductors and colored wire around her neck. They were just made-things. Tools. They were *less* than animals, for all their sophistication. Yes, the technology made SilverSide ache to know more, but they violated all her most primal urges.

She wanted desperately to break these tools.

A crisscrossing of sudden laser fire raked the under-brush. SilverSide pushed to her feet with a howl and ran again. She felt the awful heat of their weapons strike her, and she turned and twisted as she fled so that none of the beams could touch her for more than a few seconds. Even so, she could sense internal damage: automatic alarm cir-cuits overloaded and caused emergency sub-routines to be run, rerouting her nerve signals along undamaged paths to the brain.

Again her wolf shape aided her as it had before; she out-distanced the Hunters quickly. But she could still hear them, could still smell that sharp tang of steel and lubri-cants. They would track her forever, she realized, and if they did that, they would find PackHome.

You cannot allow that to happen. The First Law was plain here.

A new positronic pathway opened, glimmering. Another robot might have kept running until it ran out of power or was caught. Another robot might have been trapped by in-built programming.

The Hunters were tracking a wolf, and though she had chosen that shape, it was not the only one she could be.

SilverSide's body began to alter. The great bulk of the wolf collapsed in on itself, the body becoming much smaller. The excess mass SilverSide squeezed outward, thinning it until the alloy was as thin as she could make it.

Great, powerful wings overshadowed her now. The wings beat, cupping air.

SilverSide flew.

She was a lousy bird. She was too massive, and there was nothing she could do to alter that. She didn't fly well, and she couldn't fly fast or high, but she flew.

Her moonshadow passed over the Hunters moving through the woods below.

The WalkingStones didn't even look up. A wolf that changed into a bird was not in their experience.

"You're certain you left them behind?"

The sun was just peeking over the edge of the hills, and most of the kin had come out to greet SilverSide as, in wolf form again, she loped from the forest. KeenEye prowled the packed ground outside the entrance to PackHome. She kept looking back into the fog drifting through the shafts of light under the trees.

"I am mostly certain," SilverSide replied. One of the pups came up to her and playfully nipped her back leg. She gently nudged the pup aside, and it ran back to its mother, yelping. "I was heading south away from the Hill of Stars, not toward here at all."

"They will follow your tracks and your scent." KeenEye would not let go of the argument, but at least it was in respectful KinSpeech and not HuntTongue, where SilverSide might have been compelled to challenge her.

"I became a bird. I left no tracks, and the wind took my scent."

"You became a bird. . . ." KeenEye's stance stiffened; she crouched slightly, offensively. That said more than her words.

"You doubt SilverSide, KeenEye?" LifeCrier asked mockingly. "You saw the Egg. You've seen her kill a Hunter, which none of us could do. You saw her kill another of the WalkingStones and escape the Hunters' lightnings. We all know she's from the OldMother, and yet you scoff. I believe her, KeenEye, because I have listened to the tales of the OldMother. I have faith. What of the rest of you?"

The kin gave barks of agreement, and SilverSide could scent their pride in her. KeenEye's lips lifted, exposing teeth.

"It doesn't matter," she said disdainfully. "Bird or not, we've *still* done nothing about the WalkingStones. All we've accomplished is to anger them, and if they come *here*, to PackHome, we will all die. SilverSide might be able to kill one, but what of the rest of us?"

KeenEye's tail thrashed dirt. She fingered the necklace SilverSide had given her. "How many here have seen the bodies of kin slain by the Hunters?" she continued. "How many of you have pups who are thin because the meat is scarce? How many mothers have little milk to give the litters? We can't stand against the WalkingStones. And that is true with or without SilverSide, with or without the OldMother."

"Then we can go elsewhere," SilverSide suggested. "Give the WalkingStones this place and find another."

"Where? We've already discussed that. The other packs already watch their borders, knowing the trouble we're having. No other pack will let us into their territory."

"Then you are telling me that we *must* stay here," SilverSide said. "This is something I need to know—KeenEye, LifeCrier, all the rest of you. I do not know this world as you do. The OldMother left you the task of teaching me about the kin. *Must* we stay here?"

They nodded, howling softly. "In that, I'm afraid I must agree with KeenEye," LifeCrier said. "Our pack is already weak and small. In a fight with other pack-kin, we would all die."

That answer gave the logic circuits in SilverSide's brain the information they needed. Electrical synapses closed. It was simple.

The First Law demanded that human life must be protected. Her positronic brain, like every robot's, logically resolved inevitable conflicts to protect the many over the few. If the kin stayed here, the conflict would be human against WalkingStone. If they moved, another, uglier conflict must be confronted, and that would pit human against human. SilverSide could not kill humans.

That realization allowed her to make an unpleasant decision. "Then we will stay here," she said, "and my choice is made for me."

"What choice?" KeenEye demanded.

"The choice to fight the WalkingStones."

"We *can't* fight them," KeenEye insisted.

"I know a way," SilverSide said. "I do not like it, but I know a way."

"Then speak. *Tell* us," KeenEye said, and the insolence was back in her voice, in her stance, in her smell. SilverSide stared at KeenEye, daring the former leader to challenge her again. SilverSide let her body enlarge slightly, her already massive chest puffing out. KeenEye growled and backed away.

"Kin will probably die, my way," SilverSide said, still looking at KeenEye. "But you tell me there is no other choice that is not worse. If you tell me wrong, you may well destroy the pack. If there *is* any way for us to go elsewhere, tell me now."

"There is no way," KeenEye said, snorting. She pawed at the ground with a clawed hand. "There are other packs all around us: OneEye's, ScarredPaw's. They've already said they will kill any of our litter-kin who trespass. Ask Life-Crier—he can tell you of the battles between packs. I didn't lie. And I'm not afraid to fight. Kin die all the time—it is part of the Hunt, it is part of defending territory."

"Then it is time to hunt WalkingStones," SilverSide answered.

"It is time to challenge them."

CHAPTER 14

AROUND THE CAMPFIRE

It was difficult to hear anything above the racket Derec and Mandelbrot made moving through the woods. Derec quickly realized that there was no hope he'd be able to survive by hunting for food. He'd starve first.

They'd seen very little wildlife except during their rest periods. Otherwise, whatever animals lived here simply fled from the clamor of their passage. Shapes skittered through the trees ahead of them, birds took to the air with shrill cries. But a new sound intruded, making Derec cock his head quizzically.

"Did you hear that, Mandelbrot?"

Derec had stopped, leaning on the walking stick he'd cut from a dead branch and breathing heavily. They were struggling up a slope tangled with dense, close underbrush and tenacious, sticky-leaved vines; the place seemed to have been designed to give them trouble. The sun was already behind the hill and dropping rapidly, and Derec's legs itched wherever the plants had scraped skin through his clothing. Mandelbrot, ahead of him and sounding in dire need of an overhaul, was moving very slowly with his malfunctioning leg. The robot stopped and turned his head around, the neck grating metallically.

"I have heard several things, Master Derec. Which sound were you referring to?"

"The howling. There—you hear that?"

Very faintly, a mournful wail greeted the dusk. Another voice joined the first, then several others. The mournful chorus continued for several seconds, then went back to the solo voice once more. The forest seemed suddenly very dim and dangerous. Derec shivered involuntarily.

"That sends cold chills down my back," he said.

"There are thermal blankets in the pack," Mandelbrot told Derec. "Let me get one for you—"

Derec smiled. "It's not that kind of chill. It sounds like recordings I've heard of wolves—made before they became extinct."

The barking howls began again, echoing and reverberating among the slopes. Mandelbrot's neck joint screeched again as the robot looked upslope. "Their voices are complex," he said. "In some ways it reminds me of Wolruf's language."

Mention of the caninoid alien's name made Derec nod; he missed Wolruf, missed her quick wit and odd temper. "I wish it were, believe me. At least then we might get out of this mess. We have to find a place to camp for the night, Mandelbrot. Any level and halfway open space will do. I don't want to get caught out here in the open during the dark."

"My data banks say that even in the days before Earth was settled, most wild animals were afraid of humans. They very rarely attacked anyone without provocation."

"Well, I'm not going to count on them having been fed

the same data. Let's keep going, Mandelbrot. Maybe at the top of this hill . . . though from the size of it I'm beginning to think we should promote it to mountain."

It took them another hour to struggle to the summit. There, the trees thinned out and finally disappeared on a wind-swept, rocky ledge that, looming above the surrounding hills, gave them an excellent vantage point.

Every last muscle in Derec's body ached from the exertion of the climb. His broken arm throbbed and burned; he was breathing in quick gasps, afraid to breathe any deeper because of his ribs. Derec swung his pack down with a grimace and found the medical supplies. An EndPain injection allowed him to keep moving. Mandelbrot, every joint rasping, helped Derec inflate the tent and arrange their pitifully few supplies. Derec started a small fire in a circle of rocks, and they sat on the hilltop watching the stars appear in the dark blue of the zenith, sprinkled across the sky in their millions.

"They certainly are persistent, those wolves or whatever they are." The howls had continued to serenade them as they'd made camp. They seemed to be coming from the west, in the same general direction they were heading though several hills over. Derec sat on the edge of the ledge and tossed pebbles into the trees below, listening to them crash through the branches. He looked at the shadowy landscape ahead of them and grimaced. "Look at that. You'd figure the hills would all have to run north and south—we're going to walk five kilometers up and down for every one due west."

Derec glanced over at the robot standing alongside him. It didn't seem to have heard. "Mandelbrot?"

"I am sorry, Master Derec. I was listening to them."

"Just make sure they don't get closer." Derec threw another stone, then squinted toward the west. "How well are you seeing, Mandelbrot?"

"My night vision is very poor due to the crash damage. It is no better than yours."

"Uh-huh. Take a look anyway and tell me if that isn't a glow in the northwest, maybe four or five of those hills over. I didn't notice it before, but with the darkness—"

Mandelbrot peered in the direction Derec was pointing. "I see a patch of light reflecting from underneath clouds. . . ."

Then, for a moment, they were both silent, listening to a voice that whispered in both their heads.

All units: central computer under attack. All units . . .

The voice was very faint. It faded even as Derec tried to get the voice to respond.

"My fa—" Derec began, then stopped himself. He hated the man too much to call him that, and on Aurora it meant very little anyway. "Mandelbrot, it must be Avery."

"It is possible."

"It's more than possible. It explains everything: the distress call, the central computer not responding to the chemfets, our crash-landing—everything. He could have used a Key, jumped to the Compass Tower here, and started disrupting the city."

"Why?" Mandelbrot asked. "The first Robot City was his creation."

"He was also very disturbed that I could control it. Maybe he's decided to destroy all the others."

"It is possible, I suppose," Mandelbrot admitted. "But we will not know until we arrive."

"We have to push harder, Mandelbrot. The city's in trouble."

"Why should that concern you so much, Master Derec?"

The question sounded like one Ariel might have asked, and the reminder hurt more than his physical pain. Derec scowled. "It just does. Maybe it's the chemfets—some chemical bonding with the city that's due to them. I don't *know*, Mandelbrot. All I can tell you is that I hurt when the city hurts, and it makes me want to do something about it. Can you understand that?"

"I can, Master Derec. What you describe sounds very similar to the compulsion of the Three Laws within every robot. And if we must push ourselves tomorrow, I would suggest that you rest," the robot said gently. "You are exhausted, and I cannot carry you."

Derec wanted to argue, but Mandelbrot was right. He could feel the weariness; and the effort it took to get to his feet convinced him. "Then I'm going to try to sleep. What about you?"

"I do not know how much longer I will be able to walk. The less I move, the better. I will stand here and watch. Have a good sleep."

His dreams were haunted by his father, who could take on the shape of a wolf. Ariel was there, but wolf-Avery chased her away, and though Derec tried to run after her, his feet were leaden and horribly slow.

Derec awoke with a start. For a moment, he was disoriented and nearly panicked until the nagging pain in his arm and ribs reminded him. He opened the tent and poked his head out through the flaps.

It was still dark. Two moons were in the sky; one high, the larger one low to the west. Backlit against the moonlight, he could see Mandelbrot, standing motionless at the edge of the overlook and staring out into the night. He could hear the wolf-creatures baying at the moon.

"Mandelbrot?"

"Everything is fine, Master Derec. I was listening to them. Their voices; it is almost like a language."

"Their voices make me want to avoid them at all costs. They're probably discussing how tasty my bones and your metal would be. Good night, Mandelbrot."

"Good night, Master Derec."

He lay there for a long time in the darkness, not wanting to go to sleep. He didn't know if it was because Avery would be waiting for him in his dreams, or because he was afraid Ariel would not.

CHAPTER 15

FEINT AND THRUST

SilverSide's creator herself might have been distressed by the robot's logic. Janet Anastasi might well have been appalled and considered SilverSide's positronic mind to be hopelessly damaged. It is impossible to say.

Surely an Auroran robot would have been crippled, if not driven into outright positronic lockup, by the implications of this decision. But to SilverSide, the Three Laws were simply the morals of the OldMother, and her logic and her interpretations were not shaped by human standards, but by those of the kin.

Inclined to respond physically and aggressively to a challenge.

It took the pack another day to prepare, a long day of using their "found" tools such as sticks and flat stones, their few flint-shaped blades and planes. No one was exempt; even the very old and the very young helped as far as they were able.

After SilverSide was satisfied with the arrangements, she sent most of the kin back to PackHome after warning them to take a circuitous, long route. She sent some of the hunting kin with them for protection, not wanting to leave PackHome entirely undefended should her plan fail. KeenEye and LifeCrier insisted on remaining behind with SilverSide, and she chose another half-dozen of the pack to stay as well.

As the sun set, they said their farewells to the rest of the kin and watched them make their way among the trees. When they were gone, SilverSide howled a long challenge to the rising moons and turned to the others.

"Now, let us go find a WalkingStone to kill," she said.

The city had changed, even in the two days since she had last seen it. It had encroached farther on the forest, spilling from the valley that had confined it. Worker WalkingStones with roaring chainsaws for arms were tearing at the trees at the leading edge of the city; farther in toward the Hill of Stars, everything seemed to have changed. The ice-blue building to the west had been farther over and shorter the last time, and the flying buttresses linking it to the building alongside had not been there at all. The cluster of geodesic domes at the base of the Hill of Stars was certainly new, and an open space lush with greenery yawned under the bright lights of a slender needle tower. It was as if the WalkingStones were not satisfied with their expansion; they had to tear down and rebuild even in the center of their city.

The valley was awash in them. The wind stunk of metal; the VoidEyes in the sky above were lost in the glare.

Yet the WalkingStones' ceaseless toil impressed SilverSide, even as she growled at the sight of the naked, muddy hillsides in their path.

"They rape the land, like a male taking a female before her time," KeenEye snarled. She growled in BeastTongue: a sound of pure loathing. "There are always more of them, always more of their stone caves, always more of their lights and noise and smells."

"They leave nothing for us," LifeCrier agreed. "Is this the way the Void looks, SilverSide? Is this the way the gods live?"

"I do not know," SilverSide answered. "It is possible. I feel . . . I feel a pull to it, LifeCrier. There is something in the smoothness, in the many tools they use, in the way they move. Perhaps it is something I once knew."

"Then the gods can have the Void," KeenEye said in irreverent KinSpeech. "I hate it."

"OldMother will eat the souls of kin as we rise to the Void," LifeCrier chastised the former leader, using Hunt-Tongue to emphasize his point. "She takes us to the One Pack again, and we run in the Endless Forest."

SilverSide snapped at the two of them. "Silence!" she ordered. LifeCrier immediately moved back into the pack; KeenEye stared at SilverSide for a moment, then dropped her muzzle. "Move forward now. Quietly. We don't want to bring the Hunters too quickly."

The pack flowed among the trees following SilverSide. She brought them to a halt near the cleared section down-wind of the WalkingStones and surveyed the area.

"There," SilverSide whispered, pointing. "They will do."

The wall of a building rose several meters away, a building under construction. A group of three WalkingStones was hauling materials to a wheeled cart alongside the wall, their backs to the forest. The workers were isolated, most of the continuing work being done in a floodlit area half a kilometer away. Their head-voices were silent.

"Now," SilverSide said, and leaped into the open.

As one, the pack followed her, sweeping across the

ground like a gray wind and then falling on the WalkingStones with savage growls. SilverSide took one of them by the throat, shaking with all her robotic strength and feeling the hated thing die before it could sound an alarm. The others hit the remaining two WalkingStones in a rush.

Central! Under attack—

SilverSide heard the distress call cut off in mid-sentence even as she turned to help KeenEye and the others. She needn't have been concerned. As she had suspected from her encounter with the other worker, the kin's strength was great enough to disable this species of WalkingStone. Under the floodlights across the open field, other workers were looking at them, and SilverSide heard them alerting Central to the pack's presence.

She grasped KeenEye's shoulder. "The Hunters will be coming. We must go."

"Then we'll meet them here," KeenEye said. Her eyes were bright with the death of the WalkingStones.

"No," SilverSide said in emphatic HuntTongue. "KeenEye will destroy the pack if she does that. We've prepared for them—they will follow. I promise that. Take them; I'll follow."

KeenEye gave a howl of both challenge and triumph to the nearest workers and turned. The pack followed her back into the forest. SilverSide waited, standing over the downed workers. Yes, they were like the *krajal*. The others had turned back to their work, following the orders of Central. She heard Central call the Hunters. When she saw the first gleam of their armored skin rushing toward her, she turned and followed the path of the others back into the forest.

Behind her, she heard the crashing as the Hunters bulled their way into the undergrowth.

SilverSide snaked her way through the trees, making sure she stayed well ahead of them but left a clear path behind. Even so, the WalkingStones remained close behind her. When she finally broke through into the glade where the others waited, they were not far behind. All the kin could hear them; birds were rising in panic above the trees, and they could smell the oily stench. The kin stirred restlessly, muttering in angry BeastTalk as they milled around SilverSide.

She stood in the center of the glade, pacing. The open spot was situated in a deep valley, surrounded on all sides but one by steep slopes. "The rest of you—into the trees and make ready," she ordered. "Do not let them see you. Remember that their lightning will kill you if it touches you. I will lure them in and then run. KeenEye, you will do the rest."

They were barely in position when the first of the Hunters broke through the ring of trees, the others at its heels. SilverSide gave a rumbling BeastTalk challenge, then broke and ran when the Hunters raised their hands to her. Laser fire raked the trees, just missing her, and the Hunters lumbered into motion again. *Follow*, the voices in her head said. *Do not let the creature escape this time.*

This was exactly what SilverSide had hoped for. The hillsides formed a natural funnel; the WalkingStones had to move as a group. The WalkingStones moved across the glade as one.

And, as one and intent on their pursuit of SilverSide, they tumbled into the deep pit the kin had dug across the glade and hidden with dry grass.

"Now, KeenEye!" SilverSide cried.

The dirt removed from the pit had been piled next to it and blocked with fallen logs. Now KeenEye cut the lashings holding the logs. They rolled crazily over the edge, followed by a roaring landslide of dirt and stones. The kin pushed at the mounds of dirt, howling, keeping it cascading down on the Hunters as a choking cloud of dust rose. SilverSide could hear the head-voices wailing distress as the WalkingStones were covered under the weight of two meters of rocky clay.

When the dust settled at last, there was nothing to be seen of the Hunters. They were gone. Buried. Even the head-voices were silent.

The pack howled and wailed in BeastTalk. They clambered over the pit, stomping on the earth that hid the WalkingStones and packing it down. LifeCrier licked SilverSide's cold muzzle; even KeenEye rubbed her flank in appreciation. "We've done it!" LifeCrier sighed. "We've killed Hunters. All the kin can see the gift of the OldMother now."

The reminder served to temper KeenEye's satisfaction. The former leader only grunted. "It might seem so. But this was only one battle, LifeCrier. Only half of SilverSide's plan. There's still the rest."

SilverSide nodded in agreement and the mood of the kin darkened again. The celebration ended as they gathered around her again. "All of you must stay here to watch," she told them when they were quiet. "Central may send workers to dig these Hunters out, or it may have other Hunters to send. KeenEye, your task is harder than mine. You must watch. If other Hunters come, flee, but remember that you cannot go back to PackHome until you have lost them. No matter what, you must keep them occupied for as long as you can. If workers come, you must stop them from un-earthing these Hunters, or if you find that the Hunters can dig themselves out somehow, you must find a way to stop them or slow them down. We've not won. Not yet. We've only made the first step."

SilverSide picked up a clod of dirt and crumpled it in her hand, letting the dust trickle back through her long, clawed fingers. "Now, I must go and find this Central."

CHAPTER 16

A DEATH

"They have been following us for the last few hours, Master Derec."

"I know. I can hear them."

Derec didn't like the sound of the long, quavering howls echoing among the hills. He also didn't like the fact that the sun was just ready to set.

Their last few days had been slow and painful, but mostly uneventful. Mandelbrot's knee had seized up entirely; the robot walked with a stiff-legged limp that made their progress halting. Derec's arm was still sore and throbbing, but he nursed the remaining painkillers, taking them only when it became unbearable. He watched his own footing carefully, knowing that if he stumbled he couldn't easily break his fall. Derec would have sworn that their backpacks, light enough when they'd started out, seemed to be gaining weight as the days wore on.

He wasn't much enjoying his first days on this world. He would have given nearly anything for a hovercraft. His feet hurt, his boots rubbed his toes raw, he'd found a hundred bruises he hadn't known he'd had, and they had no idea if they'd ever see the Robot City that still adamantly refused to talk to him.

What good are the chemfets if you can't communicate both ways?

It was just like something Dr. Avery would do. More and more he was convinced that he would find Avery here, that Avery would somehow be behind it all.

Worst of all, he missed Ariel. He missed her terribly. He'd replayed their argument over in his head a thousand times. He'd come up with a hundred lines that would have made it better, if only he had a chance to do it over again. It would have been so easy.

Okay, Ariel. I'm sorry. Come with us. Please.

But of course there was no way to go back in time and tell her that. There was no way for him to turn back the clock and stop the argument before it began. It would always be there between them. The best he could hope for was that she'd be willing to forgive him when he returned to Aurora.

If he returned to Aurora.

All in all, Derec sorely regretted his decision to come to this place.

And now there were wolves.

They had been shadowing Derec and Mandelbrot since yesterday, always staying out of close range but always just on the edge of sight.

"I believe it is a territorial problem," Mandelbrot said. "I think we are just on the edge of their land and they are warning us away."

"We're not going to harm them. We just want to get to Robot City."

"That doesn't seem to be something they would understand, Master Derec."

Derec stopped and slipped the pack from his back, grimacing as the straps put weight on his broken arm. There was a compressed-air gun in the survival gear, a short-range weapon only, but the glass darts contained a deadly nerve poison. Derec felt Mandelbrot watching him as he loaded the gun and slid the holster on his belt. "They could be carnivores," he said to the robot. "I don't want to take any chances."

"I have been listening to them," Mandelbrot said. "The calls are remarkably complex."

"And their teeth may well be remarkably sharp."

"Understood, Master Derec. Still, I have been carefully watching and listening. They seem to be staying within these hills." Mandelbrot pointed to the area directly ahead of them. "One of them will come directly into view and howl to us, like a challenge or warning—that is why I believe they are telling us to turn away. What if their calls are a language? Perhaps we should avoid confrontation all together."

"How? By going a hundred kilometers around? Mandelbrot, we're both hurt. We need help, and the only help is in Robot City. Which is—we think—that way. Wolves or no wolves. I've heard the wolves, too, and it doesn't sound like any kind of language to me."

"I understand, Master Derec. Still, the voices *are* very complex: the falling tones, the breaks . . ."

"We don't have time for detours. We won't live long enough for that."

Mandelbrot nodded. Derec's insistence forced First Law overtones and Third Law obedience: the robot went silent. They began walking again.

Long shadows covered the landscape; the disc of the sun

was gone behind the hills, and the western sky was a bath of crimson. Already the first stars were up in the east, with the largest of the two moons a crescent horn high in the sky.

Derec and Mandelbrot used the remaining light to push on into the hills. The barks and yips and howls stopped ominously as they topped the first crest. When it became too dark to see the tree roots and stones in their path, they stopped. Derec unpacked the tent; Mandelbrot made a fire. "Wolves are often afraid of fire," Mandelbrot said.

"I'll remember to hire you as a guide next time we go on safari," Derec said. Firelight threw moving, wavering shadows through the trees; the wood hissed and sparked, and it was hard to see anything beyond the glare of the flames. Derec thought it worse than the darkness itself. It was easy to imagine shapes in the erratic light, and none of the shapes in Derec's mind was pleasant.

"I'll get some food started—" Derec began to say.

And then the shapes from his nightmares streaked from the woods, growling and snarling.

They were not wolves, at least not like any wolves Derec knew. They were larger than the old pictures Derec had seen: lean, gray-furred bodies and massive chests, their heads peculiarly shaped, large-skulled but with a distinct canine muzzle. They ran from the woods on all fours but reared up on the hind legs at will, slashing with forepaws—well-articulated fingers tipped with razor claws. Their eyes were red from reflected firelight, and they roared and howled and shrieked as they attacked.

The creatures hit Mandelbrot first, which very likely saved Derec's life. They ignored Derec, slamming into the hobbled robot. Mandelbrot could not move quickly enough to avoid them. The robot flailed back at them, the Avery

arm snaking like a whip. It struck one of the wolves across
the snout and there was a distinct crack of bone as the wolf-
creature yelped, rolled, and fled.

Three more struck Mandelbrot at once, and the impact,
combined with Mandelbrot's bad leg, knocked the robot entirely over. He fell into the fire, clasping two of the attacking
wolf-creatures. Sparks flared and snapped; the wolves
howled in fear and pain as they struggled to get away from
the robot's steel grasp. Mandelbrot let them go at last and
the wolves yelped and fled, their fur scorched and burning.
Mandelbrot struggled to get back on his feet, sending glowing embers flying through the air.

Then everything was confused. Derec had dragged the
gun from its holster. He squeezed the trigger at anything
moving beyond the campfire; the gun bucked in his hand.
Something big and horribly strong hit him from behind and
he went down, shouting with pain and nearly losing consciousness as he landed on his bad arm. He couldn't see
anything; his head was full of exploding blotches. Somehow
Derec held onto the gun and fired blindly. He couldn't tell
if he hit anything or not, but all at once the battle was over.
One of the wolves gave a short, high bark; the others
dropped the attack and fled into the woods.

Derec felt a metallic hand on his shoulder. "Master Derec?"

"Wolves are afraid of fire, huh?"

"I have made the correction in my data bank."

"Good. Wonderful. Now help me up."

The camp was a mess. Burning logs were scattered
around the area; the tent had collapsed. There was a long
rip in one of the packs, and several cans of food had spilled
out. "Great," Derec sighed. "We'll be up half the night fixing

things. *If* our friends don't make a return visit," he added. "Man's best friend, they aren't."

They found the body in the morning as they began their trek once more. Derec nearly stumbled over it in the underbrush. "What the—" he began, then stopped.

"Oh, no," Derec said breathlessly. "Please, no."

"What is it, Master Derec?" Mandelbrot said, limping over.

Derec didn't answer. He only stared.

The wolf-creature had evidently caught one of the stray darts Derec had fired the night before. It was a young one, a female who had evidently been watching the fight from the cover of the trees. She certainly had not been involved herself.

She couldn't have, even if she'd wanted to. Lashed around her body with vines was a primitive *travois* built of trimmed sticks, a carrier. And in one hand, uselessly, she clenched a stone knife the chipped edges of which showed the mastery of a flint knapper.

"By any god you care to name..." Derec breathed. "Mandelbrot, you were right. The wolves—they're *sentient.*"

Derec looked at the body, stricken. "And I killed one."

CHAPTER 17

IN THE HILL OF STARS

She bayed a challenge to Central from the nearest hill, for no kin would go into battle with an equal without first warning them.

There was no answer. She hadn't expected one.

Pacing along the hills at the edge of the city, SilverSide watched for several minutes, paying careful attention to the movements of the nearest WalkingStones and listening to their voices in her head.

There were several types that seemed to roam freely through the streets. SilverSide left the heights and moved down from the trees to get a closer look at them. She ran quickly across the cleared area around the spreading city and into the shadows of the buildings. When one of the WalkingStones passed her hiding place, SilverSide quickly memorized its shape and walk; once it was gone, SilverSide willed her body to change once more, patterning herself after the WalkingStone. Her head became round and smooth; her body straightened and she stood upright, letting the markings of the kin disappear.

When it was done, she took the necklace of wires from her head and laid the token of her first victory on a ledge. She walked onto the hard stone walkways and eternal daylight of the city.

SilverSide watched and listened carefully for any sign of recognition or alarm in the first few WalkingStones she passed, but none of them paid her any attention at all. As she went deeper into the steel canyons of this place, the WalkingStones became more numerous. Soon SilverSide was moving in great crowds of them, of all manner of shapes and sizes. This was certainly not the forest, where a kin could—at need—wander for a day or more without seeing another of the kin. LifeCrier's analogy, which had first sparked this idea in her, seemed more and more apt. These were *krajal*, hive-insects. They could not exist without each other. They had no individuality at all. They existed only to serve Central, and without Central they were nothing.

Their society seemed very wrong to SilverSide. Her decision now gave her no pause at all. It was right to destroy this place, despite the sophisticated technology it showed. It spoke of intelligence, yes, but of intelligence used in the wrong way. This was not logical, she decided. This was not the way of humans.

SilverSide continued on. The kin, she knew, would have been puzzled by the silence of the city: there were few noises at all beyond the hum of machinery and the sound of the WalkingStones' passage. None of them spoke in what the kin would have considered an audible range. But SilverSide heard the racket of their thousands. She listened to the WalkingStones' endless chatter in her head. Already she was missing the good smell of earth and foliage and the sounds of life. This was a dead place. This was a sterile and horrible place, and she was headed for the very heart of it.

The Hill of Stars. There, Central would be waiting for her. LifeCrier had said that the Hill of Stars was the first thing the WalkingStones had built. The *krajal* always built first a room for their queen.

The different species of WalkingStones all used different frequencies to communicate with Central—SilverSide knew that without understanding frequencies or bandwidths: each species resonated in a slightly different place in her head. Janet Anastasi had also built into her robot a primitive location device: SilverSide could listen to Central and know from which direction the transmission came.

It was easy enough to walk the streets and listen, tracking Central. None of the workers even questioned her right to be there; they ignored her, going about their own tasks.

Central was concerned about her, though. SilverSide heard a continuous stream of unanswered queries directed to the Hunters. As she approached the Hill of Stars itself, Central ordered a group of workers into the forest to seek the Hunters. SilverSide felt satisfaction at that, for it meant that Central either had no more Hunters to send or that it was not going to expend more of them until it understood what had happened. Either way, it meant that the other kin were relatively safe for the moment.

SilverSide continued on until she reached the large open plaza in which the Hill of Stars stood.

The gigantic pyramidal structure overshadowed any of the other buildings in the city, towering higher than the hills surrounding the valley. Its steep, sloping faces were pocked with windows behind which she could occasionally see one of the WalkingStones moving. The scale of the structure was something she could only now begin to understand. It was immense, far larger than anything else in this place. A fitting place for the Central, for this queen WalkingStone, she decided. There were large doors cut into each of the sides. SilverSide began walking across the plaza toward the nearest of them.

She expected to be stopped and challenged. She had prepared herself to be ready to move quickly and violently, knowing that once an alarm was raised, Central would immediately take steps to protect itself, and she would have scant minutes to finish her task.

It was almost too easy. None of the WalkingStones in the plaza made any move to prevent her from entering the Hill of Stars. Like the rest, they paid no attention to her at all. She was simply another one of the workers, going silently about her task without question—why should another of them question her right to be there? She entered into a cold dimness bounded by stone and cut with wide hallways.

There were fewer of the WalkingStones here, and most of them had a different body construction: more streamlined, with hands obviously designed for delicate work. From the orders given them by Central, SilverSide knew that these were the attendants of Central, the ones allowed into its presence. SilverSide let her body change to match their shape in a brief moment when she was alone in the hall and then continued walking, waiting.

It took only a few minutes. An order came from Central to one of the attendants who had just passed SilverSide, summoning it. The WalkingStone turned to obey, and SilverSide followed, moving with the WalkingStone along the labyrinthian corridors deeper into the heart of the Hill of Stars. In time, they passed through a set of wide doorways into a vast interior chamber.

And SilverSide looked upon Central.

The huge chamber was brightly lit from hanging lamps. Four doors entered into it on the ground level; balconies rimmed the walls to the ceiling, twenty or more stories high. In all that vast space, WalkingStones moved on all sides, but the ground floor was left mostly empty but for a cluster in the exact middle. There stood a quartet of Hunters, one at each corner of an array of eight wafer-thin, two-meter-tall rectangles, arranged like the rays of a stylized sun around a central column. The column was all black and chrome, with tiny lights blinking red and amber up and down its length. The presence of the Hunters would have been enough, but SilverSide could sense the power and energy coming from the structures.

Central. The Queen. The mind behind the Walking-Stones.

And with the Hunters guarding it, SilverSide knew that a frontal attack would not work. She altered her course in what she hoped looked to be a purposeful way, angling toward another of the exits from the room. One of the Hunters watched her, but she heard nothing in her head from Central. SilverSide left the room and went into the hallway beyond.

Had she been kin, she might have felt despair. Isolated as it was, with the Hunters around it, there seemed to be no way to reach Central. It would be a long run across that floor; before she could hope to reach the unit, she would be cut down by the Hunters' laser fire. As for the balconies . . .

She passed a glassed-in elevator rising toward the top of the Hill of Stars, climbing the outside of Central's chamber. The glimmer of an idea sparked in her positronic brain.

SilverSide stepped into the open door of one of the elevators as another of the WalkingStones stepped off. A row of marked buttons was set next to the door; she pressed one and the elevator rose swiftly up, stopping gently with a chime. SilverSide stepped out and found the nearest door leading into the central chamber. She stepped to the railing and looked down.

Far, far below in that dizzying space, she could see the sunray design of Central.

Any Third Law requirement that she protect her own life was lost in the First Law possibilities represented by the death of Central. The fact that she might die in the effort meant nothing weighed against the fact that it would save the lives of kin. SilverSide climbed up on the railing, her body changing back to wolf shape. Her powerful hind legs gathered.

She leapt.

Her robotic strength took her out over the well of emptiness. At the zenith of her leap, over the center of the space, she willed herself to change once more, letting the body expand and thin and flatten into a glider shape like the paraseeds she'd seen fall from the trees near PackHome. She sailed, soaring and spiraling down—a silent enemy descending.

For several seconds, she heard nothing. SilverSide began to think that this would work, that she would plummet unhindered down to Central.

But a worker pointed as she passed one of the balconies in her descent. SilverSide realized that there were certain things too out of the ordinary for even the workers to ignore.

Central! Alert!

The Hunters looked up and saw SilverSide.

One of the younglings heard them first. "KeenEye," he hissed. "WalkingStones!"

KeenEye growled in BeastTalk. Since SilverSide had left, she had been prowling the ground where the Hunters were buried, nervous and agitated. She'd been expecting this. She'd known that this was a foolhardy idea from the beginning. But SilverSide was the leader—there was nothing she could do about that short of challenging her again, and SilverSide was simply too strong. KeenEye gave LifeCrier a baleful, accusing glance and bounded toward the youngling.

"Go see where they are," she ordered the young male. "Quickly!"

"SilverSide hasn't had time yet to destroy Central," LifeCrier said, coming up behind KeenEye as she watched the youngling rush away. "Only a few more minutes—"

"Or perhaps she's already been killed and this is a squad of Hunters who will kill the rest of us."

"SilverSide is the OldMother's—"

"Be quiet!" KeenEye growled in savage HuntTongue. "I am tired of hearing this prattling about OldMother and the Void. SilverSide has made a mistake, whether she is from the OldMother or not."

"And what would you have done, KeenEye? Would you let us slowly starve to death? At least SilverSide is trying to do something about the WalkingStones."

Their argument went no further. The youngling came back panting. "They are workers," he gasped, his head lolling and his tongue out. "But one of them has hands like the Hunters. That one walks in front, like a leader."

"SilverSide had said that Central might send workers," LifeCrier said.

"She didn't say that they would have the weapons of the Hunters, though, did she?" KeenEye glowered. "If they're workers, then we will destroy them as we did the others. They will be expecting us here. LifeCrier, you will go to the west and circle to come behind them; I will go east and do the same. The rest of you will hide in the trees until these workers begin to dig. Then we'll hit them from all sides at once. Make sure the first one attacked is the one with Hunter's hands."

KeenEye looked at each of the small group of kin and lapsed back into KinSpeech, gruffly affectionate. "We must stop them from unearthing the Hunters. We must try to give SilverSide the time she asked for." She looked at LifeCrier last of all. "Even if it means nothing," she added. "Now— go!"

KeenEye and LifeCrier streaked away as the others melted into the cover of trees around the glade.

CHAPTER 18

ENCOUNTER WITH KIN

The wolf-creatures did not attack again that day, though Derec and Mandelbrot heard them often or glimpsed them shadowing their progress through the trees. Derec watched them, his weapon at ready but not certain that he could fire it again, not with the knowledge that they were intelligent. Once or twice, he called out to the wolves or gestured to one of them slipping past, but they never responded.

By noon, the calls had faded behind them, and they were left alone in the forest.

"I think we must have passed only through a far corner of their territory," Mandelbrot said. "The attack was simply to ensure that we came no closer to their den or whatever, and they stayed with us to be certain that we left. It is a lucky accident that our path did not lead us in the wrong direction."

"It would have been luckier if it hadn't led us to them at all," Derec answered morosely.

"We must be very careful," Mandelbrot said. "There are likely to be more tribes in the area. Master Derec, do you think that perhaps these wolf-creatures would be able to help us? Perhaps we do not have to find the Robot City."

"No," Derec replied, but the question made him glance over to Mandelbrot. "We need Robot City. Stone Age technology won't do either of us any good. Are you going to repair your knee with a flint joint? Are you going to find servos and high-grade lubricants and a new optical circuit?"

Mandelbrot was silent after that, but Derec knew that the robot was experiencing a mental quandary after their encounter with the wolf-creatures. Mandelbrot was obviously troubled by their sentience. It showed in the questions he asked, in the way that he looked at Derec's weapon, in the attention the robot paid to the movement of the wolf-creatures watching them.

Knowing the robot as he did and having seen the reactions of the original Robot City robots to Wolruf, Derec knew where the problem lay. He could almost hear balances shifting within the robot's mind.

"Mandelbrot," he said as they walked, "how do you regard the wolf-creatures? How do the Laws apply to them?"

"Are you asking if I consider them 'human,' Master Derec?"

"Yes. I suppose that's the basic question. Are they human? I know you came to class Wolruf as human."

"Positronic minds are as variable as those of humans, Master Derec. What *is* human? There are many ways to answer the question, all of them valid and all of them with shortcomings. Certainly it is more than simply the way a being looks; even among the humans I have seen there is a great variance."

Derec was shaking his head. "But every one of them you've encountered has been Homo sapiens, a bipedal, upright-walking mammal descended from apes and able to trace their ancestry back to Earth. These wolf-things, what-ever they are, aren't bipedal, aren't apes, and aren't de-scended from anything on Earth."

"That description fits Wolruf as well."

"Point taken. But you haven't answered my question yet. Let me give you a hypothetical situation: If I told old Balzac back on Aurora that Wolruf was a great danger to me and the only way to remove the danger was to kill her, would Balzac do it?"

"The danger would have to be demonstrated, Master De-rec. Your word would not be enough."

"All right, assume it was. Assume I can convince Balzac of the imminent risk. I know I couldn't order Balzac to kill a human, but what about Wolruf? Balzac's seen her walk and talk and use the computer and pilot a ship. Would he still be able to protect me?"

Mandelbrot's eyes gleamed. His bad leg dragged through underbrush, and the robot came to a halt alongside Derec. "You are asking this because you are concerned that I will not be able to protect you should these wolf-creatures attack again."

Derec shrugged. He patted his broken arm, then waggled the gun in his hand. "We're not in the greatest of shapes, Mandelbrot. Neither one of us. First, I don't want to have to use this thing, not after what we know now, but if I have to in order to stay alive, I probably will. What about you, Mandelbrot?"

The robot seemed to consider that for a long moment, and for a moment Derec was afraid that he might have in-advertently driven the robot into positronic lockup. Then servo motors whirred as it began walking again. "I have searched my data banks and checked the functions of my logic system, Master Derec, and the readouts are very erratic. My priority circuits are almost in balance. Had I never met Wolruf, had I never seen sentient alien lifeforms, and did I not have memories of Robot City in my mind, I am sure it would be different."

"What are you saying, Mandelbrot?"

"That I do not know what I would do, Master Derec. I do not know."

He could have insisted. He could have made it a direct question and stressed the importance of an answer—the Second Law would have forced Mandelbrot to answer. *"Mandelbrot, do you consider these wolf-creatures to be as human as me?"*

But somehow it didn't seem right to ask.

After all, Derec wasn't sure of the answer himself.

All of the sudden, it was too late to ask.

They had continued to walk even after the sun had set. The moons were up and bright, and Derec wanted to cover as much ground as they could before settling for the night.

Mandelbrot's comlink overheard the short-range call. "Derec," it said. "There are robots in the near vicinity." Mandelbrot's flat, emotionless voice sounded strangely dispassionate. "They seem to be searching for Hunter-Seekers that are also supposed to be in this vicinity."

Derec couldn't help the grin that split his face. "That's wonderful, Mandelbrot. Now we can finally get out of here." He focused his thoughts inward, trying to contact the robots via the chemfets in his body, but the link was still not there. "Can you contact them, Mandelbrot? Tell them there's a human in need of aid—"

Derec got no farther.

A fury in gray fur hit him from behind. Claws raked his shoulder as he was sent sprawling to the ground. His broken arm hit a root protruding from the earth. Derec screamed involuntarily as the world went dim. His attacker, a wolf-creature, had turned to attack again, snarling. Derec tried to raise himself up with his good hand and could not. The wolf-creature gathered itself to pounce.

Derec knew he was going to die.

The wolf-creature, sentient or not, was going to rip his throat out.

Derec struggled to crawl, to move. He saw a blur of metal and heard the whine of overtaxed gears. Mandelbrot had moved to intercept the wolf-creature. But the gear-whine became a wail and the robot's leg seized up entirely. Mandelbrot started to fall, internal gyros protesting, as the wolf-creature leapt.

Mandelbrot's Avery-type arm snaked out even as he fell, even as the body of the wolf-creature bounded over the robot's prone body. Mandelbrot grabbed, held, and threw. It was all he could do. The wolf yelped in surprise and pain, then the body thudded against the tree next to Derec and slumped to the ground.

The stars in Derec's head went away slowly. His vision cleared to see Mandelbrot lying next to him and staring. "Master Derec?" the robot asked. "I think I may have killed it." His voice seemed to grind from his metallic larynx, halting. Derec understood immediately that the robot was very near lockup. His one good eye was dim, and his hand was fisted tightly.

"Mandelbrot," he said desperately. "You had to do it. I would have died otherwise. I'm . . . I'm okay, I think. You saved my life, Mandelbrot. You had no choice. No choice at all. If you lockup now, you're committing a First Law offense. I need you."

Derec tried to rise and fell back again with a groan. He'd intended it as an act—it wasn't. The pain was all too real.

His discomfort stirred Mandelbrot. The eye came back to full brilliance, the hand unclenched, and the robot stood up, his left leg sticking out stiffly in front of him. Gently, he helped Derec to his feet. "Thank you, Mandelbrot," Derec said and went to the wolf-creature. It was not breathing. Up close, it was magnificent: muscular, the thick fur rich with glossy highlights in the moonlight, the face expressive even in death. Derec's gaze was caught by the forepaws. They were true hands, despite the deadly curved claws, the long fingers delicate and jointed, the thumb opposed and ideal for grasping. The creature must walk on its knuckles, he realized, for the tops of those joints were wide, flat, and bony. Except for that difference, the hands might have been those of a human.

Derec sighed. Mandelbrot was right to be bothered by the death.

The massive head lolled, the neck broken. Derec stroked the fine, gray-tipped black fur of the creature with his good hand. "You couldn't help it, Mandelbrot," he said again, knowing the robot was watching him. "You have to know that."

He stopped. His fingers had found something in the fur of the creature's neck. Derec pulled it loose. It was a necklace of colored wire. Soldered to the end of one of the strands was a small circuit board. Derec's breath hissed in with surprise. "Mandelbrot, look at this! Mandelbrot?"

Mandelbrot was no longer listening. The robot had suddenly straightened in an attitude of listening. "Master Derec! The robots I heard a few minutes ago—they are being attacked!"

From somewhere very close by, they could hear the sudden, savage howling of wolves.

CHAPTER 19

ESCAPE FROM THE CITY

SilverSide's reaction to being seen by the Hunters was swift and powered by the Three Laws. The Third Law forced her to try to save herself. Second Law demanded that she follow the orders of humans, and though she was their leader, KeenEye's commands to save the kin still carried weight; the First Law compelled her to do whatever she could to keep her people alive.

Which meant the prime consideration was that Central be destroyed.

SilverSide changed her shape as the Hunters turned to look up at her. She drew back the parafoil and thickened the body. Even as the Hunters raised their hands to fire their lasers, she became a streamlined, compact mass instead of a glider, and she dropped the last thirty feet like a massive stone, crashing heavily into the central column of Central. Laser beams crisscrossed the air where she had been; delicate circuitry smashed under her fall. SilverSide changed back to wolf form even as she rose from the wreckage of the core unit. She went to the wide panels surrounding the core and pushed with all the strength of her durable body. A panel toppled, striking the next in line—the array went down like a row of dominoes, sparking and crashing, the thunder of their destruction ringing in the cavernous room.

SilverSide fled the room, howling the ritual triumph of a victor even as she anticipated the Hunters' lasers cutting her down. It didn't matter to her. She'd done what she'd come to do.

But nothing happened; the Hunters had stopped.

Already confusion was spreading through the city—she could hear it, a thousand voices crying out in the Void-Tongue that the OldMother had given her. WalkingStones were asking Central for instructions, but Central was not replying, would never reply. The alarm was spreading out through the various levels of this *krajal*-like society.

EMERGENCY! Central core memory damaged and off-line Command program inactive: secondary routines down.

Activate supervisory backups.

Behind her, SilverSide heard the Hunters stir. She raced into the corridor beyond Central's room. There were no WalkingStones in sight there. She quickly altered herself once more to appear as one of the Hill of Stars' Hunters, depending on the disguise to give her cover as she headed for the exit from the place. She listened to the continuing dialogue in her head.

City command given to Supervisor units Alpha, Beta, Gamma. The general announcement went out first over all frequencies, then three new voices boomed in her head. The direction finder in her skull indicated that all three were in widely scattered sections of the city.

ALPHA: Normal city subroutines accessed. City functions on-line and programming reinstated.

BETA: Alert situation! Central computer destroyed. At-

tacking unit in shape of local wolf-creatures is rogue robot. Repeat, attacking unit is robot not under control of City Supervisors.

GAMMA: Alert update. Witnessing units report sophisticated shape-changing abilities. Compass Tower Hunter-Seekers programming altered to compensate.

SilverSide increased her pace as she moved toward the exit. The corridor was crowded now, the WalkingStones returning to their routines. If the Hunters were aware that she could change shape, then her WalkingStone guise was not going to help her for very long. Someone would report her presence or discover the charade through some inadvertent response.

She knew that her victory had been short and bittersweet. Yes, she had destroyed Central. She had disrupted the city, if only momentarily. But the city had responded to the challenge all too well. If she interpreted the signals correctly, there were now three sub-Centrals, all in different places, and they knew her one advantage. If she were going to win this battle, she must move quickly, find all three of these Supervisors, and destroy them.

The next command from the trio of Supervisors dashed any hope SilverSide had at all.

ALPHA: All city units: access subroutine 3067.A.296. Immediately report any units not responding. Hold that unit at all costs until Hunter-Seekers arrive. Third Law precedence invoked—city survival involved: higher priority than individual survival.

All around her, moving WalkingStones came to an abrupt halt. An instant later, SilverSide did the same; it seemed safest.

She was wrong. A simultaneous alert was broadcast from the worker WalkingStones around her. *ANOMALY!*

Hunter-Seeker unit in Compass Tower has stopped. In the same instant, all the workers in sight lunged for her.

SilverSide growled as she dropped back into her preferred wolf shape. She threw the nearest worker aside, the fragile body crumpling under her blow, and dashed through the opening it gave her. The alarm followed SilverSide as she darted from the building—she plowed through a worker who tried to block the entrance to the Hill of Stars and emerged into cool night.

She howled a lament.

Then she turned into the lumbering bird shape she had used once before, a black and sorrowing form.

Clumsily, her wings beat air, and she retreated from the city into the open sky. The false stars of the city below mocked her, and she knew there would be no hiding from the Hunters now.

CHAPTER 20

CONTACT

The uproar was furious, and mixed in with it was an occasional metallic grating, as if someone were bashing a steel plate over and over with a rubber hammer. All at once, there was a yelp of terror and a wail.

"The wolf-creatures," Derec said. "They're the ones who have been attacking the city. They're why we got the distress call. Look!" He held up the braided wire from the dead wolf-creature to Mandelbrot. It sparkled in the yellow-white light of the larger moon.

"The city does not know that they are sentient," Mandelbrot said. The robot seemed to shudder once all over. "The robots think they're just animals. They are simply exterminating them when they find them, like pests."

"This circuit board didn't come from the wolves originally. Sure, the city might think the wolf-creatures are just animals—after all, we did too. But they've obviously destroyed at least one robot already. Mandelbrot, we have to do something. Now."

Derec laid the necklace on the dead wolf-creature's body

and took his gun in his hand, his face grim. Mandelbrot's hand closed over his wrist, firmly. "No," the robot said. The odd grating slur was back in its voice. "I cannot allow you to kill them, Master Derec. I am sorry."

"Mandelbrot, you misunderstand."

"It does not matter if the robots are destroyed. That is only the Third Law and this Robot City can easily build more. I have made the decision you asked me about earlier. To kill a wolf-creature is to break the First Law."

"Please. You must trust me. I am not going to kill them." Derec tried to move his hand; the robot's grip was gentle but unyielding. "Mandelbrot, I am ordering you to release my hand. I will not kill the wolf-creatures. Do you understand that?"

Derec thought that Mandelbrot might not respond. The robot was staring at the dead wolf-creature, at the bright wire. The incident had further upset the positronic brain; Derec began to fear that Mandelbrot would freeze now, with Derec's one good arm locked in a death grip.

It would be an ignoble and curious way to end, anchored to a dead robot.

Mandelbrot's fingers opened slowly. Derec let out a breath he hadn't known he was holding. "Thank you," he said. "Mandelbrot, I'm going to need your help. I need a delicate touch and two good hands. Here—take the gun. Unload it. Quickly, we may only have a few minutes."

The battle was still going on within the darkness under the trees. In fact, the uproar seemed to have intensified. As the robot took the darts from their chambers, Derec opened his backpack and found the medical kit. Luckily, everything there was well padded and nothing had broken in his fall. He looked through the collection of vials, squinting in the dim light, and found what he needed.

"Mandelbrot, break open the dart chambers and empty out the nervekiller. Put this in."

"Master Derec—"

"It's a sedative. Undiluted, and with their body weight, it should knock them out."

Mandelbrot didn't move. His one good eye gleamed an unblinking, insistent red. "Master Derec, these creatures are unknown. Their metabolism might be so different from yours that this kills them."

"Or it may not work at all," Derec pointed out. He sighed. The sound of the nearby struggle was intensifying—he hoped there was still time. He patted Mandelbrot on the shoulder—the robot looked terrible: dinged, scratched, and battered. Having pieced the robot together from several different models and after the patchwork repairs following the crash, Derec felt pleased that the robot was still operating at all. He also hoped that he looked better, but the distorted reflection of himself in the robot's body looked just as disheveled and abused.

They needed help. Quickly.

"Mandelbrot, we can't communicate with them," Derec continued. "Twice now we've been attacked without provocation. They may be sentient, but they're also very dangerous. We need the robots. If we don't do something now, they may destroy all of them, and then they may well come looking for their friend here and take care of us."

"That is not certain."

"No, but it's probable. This is a chance that we *have* to take, one way or the other. A full-strength dose would take out a person of their general weight in two or three seconds and keep them down for an hour or two. Now—take the sedative and put it in the darts. I can't do it myself."

Derec held out the vial.

Mandelbrot hesitated, then the Avery arm extended toward Derec and its fingers closed around the vial. "Yes, Master Derec," Mandelbrot said. With delicate but quick precision, it began to do as ordered.

Mandelbrot reloaded the modified darts into the gun and handed it back to Derec. "Okay, let's go," Derec said. The shivering, challenging howls of the wolves still came from just behind the trees. Derec shouldered the backpack once more and began walking quickly in that direction. Mandelbrot followed more slowly, his left leg dragging and a distinct whine coming from his hip servomotors.

Derec broke through the trees at the top of a steep hill, the sides of which were bare dirt. Below, in a small, grassy glade well lit by the moons, a group of five wolf-creatures were struggling with four robots of the laborer type. One other wolf-creature lay dead from what looked to be a laser burn, but the robot fitted with the laser arm was already down—it was obvious that the wolf-creatures would eventually win this battle. They harried the robots, darting in with great leaps, ripping with the claws and tearing with their jaws, and then bounding away again before the robots could hold them.

As Derec watched, another of the robots slumped to the ground as a wolf-creature ripped a power connector away in a gush of violet sparks that left glowing afterimages in Derec's eyes. Mandelbrot was still struggling through the undergrowth toward him. The wolves were nearly two on one now, and Derec knew there was no time left if he wanted to save any of the robots.

He hoped this would work, but he knew that, though he couldn't say it, he was as skeptical as Mandelbrot. "The way things have gone so far..." he muttered under his breath.

He raised the gun, sighted down the long barrel, and

pressed the trigger, aiming for a gray-furred male who seemed to be the leader. A *chuff* of compressed air: in the glade below, the wolf yelped and leaped into the air. On its hind legs, it reached around and plucked the dart from its skin, looked at it, and threw it down. The old wolf-creature's gaze swept around the glade.

It saw Derec even as he fired the gun once more, hitting another of the wolves.

The old one howled and pointed. Dropping down on all fours again, it charged. Derec counted softly as he fired three more times, injecting all the wolves. Another of them, unhindered by the robots, followed the old wolf's lead and— howling—rushed up the hill toward Derec. "One, two, three, four, five, six, seven . . ."

The wolves kept coming. They looked far more angry than sleepy, and Mandelbrot was still laboring through the trees.

"Oh, Frost," Derec hissed.

The wolf-creatures were fast and powerful. He knew he was not going to be able to retreat anywhere near fast enough. He doubted seriously that he was going to be able to lose them in the darkness.

He threw the useless gun at the old one bounding up the hill.

It missed.

That figures, he thought.

CHAPTER 21

THE VOIDBEING

The old wolf-creature leaped over the edge of the hillside with the second close behind. The old one started to leap and then abruptly halted as if startled, pawing the ground with its clawed hands. The grizzled head cocked quizzically, and it growled something in its sibilant language.

But the younger wolf-creature following it had no hesitation at all. It flashed past the old one with a howl, baring its teeth and its claws flashing in mid-leap. Derec shouted and spun aside as the wolf hurtled toward him. It missed, through Derec felt the wind of its passage. The creature twisted in midair and spun as it hit the ground, kicking up dust. Derec waited for the creature to regain its balance and charge again.

There was nothing he could do. He was trapped between the old one, now snarling at him, and the younger attacker.

As Derec watched, trying to decide which way to run, the younger gathered itself again.

Whimpered.

And fell on its side. The old leader had fallen as well;

down in the glade, the wolf-creatures had also been affected, dropping to the ground in the middle of the attack. Derec sunk down to the ground himself as Mandelbrot finally thrashed through the last trees. "Master Derec!" the robot called.

"I'm all right, Mandelbrot. It worked, I think." Derec gazed down in the glade below, glad that the nights were bright here.

The remaining three robots, suddenly free, had turned to take advantage of the situation. They advanced to the unconscious wolves, raised their hands to strike and kill—

"Stop!"

Derec's shout made them pause. They turned and looked. Derec stood at the edge of the slope, letting them see him fully. "You can see that I am a human," he said loudly. "You must obey me. Come here—the wolf-creatures are no danger now."

They stopped, though they didn't back away from the wolf-creatures. Mandelbrot came up to stand alongside him. "These creatures are no danger to me or to yourselves now," he repeated. "Come here."

"Yes, human master," one of them said. The trio headed for them as Derec and Mandelbrot examined the two sedated wolf-creatures beside them.

The drug had far less effect on the beasts than it would have had on Derec or any other human. Derec went to the leader; it was still awake, its disturbingly humanoid eyes watching him. The body twitched, muscles jerking without control as it struggled to rise and either attack or flee. Derec sat down beside it and stroked the head as he might have a dog. "I'm sorry," he said. "If we could understand each other . . ."

Mandelbrot was looking over Derec's shoulder. "It

worked," Derec told the robot. "It wasn't what I expected, and I'm not sure how long it will last, but it worked. Now we need to get out of here before it wears off." Derec gave the grizzled lupine body a pat and laid the head down gently. The old one's eyes continued to follow his movements.

The three robots had reached them as Derec rose, slapping dirt from his pants. Derec tried to contact them via the chemfet link, but there was still nothing there but silence. "You're from the Robot City?" he asked them.

"Yes."

"Who is in charge there? Are there other humans? Is Avery there?"

"There are no other humans. The central computer directs all city activities."

Derec could feel his shoulders relaxing with their words, and he realized just how tense he'd been at the thought of another confrontation with his father and his twisted genius. He let out a deep sigh. "Then inform the central computer that you have found a human and will be returning with him and another robot to the city," he said. "Tell Central that we've come in response to its distress call, and that we have information for it regarding these wolf-creatures. Tell it also to open a channel to respond to Mandelbrot, the robot with me; I will communicate with the central computer through him."

The robots went silent for a moment, then one of them spoke again. "I am sorry, Master, but the central computer is not responding."

"Mandelbrot?"

"They are correct, Master Derec. There is silence on all ...just a moment." Derec saw the other robots stiffen as if listening to something only they could hear; his own chemfet link seemed to be utterly dead. He could no longer hear the central computer at all.

"Master Derec," Mandelbrot said, "the situation in Robot City has changed radically. The central computer has just been destroyed by a rogue robot. The city is now under control of three Supervisor units. I have contacted them and informed them of your arrival and the situation here. They ask that we come to Robot City as quickly as possible for consultation. The robots here will guide us, and the Supervisors will send out more robots in our direction to escort us in case the rogue attacks us. It seems very violent."

Derec was puzzled. "Surely they don't think the rogue would attack a human, Mandelbrot? And how did the city ever lose control of it?"

"That is the odd thing, Master Derec," Mandelbrot answered. "It is *not* a city robot at all. It is not even humanoid."

Mandelbrot pointed to the drugged wolf-creature.

"It looks like one of these," the robot said.

The dark bird glided over the forest, silent except for the rushing of the wind past its widespread wings. Circling the glade once and seeing nothing, it banked sharply and descended, clipping the treetops and landing clumsily on the top of the hillside overlooking the clearing.

There, under the watching moons, it changed shape and became SilverSide once more.

The Hunters were still buried below. She noted that first of all because it was most important to her positronic mind—First Law. Three WalkingStones lay here as well, and that was also good.

But the dark shapes on the ground near the Walking-Stones were kin. SilverSide howled a lament to the stars and then called for any of the other kin—there was no answer. She shifted her vision into the infrared and immediately saw warmth radiating from the ground nearby: two of the kin, and the shape of one was very familiar. SilverSide let out a glad BeastTalk cry and went to him.

LifeCrier was moving, at least. The old one had lifted himself up on his front legs and was trying to walk, though his rear legs dragged limply behind as if paralyzed. "SilverSide," LifeCrier barked in happy KinSpeech. "You've returned. Did you kill Central?"

"I destroyed it, but it did no good," SilverSide replied flatly. "What happened here? Are the others dead?"

"I don't think so." LifeCrier sank down again, exhausted, but his voice held a rich excitement. "SilverSide, there was a VoidBeing here. It had a companion, another Walking-Stone unlike any of the ones around the Hill of Stars."

"A VoidBeing? From the OldMother?" LifeCrier's words stirred odd resonances deep in SilverSide's mind.

"Not from the OldMother. No, not with that shape. From another of the gods, perhaps. The VoidBeing carried a stick that threw small knives at the kin, and a magic in the knives took away our bodies while leaving our spirits inside. I attacked it because it had the look of the WalkingStones, and I knew it couldn't be from the OldMother. But before I reached it, I could no longer move. I could only watch as it came to me and touched me. I thought it would kill me then, but it didn't. It stroked me like a mother stroking her pup and talked to me in the VoidTongue even though it seemed to know I could not understand it. Then it laid me back down. It left a short time later with the WalkingStones from the city."

Delicate balances were shifting inside SilverSide. Core programming in her positronic mind gave her a feeling akin to yearning. She could hear the echo of the first voice she'd ever heard, talking to her in the VoidTongue in the darkness of the Egg. *A human being is an intelligent lifeform. A robot must obey the orders given it by human beings.*

But this VoidBeing is not of this world, she reminded herself, *not alive as we are. It is a MadeThing of the gods, or one of the gods themselves. So it cannot be human. The kin are human.*

The feeling receded, but only slightly. There was in her a pull toward intelligence. "I must go find this VoidBeing," she said to LifeCrier.

"It's gone back to the Hill of Stars," the old kin told her. "The WalkingStones went with it."

LifeCrier struggled to rise again and this time succeeded in standing on wobbly legs. The other kin were beginning to stir as well, easing SilverSide's First Law concerns.

Until she noticed that there was one less of the kin than there should have been. "Where is KeenEye?" she asked.

LifeCrier's grizzled forehead wrinkled. "I don't know," he answered. "We'd separated the kin to better fight the WalkingStones, and she was to have attacked from over there." LifeCrier pointed into the woods behind them. "I never saw her." The others were coming up to them shakily, and LifeCrier asked all of them: "Did any of you see KeenEye during the fight?"

All the kin shook their heads.

SilverSide looked at the ground and the tracks left by the VoidBeing. It was an extremely clumsy creature; it had left a path through the trees that was as easy to follow as one of the WalkingStone's straight stone paths. An uneasy suspicion came to SilverSide. "Follow me," she said.

She ran into the cover of trees, LifeCrier and the others following slowly behind.

It took no skill at all to follow along the trail the VoidBeing had taken. The creature had broken branches underfoot and on all sides, and the ground still radiated the faint trace of heat from its passage. SilverSide saw a patch of kin-shaped warmth ahead and barked a quick hello.

"KeenEye!"

KeenEye didn't answer. The infrared red blotch didn't move. SilverSide took her vision back up into shorter wavelengths for detail, and then she saw the strange cant of the head and the odd way KeenEye was slumped on her side.

SilverSide growled, deep and warningly. She burst through the underbrush between them, hoping that KeenEye was simply sleeping as the others had been and knowing from the disquieting stillness that she wasn't.

"KeenEye?" SilverSide sat beside the body and lifted her into her arms. The head simply fell back, limp, the eyes open and unseeing; the neck was broken. SilverSide could smell the odd scent of the VoidBeing on KeenEye's fur along with the oily essence of the WalkingStones. That told her all she needed to know.

The VoidBeing had killed KeenEye.

SilverSide threw her own head back and howled her loss to LargeFace, singing KeenEye's spirit into the Void as she had seen the kin do with others who had died. From the trees, the kin—hearing SilverSide's sorrow—joined her with their own voices. The rising and falling of their song went on for long minutes, and then SilverSide let the empty body fall back to earth. It no longer held KeenEye; it was simply a dead husk.

"First we will return to PackHome," SilverSide said to LifeCrier. "And then I will come back here. If this VoidBeing lives in the WalkingStone's city, then it must be their leader."

She lifted her head and howled a BeastTalk challenge. "And if it is their leader, then it would kill all kin in the way it killed KeenEye. I must make sure that threat ends."

CHAPTER 22

BEST LAID PLANS

Derec had forgotten what a bath felt like.

"I have died and gone to heaven," he groaned as he sank back in the swirling warmth. Clouds of bubbles drifted over the enormous tub, and he lowered himself into the delicious heat until only his nose was out of the water. He could feel every bruised and aching muscle in his body starting to relax for the first time in days. Sitting up, he leaned back against the tiles, propping his broken arm (newly braced) on the edge. He motioned the attendant robot forward to scrub away the accumulated grime of his trek through this world.

Derec simply luxuriated, letting the robot do it all.

When it was over, he stepped out into the fluffiest, thirstiest towel he could imagine, allowed the robot to dry him, and put on a warm robe.

He felt soothed and comfortable as he went into the main room of the apartment.

The main room was as large and plush as the bathroom had been. Far up in one of the taller buildings of the city, immense windows on three sides offered a view of the sweeping expanse of the Compass Tower, by far the largest edifice in the city. Mandelbrot was standing there looking out at the landscape, along with another robot that Derec recognized as one of the Supervisor units. The antennae-studded globe of a witness robot hovered nearby.

"Master Derec, you look much better," Mandelbrot said, turning.

Derec grinned. "A bath does wonders, doesn't it. And I can certainly say the same for you." The dings and dents in Mandelbrot's body had been smoothed, his external linkages straightened, and his body polished. The robot's optical circuits now gleamed brightly, and when he moved, servos no longer protested.

"I am again fully operational," Mandelbrot said. "Master Derec, this is Supervisor Beta, one of the control units for this Robot City."

"Beta," Derec nodded. "There're a hundred or so questions I want to ask you."

"I can understand that, Master Derec," the supervisor answered. "Mandelbrot has told me of your journey here. First, I should tell you that the medbots who examined you tell me that you have no serious internal injuries. Your arm has been reset, and a drug that accelerates the knitting of bones has been given to you. Most of your injuries are bruises and contusions that will heal with time. You should be fully recovered within the week. As for your companion, Mandelbrot has been serviced and repaired entirely from parts in city stocks."

"For which we both thank you. But it's entirely possible that none of it would have been necessary in the first place had your central computer answered me."

Derec saw the distress his comment gave Beta; the robot's eyes dimmed briefly, and it backed away slightly. "You sent out a distress call," Derec continued, "but you wouldn't respond to our answer, either through contact via the original Robot City or via the chemfets in my body. Had you done that, we might never have needed to come here at all."

And Ariel and I might never have argued, he thought, and with the image of her that put in his mind, he felt again a deep sadness. *I have to call her. I have to apologize.*

"We deeply regret that, Master Derec," Beta was saying.

"Then why? It doesn't make any sense to ask for help and then ignore someone answering it."

Beta gave an oddly human shrug. "I agree with you, Master Derec. In explanation, all I can tell you is that this city was to be self-sufficient; there were instructions against direct contact with the original Robot City, but that does not explain why we would not respond to a human's inquiry. My fellow supervisors and I have conferred, and we assume the reason was a command in the central computer's programming. When the rogue destroyed the central computer, it also wrecked that portion of the backup units. None of the supervisors had been activated at that time; as you can see, the city is not very large or complex yet." Beta waved a glistening hand to the cluster of buildings below them. "There was no need to disperse city control. I cannot answer your question at this time, though we are attempting to reconstruct as much of the central computer's core memory as possible. If we learn more, I will inform you."

"It was Avery," Derec said with certainty. He rubbed at his damp hair with the towel. "He has the Key of Perihelion. He could have come here and programmed the central computer."

"That is possible. There is no way to be certain."

"Dr. Avery might still be in the city," Mandelbrot said

to the supervisor. "In that case, Master Derec is still in danger."

Beta gestured to the window and the horizon, where the city nudged up against what looked to be an endless forest. "This city, as I said, is very small. I doubt that a human could be in the city and not be noticed."

"Your city let a rogue robot get in and destroy your central computer," Derec reminded Beta.

"The rogue has very special abilities," Beta answered. "We have taken steps to insure that it cannot do this kind of damage again. One of those steps was to activate myself and the two other supervisors so that city control no longer resides only in one place. And as you can see, a witness robot accompanies each of us, coded with instructions to return immediately to a haven should the supervisor be attacked. That way, very little of the city's knowledge would be lost should the rogue manage to destroy one of us. There are other supervisor units waiting to take over should that happen. We are also building new Hunter-Seeker units with special detection devices."

"Great, but I doubt it'll help much. I'd make you a bet that this rogue came from Avery," Derec said. "It has all his ear-marks: inventive, cunning, and very, very dangerous. Which brings us to another problem. You've said that this rogue leads the wolf-creatures?"

"Yes. It was seen directing a pack of them that attacked workers on the edge of the city. They have given the city problems since the beginning, harassing our workers clearing the forest. As we felt them to be hindering our directives and to be dangerous both to ourselves and to any humans who would stay here, the Hunter-Seekers were directed to find and kill them."

Mandelbrot had swiveled to face Beta. "No," it said. "You cannot do that."

"I do not understand. All three of the Laws of Robotics demand it. By the Third Law, we must protect our own existence: they have damaged and destroyed units of this city. By the Second Law, we must obey the commands given to us by humans: they hinder us from following our basic programming. By the First Law, we must above all protect humans, and these creatures are undeniably dangerous. They attacked Master Derec and would have killed him had you not been there. How can there be any question about this?"

"Because it's not exactly that simple, Beta," Derec answered for Mandelbrot. "They're not just 'creatures' attacking you because you're here. I expect that they're protecting their home the same way I would. They're not just animals, Beta. They're sentient. They use tools; they have a language."

"Are you saying that they built the rogue?"

Derec sniffed. "Not a chance. They're barely at a Stone Age level. This rogue sounds more sophisticated than anything here."

"Then how did they get involved with the rogue?"

"I don't know that, but I'm willing to bet that Avery had a hand in it somewhere. The thing to do now is to figure out how to proceed without harming the wolf-creatures. There's a way to do that, I think."

"What do you want me to do?"

"The first thing that has to be done is to inform all city units to view the wolf-creatures as human. The First Law applies to them as well—you are to do nothing that does them harm. Will you do that?"

"You can do it yourself, Master Derec," Beta said. "We

have reprogrammed the city to respond to the chemfets in your body. This Robot City is now under your direction. All you need do is give us your orders."

Derec had paid no attention to the chemfets, silent and useless so long. Now he opened his mind to the sub-miniature replicas of Robot City material. He could *hear* the city now, roaring in his blood. The flood of information was almost too much to comprehend, and he hastily closed down most of the channels, leaving open only the direct links to the supervisors.

You see, Master Derec? It was Beta, talking to him via the chemfets. *All Robot City is now yours.*

Good. Derec nodded and went to the window, looking out over the rooftops and up to the summit of the Compass Tower.

"Then we'll let the rogue in if it wants in," he said. "Avery didn't know that I would come here. Even a rogue has the Three Laws built into it. Avery might be able to design a robot capable of destroying other robots, but I find it hard to believe that even he could build a robot that could knowingly hurt a human."

SilverSide watched two of the cubs wrestling on the floor of PackHome. They rolled over and over on the dusty, broken stones, growling in high-pitched BeastTalk and nipping at each other with their sharp milkteeth. Finally one of them yelped in real pain and lay on his back, paws up and throat bared in submission.

It was ritual play modeled after the adults. SilverSide could hear one of the nursing mothers chuckling throatily as the victor gave a thin howl. She lunged and snapped at the triumphant pup from behind, and it screeched suddenly, leaping high into the air as the fur on its back ruffled in fright. The pup stumbled and fell, and the adults in the cavern laughed as it ran under SilverSide's legs for safety. The pup peered out at them half-puzzled, half-embarrassed.

SilverSide reached down and lifted it in her hands. "You see, the leader always has to be ready for a new challenger," she said to it in soft KinSpeech. She stroked the soft fur and set the pup down again.

The little one ran for its own mother.

"It's always good to see the younglings playing," LifeCrier said to SilverSide as the pup started to nurse. "It reminds you that even though our spirits leave here to go into the Void, OldMother will send them back again." LifeCrier licked SilverSide's face affectionately. "KeenEye will come back one day. She is not gone forever."

"I am not concerned with KeenEye," SilverSide said. "She is dead and doesn't matter any more." It was only true—there were no emotions in her positronic matrix, only the priorities built into it by the Three Laws. Yet SilverSide sensed that her uncaring words hurt LifeCrier, and she tried to explain to the gray-furred kin. "All that concerns me is how she died and why, and what I must do to stop that from happening again. You do not understand me, LifeCrier. You cannot see what is happening inside me."

They were all staring at her now: LifeCrier, the rest of the adult kin, the younglings. Their obvious respect and dependence on her stirred the boiling cauldron inside. SilverSide felt pulled in a dozen different directions at once. Things had seemed very clear-cut and simple when she had hatched from the Egg. But now . . .

The part of her imprinted with the kin hated the VoidBeing who ruled the WalkingStones. Yet another part of her yearned to find this creature who seemed more advanced than the kin, who could fashion creatures from shiny stone and have them do its bidding.

LifeCrier had backed away a step in deference to SilverSide's rank. He lowered himself slightly to indicate subservience. "I don't understand KeenEye's death," he said. "The VoidBeing could have killed me or any of the others. Yet it didn't. I saw it raise its hands and stop the WalkingStones from hurting the kin it had paralyzed. It held my head and did nothing but stroke it. It did not seem dangerous."

"It killed KeenEye," SilverSide repeated. "I could smell its presence on her fur."

"I know. Still . . ."

"The WalkingStones seemed to obey it, you said. That would mean that the VoidBeing ranks higher than Central or these new Supervisors."

"I suppose. . . ."

"Then the VoidBeing must be an enemy of OldMother. It attacked you, even if it did not kill you. It saved the WalkingStones and left with them. It had a WalkingStone as a companion. It is an *enemy*." SilverSide recited the facts in a monotone. Around her, the kin began to nod in agreement. Only LifeCrier seemed hesitant.

Inside SilverSide, synapses closed erratically. Her positronic mind no longer resembled that of any other robot; her life among the kin had changed it far more than her creator might have expected. In that sense, she was truly a rogue. No human standards worked for her anymore. She was an alien, and she had overlaid the Three Laws with an alien morality. She could not disobey them, but her vision of them was skewed.

"I must do what best protects us," she told LifeCrier. "Nothing has changed. We still cannot leave PackHome; my attempt to destroy Central only made it more difficult to damage the WalkingStones. You tell me that this VoidBeing is a being of flesh, and flesh is very fragile and very tasty. It had its knife-stick, but even a SharpFang has its teeth and claws. If the gods had to send it from the Void, then we must have hurt the WalkingStones more than we know. Perhaps if we also kill the VoidBeing, then the OldMother will have won. What do you think, LifeCrier?—you are the one who knows the OldMother best."

"SilverSide is the leader," LifeCrier answered, using Hunt-Tongue. "If she says that the OldMother wishes us to kill the VoidBeing, then we will kill it."

CHAPTER 23

STALKING THE GODS

Derec knew what the supervisor robot wanted before Gamma entered the room. The chemfets had told him, whispering into his mind.

"We're going to have to change your name," he told the robot. "Gamma—it shows a definite lack of imagination. But it can wait. What's up?"

"There are wolf-creatures on the far hill, Master Derec. They are approaching the city boundaries."

"I'm aware of it. They didn't give us much time, did they? Is everything ready?" There was little need to ask—he could have found out via the chemfets, but somehow it seemed more reassuring to ask the supervisor. There was only so much information he could absorb from the flood the chemfets allowed him. Even if he wanted to control every function of the city, it would have been impossible.

When the chemfets injected into him by his father had first asserted their presence, Derec had thought that he was going insane. He couldn't control them, couldn't handle the eternal input. But he'd learned how to filter out most of it, learned to let the city take care of itself. The supervisors were invaluable, and the lesson Derec had been taught in the original Robot City was to delegate his authority. It was the only way to remain sane.

Derec yawned. He'd tried to sleep that afternoon, knowing the wolf-creatures would come at night, but he'd been too wound up. He yawned again, forcing oxygen into his lungs.

"Everything is set as you instructed, Master Derec." The supervisor robot, identical to its counterparts Alpha and Beta, went to the balcony high up in a building near the Compass Tower. City lights gleamed red and yellow on the robot's burnished skin. Mandelbrot came from the next room and went onto the balcony with Derec.

"I see them," Mandelbrot said. "There—just below the tree line. There are six or perhaps seven of them."

"Get your eyes fixed at last and you have to show off," Derec chided Mandelbrot jokingly, but the robot missed the humor entirely.

"I am sorry, Master Derec," he said. In retrospect, it was the only reaction Derec should have expected, but Derec suddenly knew how much he missed human company. *Ariel, especially. I need to talk to her. Sometimes I feel half-robot myself with the chemfets chattering away inside.*

There had been no time to contact her. Derec had known the wolf-creatures would come to the city again, and quickly. It was what Dr. Avery would have done, after all, and the rogue *had* to be Avery's—it just made sense.

He didn't think it would be much trouble dealing with it. In fact, his mood was rather jovial. Scrubbing away the filth of their journey through the forest and being in the city made him feel almost *human* again. He felt safe here, and with the resources of the city, nothing was impossible.

He'd be home again, soon. He'd see Ariel and patch up the rift caused by their fight.

The rogue was not a problem. The wolf-creatures he was more concerned about, but they should be easy enough, too. A general reprogramming of the city, an understanding of their language so they could communicate, and some compromise could be reached. This stupid war with the city would end.

Derec squinted into the night, cradling his sling in his good hand so that his injured arm wouldn't brush up against the railing. It was impossible for him to see anything at all. He couldn't even make out the individual trees, a kilometer and more away in the murk. The sky was overcast; even if this world's two moons had been up, their reflected light would never have penetrated the cloud cover.

"I told you they'd move," he said. "Can you see the rogue, Mandelbrot?"

"No, Master Derec, I do not. But it could still be there, back in the trees."

Derec shook his head. "No. Not that one, not if it's really the leader. If these beings are anything like the old wolves, they're pack animals. The leader would be first, or the others wouldn't follow. Remember Wolruf? Always headlong into the fray . . ." Derec grimaced. "I suppose it's possible it's already among the buildings, maybe in some other form. We might have missed it."

He shrugged. The city was alert now. The chemfets in his bloodstream fed him a continuous stream of information over the security channels. "Supervisor Gamma?"

"Yes?"

"You're certain the robots will consider the wolf-creatures human? You're certain they won't allow them to be harmed?"

"You have instructed them so yourself, Master Derec. If there were direct danger to you from one of them, I believe we would protect you first, as you most fit our programmed definition of 'human,' but otherwise, yes. We will not harm them."

"I can't stress that enough. The city can always build more robots. I don't care how many robots these wolf-creatures might destroy—I don't want them hurt. We can find some other way to coexist with them."

"That is understood, Master Derec. Mandelbrot has explained much to help us reinforce your orders."

Derec could feel adrenaline building inside him. He wanted to run back into the room and out to the edge of the city. He wanted to be there. He'd made plans to do so, but the idea had distressed Alpha, the supervisor to whom he'd first broached the subject. "That would be extremely dangerous," the robot had said, very slowly and carefully. "I do not know that the Laws would permit it. . . . The rogue robot . . ."

Derec could have argued; it hadn't seemed worth the trouble. Even Mandelbrot had agreed: the rogue was an unknown and obviously dangerous. Despite Derec's assurances that even a rogue would follow the Three Laws and thus be unable to harm him, all the robots had been noticeably "pleased" when he agreed to remain in the city. Okay. He'd play general this time, staying behind the lines and directing his forces. He noticed that the supervisors had also placed a cordon of Hunter-Seekers around his building, but he didn't comment on it.

"Give me the visual, Gamma. And make sure we're recording—we're going to need every scrap of sound these creatures make to start deciphering the language."

The wall of the building directly across from them was

a milky white, translucent plastic. Now it glowed with inner light, and a huge image of the forest gleamed there, red with enhanced infrared imaging. Derec could easily see the wolf-creatures moving cautiously through the tall grass toward the city.

"Mandelbrot," he said, leaning forward slightly and pointing to the wolf in the front of the pack. "Isn't that the old one from the glade? See—it has the same gray fur around the muzzle, the same markings."

"I see him, Master Derec."

"He might be the best one to capture. He might remember that we didn't harm him last time. He might even co-operate. Gamma?"

"I have already so instructed all units, Master Derec."

"Good. I imagine we'll have to put most of them to sleep before they'll give up this attack. They seemed rather aggressive." Derec patted his arm and the bandages swaddling the claw wounds. He watched them moving slowly toward the city. "They're magnificent creatures in their own right," he said. "Look at them. So strong and sleek; we saw what they could do to a robot."

He could see now that several of them were wearing bright wire collars: totems against the city, perhaps, or simply trophies of past victories. The sight made him nod. "Mandelbrot, you were absolutely right. They *are* human. Maybe if Wolruf were here . . ."

As the pack approached, Derec sent messages through the chemfets. Several Hunter-Seekers advanced from the out-buildings of the city in a line. Half of them carried neural disruptors hastily built during the previous day: the computer models of the wolf-creatures indicated that the disruptors would interfere with the electrical impulses of the wolf-creatures' brains and cause mental confusion. The jury-rigged models had also been prone to leakage and had disabled more than one of the robots as well. As a backup, other Hunter-Seekers loaded with sedative darts also moved toward the invaders. Worker units waited to capture one or more of the creatures in hopes of learning to communicate with them.

Derec didn't think they'd go quietly. He fully expected a bitter battle before the wolf-creatures would be overcome.

He was wrong.

Halfway down the hill, the old one simply stopped. In full view, making no effort to hide himself, he rose up on his hind legs, pointed to the Hunter-Seekers, and howled in that eerie language. The gesticulation needed no translation—it was obvious enough: *Come and get me.*

There were evidently certain universals when it came to body language.

"That doesn't make any sense at all." Derec squinted at the meters-tall image of the wolf. "You'd think a pack animal would just attack."

"They are not just animals," Mandelbrot reminded Derec.

"Yeah. And I'll bet the rogue's taught them a few sneaky tricks of its own." He grimaced. "Well, he's obviously not going to come to us. Obviously they want the fight to come to them. Gamma, let's send the Hunter-Seekers forward."

But it was not a fight they wanted. Not at all. As the Hunter-Seekers advanced, the wolf-creatures retreated. Step by grudging step. They stayed out of range of the disruptors and the darts, though Derec suspected that was accident rather than anything else.

Derec tried direct communication through the Hunter-Seekers, hoping they might understand the tone of his voice if not the words. They simply howled back at it.

He sent an unarmed worker forward, arms outstretched peacefully. When it reached the pack, they tore it apart.

At last, frustrated, he sent the Hunter-Seekers forward at a quick trot. The wolf-creatures melted back into the woods, and Derec called the Hunter-Seekers back.

As a confrontation, it was an elusive, aggravating thing. As an effort to solve the conflict, it was an utter failure.

"Frost," Derec muttered as the wall across the street went dark again and the city lights reasserted themselves. "Now just what in space was *that* intended to prove?"

SilverSide listened to the chorus of head-voices, waiting. She was just to the south of the city, having circled halfway around it from PackHome.

Already she could hear the alarm spreading as LifeCrier showed himself and the other kin at the edge of the forest to the west, and she could hear the new voice that directed the city functions, instructing even the triumvirate of Supervisors.

The GodBeing. The one of flesh, not stone.

The city was stupid. The WalkingStones had not learned. They expected the kin to attack the same way they always had, as if they could not create new tactics. She could hear the GodBeing telling the Hunters to move forward, speaking to them in the VoidTongue they both shared. *Do not kill them*, it said. *Capture the old one.*

SilverSide growled at that, pleased that she had cautioned LifeCrier only to show himself and to avoid an actual fight if he could. It was a First Law decision; SilverSide only knew that it felt right to her.

Do not harm the wolf-creatures. That was what the GodBeing said, but SilverSide wasn't sure that she believed it. SilverSide could not lie herself—the OldMother had made such a thing impossible for her—but the kin could. *Flesh* could lie, and the GodBeing was flesh.

The city's attention was on the kin now. It was time for her to move.

She had tilted and canted the dodecahedral segments of her body so that they reflected as little light as possible. Becoming a WalkingStone had not worked the last time; she knew that the city was now aware of her abilities and would have taken precautions against that type of deception. Nor had the shape felt right to her.

Still, the Third Law demanded that she protect her own existence, and to enter the city as kin would have been dangerous. The bird shape had served her well twice now; she would use it once more until she found this GodBeing.

SilverSide's decision to accept the kin had given her a definite preference for their "human" shape. She *was* kin. She might enter the city as a bird, but she would meet this GodBeing as kin.

SilverSide willed her body to change. She spread wide, dark wings, and rose quietly toward the banked clouds.

The GodBeing would be near the Hill of Stars. She felt certain of that. The Hill of Stars was the heart of the city, and the GodBeing would be placed there, perhaps in the Hill itself, perhaps even in the room Central had used. SilverSide banked and swooped, letting the wind lift her as she moved toward the glowing pyramid in the center of the city.

Lights dimmed near the Hill, then a brightness glimmered on the side of one of the buildings. SilverSide brought her wings in, let herself drop lower as her optical circuits switched to a telephoto setting.

LifeCrier! She could see the kin, their images projected on a building alongside the Hill of Stars. In her head, the

GodBeing seemed puzzled by the kin's behavior, and it ordered the Hunters forward.

SilverSide circled the area, her eyes searching.

There! The GodBeing stood on a balcony opposite the view of LifeCrier, with two WalkingStones standing alongside it. SilverSide howled softly, banked, and plummeted like a stone as the wall showing LifeCrier went suddenly dark.

The wind whistled past her as she dropped in silence.

A few meters above them, she pulled up with a savage beating of wings. The WalkingStones noticed her at the same moment. SilverSide changed instantly into kin form and dropped. The WalkingStone nearest her she picked up and hurled over the edge of the balcony—it clutched at her desperately, missed, and fell with a strange silence. The other WalkingStone, an odd one with mismatched arms, immediately planted itself between SilverSide and the GodBeing. It made no move toward SilverSide, though she knew it would not let her pass.

The GodBeing was a strange creature, she thought, its face a pasty, dead color and its fur all gathered on the top of its head and nowhere else. It concealed its body behind some strange substance so that she could not even see its sex, and one arm was bound to its body. It had no claws, and its teeth seemed to be flat and dull like a planteater's. It smelled horrible, like some obscene cross between a dead WalkingStone and a TreeWalker.

It hardly looked formidable enough to be leading the WalkingStones.

And yet . . . SilverSide was strangely fascinated by the creature. It was a being of flesh, and it ruled this world of technology. *Find intelligence*, her old programming had ordered.

SilverSide shook the feeling aside. *Protect the kin*; that was what the First Law demanded.

"I challenge you!" SilverSide roared to the GodBeing in HuntTongue, but it only shook its head, not understanding. "I challenge you, GodBeing," she said again, using the VoidTongue. The words felt odd coming from her throat and yet were strangely familiar at the same time. The GodBeing reacted to her use of the VoidTongue, its eyes going wide and startled. "Let us fight to decide who controls the WalkingStones."

SilverSide growled and shifted into the challenge stance, her hind legs gathered as if to leap, her claws extended. The WalkingStone in front of the GodBeing began to move toward SilverSide, and she snorted. It reached for her, and her jaw clamped around its arm, tearing savagely. It was like chewing on stone, but the grasp gave her leverage and she flung the robot to one side.

The GodBeing backed away, trying to escape back inside the Hill of Stars, and SilverSide moved to block it. "No," she said. "I will not allow you to run. We must fight. That is the way to decide this."

"There is no need to fight," the GodBeing said. "You will not fight me. You will move aside from the doorway." There was a tone of imperious command in its voice. Almost, SilverSide wanted to obey, and for just a moment her stance changed, becoming servile and submissive. But she shook her massive head and growled again in angry BeastTalk.

"The OldMother sent me to save the kin. You kill them. We must fight. That is the way."

The GodBeing was shaking its pasty-fleshed head. "No. I've changed all that. I've told the city to stop. Back away now. You're a robot. You have to obey me."

"I am the leader of the kin. I obey the will of the OldMother."

"Who is the OldMother?" the GodBeing asked, and SilverSide could not believe its stupidity. How could it not know the OldMother? Coming from the FirstBeast, it *must* know her.

But there was no time to question the GodBeing. From the edges of her peripheral vision, SilverSide caught movement; trebled movement. The WalkingStone she had flung aside was advancing toward her, and from inside the GodBeing's cave in the Hill of Stars, she could see two Hunters running toward the ledge and their confrontation.

SilverSide howled in fury and faced the GodBeing.

"You are afraid of me. I should be the leader. If you rule the city, then meet me. I will wait for you."

She flung aside the hand the WalkingStone laid on her and rushed to the edge of the ledge, knocking the GodBeing down in her leap. It was certainly a fragile being, for it cried out in pain as she plummeted over the side.

She willed herself to become the bird again and swooped up and away. The WalkingStones had helped the GodBeing to its feet and were watching her as she gained altitude. She watched them carefully to see if they aimed their awful fire at her, but the GodBeing held them back.

Howling her BeastTalk challenge once more, SilverSide left the city. Landing in the forest, she resumed her preferred form and sat down to wait.

CHAPTER 24

A CALL RECEIVED

It had to be one of the most frightening sounds he'd ever heard, those shivering howls coming from the throat of the huge black carrion bird. More than anything else, the fluidity of the rogue's body was terrifying. It had seemed to simply *melt* into its new shape. . . .

Watching the rogue fly away, Derec was suddenly very certain that this wasn't going to be as easy as he'd thought it would be. Not at all.

He took a deep breath of the cold night air. Cradling his arm, he went back inside.

"Master Derec, are you hurt?"

"Mostly my pride, Mandelbrot," he answered. "I suspect it'll heal slower than the rest of me."

Derec's arm was throbbing again, and his head ached where he'd hit the railing as the rogue swept past him, but none of it was as serious as it could have been. He'd seen those teeth, those claws, and he'd seen how the rogue had flung Mandelbrot aside like a broken doll. A few scrapes and bruises were nothing. Nothing at all.

Derec sat down on the couch and leaned his head back.

"We need Wolruf," he said. The city was still in an up-roar. He could hear it all in his head. Supervisor Alpha was directing the Hunter-Seekers to try to track the rogue, but Derec knew that it would be hopeless. There were too many shapes it could have taken to avoid pursuit.

"Wolruf?" Mandelbrot queried.

"Yes. Think about it. She'd understand these creatures better than we can. At the very least she'd be dealing with a canine intelligence that is—maybe—more like her own in contrast to our apish thought patterns. That's our problem. The rogue seems to believe it's one of them; their leader, in fact. Which means it's thinking like them. The rogue's logic is utterly alien. It's obvious that *I* didn't understand it," he added ruefully.

"It is still a positronic intelligence, Master Derec. It was built by a human, if not Dr. Avery himself. That much is certain. I observed it as closely as possible during the skirmish. The skin was definitely dianite, like the material of the city itself, and it spoke in Standard. There are certain givens with a positronic brain. It may even be that it will respond to the city's orders, being made from the same substance."

"Yes, Mandelbrot. It follows the Laws, or should, at any rate. I just wonder how it might *interpret* them. A pack society, a carnivore's mores..." Derec took a deep breath. "Frost, I'm thirsty." He went to a dispenser unit in the wall and ordered a drink, downing it all in one quick gulp.

"We can't understand these beings, not easily," he continued. "Wolruf has a closer affinity to them than we ever will. Besides, *you* were the one insisting that they should be treated as human. How can we do that if we don't understand them? How are we going to handle this rogue if we can't understand what it might be thinking?"

"I agree with you, Master Derec. Send for Wolruf."

"Good." Derec nodded. "It's about time I made a decent decision." *Which hasn't been since Aurora.*

Still holding the empty glass, he went out to the balcony again and stared out at the darkness into which the rogue had disappeared. The sound of the rogue's howling still seemed to echo. He felt the skin of his back prickling at the memory.

He didn't mention all the other reasons for wanting to make the call, though he knew Mandelbrot would also be aware of them, if too concerned with causing a human pain to mention them. Wolruf's outlook would help them, yes, but Wolruf would also bring a ship which would allow them to leave the world if they needed to. And Derec wanted very badly to call Ariel. He wanted Ariel more than Wolruf in many ways.

Wolruf could also bring Ariel.

He sighed again.

Derec felt in his head for the chemfet channels and called: *Alpha. Beta. Status on Supervisor Gamma.*

Beta responded immediately. *Gamma unit inactive after fall. Positronic brain has been taken to repair station and will be reinstalled in a new body if possible. Extent of damage to brain is unknown; a new supervisor unit has been activated. Alpha reports that Hunter-Seekers have lost rogue. Instructions regarding rogue and wolf-creatures?*

You will continue to regard the wolf-creatures as human, Derec answered. *The rogue is not to be harmed if you do find it, but there's no need to send the Hunter-Seekers past the city boundaries. The rogue will be back.*

Derec was certain of that much.

Understood. Derec could almost imagine distaste in the flat, emotionless response.

In the meantime, I need access to the city hyperwave transmitters. You should have coordinates for Aurora in the city memory banks. Please transmit the following message:

Ariel: Find Wolruf. Send her immediately—imperative! And . . . I'm sorry. I love you. Please send an answer to these coordinates. And Ariel—I would like you to come with her. Derec.

The message arrived at Aurora as a highly compressed squirt emanating from the Aurora system's wormhole, punched through the incredible distances and the space-time anomaly by the powerful transmitters in Robot City.

The weakened signal was received by Aurora's orbiting communications complex, the charges billed against Ariel's family's account, and transferred down to the planetary net decoded and strengthened. There it was posted to Derec and Ariel's computer terminal.

That was exactly as Derec had intended, except that Ariel was no longer there to receive it.

Someone else was.

"Wolruf? Who or what is Wolruf? You must answer me. It is extremely important."

The household robot didn't seem inclined to answer the query. The inbuilt command against revealing an owner's business was perhaps the most highly stressed program code in its memory, the Second Law priority reinforced to the best of factory's technicians' abilities.

But there was one higher priority that could always be invoked, and the speaker was *very* skilled with positronic logic. The words simply had to be carefully chosen and constantly repeated.

"It is very important that you tell me, Balzac. Mistress Ariel is not on Aurora, as you know. She has left this world and cannot help. Master Derec is in trouble; that is implied by the message. He needs this Wolruf to aid him. *I* will contact Wolruf, but I first must know where to begin looking. You must tell me all that you know. This is a First Law situation, Balzac. First Law. Ariel and Derec are in danger, and your refusal to speak increases that danger. This supersedes any previous instructions you may have received. Do you understand?"

It took an hour of careful argument and resulted in a badly damaged robotic mind. Balzac would never be of much use to its owners again.

But it *did* speak, the words halting and slurred. . . .

CHAPTER 25

DECISIONS

For the next two days, Derec checked with the city communications center every hour or so, though he knew that he would have been alerted via chemfet if a message had been received.

There was never an answer. Ariel said nothing.

That was very unlike her. Derec was certain that even if she'd been furious, she would have sent back some scathing reply. But the hyperactive frequencies were silent coming from Aurora.

He hoped that she'd simply decide to head for the planet with Wolruf, that any day a ship would appear in orbit around the world. He instructed the city to turn its attention to the sky, to search the night for the faint glimmer of a ship's drive. Maybe she was out there already, a day or two away after the jump.

But the sky was devoid of ships. Derec waited for eight days, not eating or sleeping well and leaving control of the city entirely in the Supervisors' hands after giving them firm orders: *The city is to cease any new construction and any clearing of land. Remember that the wolf-creatures are to be regarded as human insofar as harming them. Do not destroy the rogue.*

As the days passed, the wolves grew less cautious. The rogue appeared every night on the hillside outside the city, pacing the perimeter and howling in the speech of the wolf-creatures. Derec didn't need to know what it was saying; that was obvious enough. And the wolf-creatures seemed to realize that the city was doing nothing to resist them. On the third day after the rogue's challenge, the pack made a blitzkrieg attack on a party of workers, destroying most of them before the Hunter-Seekers arrived and the wolves fled. Following Derec's last orders, the Hunters didn't pursue the wolves but simply let them go back into the safety of the forest.

The rogue itself made a dash into the city on the fifth night, and it destroyed Delta, the replacement Supervisor for Gamma. The positronic brain was wrecked beyond repair; Gamma was restored to working status in a different body.

On the sixth night, a Hunter-Seeker managed to sneak up on the pack and sedate one of the wolves from a distance. But when two Hunters went to capture the creature, the rogue attacked from the shadows. The Hunter-Seekers were disabled; the rogue seemed unharmed.

It was apparent to Derec that the stalemate could not continue. It was also apparent that Wolruf, if she were coming at all, would not be there soon, and that Ariel had either never received the message or had ignored it and was not going to answer.

That left very little choice for Derec. He was entirely healed now, the broken arm knitted if still a little tender after the accelerated treatment. He had no excuses not to confront the problem directly. Anything was better than brooding.

Despite that, he was not at all pleased with the prospect.

Mandelbrot woke Derec from his sleep. "The rogue is outside the city again," the robot said softly. "I saw it in the distance, walking along the edge of the trees."

"Did you try ordering it in again?" Derec asked. With the help of the city's technical library, Mandelbrot had been trying to subvert the rogue's base programming, since it evidently had a comlink to the city. The robot had been broadcasting orders over various frequencies, but to no effect.

"Yes. In the Robot City program code once more and also in human speech using a recording of your voice. It used the comlink to growl."

"Maybe you should offer it a biscuit," Derec grumbled.

"If you think that will work, Master Derec. One moment—"

Derec grimaced. The robot was already moving swiftly toward the door.

"No! Mandelbrot, come back here. Frost, can't you tell when a person's joking? Wait a second and let me get ready." Derec rolled out of his bed and rubbed at his eyes. "It's time I went to see it personally. It's time I answered the damned thing's challenge. The rogue's right; one of us has to be in control of things."

Mandelbrot's eyes glittered at him from the night darkness. Beyond the robot, the wide archway to the balcony was open. Neither of the moons was up; the sky beyond Mandelbrot's head was dusted with stars. The wolves would be out there now, and the rogue would be with them.

"Master Derec, I do not like this."

"I don't either, believe me." Derec pulled on his pants, tugged a loose-fitting tunic over his head.

"The rogue is dangerous. It has destroyed city robots, it has damaged the central computer, it has harmed the Supervisors. It has even threatened you."

"None of which necessarily violates the Three Laws," Derec pointed out. "Not even the threat. It's in the shape of those wolf-creatures; it thinks like them, too."

"In which case it is *very* dangerous. And I must disagree. No robot in a sane state could say what the rogue said to you on the balcony. Such a statement would cause extreme reactions within my positronic potentials. Even contemplating such an act now sets up vibrations that I can sense. To actually make such threats meaningfully would be impossible. The damage to my brain would cause an immediate dysfunction if not an outright freeze."

"The rogue follows the Laws," Derec insisted.

"The rogue is insane. It must be. Its interpretations of the Laws cannot be trusted. It injured you the first time you met."

"Nevertheless, I'm going to go meet it."

Mandelbrot stepped in front of Derec, blocking his path. "Master Derec, I cannot allow that. I am sorry. The First Law forbids it."

"This is a direct order, Mandelbrot, and I've already told you your assumptions are in error. This isn't a First Law matter. Step out of my way."

"I . . . am sorry." The robot's voice was slightly slurred, hesitant; the delicate balances between the Laws shifted, but it remained in place before the door.

"Mandelbrot, the rogue hasn't harmed me. Not really. It was protecting its own existence, and it made a judgment call that it could move past me. You might have made the same decision—a small bump against the likelihood of destruction. It *could* as easily have taken my head off with those claws."

"I ... do not ... know...."

Derec saw that the robot's resolve was visibly weakening. He pressed his argument. "The rogue could have killed me in an instant, Mandelbrot. It chose not to. That tells me that the Three Laws are still functioning. And we're not going to resolve anything here unless we confront it. If we just order the city to build us a ship and leave—assuming the city's even capable of such a task at this point, and I seriously doubt that—then we've abandoned these wolf-creatures. They're going to continue to try to attack the city, and once we're gone, who knows what will happen? They may well die. We've certainly disrupted their society already, and if the city continues to grow, it will contact other packs as well. They're sentient beings, Mandelbrot. You know it yourself. I can't and won't just leave them, and just sitting here is useless."

As he spoke, Derec realized that he was also talking to himself. He *had* just been sitting there, moping about Ariel and Wolruf and doing nothing. It *was* time to confront the rogue, one way or the other. He had to face the challenge.

"Mandelbrot, I'm ordering you again to move."

The robot took a hesitant step aside. "I would like ... to accompany you."

Derec smiled. "Of course. You always need a second in a duel." Then, before Mandelbrot could say anything else: "Just kidding, of course."

CHAPTER 26

A CHALLENGE MET

SilverSide watched the city as she'd watched it every night since SmallFace was a crescent horn. The moon was entirely gone now, waiting for the OldMother to birth it once more in its endless cycle. Still the GodBeing ignored her. But SilverSide came every night and renewed her challenge.

The GodBeing would come to her. It must.

At least some of what it said had been true. The city *had* changed; it no longer pursued the kin when they attacked. Only a few nights past, LifeCrier had led the pack down to kill. Though the Hunters had come to protect the worker WalkingStones, they had not followed the pack when the kin retreated.

Then the youngling SlowPaw had been caught straggling as usual, and one of the Hunters had shot him. SilverSide had been certain that SlowPaw was dead. But the Hunters came after the body, and after SilverSide disabled them, she found that they had only made SlowPaw sleep. She had been certain that the Hunters would follow her for revenge and had been ready to lead them away from PackHome again.

But the rest of the Hunters remained in the city. The GodBeing—whose name was Derec, as she knew from listening to the city's VoidTongue—had ordered it so.

What kind of creature would stay hidden in its cave for so long? How could it hunt there, when all the game had been driven elsewhere? The GodBeing was flesh like the kin; it must eat.

Which meant that it would come out.

Most strangely of all, SilverSide could feel the urge in her to meet this GodBeing again. The remembrance of it stirred odd thoughts in her mind. She felt a pull, a yearning.

It has knowledge. It is intelligent. It is a toolmaker far superior to any of the kin. I have heard the city say that the one WalkingStone was built by this Derec.

There were moments when she did not want to fight it at all. But the challenge was demanded by the OldMother's commands inside her. Above all else, she could let no harm come to the kin, and the city harmed kin simply by its existence. She *must* control the city as she controlled the kin, and the GodBeing prevented that.

That meant it must be challenged. If it refused her that privilege, it must die.

The edge of the city was well defined, like the boundaries of a cooled lava flow. Derec stepped from a hard level walkway and with the next step, he was on grass. Outside.

He suddenly, foolishly, felt unprotected.

That's silly, he told himself. *Mandelbrot's alongside you, and Alpha's monitoring the whole thing through Witness robots. There are a half-dozen Hunters waiting back in the city; they'll get to you in seconds if anything happens. You're as safe as you can be. Besides, you're the one who insisted that the Three Laws protected you from the rogue.*

He suddenly didn't feel very confident at all.

A low rumbling came from his right. Derec turned.

The rogue was there.

It crouched fifty meters upslope where a stand of trees had been cleared by workers from the city. Perched atop one of the fallen logs and in wolf shape, the rogue looked bigger than Derec had remembered. Its claws were displayed, its mouth slightly open to reveal the metal teeth set there. It reared up on its back legs as Derec turned to it, standing perhaps a half-meter taller than Derec himself. Mandelbrot had come alongside Derec without prompting, the implicit threat in the rogue's pose forcing the robot to stay close enough to intervene.

It's a robot. It follows the Laws. Derec took a deep breath, motioning Mandelbrot back. "I've come to talk with you," he said to the rogue.

It growled, then spat out in Standard: "I have challenged you already. I did not come to talk."

"At least tell me your name."

"I am called SilverSide," the rogue answered, and Derec could have sworn there was a hint of bravado in its voice, far more inflection than any robot he had ever heard before. Whoever had programmed it had been *good.* "I am the Chosen of the OldMother, the Bane of WalkingStones. Tell your WalkingStone to leave so that we may decide who is the leader."

Derec looked at Mandelbrot, who had taken yet another step closer at the rogue's words. "Mandelbrot is compelled to protect me, SilverSide. Tell him that you're not going to hurt me, and I can send him back."

"It is no protection to you at all," SilverSide answered, and her pale eyes glanced at Mandelbrot. "I have already defeated it once. I will do it again, and then you and I will settle this."

"No, I order you—" Derec began, but it was already too late.

The rogue moved faster than Derec thought possible. If Mandelbrot had not been there, Derec would not have had a chance. Derec felt a wind as Mandelbrot shot by him and met SilverSide.

The rogue collided with the onrushing Mandelbrot in a thunderous, resounding crash. There was a blur of violent motion, and Mandelbrot was suddenly down in the dirt, his legs thrashing helplessly from a severed cable held in the rogue's claws. The rogue itself had a long scratch in its flank but otherwise seemed unharmed.

Derec opened his mouth to shout, to protest, to scream. The chemfets told him that the Hunter-Seekers were coming, but they would be too late.

Much too late.

SilverSide growled terribly, flung the cable away, and was on him. He tried to raise his hands, hopelessly. Claws raked Derec's sides as she grappled him and bore him down. "No!" he screamed. "You can't hurt me! I'm a human—"

The rogue wailed.

"I'm a human—" the GodBeing Derec cried. The word set off a bewildering spark of reactions in SilverSide's mind. *Human!* The resonance from that VoidTongue word was stunning, and SilverSide reeled from its effects.

A human being is an intelligent life form.

Intelligence. Human.

"You are *not* human," SilverSide roared in denial, but

she spoke in HuntTongue—the language of "humans"—and no answer came to her. Taking advantage of SilverSide's confusion, the GodBeing had rolled to its feet, and now she struck at it once more, intending to slash it open with her claws for its lie.

She could not. *Could* not. It was as if the OldMother controlled her hand and brought the claws back at the last instant so that she missed the GodBeing. She leapt at it instead, bearing it down again to roll it gasping in the dirt, then moving away a step so that it could stay on its back, submissive and beaten.

It either did not know to submit, or it would not. The GodBeing staggered up once more, defiant. SilverSide rushed at it again. The GodBeing screeched with pain as her arms wrapped around its chest and squeezed.

"Submit!" she whispered to it, and it was as if the OldMother's will made the words a plea. She wanted this to end. She wanted the GodBeing to go limp and end this farce.

She was so much stronger than this thing of flesh. The GodBeing was weak, weaker than the sickest of the kin. And yet it still struggled.

"No!" it shouted back, its face gone red, its eyes wide and mouth gaping open. She could smell its breath, strangely sweet. "No. You must stop this. I order it. I am a human. You must obey me."

The words staggered SilverSide as if they were physical blows. Her grasp loosened, and the GodBeing sagged to the ground. SilverSide stared at it without seeing it, all her attention on the confusion within her.

Human.

You must obey.

SilverSide howled in BeastTalk.

• • •

Somehow, he wasn't dead. The rogue was howling again like a mad thing, and, as Derec stared at it, its body was changing. The snout was shortening, the ears moving lower on the body, and the canine jaws softening. Yes, the face was humanoid, and the features were startlingly like Derec's own.

"GodBeing, I . . . I must know . . . more," it said, and he could hear the confusion in its mind in its halting voice. Positronic drift. Derec began to feel some hope. "I . . . need information."

There was someone or something behind the rogue, some shape. Mandelbrot had managed to lock his legs and rise, lumbering stiff-legged to them and impelled by the First Law. Derec saw the blow coming a moment before it landed. "Mandelbrot, no—" he began to shout, but it was too late.

Mandelbrot's closed fist fell on the rogue's neck. It went to its knees, a wolfish snarl coming from its human mouth, and now it was changing again, returning to wolf form. "No, Mandelbrot!" Derec ordered again. "I'm in no danger!"

The rogue was confused. It looked from Mandelbrot to Derec, to the forest, to the Hunter-Seekers moving rapidly toward them. It screeched, a sound of raw animal fury, its features changing rapidly and ceaselessly. Human/wolf/human/wolf.

Wolf.

It stared at Derec. "Don't go," he began, but the rogue shook its head.

Dropping to all fours, it began to run for the cover of the forest.

"Come back!" Derec shouted. "I can teach you! In the city . . ."

But it was already gone.

CHAPTER 27

CHANGELING

Below, the kin huddled on the ledge before PackHome. The pups yelped and played mock fights and nursed. The younglings old enough to be in the Hunting Pack strutted and told fanciful tales about how they had helped SilverSide kill WalkingStones. The adults simply nodded and occasionally looked to the summit of the hill where SilverSide and LifeCrier had gone.

It had been a strange fight, that of SilverSide and the GodBeing. They still did not know who had won.

"You are unhappy with me," SilverSide said in Hunt-Tongue.

LifeCrier shook his grizzled muzzle from side to side. He used KinSpeech, telling SilverSide that she needn't be so concerned. "No, SilverSide. Not unhappy with you. I'm sad that you're leaving."

"I have not decided that. I have decided nothing."

"I can smell the change in you."

"LifeCrier has the nose of a DirtDigger," SilverSide said in HuntTongue, and LifeCrier bowed his head at the rebuke.

He did not move away, though, standing his ground on the rise. They could see the Hill of Stars in the twilight, an aching brightness, and they both stared at it for long minutes.

"I saw the OldMother move in you," LifeCrier said. "My eyes are not as sharp as KeenEye's, but you and the GodBeing . . ."

"I know. I felt it."

"What will you do?"

SilverSide howled, and after a second, LifeCrier joined her. Their twined voices caused flocks of birds to rise in the trees below. "I am kin," SilverSide said at last. "I lead the litter-kin here."

"I know. No one would challenge you. You are the OldMother's Gift."

"I am kin," SilverSide repeated. "Yet . . ." She stopped and looked at LifeCrier.

"I must do what is best for kin," she said.

LifeCrier nodded. "That is all the OldMother would ever ask," he told her.

"Derec!" Mandelbrot whispered urgently and pointed.

Campfire and city lights glinted on the robot's polished body; the red gleam of its eyes glanced at Derec and then back into the night darkness beyond the city.

Derec rubbed sleep from his eyes. He struggled from under his thermal blanket and stood. The night was very quiet. Even the brilliantly lit city at his back seemed quiet, though he knew that thousands of robots were about their tasks there. The sweet odor of woodsmoke filled the air; a gentle and cool night wind tossed the mane of smoke back toward the city.

They'd been camped outside the city for the past two

nights, waiting. Each night he'd expected the rogue to come to him. The city was broadcasting an endless invitation to SilverSide. *Come into the city. You will not be harmed. The city's library is open to you. Come and learn.*

At last, it looked like it would answer the invitation.

The only question was *how*.

On the wooded crest of a hill, Derec saw the wolf-creatures. Their dark, quick shapes moved like fleet shadows under the swaying rooftop of the trees. Both moons were up; despite the city's glare and the campfire, Derec could see them quite well. Mandelbrot had moved near Derec, ready to protect him should the wolf-creatures show any hostility.

Hunter-Seekers can be sent, Alpha reminded him.

No. Not yet, anyway.

The shivering howls and barks of the wolf-creature's language drifted down toward them. Derec shuddered. In the weeks he'd been on this world, he still hadn't become used to that sound. Mandelbrot noticed and shuffled even closer. "Old racial memories die hard," he told the robot.

"The rogue is with them," Mandelbrot said. "They're gathering around it. Master Derec, I think we should have the city call the Hunter-Seekers. I am not sufficient protection for you. Regardless of whether the rogue will harm you, the wolf-creatures are certainly not bound by the Laws...."

"I've already ordered Alpha to hold them back, Mandelbrot. The wolves are no danger. Not yet. Be patient; you're the one who worked so hard to convince me they're intelligent, remember?"

"Intelligent is not a synonym for 'not dangerous,'" Mandelbrot pointed out. "You as a human should be well aware of that."

"*Hmph.*" Derec snorted. "We'll wait, anyway."

The pack had gathered at the edge of the trees closest to the city. Derec could see the rogue now, glinting in the moonlight between the pacing outriders of the wolf-creatures. Now it stepped out into full moonlight, the old one at its side. The two licked each other, nuzzling and giving playful nips. Then the rogue began walking alone down the grassy slope toward Derec and Mandelbrot.

Halfway down, the robot turned and looked back to the pack, which had gathered at the lip of the hill to watch the descent. The rogue lifted its muzzle to the wolves and gave a long, ululating lament.

The wolves chorused back.

To Derec, they sounded wild and sad.

The rogue began picking its way among the rocks toward Derec's camp once more. As it approached, the rogue's body began a slow metamorphosis. *Step*—the lupine muzzle shortened; *step*—the tail began to shorten and retract into the body; *step*—it raised up to walk on its hind legs; *step*— and the legs themselves altered, the knees beginning to flex forward.

When the robot stopped a few meters in front of them, it was recognizably humanoid in the firelight. It glanced at Mandelbrot, then at Derec.

"GodBeing Derec, I have come to learn," it said. Except for the stilted, formal grammar, its voice sounded very much like Derec's. "I have come so you may teach me of the Void from which we both fell. I have come to learn what is human."

Derec nodded. He pointed back to the city and the looming bright presence of the compass Tower. "The answers are all in there," he said. "Follow me, and I'll show you the way. Mandelbrot, if you'll take care of the fire, please . . . we wouldn't want the woods to burn." He said it mostly for the rogue's benefit, wanting it to understand that he was concerned about the well-being of the wolf-creatures.

It was difficult for Derec to give the rogue his back. He half expected it to leap on him again, biting and tearing. He listened intently for a suspicious sound behind him. Derec knew that Mandelbrot was already on edge and would respond instantly, but still . . .

Nothing happened.

Alpha, we're coming in. The rogue is with me.

We will have the apartment ready, Master Derec.

Derec began walking, then glanced back when he didn't hear the robot following. It was staring back at the forest, and as it did, the malleable face went vaguely wolfish again.

"It's your choice," Derec told it softly. "I won't force you to make that decision. Come with me or go back to them. I won't try to stop you."

The robot howled to the wolves one last time, the bestial sound eerie and wrong to be coming from that human-shaped throat.

Then the rogue turned from the darkness of the trees and the huddled pack.

It followed Derec into the eternal light of the city.

ISAAC ASIMOV'S

ROBOTS AND ALIENS

BOOK TWO

RENEGADE

CORDELL SCOTTEN

NOTABLE ROBOTS

ISAAC ASIMOV

My robot stories and novels seem to have become classics in their own right, and, with the advent of the "Robot City" series of novels, to have become the wider literary universe of other writers as well. Under those circumstances, it might be useful to go over my robot stories and describe some of those which I think are particularly significant and to explain why I think they are.

1. "Robbie"—This is the first robot story I wrote. I turned it out between May 10 and May 22 of 1939, when I was 19 years old and was just about to graduate college. I had a little trouble placing it, for John Campbell rejected it and so did *Amazing Stories*. However, Fred Pohl accepted it on March 25, 1940 and it appeared in the September 1940 issue of *Super Science Stories*, which he edited. Fred Pohl, being Fred Pohl, changed the title to "Strange Playfellow" but I changed it back when I included it in my book *I, Robot* and it has appeared as "Robbie" in every subsequent incarnation.

Aside from being my first robot story, "Robbie" is significant because in it George Weston says to his wife in defense of a robot that is fulfilling the role of nursemaid, "He just can't help being faithful and loving and kind. He's a machine—*made so*." This is the first indication, in my first story, of what eventually became the "First Law of Robotics" and of the basic fact that robots were made with built-in safety rules.

2. "Reason"—"Robbie" would have meant nothing in itself, if I had written no more robot stories, particularly since it appeared in one of the minor magazines. However, I wrote a second robot story, "Reason," and that one, John Campbell liked. After a bit of revision, it appeared in the April 1941 issue of *Astounding Science Fiction* and there it attracted notice. Readers became aware that there was such a thing as the "positronic robots," and so did Campbell. That made everything afterward possible.

3. "Liar!"—In the very next issue of *Astounding*, that of May 1941, my third robot story, "Liar!" appeared. The importance of this story was that it introduced Susan Calvin, who became the central character in my early robot stories. This story was originally rather clumsily done, largely because it dealt with the relationship between the sexes at a time when I had not yet had my first date with a young lady. Fortunately, I'm a quick learner and it is one story in which I made significant changes before allowing it to appear in *I, Robot*.

4. "Runaround"—The next important robot story appeared in the March 1942 issue of *Astounding*. It was the first story in which I listed the Three Laws of Robotics explicitly instead of making them implicit. In it, I have one character, Gregory Powell, say to another, Michael Donovan, "Now, look, let's start with the three fundamental Rules

of Robotics—the three rules that are built most deeply into a robot's positronic brain." He then recites them.

Later on, I called them the Laws of Robotics, and their importance to me is three-fold.

a—They guided me in forming my plots and made it possible to write many short stories, and several novels in addition, based on robots. In these, I constantly studied the consequences of the Three Laws;

b—It was by all odds my most famous literary invention, quoted in season and out by others. If all I have written is someday to be forgotten, the Three Laws of Robotics will surely be the last to go;

c—The passage in "Runaround" quoted above happens to be the very first time the word "robotics" was used in print in the English language. I am therefore credited with the invention of the word (and also "robotic," "positronic" and "psychohistory") by the Oxford English Dictionary, which takes the trouble—and the space—to quote the Three Laws. (All these things were created by my 22nd birthday and I seem to have created nothing since, which gives rise to grievous thoughts within me.)

5. "Evidence"—This was the one and only story I wrote while I spent 8 months and 26 days in the army. At one point I persuaded a kindly librarian to let me remain in the locked library over lunch so that I could work on the story. It is the first story in which I made use of a humanoid robot. Stephen Byerley, the humanoid robot in question (though in the story I don't make it absolutely clear whether he is a robot or not) represents my first approach toward R. Daneel Olivaw, the humaniform robot who appears in a number of my novels. "Evidence" appeared in the September 1946 issue of *Astounding Science Fiction*.

6. "Little Lost Robot"—My robots tend to be benign en-

tities. In fact, as the stories progressed they gradually gained in moral and ethical qualities until they far surpassed human beings and, in the case of Daneel, approached the godlike. Nevertheless, I had no intention of limiting myself to robots as saviors. I followed wherever the wild winds of my imagination led me and I was quite capable of seeing the uncomfortable sides of the robot phenomena.

It was only a few weeks ago (as I write this) that I received a letter from a reader that scolded me because, in a robot story of mine that had just been published, I showed the dangerous side of robots. He accused me of a failure of nerve.

That he was wrong is shown by "Little Lost Robot," in which a robot is the villain, even though it appeared nearly half a century ago. The seamy side of robots is *not* the result of a failure in nerve that comes of my advancing age and decrepitude. It has been a constant concern of mine all through my career.

7. "The Evitable Conflict"—This was a sequel to "Evidence" and appeared in the June 1950 issue of *Astounding*. It was the first story I wrote that dealt primarily with computers (I called them "Machines" in the story) rather than with robots per se. The difference is not a great one. You might define a robot as a "computerized machine" or as a "mobile computer." You might consider a computer as an "immobile robot." In any case, I clearly did not distinguish between the two, and although the Machines, which don't make an actual physical appearance in the story, are clearly computers, I included the story, without hesitation, in my robot collection, *I, Robot*, and neither the publisher nor the readers objected. To be sure, Stephen Byerley is in the story but the question of his roboticity plays no role.

8. "Franchise"—This was the first story in which I dealt

with computers *as computers*, and had no thought in mind of their being robots. It appeared in the August 1955 issue of *If: Worlds of Science Fiction*, and by that time I had grown familiar with the existence of computers. My computer is "Multivac," designed as an obviously larger and more complex version of the actually existing "Univac." In this story, and in some others of the period that dealt with Multivac, I described it as an enormously large machine, missing the chance of predicting the miniaturization and etherealization of computers.

9. "The Last Question"—My imagination didn't betray me for long, however. In "The Last Question," which appeared first in the November 1956 issue of *Science Fiction Quarterly*, I discussed the miniaturization and etherealization of computers and followed it through a trillion years of evolution (of both computer and man) to a logical conclusion that you will have to read the story to find. It is, beyond question, my favorite among all the stories I have written in my career.

10. "The Feeling of Power"—The miniaturization of computers played a small role as a side issue in this story. It appeared in the February 1958 issue of *If*, and is also one of my favorites. In this story I dealt with pocket computers, which were not to make their appearance in the marketplace until ten to fifteen years after the story appeared. Moreover, it was one of the stories in which I foresaw accurately a social implication of technological advance rather than the technological advance itself.

The story deals with the possible loss of ability to do simple arithmetic through the perpetual use of computers. I wrote it as a satire that combined humor with passages of bitter irony, but I wrote more truly than I knew. These days I have a pocket computer and I begrudge the time and effort it would take me to subtract 182 from 854. I use the darned computer. "The Feeling of Power" is one of the most frequently anthologized of my stories.

In a way, this story shows the negative side of computers, and in this period I also wrote stories that showed the possible vengeful reactions of computers or robots that are mistreated. For computers, there is "Someday," which appeared in the August 1956 issue of *Infinity Science Fiction*, and for robots (in automobile form) see "Sally," which appeared in the May-June 1953 issue of *Fantastic*.

11. "Feminine Intuition"—My robots are almost always masculine, though not necessarily in an actual sense of gender. After all, I give them masculine names and refer to them as "he." At the suggestion of a female editor, Judy-Lynn del Rey, I wrote "Feminine Intuition," which appeared in the October 1969 issue of *The Magazine of Fantasy and Science Fiction*. It showed, for one thing, that I could do a feminine robot, too. She was still metal, but she had a narrower waistline than my usual robots and had a feminine voice, too. Later on, in my book *Robots and Empire*, there was a chapter in which a humanoid female robot made her appearance. She played a villainous role, which might surprise those who know of my frequently displayed admiration of the female half of humanity.

12. "The Bicentennial Man"—This story, which first appeared in 1976 in a paperback anthology of original science fiction, *Stellar #2*, edited by Judy-Lynn del Rey, was my most thoughtful exposition of the development of robots. It followed them in an entirely different direction from that in "The Last Question." What it dealt with was the desire of a robot to become a man and the way in which he carried out that desire, step by step. Again, I carried the plot all the way to its logical conclusion. I had no intention of writing this

story when I started it. It wrote itself, and turned and twisted in the typewriter. It ended as the third favorite of mine among all my stories. Ahead of it come only "The Last Question," mentioned above, and "The Ugly Little Boy," which is not a robot story.

13. *The Caves of Steel*—Meanwhile, at the suggestion of Horace L. Gold, editor of *Galaxy*, I had written a robot novel. I had resisted doing so at first for I felt that my robot ideas only fit the short story length. Gold, however, suggested I write a murder mystery dealing with a robot detective. I followed it partway. My detective was a thoroughly human Elijah Baley (perhaps the most attractive character I ever invented, in my opinion) but he had a robot sidekick, R. Daneel Olivaw. The book, I felt, was the perfect fusion of mystery and science fiction. It appeared as a three-part serial in the October, November, and December 1953 issues of *Galaxy* and Doubleday published it as a novel in 1954.

What surprised me about the book was the reaction of the readers. While they approved of Lije Baley, their obvious interest was entirely with Daneel, whom I had viewed as a mere subsidiary character. The approval was particularly intense in the case of the women who wrote to me. (Thirteen years after I had invented Daneel, the television series *Star Trek* came out, with Mr. Spock resembling Daneel quite closely in character—something which did not bother me—and I noticed that women viewers were particularly interested in him, too. I won't pretend to analyze this.)

14. *The Naked Sun*—The popularity of Lije and Daneel led me to write a sequel, "The Naked Sun," which appeared as a three-part serial in the October, November, and December 1956 issues of *Astounding* and was published as a novel by Doubleday in 1957. Naturally, the repetition of the success made a third novel seem the logical thing to do. I even

started writing it in 1958, but things got in the way and, what with one thing and another, it didn't get written till 1983.

15. *The Robots of Dawn*—This, the third novel of the Lije Baley/R. Daneel series, was published by Doubleday in 1983. In it, I introduced a second robot, R. Giskard Reventlov, and this time I was not surprised when he turned out to be as popular as Daneel.

16. *Robots and Empire*—When it was necessary to allow Lije Baley to die (of old age), I felt I would have no problem in doing a fourth book in the series provided I allowed Daneel to live. The fourth book, *Robots and Empire*, was published by Doubleday in 1985. Lije's death brought some reaction, but nothing at all compared to the storm of regretful letters I received when the exigencies of the plot made it necessary for R. Giskard to die.

So it turns out that my robot stories have been almost as successful as my Foundation books, and if you want to know the truth (in a whisper, of course, and please keep this confidential), I like my robot stories better.

Here, in *Renegade*, Cordell Scotten has written an excellent example of why I like the robot stories. A simple question arising from the Laws—"What is good for humans?"—is developed into a complex and intriguing story.

CHAPTER 1

THE CEREMYONS

Gently soaring—basking under the sun—the two blackbodies circled far above the shimmering atmospheric irregularity that was nearing completion on the planet's surface. As high as a small mountain, the iridescent transparency, viewed from outside, covered a smooth hemispherical excavation in the planet's surface two kilometers in diameter, except for an open pie cut, a not-yet-covered sector ten degrees wide. Looking into the open sector, structures—built on ground not excavated, paradoxically—covered the entire inner area. The most striking of these structures was a tall, stepped pyramid centered under the dome.

The blackbodies floated a wingspread apart, five times the armspread of an Avery robot. Those beings—the Avery robots—were even then streaming out of the incomplete sector, evacuating the dome. The blackbodies had learned the name "Avery robot," but the name lacked meaning beyond its intonation.

"The construction was slowed by your absence yesterday, Sarco," one blackbody said to the other, "and I thank you for that. You needed the day off. Unfortunately, the effort was only slowed. It would have benefited by a complete interruption."

"You are a rascal," the other said, his red eyes gleaming like burning embers set deep in a black demonic body. "I'll bet you arranged for an Avery to cut me loose during tether last night. At least they've learned not to blow us up."

The blackbodies appeared identical in form: a large white hook protruding from above deep-set, luminous red eyes; a lacy silver frond languidly waving at the other end; but bodies otherwise devoid of visible detail except as flying winged silhouettes. Wrinkles in the skin, if any, and other possible lines of demarcation were lost in the soft blackness.

"You were cut loose?" the first said.

"Don't play the innocent, Synapo. Someone cut my tether last night, and by the time I drifted into sunrise, I was over Barneup. It took me all day to get back. Have you ever tried to grow a new hook while underway?"

"You do look a little beat. But then so am I. Trying to make sense of Wohler-9 is exhausting, and so far he's the best of the Averies. I learned very little today. We could both do with early tether. I'll see you in the morning, Sarco."

"Wait up! You're not getting off that easy."

But Synapo had already balled and was dropping, if not like a rock, still at an appreciable rate that put him out of earshot in a trice. Sarco sighed—a soft gentle emission of pure oxygen with a faint trace of unreacted ammonia—but did not follow immediately.

As Synapo approached the surface of the planet, he began braking, unfurling from his collar the tough filmy hide of his reflector, letting it flap and rattle in his wake as it dragged at him like a sea anchor. As he neared the trees on the side of the domed transparency away from the open sector, he sealed the gores of the thin, shiny reflector, sealing all but his head inside, leaving his hook and eyes protruding from the underside.

With gentle bursts of compressed hydrogen, he began to inflate the reflector, dissipating his momentum and slowing his descent until he was barely drifting downward. Ten meters above the top of a tall conifer, he let go his chitinous hook, letting out the tether of tough, stringy hide until the hook was dangling below a sturdy limb. A final burst of hydrogen filled the reflector, erasing the last crease to leave a smooth, unblemished, mirrorlike surface. The tether twanged taut, caught between the now buoyant silvery balloon and the hooked limb of the tree.

Synapo began the luxurious process of uncoiling his tense fibers, drifting into deep tether as he lay suspended within his own skin. His storage cells were not sated with a day's thermo-electric output from the sun's radiant heat as they normally would have been if the aliens had not been disturbing the atmosphere; but little of the radiation he had been exposed to that day had escaped the nearly perfect blackbody absorption of his other skin. That energy was all there, save only the small expenditure for intense thought and languid motion, and the large expenditure for electrolyzing water and compressing hydrogen; and the unusual expenditure that day to converse—if it could be called that—with Wohler-9. Still, he had a sufficient reserve of juice left in his cells. It would take little to get him through the night, just that amount needed to maintain body temperature, to make up for the minuscule amount of energy lost by radiation from his silvery hide.

Sarco stayed aloft until Synapo tethered. Then he balled and dropped and tethered nearby so as to confront Synapo the next morning, first thing.

The Avery robots continued to stream from the open sector of the dome like ants abandoning an anthill. Dusk was coming on rapidly, but night would not hamper their operations.

Wohler-9 stood just outside the open sector. He had watched Synapo and Sarco drop, but had not distinguished them from the rest of the blackbodies which, a half-hour later, began to fall from the sky like the gentle descent of a black snow that melted to bright raindrops as it neared the surface, raindrops inversely and miraculously suspended above the trees in defiance of gravity.

When the tiny amount of absorbed sunshine began to warm Synapo's reflector the next morning, he awoke and began to deflate. When his hook dangled free, he sucked in his tether and drifted to the ground, gently bouncing off the outer foliage of the tree.

When he reached the ground, he unsealed the front seam of his reflector and pulled it around him like a bath-robe to preserve his body heat. On his two short legs, he waddled through the forest to a small brook. Sarco was already there, having breakfast and waiting for him. His hook was turned to the back in nonaggressive posture, which was a good sign. Still, he was having breakfast. You could hardly expect anything else. Anger cannot abide alongside intense creature satisfactions.

During the night, the feathery cold-junction that protruded from Synapo's rump had warmed, and the millions of hot junctions distributed throughout his lampblack hide had cooled, so that both cold and hot junctions were now at the same median temperature; and he had fasted throughout the night. Now as he backed up to the brook beside Sarco, drew his reflector tight across his back to bunch it in front of him, and squatted to dip his cold junction into the icy water, he sighed contentedly as the fresh juice flowed into his storage cells. That fresh shot each morning was the best juice to be had all day.

Neither spoke, which was the custom at breakfast, nor would they speak until they were again on the wing. Speaking, unless forced by exigencies—such as the discussion with Wohler-9—was strictly a waste process, using the oxygen discarded from the electrolytic production of vital hydrogen. Electrolyzing when their hydrogen sacs were full, merely to generate oxygen for speaking, was a luxury they seldom permitted themselves and a necessity only under the rarest of circumstances.

That morning, however, Synapo again planned to allow himself only an hour on the wing before he resumed his discussion with Wohler-9. He timed it so that he could watch the Myostrians at work, as he had for the past several days. He was depleting his cells to well below what he found comfortable—he went around continually hungry—but at least he would be generating hydrogen during the discussion and not wasting juice as he would be otherwise. That was small comfort as his store of vital energy dropped lower and lower. But Synapo felt that discussion was vital, not for what it had revealed so far, but for what it promised to reveal in the future.

With breakfast over and the gores of their reflectors tightly rolled into black ruffled collars, they began the long climb to charge altitude. Synapo, with Sarco following, slowly circled upward with languid but powerful strokes of his great wings. He kept the hemispherical iridescence centered below, so that when he finished his short charge, he could drop rapidly to the open sector where he could see

Wohler-9 still standing vigil, right where he had been as Synapo dropped to tether the evening before.

When they reached a comfortable altitude, Synapo slowed his flapping and rolled onto his back, a wingspread below Sarco, giving the other the dominant position as was his right as interrogator. That had been the status of their conversation the afternoon before when Synapo had terminated it unilaterally.

"Now, Sarco, you were saying?"

"Forget that," Sarco said. "My tether was cut, and I was fuming yesterday evening, but it's no big deal. A new hook and a night's rest and it's the same as forgotten."

Good, Synapo thought, *but it wasn't an Avery, it was my own burning breath which sent you into far sunrise.* He wouldn't have stooped to such a childish trick if the situation hadn't warranted it. The thought of that piece of unstatesmanship lingered, unsettling his conscience.

"What is important," Sarco continued, "is getting the weather back under control and stopping the godawful screeching of those tin aliens on hyperwave. The weather I'll have under control as soon as my people finish neutralizing that node below. I figure to have the compensator complete day after tomorrow.

"But the hyperwave noise is about to drive us all nuts, Synapo. Haven't those metal morons heard of continuous modulation?"

"Of course. That's the way they arrived," Synapo said. "But their discrete modulation of hyperwave and our small discomfort with the crosstalk on our continuous channels is a minor problem. The real problem is your construction of the node compensator. It's a mistake, Sarco. You'll have deactivated the aliens only temporarily. And if I'm right, as I am more and more sure I am, you'll have succeeded merely in deactivating a bunch of servants, and probably not for long, but you will have irritated their masters sure as the Great Petero is our guide."

"And the Cerebrons, what have they come up with? The Myostrians are at least taking action."

(In some contexts, the plural Myostrian tribal name is better translated as Myostria, and the racial name Ceremyon is better translated as Myoceron to reflect the Myostrian point of view.)

"We had a caucus yesterday afternoon," Synapo said. "All agree I'm close to a breakthrough with Wohler-9. Whatever you do, don't close the compensator. You've already achieved better than 95% compensation. Meteorologically, you've already won."

"You've got until sunpeak day after tomorrow to achieve your breakthrough, Synapo."

There was no point in arguing further. Synapo rolled out from under Sarco and drifted off to the left while climbing a temperature gradient to a slightly cooler stratum. That inverted gradient so early in the day was a measure of the meteorological disturbance—the residual effects of the alien creations—the completed dome would eliminate.

After an hour of charge, he was still quite hungry, but nonetheless he balled and dropped, wind whistling through the feathery frond of his cold-junction, until he neared the top of the dome. Then he slowly spread his wings, braking in a swoop that carried him on a complete circular inspection of the dome.

He made one more pass around the dome, lower now, looking for any sign of spacetime instability. Why did he care? The dome could have leaked like Nimbar and it wouldn't have mattered to him. It was a habit, though, a matter of professional pride, pride in his race, pride in

Sarco's people and the technology they shared with the Cerebrons.

As he rounded again toward the open sector, he braked to a slow gentle glide and, stirring hardly a wisp of dust, came to rest beside the Avery robot who called himself Wohler-9.

He now had a fairly good idea what an Avery robot was. He had a modest grasp of the language called Galactic Standard, and even though it was certainly not standard in their part of the galaxy, they had become aware of it from the occasional bursts of discrete hyperwave that had reached them beginning centuries before. Translation of the language had been slow and incomplete, lacking anything that might have served as a Rosetta stone, but they had acquired a feeling for the language, in terms of the mathematical development of the species, and then with Wohler-9 on hand—not quite an analogue of the Rosetta stone—their fluency had progressed to the modest state Synapo now claimed.

"Good morning, Wohler-9," Synapo said.

The robot slowly swiveled his head until the eyes bore intently on Synapo, but otherwise he gave no sign of recognition. That did not distress Synapo. In fact he expected it. He now knew that the robot did not consider him a master, and so he was not worthy of attention unless he somehow violated the robot's basic programming: a prime directive and three guiding principles.

The prime directive was to erect the monstrosities that had played such havoc with their weather by energy and particulate emissions, and which were now covered and almost neutralized by the compensator. The disturbance had been almost as great as that caused by the impact of a giant meteor a quarter-century before.

The function of the monstrosities was still not clear, other than being creations for the masters. With their benign weather—brought under control eons before—the notion of shelter and buildings, if it had ever existed, had long since disappeared from the racial memory of the blackbodies, lost in prehistory.

"You properly informed your masters of our interference and asked for assistance more than a hand of days ago, if we translated your message correctly. Each day I have asked if you have received further instructions among the numerous messages that we have monitored in both directions. Your responses thus far have not been reassuring. But now we have reason to suspect that you have received some clarification of the situation, if we understand a message you received yesterday morning. I informed you of that message yesterday afternoon. I now ask again. Have you received further instructions?"

Still the robot did not answer. He had swiveled his head back to watch the procession of robots and vehicles passing out of the dome, heading north across the plain bordered by the forest.

"We will complete the compensator—the dome—tomorrow, thwarting your prime directive," Synapo added.

That brought a response. Wohler-9 turned to face Synapo.

"Miss Ariel Welsh will deal with you when she arrives this afternoon," Wohler-9 said, and swiveled back to watch the evacuation.

There was no point in attempting further dialogue. Synapo took off and headed for charge altitude and a Cerebron caucus.

CHAPTER 2

THE DOMED PIT

Ariel Welsh, in her typical fashion, came in too fast on a trajectory that was accordingly too flat, and she skipped off the planet's atmosphere like a flat stone hitting the surface of a mill-pond.

"Darn," she said, which seemed to understate the situation somewhat. She turned the controls over to Jacob Winterson, saying, "Here, you do it."

"You should have asked me earlier, Miss Ariel," the robot said. "You must save yourself for the negotiations with the aliens. But I do have a few suggestions with regard to your approach trajectories in general, which should benefit . . ."

"Put a lid on it, Jake!" Ariel said impatiently. Nonetheless she watched the robot closely and with a great deal of admiration, not only for his style of piloting but for his superb appearance as well. She particularly liked to watch his biceps flex.

She had acquired the robot only months before, the

whim of a spoiled rich girl, teasing a jealous boyfriend and rebelling against the mores of a bigoted Auroran society.

Robots like R. Jacob Winterson were not popular on the planet of Aurora. Neither the men nor the women of Aurora wanted to be upstaged by the perfect comeliness and superhuman strength of a humaniform robot. *Humaniform* was the term their creator, Dr. Han Fastolfe, had used to describe them, searching for a better term than *humanoid*, which hardly sufficed to describe Jacob. The Avery robots, like the one she had once known as Wohler on the planet Robot City, could also be described as humanoid, but they were a far cry from Jacob.

The simulation of a well-muscled body that was Jacob Winterson was a reflection of that era when bodybuilding was the vogue of a stagnant Auroran society.

She watched him now as he plugged himself into the ship, a small two-man jumper with a cockpit just big enough for the two of them. She should have used the ship's computer to set up the proper approach trajectory, just as he was about to do, instead of coming in cowboy fashion, hands on.

She watched the thick muscles at work in his bull-like neck, watched the flexing of biceps the size of piano legs, corded by thick veins reaching across his powerful forearms.

She had prevailed upon the ancient Vasilia Fastolfe, the estranged daughter of the famed Dr. Han, to delve deep into the catacombs below Aurora's Robotics Institute and bring out Jacob from among the thirteen humaniforms left over from the aborted campaign to sell them to a recalcitrant Auroran public.

She had never seen Jacob naked, though Derec didn't know that. Vasilia had brought him up from the depths fully clothed. And then he seemed so real—so alive in the human sense—that Ariel had never explored beneath the surface of the ample wardrobe she had provided him. It seemed too much an invasion of privacy.

The idea appealed to her, she had to admit, but not so strongly as to overcome her loyalty to Derec. In her mind, her teasing was not a form of disloyalty, no matter how miserable it made Derec. Like the myriads of young women who preceded her, she had no idea how miserable it really made him or she wouldn't have teased him.

On their third orbit, Jacob located their destination: the beleaguered robot city Wohler-9 had described by radio after they had jumped into the system. Derec was apparently not in the city at the time. Ariel had counted on hearing Derec's voice.

Their destination was the second-largest iridescent domed pit they had seen on the planet, and the only one with a pie-cut of city buildings that extended to the center of the shimmering pit.

Jacob laid in a trajectory that would bring them through the atmosphere to a landing on the open plain half a kilometer north of the dome and near the path of evacuation of the Avery robots; and then, with the help of the jumper's computer, he executed the maneuver flawlessly. They disembarked less than fifty meters from the line of evacuation and commandeered a large courier robot carrying two packages.

"Return to the city," Ariel said as she sat down on one of the packages and motioned Jacob to sit down on the other one. She would like to have said, "Take me to Wohler," but the nonpositronic brain of the courier would not have been capable of interpreting and executing that command.

As they neared the open sector of the dome, towering a

kilometer above them, Ariel said, "Can you raise Wohler on the radio, Jacob?"

"I have, Miss Ariel," Jacob replied. "He is standing over to the right of the opening in the dome." The robot pointed and said, "There by that large open lorry."

Up close, the paradoxical nature of the huge iridescent bubble became more dramatic as Ariel looked down through the flickering wall of the dome into a pit that seemed to underlie a city built on solid ground. Looking through the wall and the opening at the same time, the city seemed to float above the excavation. It left her feeling decidedly uneasy.

"Take us to Wohler," she said to the courier. They disembarked at the lorry and walked up to Wohler-9, an imposing gold machine standing at the front of the lorry and facing the stream of evacuating robots.

"I am Ariel Welsh," she said.

"I know," said Wohler-9.

"What is going on here?" Ariel asked.

"We are moving the necessary materiel for construction of a second Compass Tower and city on the other side of the plain, five kilometers away."

"Why?"

"This dome will soon be closed by the aliens, blocking all traffic into and out of the city."

"Why?"

"That is not clear."

"Where is Derec Avery?"

"I do not know, since he is not on this planet."

Ariel took a moment to absorb that. "When did he leave?"

"He has never been here," the golden robot replied.

Now she felt slightly ill. She had misunderstood that

weak relay from a central computer, which had led her to believe Derec would be here. She had to keep talking, or scream. She had thought she would see him so soon.

"Are all the supervisors here ninth generation?" she asked.

"No. I am the only ninth. All others are eighth generation."

"How did that come about?"

"Wohler-1 sacrificed himself to rescue you from the side of Robot City's Compass tower during a life-threatening thunderstorm, Miss Welsh."

The Burundi's Fever Dr. Avery had exposed her to—amnemonic plague, so-called—had robbed her of the links to her memory. The memory had still been there, but she had lost the connections to it. Derec had helped restore those links by providing clues from their mutual experiences. That particular experience involving Wohler-1 must have been exceptionally potent, for now her mind orchestrated that clue into an unnerving symphony of emotion as the experience condensed into consciousness. The guilt of causing the termination of that magnificent golden robot, laid on top of her misunderstanding of the relayed message from this planet, left her momentarily faint.

She swallowed hard to regain her composure and then said brusquely, "What is the nature of the dome? Why not simply destroy it?"

"A simple demonstration will suffice to answer your question, Miss Welsh," Wohler-9 replied.

He unclipped a meter-long, chrome-plated crowbar from the side of the lorry and started walking toward the edge that bordered the right side of the opening in the dome's glimmer.

Ariel and Jacob followed him, and as Ariel approached

the interior of the dome, getting a little ahead of Wohler-9 in her impetuous fashion, she could see up close the soft blackness of the lining, a blackness that demarcated the end of the ground and the beginning of what seemed open space. Looking down at it sent her into a dizzying subjective vertigo. She seemed to spin in that black space as it drew her down, sucking at her mind.

"Under no circumstances come closer than half a meter, Miss Welsh," Wohler-9 said as he casually moved his arm in front of her. With that warning she seemed to come to her senses, and she moved back out so that she was facing the edge from a distance of a few meters; her head cleared, and from that position she could now see along both the inside and outside walls.

Wohler-9 then approached the edge of the wall to almost that half-meter limit himself. He stopped then, facing the inner wall, and said, "And don't become confused. The wall may seem deceptively far away."

He took a baseball batter's stance then, and with a lusty swing that brought the crowbar around in a horizontal arc perpendicular to the wall, he struck the edge of the dome with the middle of the crowbar. Without a sound, the edge of the dome, like the edge of a supersharp tool, cut the crowbar neatly in half. The far end of the crowbar sailed off. The near end stayed firmly in Wohler-9's hands as he completed his swing.

Then he casually tossed the remnant toward the inside wall.

Ariel's eyes had naturally followed the flight of the far end of the crowbar until it hit the ground and stopped skidding. She looked back just as Wohler-9 tossed the piece left in his hand toward the interior blackness.

That piece seemed to curve in toward the blackness a

fraction of the distance it would have traveled if he had tossed it straight up in the air with the same force, and then it came shooting back out on a parabolic course obviously calculated to hit no one. It landed behind him a distance equal to the distance it would have traveled in front of him if the wall had not been there.

"Now, a second demonstration will point up and clarify the dome's external characteristics," Wohler-9 said.

He picked up the half-crowbar that had just sailed back out of the blackness, walked over, tossed it into the lorry, and then unclipped two sections of a tubular pole from the side of the vehicle. When he fitted the two sections together, he had a pole about five meters long. From a locker he took a large piece of white cloth that he unfolded and tied to the pole to form a square flag a little less than four meters on a side. With the flagpole in hand, he walked along the outside of the dome until he was three or four meters from the edge of the opening. Ariel followed him.

They were walking along the edge of a deep, shimmering hemispherical pit two kilometers across and a kilometer deep. From that viewpoint there was no evidence of the city that they knew existed inside the shimmer.

"Under no circumstances let any part of your body touch or project into the transparent dome," Wohler-9 said. "That part of you would go through and never be the same again. Now observe the flag."

He pushed the flag through the dome's glimmer. It seemed to disappear.

"Perhaps it appears to be gone," he said, waving the pole, "but look carefully at the far side of the pit."

At first Ariel could see nothing unusual on the other side, but after a moment, after looking more carefully, she finally saw a tiny white flag waving, far away, two kilometers away, on the other side of the pit.

Wohler-9 laid down the pole so that it still projected into the dome. It did not lie flat on the ground. The near end hung suspended, slanting into the dome at the ground. The tiny flag on the other side of the pit had disappeared into the grass.

"Two further observations," Wohler-9 said, "for which we'll use the lorry."

He left the pole projecting into the dome, retrieved the other half of the crowbar from the deep grass, tossed it into the lorry beside the first half, and stepped in to stand at the driver's station. Ariel took a seat immediately behind the golden robot and Jacob stepped up to stand beside Wohler-9, who immediately took off down the west side of the dome, staying well away from the edge of the pit.

They were almost halfway around the dome before Wohler-9 spoke again.

"We should be coming to it now," he said.

And then Ariel saw the white flag lying in the grass with the pole sticking out of the dome a few centimeters above the ground.

Wohler-9 stopped the lorry.

"You don't need to get out."

He stepped down from the lorry, picked up the pole carefully, as though it were a fragile memento, walked back, and offered the flag end to Ariel.

"Take hold of the end," he said.

When she did, he moved his end as though to bend it in her grip, and it snapped in two.

"Passing through the dome distorts the crystal structure, setting up fault lines with very little strength. Now one last observation, this time inside the dome."

He drove back the way they had come and then drove through the opening, close to the right side. The traffic pouring out of the dome gave way smoothly, shifting to its right to accommodate the lorry, as though a computer were directing all the traffic—which it was, of course: the city central computer.

"We'll take the perimeter route to avoid bucking the traffic coming down Main Street," Wohler-9 said, "even though it will be a little longer this way, half-pi-times longer."

Wohler-9 drove rapidly to a point half-way around the perimeter of the dome. He stopped at the same wide street: Main Street, which approached the dome as close as any. Ariel looked back down the street and saw the Compass Tower framed in the opening of the dome.

Wohler-9 led them now to the dome wall opposite the end of the street and handed Ariel a pair of binoculars as he pointed to a small bright object in the soft darkness of the inner wall.

Ariel put the binoculars to her eyes, and with the focus wheel at the infinite setting, she could just barely make out a shape that had the appearance of a small two-man flier headed toward them with its landing lights on.

"This is our final test of the dome, which we began earlier this afternoon," Wohler-9 said. "Right now the flier is held by the gravity of the black concavity at a virtual distance of four kilometers. It is headed toward us, but held motionless by the black concavity with the flier's impulse engines throttled back to 75% capacity, equivalent to an acceleration of ten gees. We plan to bring it in now. Its fuel is almost depleted."

Ariel had a hard time taking the binoculars away from her eyes. She turned to hand them to Jacob.

"Here, I want you to record this," she said. "I want you as a witness. Derec's not apt to believe any of this."

"Thank you, Miss Ariel," Jacob said, "but with my 50-power binocular vision I have already recorded the unusual operation of this flier."

Ariel was tired. It had been a long day already. Altogether too much for one day. Too much sensory stimulation, too many strange ideas, too much emotion. She missed Derec and felt inadequate to the challenge presented by this alien world.

"Unless you have further exhibits and demonstrations, Wohler," Ariel said, "I would like to shower and freshen up. Later, after some dinner, you can give me a detailed report."

"I have just ordered in the flier, Miss Welsh," Wohler-9 said. "We shall now proceed immediately to your apartment."

As they drove down the broad street toward the Compass Tower, the faint sound of the flier grew louder. Ariel turned to watch its lights growing brighter now in the soft darkness surrounding the city. She had a hard time taking in everything she had seen in the short time she had known Wohler-9.

Then she could see the flier growing larger with her naked eye, until it came hurtling out of the wall and screamed by overhead, spiraling up over the Compass Tower and out the opening in the dome.

CHAPTER 3

WOHLER-9'S STORY

THE LAWS OF ROBOTICS

1. *A robot may not injure a human being, or, through inaction, allow a human being to come to harm.*
2. *A robot must obey the orders given it by human beings except where such orders would conflict with the First Law.*
3. *A robot must protect its own existence, as long as such protection does not conflict with the First or Second Laws.*

Han Fastolfe, An Introduction to Robotics, Chapter 1, Ancient Technology.

"Now, Wohler, I would like to hear this from the very beginning," Ariel said.

She had just sat down to eat dinner. They had arrived at the apartment an hour before—a small two-bedroom flat on the second and top floor of a small building on Main Street, halfway toward the opening in the dome from the Compass Tower.

Jacob stood quietly in a wall niche near the entrance to the apartment. Wohler-9 was standing attentively on the other side of the table from Ariel.

"I was the seventh and last of the supervisors to arrive by Key teleportation on the morning of . . ." Wohler intoned when Ariel interrupted him.

"No, Wohler, not in quite that much detail," she said.

"You do not want it from the very beginning, Miss Welsh? You would like more of a summary?"

"Yes. And confine the summary to your interactions with the aliens and their erection of the dome."

"Very well. We began cityforming the planetary surface with construction of the Compass Tower on the open plain one-point-zero-two kilometers from the nearest forest vegetation.

"We had progressed to the third floor of the Compass Tower when an unusual incident involving a witness occurred at the edge of the forest."

Ariel interrupted him. "A witness robot?"

"Yes, Miss Welsh. To alert us to the migration of planetary life into the construction arena, we had established a rapid circular patrol of twelve witnesses on a perimeter two kilometers in diameter centered on the Compass Tower.

"The unusual incident involved destructive bisection of a witness as it passed near the forest."

"Bisection, Wohler?"

"Yes, Miss Welsh. The witness was cut in half. Just before the incident, that same witness had been observing the flight of several of the aliens we now call blackbodies to a point near the forest about twenty meters above where the incident occurred.

"Those observations by the witness constitute its last transmissions to core memory over the comlink."

"Switch to memory detail, Wohler," Ariel said quietly.

"The blackbody flight pattern began just after the preceding witness had passed by. A blackbody would fly to a point about twenty meters above the incident point, stall out, collapse into a ball, and drop to five meters above the ground. At that point it would spread its wings and resume flight, swooping down and back up into the air, narrowly missing a collision with the ground.

"A careful inspection of the witness's transmission shows a faint shimmering in the air coincident with the blackbody's resumption of flight. The shimmering progressed rapidly toward the ground from the point of flight resumption. The performance was repeated by a succession of blackbodies, and as the witness approached closer, it became apparent that on each cycle, the shimmering proceeded not only to the ground, but also back up, traversing the perimeter of a thin vertical area that grew taller with each successive pass. The pattern was repeated rapidly by twenty-one blackbodies before the witness arrived. The blackness we see from the inside was not visible to the witness as he approached. He was looking at the blackbody construction almost edge-on, but slightly outside, moving in for a close-up view."

"The record ended at that point, of course," Ariel said.

"Yes. Since that time, witness records show that to be the pattern of blackbody operation in constructing the dome. As the construction progressed, the intersecting arcs traversed by the shimmer, and the point to which the blackbodies flew to begin each pass, rose in the air until it reached its present location. That operation now begins at midmorning at a height of a little more than a kilometer directly over the Compass Tower and lasts for one hundred twenty passes of the blackbodies, which generally takes a little over an hour."

"Hour?"

"An ancient term from the vocabulary file. It means one-twenty-fourth part. The blackbody I conversed with used my access to central's files to search for an exact translation of their terminology, one-twenty-fourth part of the period of planetary rotation."

"And do they divide that further, as we do with our centads?"

"Yes. Their next division, into sixty parts, can be labeled 'minutes' according to central. The conversion of those units into our decads and centads gives, for the hour . . ."

"I am quite capable of making that conversion, Wohler."

"Thus construction of the dome begins each day at ten AM, and . . ."

"Ten AM?"

"At ten hours antemidday, or more exactly in the ancient terminology, ante meridiem, being before noon. Their day is divided into two twelve-hour parts: AM, before noon, and PM for post midday or after noon."

"Didn't it seem odd to your alien that he could find terms that seem to describe their technology in our ancient history files?"

"No. By my recording, specifically in that regard, he remarked, 'How satisfying to find our own circadian rhythms—the metabolic divisions of our natural clocks—so faithfully reproduced in another species.'"

"It seems darn odd to me," Ariel said. "But to get on with this, at the time of the incident, the witness robot was sliced in half by the first elements of the present dome as its momentum carried it past the edge, just as the crowbar was cut in half earlier today."

"Yes," Wohler replied.

"You had had no interaction with the blackbodies until then," Ariel said.

"That is correct."

"But then you began a dialogue."

"No. Not immediately."

"But not to do so was to violate the Third Law, Wohler."

"On the contrary, Miss Welsh, we chose to comply with the Third Law by retaliation."

"But, Wohler, that violated the First Law, which protects intelligent life."

"No, Miss Welsh, it does not. It protects humans."

"It protects Wolruf."

Wolruf was a dog-like alien, a friend of both Ariel and Derec. They had been through several unpleasant experiences together, starting with an alien pirate by the name of Aranimus who had held all three of them prisoner at one time. That was when they had first met Wolruf.

"But only because Master Derec chose to make an exception," Wohler-9 said. "Dr. Avery's original programming made no such exceptions. The first law now protects humans *and* Wolruf. But our definition of a human being is quite narrow. It certainly does not include the blackbodies."

Dr. Avery was Derec Avery's father and the erratic, egocentric scientist who had created the original planetary Robot City. He had suppressed his teenage son's memory and subjected him to irrational experiments in bizarre situations on and off the Robot City planet. Derec had learned a great deal about himself, but Avery left Robot City without restoring Derec's memory.

"Proceed, Wohler," Ariel said. "How did you retaliate?"

"We attempted to stop construction of the dome by intercepting the flight path of the aliens, ramming them with a one-man flier, but it was not entirely successful. The alien was destroyed, but so was the flier and the robot pilot. Spectrographic and flame temperature records support a hydrogen explosion as the cause of failure."

"So then you started a dialogue," Ariel said.

"No. Logic dictated that we determine why a hydrogen explosion caused the failure, so we decided to trap and examine an alien.

"At night, the blackbodies convert into silver balloons which they anchor to the tops of trees. We successfully captured one which had anchored to a tree on the very edge of the forest five kilometers away. We easily unhooked its anchor line after cutting the tree down.

"However, in order to examine the alien, it was necessary to first remove the balloon which surrounded it. Again a hydrogen explosion destroyed the alien and the surgeon when he attempted to cut the balloon away with a laser scalpel."

"It figures," Ariel said with a sigh. "So then you initiated a dialogue. Surely."

"No. One or more of the aliens had been confronting robots all around the Compass Tower construction site for three and a half days, but our programming did not require us to grant recognition, and we were, of course, quite busy erecting the Compass Tower, which had to be completed before work on the general city could begin. Understandably, we paid no attention to their confrontations, until I personally was confronted by one of the blackbodies. That happened immediately after we lost the surgeon and his laser scalpel. It then occurred to me, when I was confronted, that by conversing with the alien, I might find out what the surgeon was seeking, and I was then compelled by the Third Law to do so. The Third Law says . . ."

"I know, I know," Ariel said. "So then you initiated the dialogue."

"No. Surely it is clear by now, Miss Welsh, that the alien initiated the dialogue."

"So it seems," Ariel said with resignation coloring her voice. "I wouldn't want it any other way."

"On the contrary. It is now quite apparent that if I had initiated the dialogue earlier . . ."

"You're quite right, Wohler. But you need not feel bad for all that."

"I understand technically that you can be affected in that manner, but I am incapable of experiencing such an emotion, Miss Welsh."

"Clearly," Ariel said. "Clearly. Now what has your dialogue with this alien revealed?"

"Not a great deal, Miss Welsh. I have spent most of the time teaching him Galactic Standard, since I have no linguistic capacity for understanding his language. And teaching him has been most difficult because of that lack of linguistic knowledge. But he seems now to have a rudimentary knowledge of our language, which should prove useful in your dialogue with him."

"I take it you are speaking of a male alien, then?"

"I loosely ascribe that gender, but it is more a description of his manner and conduct, a similarity to the attributes of a male human, which I perceive by the behavioral differences between the males and females of the human species."

"Male chauvinism in a robot? Is that what I am detecting, Wohler?"

"Not at all, Miss Welsh. My analysis is quite objective."

"On the contrary, Wohler. I would say it is quite pro-grammed, and of the Dr. Avery variety. But let's get on. What else did you learn?"

"In reviewing my records," Wohler replied, "I found that I taught the alien our language and much about humans, but learned little about them, other than the fact that the construction of our city is disturbing their equilibrium. He used the terms *inversions* and *puncture nodes* and *abnormal thermoclines*, but the terms have little meaning for me, and so little meaning for me to pass on to you."

"The terms do not help me a great deal, either," Ariel said. "Do they mean anything to you, Jacob?"

Up to that point, Jacob in his niche had not entered into the conversation, nor moved at all. He had appeared frozen in position. Now his head gave a little twitch. A glimmer came into his eyes.

"They are meteorological terms, Miss Ariel," Jacob said.

"Like in weather?"

"Yes."

"We're disturbing their weather!" she exclaimed.

"It would seem so, Miss Ariel," Jacob confirmed.

"Wohler, I must speak to this alien—now, tonight."

"That will not be possible, Miss Welsh," Wohler said. "He has already retired to his balloon."

"What to do, Jacob?" she said in exasperation, as much to herself as to Jacob. "What to do?"

"It appears you can do nothing until morning, Miss Ariel," Jacob said.

"How do we contact him in the morning, Wohler?" Ariel asked.

"I know of no way to contact him, Miss Welsh, nor to lead you to him. I can't tell one of the blackbodies from another. And even if I could, they are seldom on the ground except at night, and then they are isolated in a hydrogen-filled balloon."

"So what do we do?" Ariel asked.

"We must wait for him to come to us."

"And when will that be?"

"He generally comes to the west side of the opening in the dome each morning."

"That reminds me, Wohler, pass the word over the com-link that all future references to time of day and passage of time in general are to be expressed in alien terminology. I want to become accustomed to their way of thinking. When in Rome, do as the Romans do.

"So when will this blackbody come to the dome?"

There was a pause before Wohler replied.

"I beg your pardon, Miss Welsh, but the encyclopedic file shows nothing regarding behavior under either *Rome* or *Romans*."

"Forget that, Wohler. Just an old saying. I wouldn't know a Roman if I saw one. Answer my question please."

"He comes to the dome near ten AM each morning, just before the aliens begin their construction work. He seems to be inspecting that effort."

"A good supervisor," Ariel said.

"No. I have the impression that he does not approve of the construction; that it is being performed by a tribe to which he does not belong. His terse comments seem to be more a critique of their work in an artistic sense."

Ariel did not sleep well that night. She longed for Derec to be there beside her, and she was homesick as well. Compared to this alien planet with its insidious dome and its blackbody creatures straight out of hell, Aurora seemed the most desirable of places: comfortable and quiet, typical of

Spacer worlds. She longed for its cultivated farms and green fields, its open, hardly discernible cities with their mani-cured lawns and gardens, its junk food shops and under-ground malls where she and Derec had had such fun with their friends. It startled her then to realize she had had fun. She had ignored the old friends who had ostracized her, but the new ones—though they might still covet her wealth as much as those old ones—had been genuine fun.

And fun with Derec. She yearned to see him intensely; she missed him so.

She had become quite fond of Jacob and didn't think of him as a robot with her fun mind, for he was fun to be with. He had a wry way of saying things that was quite amusing, and Ariel suspected he had cultivated it for that very reason, but of course, he would never admit that he had the faintest conception of human humor. Yes, she had become quite fond of Jacob.

But it was Derec she longed for: his pinched face, his skinny frame. Typically male, his rapid teen growth had sac-rificed meat and breadth to bones and height. Yet she could still look down on him by several centimeters. But she had stopped growing, while he would probably reach and pass her as he filled out. For the time she had, she was going to enjoy being taller than he and use it to advantage whenever that seemed appropriate. She loved teasing him. He was so loveable.

And she slipped off into a lonely, scary dream.

CHAPTER 4

DIALOGUE

Synapo had never drained himself quite so low before. The musculature of the legs particularly seemed weak as he walked toward the brook that morning. He had exhausted the fat juice cells for long-term storage around his chest and waist and buttocks and now he was drawing on the prompt supply cells that fed his muscles. And those in his legs were nowhere near as plentiful as those that supplied the large pectoral muscles that powered the downbeat of his wings. The legs were always the first to go. That was an old Myostrian saying that Sarco and his ilk were fond of iterating for some reason beyond the fact that it was true.

And the truth of that adage was never more apparent than when he had started for the brook that morning. He had actually felt sort of faint after the long inactivity of a night's tether.

Sarco had already left. That became apparent after breakfast as Synapo climbed to optimum charge altitude. Sarco was already on station in Synapo's favorite space immediately over the center of the compensator. Naturally,

Sarco would be the only one of both tribes not to recognize that and defer to him. It was the first time he had violated that space without permission.

Yet, the times were unusual; old, little-used protocols were easier to violate than those reinforced by continual use. The concept of preferred location was not a natural one with the Cerebrons as it was with the Myostrians, who tended to stay in one location for long periods in the process of constructing and destroying weather node compensators like the domed glimmer below. The Cerebrons did not normally spend the night on the ground, but instead tethered their reflectors together in large drifting nightpacks by interlacing their hooks. They were normally nomads, continually roaming all over the world in the state of deep cogitation that had brought their race to the intellectual heights it now enjoyed.

The last time they had anchored for any significant period of time was when both tribes were battling the weather effects of the great meteor fall a quarter-century before the aliens arrived.

Thus, preferred space was the Cerebron equivalent to the Myostrian preferred location. The preferred space was naturally toward the center of the pack, and the most exalted was dead center where the less taxing audio communication reached the greatest number of Cerebrons—and the surrounding elite first—and where the more taxing radio communication reached all the Cerebrons with the least expenditure of energy.

When the two tribes interacted—as they were doing now, and as they had during the meteor incident—the dominant tribe tended to be the Cerebrons unless the Myostrians had an unusually aggressive leader, and up until that morning, Synapo had been the more aggressive in their interaction despite the fact that it was Sarco and his Myostrians who were aggressively building the compensator. That was to be expected. Synapo would have been a little alarmed—contrary to the tenor of his words—if the Myostrians had performed otherwise.

So in the context of past behavior, it was surprising to find Sarco—with his hook pointed aggressively forward—on station in Synapo's space. The natural disposition of both tribes was peaceful, so Synapo meekly left his hook pointed aft and took up his station two wingspreads to the right of Sarco as Sarco circled around the center of the dome far below.

"You are on the wing a tad early, Sarco," Synapo said.

"I watched the alien land last night," Sarco said. "And monitored its jump into our zone two days before. That, perhaps, explains their discrete modulation of hyperwave. But not entirely. The metal monsters phased in with continuous modulation. How do you explain the jump? Do we have two different sets of aliens?"

"No. Not if I understand what Wohler-9 was telling me. This new being is clearly a master of the metal ones."

"Well, this morning, I'm joining you. I'll be able to observe the construction almost as well from your station as from mine. And though I care not a whit for either set of aliens, it would be a shame to destroy life unnecessarily. I want to see for myself how you handle them."

Synapo said nothing further for the rest of the short charge. He was already exhausted by the endless days of talk and the surfeit of poisonous oxygen that he felt compelled to hold in his sacs. But he continued to carry his hook aft so that Sarco would know that his silence was not intended as an affront. He could afford to allow Sarco to dominate this brief morning charge. But that was all he could allow him.

They balled and dropped as Sarco's people were forming up for construction. Synapo had not intended for Sarco to get ahead of him, but from habit set by the short time the aliens had been on their world, Synapo opened on glide path in his usual manner, which took him on a high circular pass around the dome.

Sarco chose to go in directly. By the time Synapo realized that Sarco was not following, it was too late to correct his error, but he circled tight, high up, and began to dive well before he had completed half the circle. Synapo watched him through the transparent dome as Sarco made a fast, powered approach and an aggressive landing: a powered stall a half-meter above the ground with his wings spread to their full ten-meter breadth as he came to rest only two meters from the aliens.

Synapo mentally cursed Sarco, but restrained himself and did not radiate his feelings as he might well have had he known the aliens could not receive his broadcast. A cloud of dust obscured Sarco and the aliens as Synapo came in on a flat gentle glide path and settled to the ground well inside the cloud. He knew he was more majestic in the air, but he also knew his approach would be obscured by Sarco's dust, so he chose to come in closer even than Sarco. Still, his approach was executed so adroitly he added not a whit to the ball of dust that was already rapidly dissipating.

There were three aliens: Wohler-9, a nonmetallic being a head shorter, and a third being as tall as Wohler-9 that Synapo took to be nonmetallic until he detected the neutrino radiation that characterized Wohler-9 and microfusion in general. He had to conclude that despite the deceptive appearance, the third alien must be of the servant tribe,

although he knew that quick generalization might be diplomatically embarrassing if it proved wrong.

Sarco at least had the good sense not to open his oxygen vent prematurely. And it was apparent that Wohler-9
was confused and not able to distinguish between Synapo
and Sarco. The robot's eyes kept flicking back and forth
between the two of them.

"Good morning, Wohler-9," Synapo said.

There was no hesitation, no ignoring Synapo this morning. Wohler-9 swiveled his head and rolled his eyes around
ahead of that motion so that they came to rest on Synapo
well before the head caught up.

"This is Miss Ariel Welsh," the robot said as he gestured
with a rather grand motion toward the diminutive alien,
who stood hardly as high as Synapo's shoulder joints.

And with a nod, Wohler-9 dismissed the other alien as
a servant beneath consideration, a fact confirmed by his
words.

"And this is the humaniform Jacob Winterson, Miss
Welsh's personal robot."

The validity of Synapo's generalization was reassuring
as was his initial reaction to the small alien's unimpressive
appearance. But Wohler-9 had failed to introduce Synapo,
a breach of etiquette not easily forgiven, which was not
reassuring.

Still, the robot was only a servant and perhaps not as
well schooled in diplomacy as the small master, who was a
she, a member of the subordinate clan of the dominant tribe.
Synapo had guessed she would be from his earlier conversations with Wohler-9.

Yet that was also disappointing since he would still not
know, after all the interminable discussion that would surely
take place, how dominant that other clan was and whether

that other clan would also dominate the tribes of his world if this Miss Welsh did not prove to do so. She was certainly not very imposing.

But her personal robot was imposing, and he was only a servant. That left Synapo with nothing to go on at that point but superficial appearances, which he knew from long experience to be untrustworthy.

And then, to Synapo's astonishment, Sarco was talking.

"Welcome to our world, Miss Ariel Welsh," Sarco said. "My name is Sarco, which is as close as we can come to a translation into your language. I am leader of the Myostria."

That caught Synapo by surprise. He had not really expected Sarco to be fluent in the language. Sarco had a better command of the language than Synapo would have thought possible from the brief radiated lessons he had given the Cerebrons. Sarco had obviously monitored those lessons, but he could only have picked up the audio patterns by special tutoring from one of the Cerebron elite.

And that, too, disturbed Synapo. Someone of the elite must be striking for dominance, and hard enough to risk undercutting Synapo in his rivalry with Sarco.

Synapo was so caught by surprise that before he could say anything, Sarco, with a gesture every bit as grand as Wohler-9's, said, "And this is Synapo, leader of the Cerebrons."

Sarco's introduction could be taken two ways. Synapo hoped the small alien placed Sarco's relationship to him in the same pattern as Wohler-9 to her. Had Sarco intended that to be the case? Had he misjudged Sarco's behavior during charge that morning?

"Yes, Miss Ariel Welsh. Welcome to our world," Synapo said.

The small alien turned away, shaking all over, after suddenly putting her hand over her primary and secondary vents. She was obviously caught in a fit of ague.

Wohler-9 studiously ignored her condition. The only reaction of the other, the humaniform, was a slight upward curvature at the corners of the robot's primary vent. Her behavior and theirs confused Synapo and led him to wonder about the efficacy of the robots as suitable servants. Surely one of them should have done something to ease her paroxysm.

She recovered quickly, however, and turned and said, "I am pleased to meet both of you," and then she put one hand to her front, the other to her back, and doubled over at the waist, which led Synapo to wonder if she had now suddenly been caught by a cramp like that which sometimes caught him when he was carrying too large an inventory of oxygen, as he was at that moment. But unlike her, if a cramp hit him in this situation he would suffer through and ignore it. That gave him a nice feeling of superiority.

CHAPTER 5

IMPASSE

Ariel finally got control of herself and with a sober face, turned back to face the aliens. Their frightening appearance had almost paralyzed her until that first one, Sarco, had spoken.

Wohler-9 had pointed them out before they began their drop, while they were still lazily circling above the center of the dome.

And then that first one had landed, coming in so fast it seemed like he could not possibly stop in time, and then unexpectedly spreading his wings so wide he engulfed them all in a jet black space absolutely devoid of any detail, as though they were suddenly and inexplicably thrown into the featureless black concavity of the dome.

When he retracted his wings, they seemed to melt into his sides and disappear in the soft blackness. The contrasts of color—or lack of it—heightened the disturbing appearance of the alien: the vicious white hook that could obviously disembowel a human in one neat stroke, and the disconcerting red glow of the sunken eyes that gave her the feeling she was peering deep into the bowels of hell.

Then the other one arrived, much more decorously than the first, and when he opened his mouth, she was immediately transported back to Earth, to Webster Groves, one of the caves of steel that she and Derec had once visited. And then the first one so confirmed that impression, she could hardly contain herself.

And when the second one, the one called Synapo, had said, "Yas, wekkom to ah wuld, Miz Ahyahl Wilsh," she had to turn away to suppress her laughter and an incipient sneeze caused by the tingling in her nose from the faint odor of ammonia they exuded.

She could hardly contain the delightful relief that came with the knowledge that these demons had a comic side. They were just naturally provincials of a Webster Grove persuasion. Wohler-9 could not possibly have given them that accent.

She recovered quickly, however, and without sneezing, she turned and said, "I am pleased to meet you both," and then she bowed. "This is an historic occasion, which we shall surely carry with us always. It saddens me that such an important meeting must be marred by discussion of the discordant incidents that have occurred before we can explore the great potential for harmony in the future relations of our two species."

She steeled herself to put his reply in the framework he surely intended, and she found she could quite easily ignore the thick accent and concentrate on only the meaning.

"We are equally saddened," Synapo replied.

"The protocol of my species in this situation suggests that you should select the first topic for discussion," she said.

Immediately Synapo said, "Explain the square root of minus one."

His reply seemed completely at odds with the discussion she thought was going to take place. She was not schooled in mathematics and was expecting more diplomatic double-talk. She hesitated for just a moment, and then turned toward Jacob and said, "Jacob?"

Immediately Jacob said, "The square root of minus one is a member of a class of numbers that cannot be given substance except in a specific context. In this case, one such context is the interrelationship of space and time, in which the measurements of time must be multiplied by the square root of minus one in order to properly relate them to the measurements of space."

"Or the reverse," Synapo said. "A quite satisfactory answer to a simple question, but then one must start simple and work toward the complex. And now what is your pleasure, Miss Ariel Welsh?"

That sort of drivel isn't going to get us anywhere, Ariel thought. *Let's get right to it.*

"Why have you isolated our city, enclosed it under this big dome?"

And as she gestured toward the dome, the first shimmer that morning—the first pass of the Myostrian construction—shot down the edge of the wall with a faint crackling and disappeared into the ground.

Ariel jumped, startled. With the edge of the dome off to her left and to the rear, she had turned slightly as she gestured and had caught the shimmer at the corner of her eye before the sound reached her ears. Being to her back, though, it had startled her more than if she had been facing the edge.

Sarco said, "Ah, my people have started work."

Synapo said, "My colleague Sarco informed me yesterday that the node compensator—this dome—will be completed tomorrow, so that leaves us little time for negotiation. He further informs me that the dome is necessary in order to properly control meterological conditions. The particulate emissions and the radiation and convection of thermal energy from your creations are seriously disrupting the weather of our planet, and thereby disturbing our mental processes and our emotional equanimity."

The source of Synapo's linguistic training came sharply into focus. He talked exactly like a Robot City supervisor. Only Wohler-9 could have downloaded all those big words.

What had he said about work on the dome? It escaped her as she zeroed in on his last sentence.

Jacob was right. The aliens were concerned about the weather and talked as though they were actually controlling it. Spacers and Settlers also talked about the weather a great deal, but so far had not been able to do much about it.

"You control the weather?" she said.

"Of course. It is essential that unruly airflow not disturb our cerebrations. How can one think when he is being bounced about in a turbulence? Your creations generate a puncture node of the worst sort.

"But now I believe it is our turn. And I suppose we must dispense with going methodically from the simple to the complex, as I had intended.

"What vital purpose do your creations serve? What ends justify the killing of two of our people—first, a Myostrian in legitimate pursuit of an assigned task, and then a Cerebron who was peacefully tethered and surely in no way interfering with your obscure endeavor?"

Ariel knew that, on balance, the destruction of a witness robot was hardly equal to the death of two intelligent beings. But she had heard that a good offense was the best defense.

"And in the pursuit of that task of questionable legitimacy," Ariel replied, "your Myostrians created something that sliced one of my people in half."

She didn't really think of a witness robot as *people* but the black bats—or as Wohler-9 termed them, the blackbodies—didn't need to know that.

"I respectfully remind you that it was your creations that caused the Myostrians to start construction of the compensator," Synapo said. "I ask again: what purpose do those creations serve? What further threat to our equilibrium lies beyond the disturbance of our weather?"

It was a legitimate point, which caused her to reevaluate what was serious and what was not, who had provoked whom, and when, and how. Perhaps the weather was of equal importance to sentient life in their minds—perhaps the weather was their life.

That thought, coupled with the observation that, while he was talking, he had slued his hook around so that it pointed forward, like that of his companion, caused Ariel to reconsider the gravity of the situation. Even though she didn't know for sure what that rotation meant, it didn't seem to bode any good and might even be considered somewhat ominous, taken with the quiet way he had made his last pronouncement.

She had let their provincial accent distract her, which may have caused her to consider this confrontation less serious than it really was. She had known how serious the situation was well before the meeting, and her anxiety had steadily increased until the moment of confrontation. How had she let the circumstances of their meeting so distract and deceive her?

The shimmer at the corner of her eye at that moment and the crackling sound that accompanied it marked the pass of a Myostrian far above and brought her attention back to the construction of the dome. She noticed then that, while they had been talking, the edge of the dome had progressed toward the center of Main Street, closing the opening by at least two more meters on that one side, probably four meters considering both sides.

The city robots had extended Main Street into a road across the plain to facilitate their exodus. The two edges of the wall were not far from the edge of the road itself, four lanes wide where it exited the dome.

It was then Synapo's earlier comment came to the front of her mind: *My colleague Sarco informed me yesterday that the node compensator—this dome—will be completed tomorrow, so that leaves us little time for negotiation.*

She had not forgotten it. It had simply been overlaid by a surfeit of sensory stimuli. It was difficult to take in all the data and digest it in proper order. But clearly they were in the midst of a negotiation in which she had reasoned herself into a corner, a fact that she must honorably acknowledge in the presence of these aliens; and time was running out.

Perhaps that acknowledgement alone would buy her some time. A diplomat might have been duplicitous at that point, but Ariel had recognized earlier that she was no diplomat. You take in the data, you analyze it, and you proceed accordingly.

"Your argument is sound," Ariel said. "It takes only a brief moment—having now all the facts—to recognize that we are the offenders and you are the offended. We ask for your patience. We ask that you stop construction of the dome while we consider how we may resolve this dilemma, leaving neither of our peoples with further injury and with harmonious relations restored."

She recognized that wasn't quite right. Their relations had never been harmonious. That was her minor concession to the duplicity of diplomacy.

Neither of the aliens said anything, but Ariel knew something was going on. Standing side by side, they had turned their top sections so that their hooks and eyes confronted one another briefly. Then they turned back to confront Ariel.

"We agree to a one-day delay in the construction of the compensator following completion of today's effort. We will meet again tomorrow as we met today."

Ariel felt a touch on her elbow and half turned as Jacob bent over to say softly, "Would it be helpful to know the present stability of their weather?"

"I don't understand," she said, just as softly.

"How effective is the dome in its present state?" Jacob asked. "That data will enter into our reckoning of possibilities for resolution of the dilemma."

"Ninety-nine-point-two percent compensation including the improvement allowed by consideration of both positive edge effects," Sarco said before Ariel could ask.

Ariel understood then why Jacob had asked the question.

"Could you live with that if we caused no further deleterious effects?" she asked.

"Yes," Synapo said.

As though not to be outdone by Ariel's lieutenant, Sarco asked, "Why do you discrete or jump modulate hyperwave when the signal fidelity and freedom from noise is so much better with continuous modulation?"

That time Ariel didn't hesitate a second. She looked at Jacob and said simply, "Jacob?"

The reply by Jacob was delayed by a distraction at that point. A small, tight, luminous green flame, no more than ten centimeters long, bloomed in the blackness a few centimeters below Synapo's eyes. But he said nothing.

Jacob was distracted only momentarily—just long enough to register the spectrum and flame temperature of pure hydrogen co-blended with pure oxygen and a trace of ammonia.

"We are not familiar with continuous modulation," Jacob said.

"Strange. You teleport with both types of transition," Sarco said. He seemed not to be disturbed by fire from Synapo. "You yourself jumped here in discrete mode, and Wohler-9 phase condensed here in continuous mode. Do you not recognize the parallel with hyperwave?"

"I am not an expert in these technologies," Jacob replied. "We can only take your question under advisement."

As though to avoid further discussion, Synapo turned abruptly, and with a short wobbling run and an awkward hop, he flapped into the air and started gracefully into a great climbing turn. Sarco hesitated only a moment and then turned, wobbled, and with an even more awkward hop, quickly followed him. They were soon far above the dome.

At the end of the dome construction activity that day, the edges of the dome had just started cutting into the four-lane road.

CHAPTER 6

INTRIGUE

Immediately after the meeting, Synapo climbed more rapidly than usual to charge altitude. He kept his hook aggressively forward—something he almost never did when he was climbing to charge, and he paid no attention to Sarco, who was climbing in his wake—again something neither a Cerebron nor a Myostrian did when there was the least possibility of someone sharing the climb.

In short, he was exceedingly irritated with Sarco, and he wanted Sarco to know it. As he climbed, he radioed the local Myostrian weather station for the optimum altitude in the compensator's zone, the corresponding stability quotient, and the forecast for the afternoon. He had some deep cogitation to do, and he wanted optimum conditions in which to do it.

First, there was the matter of internal tribal dominance. That took precedence over Sarco's unsettling behavior—he would get to that—and the assurance he had given the aliens that he could live with a compensator efficiency of 99.2%. Sarco had not questioned his conclusion—by Nimbar, he better not have—but Synapo wasn't all that sure in his own mind how the Cerebrons might react to it. They were much more sensitive to small disturbances in the weather than were the Myostria.

The weather was important, but in the short term, it was the possibility of one of the elite striking for tribal dominance that had him most concerned. There was a definite hierarchy throughout the Cerebron pack, but it was exceptionally rigid among the members of the elite, who currently numbered eleven. If one of them were striking and involved him now, it could seriously undermine his relations with Sarco and his negotiations with the aliens. That was his primary concern. He thought of himself more as a statesman than as a mere politician. By the time Synapo had climbed to charge altitude, he knew how to proceed.

When he leveled off on station, he radioed Neuronius, his second in command, and as he summoned him for conference, he noted with satisfaction that Sarco had taken up his customary station: fifty meters below in a fifty-percent-tighter circle. Sarco had called to him only once on the way up, and Synapo had ignored him.

Now as Neuronius approached, did Synapo note a more casual, less deferential stroking of his wings? The striker would surely be his second in command. Yet, unlikely as it might be, it could be anyone in the pack. Once, a hand of centuries ago, a young, midpack rabble-rouser had struck successfully, destroying the elite—that is, the elite structure—and generally upsetting the entire hierarchy as he brought in his own lieutenants from up and down the pack. He had proved to be one of the better administrators. And Synapo was in his egg line, twice removed.

Neuronius rolled into conference beneath him, hook properly reversed. Synapo's hook was still set aggressively.

It would stay that way the rest of the day. There would be no more meek, deferential conferences with Sarco or anyone else until these affronts and possible strikes were resolved.

Synapo got right to work on Neuronius.

"It comes to me on a zephyr that someone is trying to supplant you in the hierarchy, Neuronius." He put it casually as though he were an unconcerned, indifferent observer.

He was looking for Neuronius's immediate reaction, a slight tremble-twitch in the hook, a faint flicker in the redness of the eyes, an ever-so-slight fanning of the cold-junction, the uncontrollable body language that one displays before one can steel himself to the shock of the unexpected.

And there it was: a slight wave in the silhouette on the right, a bunching of the right deltoid muscle—the one that pulled up the right wing and readied it for the power down-beat. That was a typical guilt reaction. Not a reaction in response to fear, the fear that someone was trying to supplant himself, Neuronius; but instead a response to guilt concerning his own ambitious plans. That guilt could lead to fear later as Neuronius pondered what Synapo's remarkable intuition might lead to; but at the moment it was only a symptom of guilt.

Synapo knew then the shape of things within and without his tribe. He could scheme up suitable responses. Anticipation of the cerebral exercise involved, the challenge, filled him with keen anticipation. Nowhere was there room for fear, for anticipation that he might fail.

Neuronius was a threat he could meet head on. And Sarco was an excellent engineer and an able administrator, but not the political animal that he faced in a tussle with Neuronius.

Synapo listened keenly to Neuronius's answer to the needling remark.

"I do not fear such a change if that Cerebron can serve you as ably as I," Neuronius replied.

Ah, suitably servile. He was not yet ready, not quite sure of himself. That called for a less aggressive response, at least for the moment.

"We meet again with the aliens tomorrow morning," Synapo said. "I want you and Axonius to accompany me."

Axonius was third in the elite hierarchy, next in command after Neuronius. It was essential that Axonius witness the ineptitude of Neuronius and discredit him with the elite. Exactly how that would come about Synapo was not sure, but he did not lack confidence in his ability to carry it out in some fashion during their meeting with the aliens or later. Neuronius was not yet ready for command decisions and might never be. Synapo had merely to show that to Axonius and simultaneously educate Axonius in the difficulty of command.

Further, it would not hurt to condition Neuronius in the direction that would encourage ineptitude; that was not statesmanlike, perhaps, but certainly the political thing to do. Synapo had only to enhance what was already natural. Neuronius was by nature a haughty beast who acted as though he were infinitely superior to all those below him in the Cerebron pecking order. Synapo had only to encourage and assure him that the aliens were also to be included in that inferior category.

He made it seem as though he were asking Neuronius's advice, confiding in him, passing confidential information to him beyond that which he had provided the Cerebrons in caucus, and by bits and pieces he led Neuronius to the conclusion that the aliens were weak and ready to capitulate and leave the planet. He was careful, however, never to say that directly but merely to imply it by innuendo.

Synapo was ready then for the next meeting with the aliens.

CHAPTER 7

CRISIS

"How do we stand right now, Wohler?" Ariel asked.

She and the two robots had just left the meeting with the aliens and were traveling down Main Street in the lorry, heading for the apartment. The street lights stretched ahead toward the Compass Tower like a string of illuminated pearls in the dim light of a late dusk, the permanent dusk created by the dome.

"In what respect, Miss Ariel?" Wohler asked.

"With respect to the city, Wohler. The dome will be closed day after tomorrow unless we can get through to those monsters. What are you doing about it?"

"We are moving the necessary materiel for construction of a second Compass Tower and city on the other side of the plain, five kilometers away."

"Yes, I believe those were the very words you used earlier," she said. How could she be irritated by a machine that, given the same stimulus, came up with the same answer? "So your grand plan is to hop all over the planet, a jump ahead of the aliens, constructing Compass Towers and cities—weather nodes—while they follow along behind neutralizing them with their domes?"

Was she still feeling guilty about Wohler-1 and taking it out on this poor machine that wouldn't know it even if she were?

"We tried first to neutralize them and lost a pilot robot and flier," Wohler-9 said, "and then we tried to learn more about them and lost a surgeon and laser scalpel."

"You could have learned a lot more about them by just talking to them."

"That has not proved to be true, Miss Ariel, and did not seem to be necessary at first since they destroyed only that one witness. They did not interfere with our endeavor once we enlarged the patrol circle to avoid construction of the dome. It did not appear they were violating our governing laws nor interfering with the Prime Directive until their construction work began to circle inward—to close the dome. Then we did begin to talk, and they succeeded in learning our language, but we learned very little except specialized terminology which you have now determined to be meteorological in nature."

"What about the central core?" Ariel said. "You'll surely not leave that behind."

"No, Miss Ariel. Our control computer's mainframe is mobile. When the blackbodies begin construction on the last day, we'll move it out to serve the new city."

"Which will then shortly be covered by a dome."

"Yes. That was why we hyperwaved Robot City for help."

"Come upstairs with us, Wohler," Ariel said as Wohler-9 pulled to the curb in front of the apartment building.

When they walked into the apartment, both Jacob and Wohler-9 headed for wall storage niches.

"Jacob," Ariel said, "would you rassle up some lunch for me? See if you can get a crisp garden salad out of that thing. And then sit down at the table. I'll freshen up and be right out."

When she came out, the salad and a glass of milk were waiting on the table; Jacob sat across the table from where he had set her place, and Wohler-9 was standing in his niche.

She felt uncomfortable when the humaniform, Jacob, stood in a niche. Her Auroran upbringing made it seem natural for Wohler-9 to do so. That was where he was supposed to be when he wasn't doing some task for her. And she should have felt exactly the same way about Jacob, but his appearance didn't allow it.

"Now," she said as she began eating, "our most pressing problem is how to carry out the objective of making this planet suitable for human life and at the same time avoid disrupting the weather. The weather does seem to be the main concern of the aliens.

"However, that's too tough to handle during lunch. It will ruin my appetite and upset my digestion.

"Let's talk instead about the hyperwave noise, the other way we're apparently disturbing them. I can understand the weather problem, sort of, and even have a glimmer of what a puncture node is—hot air punching up through a cold air layer, I suppose—but I've got no idea what they mean by discrete and continuous modulation. What's that all about, Jacob?"

"I'm not sure myself, Miss Ariel," Jacob said. "I am aware of only one type of modulation of hyperwave: that which the alien called discrete. Nor had I drawn the connection of hyperwave modulation with jump technology, which permits us to travel through hyperspace. Were you aware of such a connection, Wohler?"

"No," Wohler-9 replied, "but I was aware that teleportation using a Key to Perihelion is technologically different from jump teleportation."

"This seems to me a minor problem involving new technology that we obviously should have been aware of," Ariel said in true managerial style. "Get to work on it, Jacob."

"Very well, Miss Ariel," Jacob said. "Where would you suggest I start?"

For a moment Ariel thought that perhaps Jacob was being sarcastic, and then she realized that could not be the case. He was just a robot. Still, could the Robotics Institute have included an optional sarcastic module for the positronic brain of their humaniforms? Not likely. But it was an interesting thought that diverted her from these pesky engineering problems. They were more Derec's forte than hers. Social problems, people problems, sarcastic positronic modules; all those she doted on. Not pesky problems with meteorology and hyperwave.

She was quiet for awhile. Jacob at the table, and Wohler-9 in his niche, said nothing.

Then she said, "Wohler, is there a Keymo on the planet?"

"Yes," Wohler-9 said. "Keymo, eighth generation, is in charge of Key control."

"There's your lead then, Jacob," she said. It was merely a people problem—robot problem—after all. "We want to develop continuous hyperwave modulation. Synapo said there was a connection between continuous hyperwave modulation and Key teleportation. Keymo on Robot City manufactured the Keys. Keymo here, in charge of Key control, of all those here, should be most familiar with Key teleportation and the one most likely to fathom continuous modulation.

See if the two of you can't cobble up some equipment to implement it."

"Very well, Miss Ariel," Jacob replied.

"Wohler," Ariel said, "find Jacob a comlink cartridge, plug it into him so he can find Keymo on his own, and then come back and help me. With your knowledge of the aliens, we've got to figure out a solution to this dome problem."

Jacob and Wohler-9, when not conversing audibly, close at hand, had been communicating with their cumbersome, long-distance, radio frequency systems. The comlink cartridge would hook Jacob into their more sophisticated, short-range, microwave telephone network.

"Very well, Miss Welsh," Wohler-9 said.

Ariel did not hold out much hope that Keymo and Jacob would come up with anything significant. In her experience, ordinary robots just weren't creative. Yet there was that extraordinary exception: that brief period on Robot City when Shakespeare's Hamlet had lived again, supported by robot actors, and the robot Lucius had created his artistic masterpiece, the dynamically chromatic edifice called Circuit Breaker.

A half-hour later Wohler-9 returned.

"Did Jacob locate Keymo?" Ariel asked.

"I believe so," Wohler-9 said. "He had contacted Keymo over the comlink before I left."

"Good. Does this apartment have a memory projector?"

"Yes. The niches are equipped with sockets, and that wall serves as the screen."

"Just what we need. How many times did you meet with the alien Synapo?"

"Thirty-four."

"How long each time?"

When Wohler-9 began reciting the list that contained the time for each meeting, Ariel interrupted him.

"On the average!" she said.

"Forty-two minutes," Wohler said.

"I'll not have time to go over all that before tomorrow morning. Yet I desperately need some clue as to how we may resolve this dilemma.

"Wohler, while I'm thinking how to screen that material rapidly, download to central core just the dialogue of your meetings with Synapo, and get a printout back to me as soon as possible."

"Download in progress," Wohler-9 said.

A fraction of a minute later, while Ariel was still pondering her problem, Wohler-9 said, "Download complete."

A couple of minutes later, she said, "I really don't know what I'm looking for, but I do know what I'm *not* looking for. Wohler, delete all sections of the meetings dealing with linguistics and play back the rest at double speed."

She could understand neither Wohler-9 nor the alien at that speed. Then when she slowed it down so she could understand Wohler-9, she still couldn't understand Synapo's Webster Grove accent. She finally slowed it down to normal and could understand most of what Synapo said, but not all. She refused to slow it any further.

Just as she didn't hope for much from Keymo and Jacob, she really didn't expect to get anything much out of listening to Wohler-9 and Synapo. But it did keep her conscious mind actively on the problem and left her subconscious mind to free-wheel on all the correlated branches of the main subject.

Neither her conscious mind nor her subconscious mind contributed anything of significance during an inquiry that became dull and dragging after the novelty of watching and listening to a giant bat wore off.

The courier from central core arrived with the printout of the dialogue late in the afternoon, and with that interruption, Ariel decided to take a break and eat an early dinner. She had heard nothing from Jacob and realized she had been expecting him to return for dinner, when there was really no reason why he should, since he didn't eat and merely kept her company when she did. Still, it was a habit she had become accustomed to, and she missed him now that she was deprived of that pleasure.

Was it Jacob she missed, or really Derec? She had only to ask herself that question, and the longing to see Derec and the flood of homesickness for the beautiful estates and green farmlands of Aurora overwhelmed her.

She tried to put it out of her mind as she ate a lonely dinner, but it was not possible. Her mind rebelled from the magnitude of the problem that faced her on this alien world, and while she ate, she wallowed in her loneliness and homesickness, and before she finished eating, tears of self pity were trickling down her face.

As she finished eating, Wohler-9 asked, "Are you in pain, Miss Welsh?"

Ariel wiped her tears away with a napkin. "No, Wohler. Just lonely."

"Does my presence relieve your loneliness to any degree?"

"No."

"To what degree did my assistance this afternoon serve in the preservation of the city, Miss Welsh?"

"Very little, I'm sorry to say," Ariel said. "Why do you ask? Did you expect otherwise?"

"Certainly I had hoped otherwise, Miss Welsh. I proceed

at all times in the direction that best serves the Prime Directive, if that does not violate the more compelling laws that govern my behavior.

"I have been neglecting my supervisory duties in the construction and operation of the city, Miss Welsh, for I concluded that your imperative best served the Prime Directive. If that seems no longer to be the case, I must return to my duties, which are currently spread among the other six supervisors."

"Very well, Wohler. Return to duty."

"I will clear the dinner table, request a maid to serve you in the future, and then take my leave."

"I'll clear the table, Wohler. And a maid won't be necessary. Jacob will suffice."

"But he is on another assignment, Miss Welsh."

"We'll handle it, Wohler. Just raise Jacob on the comlink, tell him to get back here no later than ten PM, and then leave."

She was anxious to be alone. Wohler had begun to get on her nerves, Wohler and that alien she had felt compelled to watch and listen to all afternoon.

"Will you be needing me at the meeting tomorrow morning?" Wohler asked.

"No. Did you get hold of Jacob while you were chattering there?"

"Yes, Miss Welsh. He will be here by ten PM."

"Then leave, Wohler."

Despite her warm feelings for Wohler-1, she was fed up with this Wohler-9. Yet in his dialogue with the alien, she felt there had to be some clue to the aliens, to their behavior, to their needs, to their culture, a clue to something that would make the aliens and humans compatible so that this desirable planet did not have to be abandoned and bypassed in the future.

She turned to the printout the courier had delivered before dinner.

Strange how that archaic form of transmitting information—the printed word—had stayed around so long. Yet was it so strange when that marvelous instrument, the human brain, was taken into account: the speed with which she could assimilate the words and conjure related images, the speed with which she could scan the pages?

She quickly thumbed to where Wohler had left off in his projection that afternoon and scanned through the rest of the dialogue—ten times the volume they had covered that afternoon—and she did it in less than two hours. And got more out of it, by being able to easily and quickly replay, fast forward, skip, and ponder over the significance of a phrase, a word.

It was true that central core had eliminated the alien's accent—and certainly that had speeded things up—but the true efficiency came with the printed word itself: the strange archaic telepathy that extracted alien ideas from an alien mind and moved them into hers.

Yet despite the ancient beauty of the printout, nothing of significance came from its perusal, no more than had come from the boring afternoon with Wohler and the memory projector.

Still, her intuition told her there had to be a solution. She just wasn't looking at it right, or with the proper frame of mind, or in the proper place. If not the dome, where on this weird world was she supposed to look? The city was the problem, a weather node the aliens had termed it, an aggravating, uncontrollable irritant, like a grain of sand in an oyster.

And the aliens were coating it, smoothing it, to relieve the abrasion, like an oyster coats the sharp edges of a grain of sand with iridescent nacre, mother-of-pearl. Now she was even beginning to think like an alien. This world is an oyster and the city and its dome are a pearl. Oyster World. Pearl City. She had christened a world and a city.

And she had gotten no further by the time Jacob returned at ten PM.

"Well, you're finally back," she said when he came in. "What did Keymo have to offer on the hyperwave problem?"

"Very little, Miss Ariel," Jacob said. "Neither of us could see how Key teleportation technology could be applied to modulation of hyperwave signals."

"Did you examine the parallel dichotomy of hyperspace jump technology and discrete modulation of hyperwave? That parallel connection should provide clues to the connection between the Key and continuous modulation. Right?"

Ariel had first heard the word *dichotomy* on the way to Oyster World, when Jacob had used it; and she had been wanting to use it ever since. It had such a ring of erudition. Now she had played it back to him.

"You suggested only that we look for a connection between continuous modulation and Key teleportation. Neither of us could see any during a lengthy discussion which concluded only a half hour ago."

You dummy, she thought, *the creative process is primarily a matter of drawing correlations*. If there is a connection between discrete modulation and jump technology, as the aliens claim, you must first ferret out and understand that connection. Then maybe you can deduce what continuous modulation is by examining Key teleportation for the parallel connection the aliens say exists there. She thought she had made that clear before he left. He, too, had heard everything the alien had said.

"Tonight, while I'm sleeping," Ariel said, "examine everything in your memory concerning jump technology and discrete modulation of hyperwave. Go back and forth comparing the two at every point. Look for similarities. Correlate one with the other. And give me a report in the morning of all instances where you see a similarity between the two."

"Very well, Miss Ariel."

She retired to bed then and thought how she would like to see the full musculature of Jacob without his clothes on. And that made her feel guilty, and her longing for Derec came rushing in, the longing she had been pushing from her mind all evening that had probably brought on the unmaidenly notions concerning Jacob.

She went to sleep, and sometime during the long night, she dreamt of playing in a verdant Auroran cornfield with her personal robot as she had when she was a child, and then the robot became Jacob, and they were running and laughing as he chased her down the rows of tall green plants waving in the gentle breeze, and gradually he was no longer chasing her but waiting for her at the end of the long row, far away; yet it was not Jacob; and then she realized that Derec had come to Oyster World, and he was standing there with his arms outstretched, waiting for her. Joyfully, she ran toward him down the long rows of waving green.

She awoke, and it was morning, and she was indeed on Oyster World. But Derec was not there.

CHAPTER 8

THE WOLF PLANET

"I'm grateful you took the time to come," Derec said.

He glanced at his companion sitting next to him in the runabout.

"Wouldn't 'ave,'cept 'u sounded urgent," Wolruf said.

They were heading east on Main Street toward Derec's apartment. He had just picked up Wolruf at the wolf planet's primitive spaceport at the west edge of the robot city.

Wolruf had arrived in the *Xerborodezees*, a *Minneapolis*-class hyperspace jumper that the wealthy Ariel had given the small alien the year before to speed her return home. The *Xerborodezees* could accommodate ten passengers, and as it turned out, it was the only way that Derec and his robotic companions were going to get off the planet. He had accidentally demolished his means of transportation when he arrived.

Wolruf was the size of a large dog with sleek, well-groomed, brown and gold fur; and she was shaped like a dog except for the fat-fingered hands and the flat face which, despite its flatness, bore unmistakable lupine characteristics.

Farther east on Main Street, a half-kilometer beyond Derec's apartment, a large pyramidal edifice—the Compass Tower—was at that moment strikingly displayed in a glowing frame, red-shafted by the morning sun still hidden behind it.

"You mean Ariel," Derec said. "I sent my call for help through Ariel."

" 'u signed it. Not Ariel. Wouldn't 'ave come if 'u 'adn't signed it, 'Situation desperate, Derec.' Goin' call 'u 'Desperate Derec' from now on."

She gave a funny gargling bark, not a growl, more a sharp rattling gargle, as though her throat were laden with phlegm.

Derec had become so accustomed to her in times past he had forgotten that extraordinary chuckle and her uncommon treatment of Galactic Standard. The imperfections in her pronunciation of Standard had regressed somewhat during the past year on her home planet, but her rolling of the letter "r" had been almost entirely eliminated after prolonged exposure to Ariel and Derec, and that improvement seemed to be still largely in place except for a trailing burr. The left-out and chopped-off pronouns, the missing aitches, and the sibilant hiss for the "zee" sound were still evident. And the " 'u" pronunciation of "you"—not at all an "ooh" sound, but a sort of choked and swallowed bark that masked off the initial "y"—could only come from the throat of a lupine alien, something a human was unlikely ever to match.

"I'd never label this situation desperate," Derec said. "That's not the message I sent. I contacted Robot City on my internal monitor link, and they hyperwaved our house computer on Aurora. At least that's the routing I set up. I expected Ariel to relay my message to you, but that doesn't sound like Ariel, either. Sounds more like someone with a vital interest in this planet, which is nobody I know of."

"Doessn't matter 'ow I 'eard. 'u succeeded, I'm 'ere. Now what's so desperate 'u've got to call 'alf across the galaxy?"

"I've got a rogue robot on my hands, Wolruf."

"Doessn't follow the Lawss of Robotics?"

"Yes and no. It's got the laws but doesn't seem to know for sure what a human is. It's like a darn chameleon. The way I've got it figured, it changes itself to match as best it can whoever it thinks might be human at the moment."

"Like Mandelbrot's arm?"

"Yes and no. The stuff it's made of isn't as coarse as the Robot City material. Its cells are a lot smaller than the variety in Mandelbrot's arm.

"I've got the feeling we're seeing micromolecular robotics here; and I've got no way to reprogram it. It's self-programmed and seems to imprint like a newly hatched chicken at the drop of a hat, and on anything it takes a mind to."

"So 'ow can I 'elp?" Wolruf asked.

"It had a wolf form when I first arrived. It was the leader of a pack of intelligent wolf-like creatures which it must have thought were human. They were attacking the city's Avery robots. The wolf robot gutted one of the Averies. Robot City relayed their call for help over my internal monitor.

"When I got here, it imprinted on me, after giving me a really hard time—and I mean a *really* hard time. It was still humanoid when I left it this morning, and soaking up information from the city library like a second-generation Settler on a mission to Earth."

"What iss it 'u think I can do?" Wolruf asked.

"It was wolf-like when it came into the city, after I arrived, and then it imprinted on me. Now it's coming along a little too fast, too much personality change too quickly. With your wolfish characteristics, you make a natural model for imprinting, a nice compromise between wolves and humans."

"Amazing! Why do 'u 'umans persist in thinking of us ass wolves? There'ss a species on my world—the dongeedows—that arrr a great deal like the gorillas in 'urrr ssoos, but I don't think of 'u . . . now wait a minute. I take that back. 'u arrr beginning to resemble a dongeedow a great deal."

She gave that phlegm-rattling gargle again. And yes, the trailing burr was definitely still part of the pattern.

"You can joke all you want, Wolruf, but I don't regard this situation as very humorous."

Derec was not in the best of spirits. It was good to see Wolruf again, and that had cheered him momentarily. They had known each other for a long time, ever since she had been more or less a slave—an indentured servant—of the alien pirate Aranimas. Derec had freed her with the help of Mandelbrot, the robot he had put together from the pirate's supply of spare parts.

But Wolruf was hardly a stand-in for Ariel. Just seeing a good friend like Wolruf made him yearn for Ariel even more. If it had just been her and not Wolruf who had run down the ramp of the *Xerborodezees*, life wouldn't seem so grim right now.

He shouldn't have reacted adversely to Wolruf's weak attempt at humor. He should at least give her credit for trying. But he missed Ariel, and he wasn't about to let anything cheer him up.

" 'u arrr in a foul mood," Wolruf said. "A rogue robot couldn't make 'u feel that bad. Why issn't Ariel with 'u?"

It was eerie the way Wolruf could sense his mood, interpret it, and put her finger on what was bothering him.

"Let's not go into that. Let's just say she wasn't too pleased with me when I left her on Aurora. So she's probably pouting back there in a snit."

And he added as a bitter afterthought, "With her playboy Winterson. You've never met him. Jacob Winterson. As revolting a bundle of simulated muscle as you'll ever see."

"A cyborg? Like Leong?"

Wolruf was referring to Jeff Leong, a young man whose brain had spent a rather unpleasant period in a mechanical robotic body while the Avery robots on Robot City had repaired and healed his damaged human body.

"No, a humaniform robot," Derec said. "Looks exactly like a human. Almost impossible to tell from the real thing."

" 'u're jealous of a robot?"

Wolruf gave that phlegm gargle again.

Derec said nothing. The conversation was veering in an unpleasant direction.

"Ah, a sorrr point," Wolruf said. "My apologies."

"We're here," Derec said as he pulled the runabout to the curb in front of the apartment.

He looked up anxiously to the second floor.

" 'u're expecting trouble?" Wolruf said.

She was reading his mind again.

"No. Mandelbrot would have phoned me," Derec said, not quite truthfully, for he did feel just a shade anxious as he got out of the small vehicle. Mandelbrot and SilverSide didn't seem to understand one another. Perhaps he should not have left a robot to babysit another robot.

But everything seemed normal when they walked into

the small two-bedroom apartment on the second floor. Mandelbrot was standing in his storage niche in the wall near the door. SilverSide was plugged into Derec's terminal and didn't even turn around when they came in.

"Impressive," Wolruf said, her eyes going wide as she stared at the robot at the terminal. " 'e's certainly got 'urrr scrawny shape."

SilverSide's lustrous silvery exterior only appoximated the details of Derec's appearance, but in size and proportions, it was, indeed, an excellent approximation.

Wolruf was exaggerating, of course. Derec was not scrawny. He was thin, but well endowed with sinewy biceps and with the hard plates of muscle across chest and abdomen typical of an older teen's torso.

But with that humorous barb, Wolruf had hit that sensitive nerve again. Derec did feel inadequate whenever he thought of Jacob Winterson.

"Everything under control, Mandelbrot?" Derec asked. He had walked to the center of the room, hesitated when SilverSide did not respond to their entrance, and then turned to address Mandelbrot.

He got no answer from the robot in the niche.

"Mandelbrot!" he repeated.

"Oh, yes, Master Derec." SilverSide unplugged and turned to face them. "Everything is under control."

Derec glanced at SilverSide and then turned to walk toward the niche as he said again, "Mandelbrot, you okay?"

"He's fine," SilverSide said. "I deactivated him."

"You what?" Derec's voice reflected his astonishment that SilverSide would have had the temerity to shut down Mandelbrot's microfusion reactor, risking partial loss of positronic memory.

"When you're not around, he tends to give me unwanted

advice," SilverSide explained. "Here, I'll bring him back up, since it apparently displeases you to have him down."

"It does a lot more than displease me." Derec's voice shook with anger. "And stand back, I'll reactivate him myself."

SilverSide stopped. He had started walking toward Mandelbrot's niche.

"Don't you ever—I repeat—" and now Derec's voice was strident, grating, "don't you ever deactivate Mandelbrot again."

"Certainly not," SilverSide said, "if that is your wish, Master Derec."

"That is most certainly my wish."

"Very well, Master Derec."

Derec had walked to the niche, and now reached around to swing open a plate set flush in Mandelbrot's back that covered a switch panel. Carefully, watching for Mandelbrot's reactions at each step, he reactivated the robot by flicking switches in a definite sequence.

Stabilizing the microfusion reactor was the most delicate part of the activation procedure and took the most time—almost half an hour. The robot's eyes were designed to guide that operation, changing color in the spectral sequence whenever it was safe to move on to the next phase—from black through purple, blue, green, yellow, orange, red, and finally back to colorless black—Mandelbrot's switch-induced standby state.

Completely ignoring Wolruf, SilverSide had gone back to the terminal and plugged himself in again after his exchange with Derec.

Wolruf had curled up on the davenport and was fast asleep when Derec finished.

Battery backup should have provided the low power

needed to protect Mandelbrot's positronic brain from serious harm, but there was always the possibility of a loss of long-term memory during the nanoseconds required to effect the switch from one power source to the other. Derec would never know until the gap revealed itself, perhaps at some juncture when that particular memory would be urgently needed.

As he pressed the power-reset button, he cursed himself for having left the two robots alone together. Mandelbrot's eyes lit up with a red glow that pulsed rhythmically.

"How do you feel now, Mandelbrot?" Derec asked.

"Normal. The wild one deactivated me. I didn't realize what he was doing until too late."

The robot gave a small shudder.

"Was that a Third Law reaction just now?" Derec asked.

"I believe so, Master. I didn't protect myself properly as the Third Law directs. I felt a momentary disturbance upon reaching that conclusion, which must have sent an associated potential wave through my motor control system. Is that the way it appeared?"

"Yes. I just wanted to be sure that it was not some damage from deactivation," Derec said. "Ah, Wolruf, you're awake."

Wolruf yawned and stretched. "Mandelbrot okay?"

"It would appear so, except for a normal Third Law reaction," Derec replied.

"It looks ass though anotherrr imprinting may not be ass likely ass 'u 'ad thought," Wolruf observed.

The small hairy alien was looking at SilverSide, who was hunched over the terminal and seemingly absorbed in the information that was flowing into his brain.

"SilverSide has apparently put you down as an inferior," Derec replied, "a variation on this planet's wolf species."

"That was my conclusion," SilverSide said as he unplugged and swung around in the swivel chair to face them, "and I have been unable to find any 'Wolruf' biographical file or anything to contradict that conclusion.

"Would you tell me all about yourself, Mistress Wolruf?" SilverSide requested.

"No!" Derec said emphatically. "Not now. Plug back into the library. The rest of us have got some things we must take care of now."

SilverSide turned back to the terminal, and Derec motioned for the other two to follow him outside.

When they were standing by the runabout at street level, Derec explained.

"As I suggested to you earlier, Wolruf, he's coming along too fast now. Deactivating Mandelbrot confirmed that in my mind. I'd consider that a violation of a sort of corollary to the Third Law. How does a robot view that, Mandelbrot?"

"The Laws are not infinitely rigid," Mandelbrot said. "They are surrounded by side potentials that create what I can only call soft boundaries, foothill potentials that lead to the ultimate peak. The First Law has the hardest and sharpest boundaries of all, but even so, those boundaries are not absolutely and infinitely sharp."

"Are you saying he violated the Third Law?" Derec asked.

"No, but he did something I would never do except to protect a human or myself."

"Maybe 'e was protecting 'imself from 'urrr ideass, Mandelbrot," Wolruf said.

"Not likely," Mandelbrot said. "I do not consider words and ideas to be a source of injury to a robot."

"But he is in a very sensitive and impressionable state

right now," Derec said. "And that's another reason I want to get him out of the city and back to the forest where I found him, where he's apt to be more comfortable and less perturbed by strange stimuli.

"We'll take the runabout to the east exit and walk the rest of the way. It's only a couple of miles to the place I have in mind; there's a small grassy clearing in the forest near a clear pebbly brook—very peaceful and quiet. You and the wild one can trot along behind until we get to the east exit, Mandelbrot. Then we'll all walk."

"Very well, Master Derec. Shall I get the tent and other survival gear from the storage locker?"

"Yes."

Derec could not remember his childhood. He knew that somehow it must have been different from that of other children on Aurora, for he did not have the natural feel and easy, confident way of handling robots that was so much a part of a normal Spacer's personality, something acquired beginning in earliest childhood. In all the nurseries and homes, robots were the only nannies to be found. On Aurora, for instance, the closest any adult ever got to a child was the human who supervised the nursery nannies.

Had he been raised by a human nanny, maybe even his own mother? Had that been a still earlier experiment of his eccentric father, Dr. Avery? Derec knew in intimate technical detail how robots worked—he was an expert roboticist—but he did not have that natural insight into the positronic brain that almost all Auroran children had by the age of five.

The only robot Derec felt really close to was Mandelbrot. It wasn't a matter of trust or distrust. Robots were what they were programmed to be. You could trust even the Avery robots that built Robot City and the other robot cities, like the one here on the wolf planet, if you knew who had last worked with their insides. The only time you couldn't trust them was when someone like the irrational Dr. Avery deliberately altered their programming. He had, for instance, excluded Wolruf from protection when he revised the programming of the Robot City robots.

But Derec seemed to lack the upbringing to deal naturally with robots—Mandelbrot being a possible exception, or as much of an exception as to make it a rule—and now he was confronted with SilverSide, a being he had concluded from behavior and appearance must be a robot, yet a robot as unpredictable and unsettling as any he had ever dealt with.

Like the Avery robots—and like Mandelbrot's control of his arm—SilverSide had the ability to change shape by changing the orientation of his cells, which themselves appeared to be tiny robots—microbots—even smaller than the cells of Avery material. Derec had pretty well established that those microbots, during a metamorphosis, were being reprogrammed by SilverSide's positronic brain, much like some living organisms—lizards and amphibians—seem to reprogram their own cells in order to grow a new limb or a new tail.

Yes, he was quite uncomfortable with SilverSide, and as he went around gathering up supplies for their outing, he realized for the first time that he had begun to consider SilverSide actually dangerous. He had never felt that way about any robot before, not on Aurora or anywhere else.

The fact that Mandelbrot's remarks had distracted SilverSide and reduced his efficiency did not seem to be a reasonable cause, logically arrived at, for the quite serious offense of deactivating another robot. Robots could not go around knocking one another out—seriously risking amnesia in the victim—simply because the victim had been a source of distraction, no more than people could. SilverSide had done something Mandelbrot "would never do," to use Mandelbrot's own words.

SilverSide was an alarming phenomenon, yet exceedingly fascinating. Derec knew the robot should probably be deactivated, but that was a step Derec could no more take than could many other scientists who were on the cutting edge of their disciplines and involved in experiments dangerous to the society they lived in.

CHAPTER 9

INSIGHT

While she was eating breakfast, Ariel queried Jacob on the results of his nightlong cogitations.

"I have made a list," Jacob said, "of the technical features that jump technology and discrete modulation of hyperwave have in common. Would you like me to project it on the screen?"

"Heavens, no," Ariel said. "I don't understand that stuff. Transmit your list to Keymo over the comlink; see if he can deduce a parallel list that allows him to predict the characteristics of continuous modulation from the characteristics of Key technology, features they would likely share.

"And tell him I'd like an answer well before we go to the meeting with the aliens."

She finished breakfast and stepped out onto the small open balcony to sample the fresh smells of morning. And she was assailed instead by the sterile, leftover smells from night in a brand new city; not even the yeasty smell of baking bread that characterized the city of Webster Grove at any time of day and was certainly to be preferred to the ozone and machine oil of Pearl City.

Until that moment she had not really come to grips with how much she disliked cities. She had put up with Robot City, and with Earth's caves of steel, and now with this city, just to please Derec, disliking it all the time but kidding herself into thinking she was having a great time.

She disliked cities, any city, and she disliked them most in the morning. Without thinking, she had expected to sample the new-mown hay of Aurora. Instead she was oppressed by the smells of a city she disliked intensely and yet was compelled to try to save. The thought of that negotiation, less than two hours away, lay—in its anticipation—not like an idea in her mind, but like a brick in her stomach.

With her nose wrinkled and breakfast roiling her gut, she turned and went back inside to dress for the meeting.

An hour later, she was dressed and sitting in the living room, still groping for some solution to the dome problem. Jacob was standing in his niche. She even preferred that in her present mood. She wanted no distractions this morning.

Quite edgy, she decided she could wait no longer for Keymo to communicate with her. She needed a solution to take to the meeting, any solution, even one for a minor problem.

"Jacob, raise Keymo on the comlink," she said. "See if he's come up with anything on the hyperwave bit."

"Keymo reports some limited success," Jacob said. "He can now see certain features of Key teleportation that he had not seen before, features that might potentially serve as a method of instantaneous communication quite unlike current hyperwave communication."

"Good. Could it be called continuous modulation?"

"Yes. But it modulates a sort of hybrid wave, not hyperwaves as we know them."

"Good. That seems like a small distinction." Particularly since she didn't know what any of it meant. "That must be what the aliens are talking about.

"Let's go," she said.

"We're well ahead of time," Jacob said.

"Drive slow," she said as she walked out of the apartment with Jacob trailing closely behind.

He had requisitioned a small nonautomated runabout the night before, but not without some difficulty. With the evacuation at its peak, transport vehicles were in short supply.

Main Street was bumper-to-bumper with traffic, but it was all moving briskly so that Jacob, following her instructions to drive slowly, parted the traffic like a rock in a turbulent river. All eight lanes were flowing northbound to expedite the transfer of materiel.

Still, they arrived at the dome opening at 9:40 AM, more than twenty minutes ahead of time. At the dome opening, the street narrowed to four lanes and then turned into a dirt road a few meters north of the dome.

Wohler-9 was already standing vigil on the west side of the opening where the meeting with the aliens would again take place. This time she did not plan to make Wohler-9 a participant.

"Drive on north, Jacob," Ariel said. "I don't want to appear anxious."

She knew she must sound inconsistent, edgy to leave one moment, reluctant to arrive the next. She had to remind herself that he was just a robot and couldn't care, and so didn't judge her one way or the other. It was a good thing. She already felt inadequate enough.

Ten minutes later, Jacob said, "We are at the halfway turn-around point, Miss Ariel."

She had been deep in her dome problem, still unable to think of anything that could serve to stall the aliens further. The closure of the dome seemed inevitable.

"Fine," she said and glanced at him. "Let's turn around."

For just a second, a quick thrill of affection for Jacob coursed through her mind. He was such a handsome hulk and so thoughtful and caring.

He was clad in an attractive, short-sleeve top of loose weave that she had picked out. She had selected it for this occasion because of its casualness. She was clad informally as well. She didn't want the aliens thinking she was toadying up to them, no matter that they might not be able to classify her attire one way or the other. It was more a matter of establishing the proper frame of mind—in her mind.

She reached over impulsively and patted him on the forearm. She put out of her mind the thought that he was incapable of not being thoughtful and caring, incapable of acting otherwise, and programmed so. And he was a handsome hulk.

He gave her a quick glance in turn.

"Is there something else, Miss Ariel?"

"Oh, yes, Jacob. There is. I just hadn't anticipated it back on Aurora when I first asked for your companionship."

After all, he was only a robot. She kept telling herself that, over and over.

"Then I can be of further service?" Jacob said, questioning.

"You could, indeed, Jacob. It's just that I can't accept that service, no matter how delightful I might find it."

And then there popped into her mind the image of Derec, waving, standing far away at the end of a long row of waving green corn. And she wondered where that memory came from. She had never been in a cornfield with Derec. Not that she could remember.

And that brought her back to her present responsibility, which was more an obligation to Derec, to carry out his wishes, for she had only negative feelings for the robot city otherwise.

Still, the obligation remained.

"Do you see any sign of the aliens, Jacob?" she asked.

"Possibly," Jacob said. "I see three blackbodies that have just descended into a circular flight pattern around the dome."

"Can you time our return so that we arrive just after they have landed?"

"I will endeavor to do so."

He succeeded.

She got out of the runabout, walked over to face the aliens, and decided not to bow. Jacob stood to one side and slightly behind her.

Affecting a faint note of haughtiness, she said, "Good morning, ambassadors."

They had called themselves *leaders* the day before, but she refused to use that term for fear they might misconstrue themselves to be her leaders.

"Gud mahnin', Miz Ahyahl Wilsh," the middle alien said.

Ariel could not help smiling broadly. The Webster Grove accent took her by surprise again, but she immediately set her mind to eliminate it from consideration so as to avoid the less-than-serious attitude she had briefly lapsed into the day before.

"This is my assistant, Neuronius," the middle alien continued, bunching on the right side what looked like a shoulder in silhouette, "and this is my third in command, Axonius," and he bunched his silhouette on the left.

Ariel responded by inclining her head in the appropriate direction as each was introduced, a casual, restrained acknowledgment short of a pronounced nod.

The alien did not use the grand gesture that Sarco had used the day before when he had introduced Synapo, but it still left Ariel wondering whether she was dealing with Synapo or Sarco.

Here she was, on thin ice already, and the meeting had just begun. She guessed that it must be Synapo. It was he who had dominated the meeting the day before. On the other hand, these others were subordinates. They did not rate the grand gesture, even if this were Sarco.

She had nothing with which to parley except the analysis of hyperwave modulation that Jacob and Keymo had concocted at her prodding. And if this were Synapo, and if she had construed properly—that his green flaming the day before was an impatient assessment of Sarco's complaint—then it must have been a trivial complaint in Synapo's mind and not much of a bargaining chip for her side.

Not knowing for sure whom she was dealing with, she decided to stall.

She said, "I trust that you have now concluded that closing the dome does not have any immediate importance since it is already ninety-nine-point-two percent effective."

"On the contrary, we feel it would be better to close the compensator and to completely enclose any such creations in the future," the alien replied. "Although the emissions from the creation that Wohler-9 calls a city have been brought under control, we are still concerned, for the city may merely be a harbinger of worse things yet, things that lie off-world and are yet to be inflicted upon us."

"I can assure you that no such dire things exist. We merely want to share this planet with you and are quite willing to go to great lengths to ensure our mutual compatibility."

"That would be more reassuring if it were to come from a leader. That would be a member of your *he* clan, if I downloaded Wohler-9 correctly."

Another male chauvinist like Wohler-9, Ariel thought. This big bat had to be a male. Clearly.

The entire universe was filled with insufferable males.

"Not necessarily. Women—our *she* clan as you describe them—have often been leaders, and able leaders, functioning quite as well as men—our *he* clan."

"But most leaders are still members of the *he* clan. Is that correct?"

"Yes," Ariel was forced to reply.

The discussion was certainly not going well. Ariel decided to risk her only bargaining chip in an effort to turn things around.

Without giving the other a chance to respond, she said, "But let's get back to the main points of our discussion, the things we have been doing that are disturbing to you. We do not wish to disturb you in any way and are willing to go far to ensure that that does not occur.

"For instance, we can change our modulation of hyperwave from discrete to continuous so as not to disrupt your listening comfort."

A small flame of irritation shot from beneath his eyes, smaller than the day before, but still a respectable, quite noticeable, luminous green jet.

"Sarco!" he said like he was uttering a curse. "That hyperwave disturbance is not important enough to discuss here. My esteemed colleague is a music lover and prone to give those minor disturbances more attention than they deserve."

She had shot her wad, and at the wrong alien.

"Still," she said, "that does show how far we are willing to go to avoid disturbing your people. That should reassure you as to our intentions."

"Proper reassurance can only be supplied by your leader."

With strangely mixed emotions—longing and irritation inexplicably intertwined—she thought, *I am the leader here, mister bat, and you're stuck with me. But I wish my darn partner were here instead of way off cruising down some alien cornfield.*

She didn't stop to question where that strange image came from—the vision of Derec at the other end of a green, green cornfield; the yearning for Derec was too intense; and then the answer to the dome problem struck her with that marvelous insight that can come only from one brain hemisphere communicating with the other, passing on the subconscious machinations of the one that are hidden from the other.

For the first time, she felt in command of the situation.

CHAPTER 10

NEURONIUS STRIKES

Synapo was growing impatient with the *she* alien. The discussion was becoming tedious and unrewarding, and at the same time had not yet provided a suitable circumstance for embarrassing and discrediting his striking subordinate, Neuronius.

It was becoming more and more obvious that the small alien was in no sense a leader; that Synapo must somehow contrive to bring to his world a true leader of the aliens. In the meantime, he would have to direct Sarco to close the compensator and to start construction of the next one if, as he suspected, they were beginning to construct a second city on the other side of The Plain of Serenity.

Those were the thoughts that had led up to his last remark, and now the small, tedious alien was speaking again.

"There is no need to bring another leader to this world. You are looking at one. I had hoped to continue with the construction of our city, but that appears now to be impossible in view of your irrational fear that we have some insidious and covert plan to irrevocably disturb this planet."

The manner and bearing of the little alien had changed; her voice had taken on a different timbre. Had Neuronius noticed the subtle changes?

He discounted her attempt to belittle them by use of the adjective *irrational*. Disparagement was a not uncommon diplomatic ploy that was sometimes effective, but not often so, yet still worth the gamble in her case. He recognized that, but would the haughty Neuronius recognize her ploy and properly discount it? Or would he let irritation distort his analysis?

And would Neuronius recognize those subtle changes in her demeanor that were pure telepathy, transmitting information more effectively than the spoken word.

"We have other, more compatible methods of cohabitating with you on this planet," she continued. "The city under the dome in its present state would be essentially deactivated and serve merely as a coordination and communications center for the new effort."

She had switched diplomatic techniques, discarding the superior, haughty manner—every bit as haughty as Neuronius—and was now the companionable, friendly tactician. That was indeed the sign of a genuine leader. Would Neuronius recognize that and be able to switch tactics himself?

She had abandoned her mission's preferred goal, apparently, and was regrouping around an alternative; again the sign of a true leader with full authority to make important field decisions.

"Please describe this compatible method of cohabitation," Synapo said.

"Let me first ask a question. Do I, by myself, constitute a weather node, or my companion Jacob here, or our vehicle here with us in it?"

She had inclined her head toward the servant and pointed to the creation behind her, the vehicle.

"No," Synapo replied. "None of those entities, singly or together, create a weather node. The thermal disturbance is too small and quickly dissipates."

"Good," she said. "We will switch, then, from an urban, energy-intensive mode to an agricultural, labor-intensive mode; from a centralized society to a dispersed society; from industrial products to agricultural products; from robot cities, which you feel compelled to cover with domes—your node compensators—to robot farms that you will find completely benign."

Wohler-9 had not provided the agricultural and farm terminology, so Synapo could not immediately translate the small alien's words. He had to extrapolate from all that he had been told by her and by Wohler-9 and from all the previous data he had acquired by monitoring the aliens' hyperwave transmissions, but still it took him only a moment.

"By agriculture you mean the intentional cultivation of grasses and other plants like those growing on The Plain of Serenity and in The Forest of Repose; and by farms you mean the land subdivisions where this takes place. Is that correct?"

"Yes," the small alien replied.

"We have been exceedingly patient with your invasion of our world. You did not inquire whether this was a reasonable thing to do, nor negotiate ahead of time a suitable program for doing so, and when it did not prove to be reasonable, and we took steps to isolate the disturbance in as minimal a way as possible, you killed two of our people.

"Yes, we have been patient beyond any reasonable translation of that word, and now I'm going to ask that you be as patient with us today as we have been with you these many days past. Your patience will be tried, not by violence and death—as ours has been—but by boredom and ennui as we carry out, as we must, the rituals of our government as they were set up uncounted millennia ago.

"At that time an ancient Cerebronian philosopher by the name of Petero observed that all of our levels of government were filled by incompetents, that indeed government officials rose to their ultimate level of competence and then one level beyond, where they then remained, incompetent, for lack of ability to advance further.

"The observation was so striking and so self-evident that it became known as Petero's Principle, and all government was immediately reorganized to include the *strike* factor, whereby any official may be declared incompetent and displaced merely by a subordinate showing greater competence at that higher level.

"That, by definition, proves that the former official was incompetent, that is, not as competent as he could have been; and the process of proof, whatever form it takes, is known as *striking* for the higher position.

"So I now turn responsibility for these proceedings over to my subordinate, Neuronius, so that he may evaluate and respond to your proposal."

As he made the last statement, Synapo graciously gestured in Neuronius's direction and carefully watched his subordinate for involuntary reflexes, the body language, the telepathy that would tell him what was going through his subordinate's mind.

And if Axonius were competent for command, he would also be studying the mindset that Neuronius would be body-casting—broadcasting with his body. And Axonius would take that into consideration when he finally rendered his detailed analysis and final judgment of Neuronius in a caucus of the Cerebron elite.

So in a sense, not only Neuronius and Synapo, but Axonius as well, was on trial, for it would be the Cerebron elite, in caucus, who would render the final judgment that would restructure the government of the Cerebrons, if this immediate negotiation proved to be a decisive node in their history.

And in that negotiation with the aliens, Axonius must be the tie splitter—on the spot—if Synapo and Neuronius disagreed. Axonius could be placed in a quite delicate position. He could literally be dumped from the elite if he made a wrong decision, no matter how the contest between Synapo and Neuronius came out.

However, Axonius did have one factor going for him: he had nine votes in a caucus that would exclude Synapo and Neuronius. Each member of the elite had votes corresponding in number to his position in the hierarchy.

So now, all of this was surely going through the minds of the other two Cerebrons as Synapo turned to Neuronius to obtain his response.

The bodycast was not good. Neuronius radiated confidence, and that must surely have an effect on Axonius, which could make things difficult for Synapo if Neuronius took a contrary course.

"Miss Ariel Welsh, you plead a good case for the cause of your people," Neuronius said. "Perhaps I do not fully understand all that you said, but my mentor is an excellent instructor who has never failed me thus far, so I'm reasonably sure I understood the gist of your remarks.

"You radiate confidence and sincerity and all the other aspects essential to the execution of leadership, so you can surely not be found at fault in that regard.

"And your proposed change to the labor-intensive mode of agriculture seems—on the surface—benign, as you so eloquently describe it.

"The node compensator is operating at ninety-nine-point-two percent efficiency, and that has proved acceptable in Cerebron caucus, so that certainly is a point in your favor.

"And neither you nor your servant, taken individually, nor the small collection represented by one of your loaded vehicles—all small thermal emitters—constitute a weather node, as my mentor has concluded.

"Those are all positive arguments that weigh in your favor, but we must counterpose on the scale the few negative things which argue against your proposal before we can assess which way the scale finally tips.

"And surely weighing in against your proposal are the deaths of our two colleagues, and in the particular case of the last fatality, the passive state of our colleague before his death—in tether, a grim way to die without being able to defend one's self. How many more deaths of Ceremyons lie in the future?

"Yet those deaths—which can be largely attributed to misunderstandings by incompetent servants—and the small likelihood of more deaths in the future, do not tip the scale against you.

"Now we must weigh the true nature of the agricultural mode and the supporting, partially compensated, city nodes, and there is where we stumble.

"We know nothing about the agricultural mode except your reassurances of its serene harmlessness, nor do we know what additional emanations may find their way out of the opening in the city compensator.

"You term our fears irrational, when any rational being,

considering your past performance, must judge your actions to be frightening and such fears to be well founded.

"We mourn our dead colleagues, and we are ever so uncertain concerning the nature of your proposal, so we have no choice but to vehemently oppose your further occupation of our planet. We do not consider your intentions benign, Miss Ariel Welsh, not by a hooked eye."

Neuronius hunched his wings and fell silent.

The fool, Synapo thought. *He has just cast himself from the elite. There is little doubt of that. And just as I suspected, he reacted to the small alien's haughty disparagement when she used the term "irrational." It weighed in heavily with the fool's own irrationality, his basic paranoia, which I have long suspected.*

Thank god for the level-headed Axonius.

Now it was time for Synapo to cast his own vote.

If he agreed with Neuronius, he would only have to say so, and Axonius would be off the hook. For Synapo to register his opposition, he had only to ask Axonius for his opinion.

Which he did.

"And how say you, Axonius?"

For the second time that morning, Synapo felt some misgivings. Axonius's body language showed fear and irresolution when he should have been exuding confidence and decisiveness.

"Clearly," Axonius said, "Neuronius has properly assessed the situation and has come to a remarkably astute conclusion."

Synapo was stunned. His clever strategy had backfired completely. His attention this past year had been too much on the paranoia of Neuronius, and he had failed to properly assess Axonius, who had always seemed such a reliable lieutenant. That was where Synapo had gone wrong, perhaps: the difficulty of properly assessing someone you basically like and who invariably agrees with you.

It was a mere formality now. Synapo was foremost a statesman and a loyal Ceremyon; and a politician only when it wouldn't hurt the tribes.

He could have opposed his two subordinates, and the elite might grudgingly have supported him, but then he would have presented to the aliens the picture of a race and a government in disarray. It was more the position of the elite to acknowledge that disarray after the fact and to show magnanimity toward the aliens and flexibility in government by reversing the decision of their agents.

"We agree, then," he said. "It pains me, Miss Ariel Welsh, but your proposal cannot be accepted. In our short acquaintance, I have come to admire and respect you—your forthrightness and courage and unfailing good humor. May all those attributes stand you in good stead as you take this painful decision back to your people."

He was finished as the leader of the Cerebrons unless he could get this decision reversed in caucus—and in a caucus truncated to nine members with the nine votes of Axonius weighing in against him.

CHAPTER 11

S.O.S.

Immediately after the meeting, Ariel and Jacob returned to the apartment. Jacob started toward his storage niche, but Ariel forestalled him.

"Fix a large garden salad, Jacob," she said, "with thousand island and a couple of glasses of milk. Set the table for two. And then join me. It won't hurt you to act human for a change, like you're enjoying my company. That's an order."

"That is an order not difficult to comply with," Jacob said.

"Do you like thousand island dressing?" Ariel asked.

"Whatever pleases you, Miss Ariel. Lacking true taste buds, I really have no preference."

"What a shame. You're missing half the pleasure of life."

"Experiencing the pleasure of taste has never been my privilege. But of course," he added swiftly, so as to preclude generating displeasure for Ariel, "neither have I missed it."

"Did you have any reaction to the meeting this morning, then? Pleasure, displeasure?"

"My positronic potentials registered a sharp disturbance when it was apparent that the aliens were not going to endorse your proposal. I was reacting, however, not to a subjective or objective analysis, but to the knowledge that you were going to be intensely disappointed and in a quandary as to how to proceed."

"You have certainly analyzed my reaction correctly. Quandary is the operative word. I've held off calling Derec until now because I wanted to be able to tell him what he had to do rather than have him tell me what I had to do."

Jacob keyed the food processor and received a head of lettuce, two tomatoes, a cucumber, a handful of mushrooms, a block of cheddar cheese, a block of ham, a package of bacon bits, and a package of croutons. Derec had done a great deal to improve food processor technology while he was on Robot City.

"I really had a darn good chance of being in the driver's seat," Ariel continued. "When that farm inspiration came to me, I really thought it was the answer. I really thought old Synapo would buy it."

She didn't say anything more then. The vision of green Auroran truck farms and golden wheat fields had come to mind. She could see the robots moving down the green, weedless rows, harvesting lettuce, tomatoes, cucumbers, the very things Jacob was taking from the food processor.

Those same farms would flourish equally well right here on Oyster World. This world could be the breadbasket for this part of the developing galaxy. And without interfering with the aliens at all. There would be no need for expensive and energy-wasting food processors in this part of the galaxy if all one wanted was a simple green garden salad.

She had failed to create the same image in Synapo's mind. But how could she have succeeded? How was he to understand something that was as alien to him as his government was to her? She had been expecting too much.

Yet was his government so strange? She herself had seen many instances on Aurora—city governments with their bureaus and committees and councils—which Petero's Principle fit perfectly: all positions filled with incompetents, almost without exception.

"I guess it's not so strange that the aliens didn't buy my proposal," she said. "They are aliens and can't possibly think like we do. Yet their government makes sense, odd sense, mind you, as you might expect coming from aliens. Nothing a bunch of humans would ever come up with. It makes too much sense.

"And I guess it's just wishful thinking to expect Synapo to change his mind. So when you think about it, I guess I'm not really in a quandary, am I, Jacob?"

"So it would appear, Miss Ariel," Jacob replied.

In a process that was too fast for the human eye to follow, he had torn the lettuce into bits, sliced the tomatoes, and had diced everything else except the bacon bits and croutons. Now he was tossing, in a large bowl, everything but the ham, cheese, bacon bits, and croutons.

"They'll close the dome tomorrow," Ariel said, "and we'll be camping out."

"That seems to be the only logical deduction."

"So I've got to call Derec for help, right?"

"Quite so," Jacob agreed.

"How do I do that?"

"I do not have personal knowledge of that function. I will check with Wohler-9 using the comlink."

At the same time, he keyed the food processor for milk and thousand island dressing.

Ariel said nothing, and then, while he set the table, Jacob reported from the comlink.

"Avernus-8 supervises Mr. Avery's special monitor link."

"Tie in to him," Ariel said.

"I now have Avernus-8," Jacob said.

"Tell him to transmit the following message to Derec."

Ariel hesitated, thinking, while Jacob finished putting everything on the table. He had topped two bowls of salad with diced ham and cheese, ladled out a generous dollop of thousand island dressing onto each, and then sprinkled on the bacon bits and croutons.

Then she said, "No. Ask him first what's special about Derec's link, how does it work?"

She sat down at the table and motioned for Jacob to do likewise, and they both began to eat.

"Avernus-8 says that the connection with Derec's internal monitor is not made over hyperwave," Jacob said. "It is a special system Dr. Avery developed. The equipment is mounted on the mobile platform supporting the computer mainframe and on the mainframe's backup platform, but is accessible by all seven supervisor robots."

"And who has detailed technical knowledge of the system?" Ariel asked. "User's manual, wiring diagrams, maintenance manual?"

"Avernus-8 and the technician on each of the two computer platforms."

"I'll bet a pewter button that Derec's special link does use hyperwave, but unlike it's ever been used before. It's not common, ordinary discrete modulation.

"Dr. Avery has beat us to it, darn it. He's already invented the aliens' continuous modulation.

"Jacob, hook Keymo into your comlink connection, and

tell Avernus to describe Derec's monitor system to him. See if the two of them don't agree that it's continuous modulation of hyperwave as Keymo would define it."

That connection and analysis took a little longer than quick, but still consumed less than two minutes.

"Avernus-8 replies in the affirmative," Jacob said. "To communicate with all robot cities, Master Derec's internal monitor metabolically manipulates hyperwave in a manner similar to what Keymo describes as continuous modulation."

"Bingo," Ariel said. "Derec does it and doesn't even know how he does it. And I don't need to know anything about engineering to do engineering. Tell Avernus to ring up Derec and give him this message:

"CRISIS HERE ON OYSTER WORLD. YOU MUST IMMEDIATELY REPROGRAM AVERY ROBOTS. I ALSO HAVE A BIT OF IMPORTANT ENGINEERING TECHNOLOGY TO TEACH YOU, DUM-DUM. IN FACT, YOUR OWN INTERNAL ENGINEERING, SO COME AT ONCE.

"Sign it: LOVE, ARIEL, and ask for confirmation."

For ten minutes Jacob said nothing while Ariel forked salad into her mouth and mooned over Derec. With that wild imagination one has when extrapolating hope, she visualized Synapo meeting with her before Derec arrived, telling her the aliens had changed their minds and would accept her proposal. She would then be the aliens' kind of Leader.

No matter what, the robots would have to be reprogrammed. They weren't going to build any robot city on this planet.

While they were finishing their lunch, Jacob broke the silence.

"Avernus-8 has received this reply from Master Derec:

"ON MY WAY, SMARTY PANTS. LOVE, DEREC."

She spent the rest of the afternoon on the balcony,

which overlooked Main Street, sitting in the subdued light of the perpetual dusk under the dome, reading a book of poems she took with her whenever she traveled: *Selected Poetry of Old Earth*.

It was an ancient book, bound in soft brown imitation suede, and printed in a small, graceful font on one side of thin, translucent, parchment-like paper. It was the only thing her mother had ever given her that she truly treasured. Juliana Welsh had given her a lot of expensive things: clothes, jewelry, cars, fliers, jumpers, but seldom anything with the taste and thought that was reflected in the selection of that little book. She wondered if her mother had picked it out or had merely asked one of their robots to pick up something via the hyperwave shopping service.

She came to a very short poem she had forgotten, but when she reread it, it seemed like a piece of wisdom that might apply at almost any time in a person's life—Robert Frost wisdom:

The Secret Sits

We dance round in a ring and suppose,
But the Secret sits in the middle and knows.

That's what she seemed to be doing. Dancing around the solution to the problem. She had come so close to the answer in that meeting with Synapo and his lieutenants. He had said as much with that elaborate apology he had left her with, as though he would have done things differently if it had been left up to just him. In that case, would he really have bought her proposal?

She looked up every now and then to stare at the opening in the dome. It made her uneasy. What if they could suddenly close it and trap them all inside that insidious blackness? There would be no way out, no way that human technology could provide.

But she didn't want to camp out, and she certainly didn't want to spend any more time in that tiny, cramped, two-passenger jumper than she absolutely had to.

After dinner Jacob rigged a viewing screen on the balcony so she could spend the evening keeping an eye on that critical opening in the dome while she watched a library tape of an old hyperwave drama involving Elijah Baley, Gladia Solaria, and the robot Daneel Olivaw.

She could not see the dome opening when she looked up. The starshine in the black sky was not bright enough to be seen through pupils contracted by the illumination required to present Elijah Baley in all his glory. But she could see the lights of the robot traffic far out on the plain, traffic that was now diminishing as the materiel transfer neared completion.

When she went to bed, she posted Jacob on the balcony with instructions to call her immediately if he saw any change in the size of the dome opening.

In the middle of the night, she dreamt that she was trying to escape from that black void inside the dome, piloting her hyperspace jumper with the monster Synapo sitting beside her in the cockpit, heading on a course that would take them down Main Street with the Compass Tower far in the distance. But she was still out in the void, hanging motionless at least a kilometer from where Main Street began, with her throttle pushed to its limit; and stretching away from her toward Main Street were long, long rows of waving green corn; and standing at the end of Main Street, far away down those rows of corn, was Derec waving and beckoning for her to come to him. She turned to look at

Synapo in the midst of a feeling of disoriented horror, and a crimson flame shot out of the blackness beneath his luminous green eyes and burned her hand.

She awoke drenched in perspiration, her hand resting painfully on the sharp corner of the nightstand beside her bed. She finally drifted back to sleep, yearning for Derec to be there in bed beside her, but back on Aurora, not there on Oyster World.

By ten o'clock the next morning, the materiel transfer dwindled to a halt, and with their limited possessions piled in the runabout beside them, Ariel and Jacob stood outside the dome at the meeting site, keeping vigil with Wohler-9 and his lorry, waiting to witness the final closure of the dome.

Five minutes passed—10:05 AM—and no blackbodies had shown up to send their shimmering additions down the edge of the dome, then a half hour, and then an hour, and still no construction activity.

There weren't even any signs of preconstruction activity like the long line of blackbodies that had formed on other mornings heading toward the apex of the dome opening, like an outspiraling thread unwinding from a black hole, from a spherical black mass that from far away could not be resolved into individual blackbodies basking on the wing in the light of the sun.

There was no dull black ball in the sky this morning. The blackbodies were up there like every other morning, but unlike construction days, they were loosely dispersed from horizon to horizon, languidly circling, soaking up the sun's radiation.

Ariel and the two robots sat there all day waiting for something to happen and nothing did: no construction activity and no visit from the aliens to explain the lack of activity.

Ariel ate lunch and dinner from supplies Wohler-9 had stashed in the lorry for her, supplies that were to last a month to give them time to get the Oyster World dilemma resolved.

Derec was due to arrive in three days: one day to get far enough away from that other planet to allow the jump through hyperspace, and two days to travel in from the jump arrival point, the nearest clearsafe in the Oyster World zone.

They spent the night in the open. Ariel slept on the long back seat of the open lorry under the stars of a cloudless sky. She refused to spend another night under the dome with the threat of its imminent closure literally hanging over her. One night like that was enough.

CHAPTER 12

WOLRUF STANDS INSPECTION

They arrived at the clearing well before noon, following a large animal trail Derec had discovered and explored with Mandelbrot a few days before. Although the forest cover discouraged the growth of dense underbrush, there were scattered patches that occasionally blocked the trail for homo sapiens, low branches that the animals who had made the trail—possibly SilverSide's erstwhile associates—simply walked under.

The trail was clear now, of course. When they had first explored it, Mandelbrot had simply fashioned his arm into a machete—the arm that was made of Robot City material—and cleared the way with a motion that bore some resemblance to a buzz saw.

This morning Derec led the way, with Mandelbrot next, then Wolruf, and finally SilverSide bringing up the rear. SilverSide kept up a steady conversation with Wolruf during the hour that it took to reach the clearing.

Derec could hear the buzz of conversation but was too far in front to make out what they were saying. When he reached the clearing, and as they approached, he could hear them clearly but still couldn't understand them. They were no longer speaking Standard.

Mandelbrot was already erecting the tent as Wolruf walked into the clearing.

"I don't believe this," she said. " 'ees already speaking my language. Not fluently 'et. But give 'im another decad and 'e'll be speaking it like a native."

"Yes. He has a marvelous affinity for new knowledge," Derec said. It made him uneasy, that affinity.

Derec gathered some stones from the brook and built a fireplace. Wolruf put the inside of the tent in order. Mandelbrot gathered firewood.

SilverSide disappeared. It wasn't until Derec finished construction of the fireplace that he noticed SilverSide was gone. Wolruf was fast asleep in the tent on one of the cots she had erected. She really wasn't much of an outdoors person, not at all like Derec in that respect.

There was no point in looking for SilverSide. This was his habitat far more than theirs. They might never see him again.

The thought of that filled Derec with dismay. He had become vitally interested in the strange robot—a fascinating study in alien robotics. He had learned a great deal merely by association, but he needed to learn much more, including its origin and the purpose of its original programming.

And he had sucked Wolruf into the problem as well. He had brought her "half across the galaxy" as she had so emphatically pointed out. How was he going to explain that he would not need her services any longer? That she had come all this way for nothing!

When Wolruf awoke, she took the news of SilverSide's disappearance quite calmly.

"Good," she said. "Can I go 'ome now, back to civilissation? Can we at least go back to the city?"

"He'll come back," Derec said more confidently than he felt. "We'll at least stay overnight. He might not come back to the city, but he'll come back here."

They spent a quiet afternoon. Derec read. Wolruf slept. Mandelbrot stood guard, just outside the clearing, facing away from the campsite, with his back against a tree on the other side of the brook. SilverSide would have a hard time getting at his switch panel that way.

After dinner, after it got dark, hoping to attract SilverSide, Derec built up the fire so that it lighted the entire clearing.

Mandelbrot stayed at his guard post. Wolruf dozed in the warmth of the fire. Derec thought about Ariel, and that brought him to Jacob Winterson and, putting Jacob out of his mind, brought him back full circle to worrying about SilverSide.

The fire died down. Derec was talking when Wolruf quietly laid a hand on his arm and pointed across the fire to the other side of the clearing, the side away from Mandelbrot's guard post.

There—just inside the clearing, in the faint light of the dying fire—were two gray wolf-like shapes, sitting on their haunches. When he looked at them, the firelight caught the backsides of their eyes and came back at him as a ghostly green glow. That must have been how Wolruf had seen them in the first place; they were otherwise almost invisible.

"Master Derec," Mandelbrot called softly from behind them, "we are surrounded by animals circling around the campsite. Should I take any action?"

"Can you suggest anything suitable?" Derec asked.

"Not at the moment," Mandelbrot replied.

"Stay at your post then," Derec said.

"I 'ate stuff like this," Wolruf said. "Why do you alwayss 'ave to bring me along?"

Just then the shape on the right threw back its head and howled, long and piercingly, letting it trail off slowly into a series of soft sobs.

That howl was answered by an identical howl from the forest that seemed to progress halfway around the campsite before it, too, sobbed to a finish.

The two shapes rose then and trotted toward the campfire. The one on the left was smaller, Wolruf's size, and as they approached the campfire, its form became silvery while the form of the other, standing a meter at the shoulder, became more distinctly mottled black and dark gray.

After coming well into the light of the fire, the larger beast turned and loped into the forest. The small silvery beast came around the fire and sat down on its haunches beside Wolruf.

"That was LifeCrier," the small beast said. "He wanted to inspect Wolruf."

"SilverSide?" Derec queried.

"Yes. Surely you can tell it's me. The imprint is quite realistic."

"And did I pass muster?" Wolruf asked.

"I wouldn't be here if you hadn't, Mistress Wolruf," SilverSide replied.

She had achieved a remarkable likeness to Wolruf, considering that the robot was an organometallic construction from coarse cellular microbots. The flat face, the pointed ears, the fingered forepaws were all in character. She had even achieved a good simulation of the fur without creating individual hairs.

"I think the wolves have gone, Master Derec," Mandel-brot informed them.

"I would suspect so, Mandelbrot," Derec said. "Silver-Side is back. Perhaps you should come and meet her in this new form."

Mandelbrot crossed the brook and walked up to the fire. He hardly glanced at SilverSide.

"Would you like me to build up the fire, Master Derec?" he asked.

"Yes," Derec said, "and then perhaps you should resume guard duty. Other beasties may come calling, some that are not so friendly."

Those that had just left had not been nearly so friendly at one time, Derec recalled.

"And SilverSide, you might post yourself on the other side of the campsite, but don't stray so far into the forest this time."

"Mistress Wolruf?" SilverSide said, questioning with a rising inflection.

"Yes?"

"Are those your wishes?"

"Of course."

SilverSide's fealty had clearly shifted to Wolruf.

Derec slept well until the middle of the night. With SilverSide back in the fold, his attention had shifted to him-self, and he went to sleep yearning to be with Ariel. The gentle snore from the cot next to him reminded him of Ariel and aggravated the desire, but it was not enough to keep him awake long.

That night he didn't dream of Ariel or of anything else. The short hike, the outdoor environment, and the relief connected with SilverSide's return promoted sound sleep, and he didn't stir until shortly before dawn, when he was awakened by Avernus's call over his internal monitor, transmitting Ariel's call for help.

CHAPTER 13

THE VOTE ON SUPERIOR COMPETENCE

Immediately following the last, disastrous meeting with the aliens, Synapo had circled up to charge altitude with Neuronius and Axonius trailing far behind. He was looking neither to left nor right nor up nor down. His eyes were open but staring straight ahead—staring, unseeing, out of a mind closed down by shock.

So when he arrived on station, he was surprised to see Sarco there ahead of him, circling in Synapo's space, hook set aggressively forward.

Although it was virtually unheard of and highly unethical to communicate political matters by radio, Neuronius must have done just that, radiating Synapo's defeat for all to hear, while Synapo, in shock, had his sensory equipment shut down. Else why would Sarco be up here already, contesting Synapo's dominance?

So, indeed, it had been a conspiracy; and it involved not only Sarco and Neuronius, but Axonius as well.

Synapo ignored Sarco, and with his hook set aggressively forward, he winged Sarco out of the way and took up his station in a tight circle immediately over the center of the compensator.

"What's up?" Sarco said, meekly yielding the space. "You don't seem happy."

Synapo said nothing.

"What happened down there?" Sarco asked again, putting more insistence into his voice.

"You should know," Synapo finally said. "One of your Cerebron toadies has already radioed you."

"What are you talking about? Nobody has radioed anything; and I can't stand toadies, least of all a Cerebron."

"Neuronius? What about Neuronius?"

"Neuronius coached me in pronunciation of the alien language. Does that make the poor soul a toady?"

"Poor soul, my hook. He was just trying to stir up trouble between you and me; if you somehow don't relish that idea, then he was using you, Sarco, and you must be exceedingly naive."

"I must admit I thought it was an elegant idea, using your second in command to advantage in our rivalry. But, Synapo, it has always been a friendly rivalry."

"Neuronius is striking, Sarco. And with Axonius on his side. Why do you think I took them both with me and excluded you rather unceremoniously?"

"Frankly, I didn't know, and you didn't appear to want to explain. So what did happen down there?"

"Neuronius made a wrong decision involving the aliens, I reversed him, and Axonius sided with him. It was as simple as that."

"That doesn't sound like Axonius, Synapo. Give me the details. You three have involved all the Myocerons. You can't expect me to sit idly on the sidelines."

"Axonius had you fooled as well, eh?"

With that slight dig, Synapo proceeded to describe the meeting in detail. Before the end of the long account, Sarco had rotated his hook so that it pointed passively aft, expressing silently but eloquently whose side he was on.

When Synapo finished, Sarco asked, "When are you having your caucus?"

Synapo had put off that decision until Sarco prodded him. His mind had been so paralyzed he had not worked out a plan of action during his slow climb to station.

"One hour from now," he replied, making a quick decision.

"I hereby exercise my right as leader of the Myostria," Sarco said, "and proclaim that caucus to be a joint gathering, a Cerebron caucus and a Myostrian hearing. Please announce it as such to your people, and I will do the same for mine."

It was an historic occasion. A joint gathering of the elite of both tribes was something that occurred only once a decade or so, if that often.

In an ordinary Cerebron caucus, Synapo would be on station circling lazily above the center of the compensator in a large, loose circle with the other members of the Cerebron elite flying to right and left, above and below, a wing-spread apart.

In the larger assembly of a joint gathering, however, the flight caucus was not compatible with clear and audible communication, so a grounded gathering was held on the high crags atop The Cliff of Time—a ninety-meter escarpment that cut across the intersection of The Plain of Serenity and The Forest of Repose eight kilometers to the northeast of the robot city and its node compensator.

Synapo, with his hook set forward, stood on the highest crag while the other ten members of the Cerebron elite stood below, facing him in a line on a slightly tilted table of flat granite. Their hooks were all set aft.

Neuronius stood in the middle of the line immediately below Synapo, Axonius stood to his right, the next in rank stood to the left of Neuronius, and the other members of the Cerebron elite stood right and then left in descending order of rank in the hierarchy.

Sarco, with his hook set aft, stood on a nearby crag on Synapo's right, above the same rock table, with his elite gathered below him in similar fashion and within easy earshot of Synapo.

In addition to Sarco, there were fourteen other members of the Myostrian elite. It had been temporarily expanded to handle the increased load imposed by construction of the huge node that compensated the weather effects of the robot city.

"As you all now know," Synapo said, opening the joint gathering, "we are in a strike situation, not only at the highest command level in the Cerebron elite, but with regard to our world in general, for in all fairness, we must regard the invasion by the aliens as a strike for cohabitation of a world which we have previously regarded as strictly our own.

"To regard the presence of the aliens in any other fashion is not to give them their just due, for we cohabit now with many lower forms of life. The aliens may simply be another inferior species seeking peaceful coexistence.

"On the other hand, that may not be so. We must consider the possibility that we are seeing a superior race and may be bargaining from a disadvantageous position, trying then to retain cohabitation rights ourselves.

"The Cerebron elite and the leader of the Myostria were all familiar with this philosophy of negotiation and with the details of the discussion that had already taken place as we undertook further discussion with the aliens this morning.

"By this morning, however, it had come to my attention that Neuronius was striking for command, so we entered this latest meeting with the aliens under slightly different circumstances.

"If conditions were appropriate, it behooved me to give Neuronius his chance to prove competent in command, to possibly prove superior competence in our continual striving to avoid the pitfalls that beset a governmental hierarchy described by Petero's Principle.

"The Cerebron caucus has been called this afternoon to judge that competence, while remembering our delicate situation with regard to our cohabitation with aliens."

Synapo then summarized the discussion with the aliens that had taken place that morning up to the point when he had turned over control of the negotiations to Neuronius.

After calling upon Neuronius to defend his response to the aliens' proposal, Synapo sailed down to the table rock to stand a pace in front of Neuronius, who then sidled out from behind Synapo, and with an awkward hop and a powerful flap of his wings, arrived at the position on the topmost crag that Synapo had just vacated.

"Cerebrons, your challenge this afternoon is not just a matter of judging day-to-day competence of command. The matter is far larger than that. You must also judge competence in assessing and establishing the rank of the Ceremyons in a galactic hierarchy that includes the invading aliens."

His body language radiated confidence, even arrogance.

"There are many facets of superiority of one race with respect to another, but the fact of most concern to us should be whether we are superior enough to eject the aliens from our planet. All else is the weak juice of the soft, degenerate culture Synapo would have us embrace.

"That summarizes the results of my cerebrations, and I responded accordingly. There is no point in subjecting you to useless rhetoric. I told the aliens that we could no longer tolerate their presence on our planet and terminated the negotiations."

Synapo was stunned for the second time that day. That last was a brazen lie. He, Synapo, had terminated the negotiations that morning. For Neuronius to lead the caucus to believe otherwise was to presume the outcome of the forthcoming vote.

Neuronius paused for just a moment and then continued, "However, I did not tell the aliens how I propose to ensure their removal. Threats merely alert the enemy and eliminate the element of surprise.

"But to this caucus I suggest—and strongly recommend—that we immediately remove them the way one of their number accidentally and effectively removed himself from our world—when he blindly ran into the edge of an embryonic compensator."

Neuronius paused for a moment. Then he dramatically rotated his hook forward.

"I suggest we ship them all into the black eternity that lies beyond space and time, where those two part company in the bowels of a node compensator."

Neuronius stood silently on the crag for a moment, and then sailed down to the table rock and waddled back to his place in the line behind Synapo.

For a while the silence was disturbed only by Neuronius, by the rustle of his wings and the soft slap of his feet against the table rock as he moved to resume his position in the line.

Finally, when even those sounds were complete, the only thing to be heard was the soft sigh of excess oxygen being vented here and there among the assembly.

Synapo was appalled by the suggestion, so disconcerted he had a hard time taking it in.

Finally, he spoke again from his position on the table rock.

"Axonius, I appoint you temporary Chairman of the Caucus, for the purpose of stating your position, taking other statements from any who may care to speak, and finally tallying the Vote on Superior Competence."

That was the standard statement to make at that point in the proceedings; and that was fortunate, for he could not have trusted himself to say anything else after Neuronius had presented such a quixotic solution to the alien problem.

Axonius now flew up to the topmost crag.

Neuronius had impaled Axonius on the horns of a terrible dilemma, unless Synapo had completely misjudged the younger Cerebron. Axonius was an opportunist—that had become clear that morning—but he was not a killer.

Synapo knew exactly what was going through Axonius's mind and could sympathize with him and feel his anguish—a terrible anguish his body language clearly bespoke: the flicker in his eyes, the slight flutter of his cold-junction, the tight way he was hugging his wings to his body.

Axonius was finished. The only way he could possibly save his position in the elite after the foolhardy position he had taken that morning was to vote for Neuronius and hope that he would win. Yet he was a gentle being and could not honorably endorse the violence recommended by Neuronius. He had misjudged Neuronius, and now he would have to pay the terrible penalty for that unfortunate error.

Synapo wondered how well Axonius would handle it.

He wanted to see him unbowed by defeat, wanted to feel he had not completely misjudged him.

"Honorable leaders, fellow Cerebrons, fellow Ceremyons, I am placed this afternoon in an exceedingly awkward position."

Good, Synapo thought, *that's the first promising observation I've heard from a Cerebron all day.*

"This morning," Axonius continued, "it was my opinion that Neuronius spoke from a position of superior competence in his assessment of what should be the posture of Ceremyons if we are to insure our proper place in the galactic hierarchy, to use his terms.

"It was not a decision arrived at lightly. I have great respect for our leader, and have never before seen him come to an erroneous judgment. He is completely right in pursuing a policy of peaceful cohabitation with all life forms on our world.

"But is he right in applying that same policy to any galactic species that may take a notion to inhabit our planet? How can we determine and judge the intentions of an alien species without conducting an experiment and risking our survival in the very process of the experiment?

"It is an unfortunate dilemma which risks, on the one hand, prejudging and punishing an alien species without a hearing, but on the other hand, risks our very survival not to do so, not to prejudge.

"Mine was not a decision arrived at impetuously this morning. We have all been pondering the problem and updating our cerebrations with each report of the negotiations by our leader.

"So this morning, the risk to our survival seemed overwhelming, and I favored the position of Neuronius as being the more competent exercise of leadership.

"I shall not dwell unduly on the remarks of Neuronius this afternoon, and will merely conclude by saying that I cannot in good conscience endorse them; they do not reflect competent leadership."

His hook had remained pointing aft throughout his remarks.

He hurried on then, no dramatic pauses, words tumbling out of his mouth in an effort to somehow put distance between himself and his own pronouncement.

"Would anyone else care to make a statement?" he said.

Synapo was proud of Axonius. Almost ready to forgive him. Axonius had stuck courageously to the position he had taken earlier that morning and yet had denied Neuronius that afternoon.

Synapo, like everyone else, was expecting any further remarks to come from the Cerebron elite before Axonius called upon him for a final statement, giving him the traditional privilege of last remarks before the vote.

So they were all surprised when Sarco spoke up, standing on the crag to Axonius's right.

"Honorable chairman, under ordinary circumstances any remarks that I might make to a Cerebron caucus would be off the record unless I were called as an official witness, which I have not been this day. In fact, quite the contrary. The Myostrians are here because of Leader Privilege which I exercised, recognizing this meeting to be of vital concern to the Myostria. This is our world as well as yours, Cerebrons, and ordinarily decisions affecting our mutual welfare are jointly arrived at by friendly discussion between the leaders of the two tribes.

"Today, a matter of vital concern to both tribes is unavoidably going to be decided by the exclusive vote of a

Cerebron truncated caucus, without our leader being able to participate in the decision.

"You can understand my concern, then, and the reason I ask to be considered an official witness in your proceedings. How say you, Mr. Chairman?"

"So noted and recorded, Honorable Leader," Axonius confirmed.

"My remarks will not be brief, yet neither am I given to excessive rhetoric. I am fortunately not constrained by the extraordinary position Axonius finds himself in. Quite the contrary. I feel compelled to dwell at length on Neuronius's position this morning and his remarks this afternoon."

As he was concluding those words, without pausing, Sarco slued his hook around until it pointed forward.

"Taking the last first, his final statements this afternoon confirm what I have long suspected: he is a paranoid psychopath with a cunning way of hiding his affliction by artful words and soothing flattery until the hook needs be set.

"Then his pent-up fears and irrational solutions come bursting forth, as we witnessed in stunned silence this afternoon. If you were not stunned, Myocerons, then you need to examine your own state of mind.

"Axonius obviously was, and his introspection guided him accordingly. Neuronius had him deluded with the promise of honorable ascension until this afternoon, when all the honor evaporated in the course of an irrational grab for power.

"I can understand Axonius's reasoning at this morning's meeting with the aliens, but a true leader has to look deeper than Axonius did and reason rationally—as Neuronius did not—to find the ultimate solution to problems: that solution which looks beyond immediate and easy resolution.

"Typically, Synapo summed it all up quite concisely in

his opening remarks this afternoon—somehow we can always count on him. Neuronius could have spared us all a lot of grief, if he had just been listening and taken heed, if he had just been listening to Synapo's daily reports these past few days and taken heed.

"Setting honor aside—and the honor is quite as compelling to Synapo as the logic—to strike blindly as Neuronius recommends is to possibly kick the toe of a giant who then, as Synapo suggests, may not be so willing to cohabit, and might even shuffle all Myocerons into their own version of a space-time partitioner or, perish the thought, some even more malevolent and painful form of annihilation.

"To not strike blindly, but instead, to try to understand the aliens—and I am already impressed by their small leader and think I understand their intentions—is to soothe the giant under the worst of circumstances or to help and minister to a lesser species under the best of circumstances. Both are honorable directions for the Myoceria.

"Neuronius has sorely misguided you, Cerebrons.

"Synapo has already shown you the way. I have merely reiterated what he so concisely and clearly pointed out.

"Please do not fail him."

A silence as keen as that which followed Neuronius's last statement now fell upon the assembly.

Axonius seemed in no hurry to break the silence; instead he seemed to be providing a space for the Cerebrons to ponder Sarco's remarks.

Finally he said, "Are there any others who would like to make a statement?"

But now he waited not at all before he said, "If not, our Honorable Leader is here provided the traditional last words before the Vote on Superior Competence."

"I have nothing further to add to my colleagues' remarks," Synapo said and turned his hook until it pointed aft to accept humbly whatever the Cerebron elite might decide.

Axonius took the vote by radio ballot: secret and unanimous.

CHAPTER 14

BEARER OF GLAD TIDINGS

When he heard Axonius announce the favorable results of the unanimous vote, Synapo immediately took flight, circling up and up into the calm sky, matching that calmness with the cold detachment he had induced in himself as Sarco was speaking.

He was not surprised when Sarco joined him, and he was grateful to Sarco for the power of his oratory, but he wanted to be alone, and he had been on the point of ensuring himself that solitude when he detected Sarco close behind.

With Sarco close at hand, expecting some kind of dialogue, he could not balloon himself into isolation as he had intended; that would show neither tact nor the genuine gratitude he felt.

So he merely climbed to a safe ballooning altitude and then started circling in position, waiting for Sarco to catch up.

"I know you want to be alone," Sarco said, "and I'll not

intrude on your time but for a brief moment, just long enough for a word of warning."

"You're not intruding, old friend," Synapo said, "and rushing off as I did may have made me appear ungrateful for the service you rendered at the gathering. But I am truly grateful and might not have won the endorsement of the elite if you hadn't made that impassioned speech. You deserve to be where you are, Sarco, the very antithesis of Petero's Principle."

"I didn't come up here to be praised, you old jet, but to warn you about Neuronius."

"You and the elite have taken care of him, Sarco."

"For the moment, perhaps, but maybe not even for the moment. He's dangerous, Synapo."

"Neuronius? Dangerous? To himself maybe. He certainly confirmed that today."

"No, to you, Synapo."

"I think not. He's devious, and a liar, and not to be trusted, but hardly dangerous otherwise."

"He was standing in back of you," Sarco said. "You couldn't see his body language, his undisguisable reaction to that last bit of terse, indirect language Axonius used to describe his competence to guide the caucus.

"But I was watching him intently, Synapo, then and again when I gave my harsh assessment of him. He may even be dangerous to Axonius and to me, but he's going to hold you responsible for his downfall, and you're the target he'll be focusing on."

"Perhaps, but there's little you or I can do about that," Synapo said. "His danger to the future of the tribes, at least, has been eliminated by his departure from the elite. That was my primary concern."

"He's still a danger to the tribes so long as he can get at you and me. And what about Axonius? Where does he stand in the elite now? He helped save your hide."

"I'm not sure at this point. This has been a rather full day. I'm too exhausted to think clearly now."

"I was impressed with his handling of the caucus, Synapo."

"And so was I."

"I'll leave you now. May Petero guide your deliberations."

"You agree that the alien proposal for cohabitation should be given a fair trial?"

"I'll not argue that," Sarco said, "not after what you've been through. Yes, we'll postpone closure of the weather node compensator indefinitely."

He glided away. Synapo balled and immediately closed and inflated his reflector to its full extent, suitable for high-altitude cerebrations.

Although his storage cells were still critically low, and though his cerebrations in reflection mode would use a modest amount of juice, he could recharge to full capacity as he leisurely beat his way back from wherever the gentle air currents would take him during his silvery ruminations.

His first step in the direction of those ruminations had been taken when he reached stable altitude, and with only his hook, eyes, and primary vent protruding beneath the balloon, he surveyed the vast panorama.

The Ceremyons were far below him at optimum charge altitude, replenishing their juice stores in random flight circles that covered the globe in a loosely dispersed pattern up to the dusk band.

The dusk band was creeping toward him from the east—powered by the natural rotation of his world and his slow easterly drift—delineating day from approaching night that was just barely visible as a thin black crescent sliced from the edge of the globe.

From such high altitude, he appeared to have drifted very little from the point where he had ballooned. The compensator with the pie-cut sector lay only a small way to the west.

He closed his eyes, purging his mind of stress and strain which gradually faded away to a calm serenity.

And he slept.

He awoke to a star-studded frame surrounding the jet black circle of the planet. And his mind went immediately to Axonius, and to the answer to the question posed by Sarco as they parted that afternoon.

He would keep Axonius as his second in command. To discard a competent aide who was now all the more valuable for the lesson he had just learned, and all the more loyal for the gratitude he could not help but feel, would be to exercise a petty vengeance that was not characteristic of the statesman Synapo.

That resolved the tribe's hierarchical question, and the aliens had proposed a course that they felt promised harmonious cohabitation. He had no more problems at that moment, questions perhaps, but no problems, for he did not consider Neuronius a problem apart from the day-to-day governing of the Cerebrons; and the only worthy question that remained—the question of the possible superiority of the aliens—he could do nothing to answer right then.

Their small leader would make a friendly pet but was in no wise a threat, no more so than the servants, the Avery robots. The only question that remained was how did the small leader fit into the alien hierarchy, that part that still lay off-world.

He could do nothing to answer that question now. With a serene mind, he went back to sleep.

He awoke with his back to bright sunlight as he tossed quietly in the gentle turbulence created at the juncture of land and sea. Far to the west he could see the large node compensator with its pie-cut sector visible only as a small departure from perfect sphericity on the right side.

He deflated then, contracting the outer silvery surface of the six gores, and by that contraction, rolling the paper-thin hide into tight black rolls as the gores unsnapped at the continuous tongue-and-groove that kept them locked to one another while inflated.

The fluttering of the hide as he dropped through the thin air of the stratosphere was no competition for the powerful pull of the thin layer of smooth muscle that lay just below the silvery surface. Soon, all that was left of the balloon was a six-segment collar, visible only as a small bump in the black silhouette.

The ocean was still far below when he spread his wings at optimum charge altitude and started flapping with powerful strokes toward the compensator. Despite the night's metabolic cleansing—the destruction and purging of waste products that constitutes rest—he felt stale and overworked. He missed that fresh shot of juice he had become accustomed to during the construction of the compensator, when he dipped his cold-junction into the icy water of the brook upon deflating in the early morning.

That was the only aspect of Sarco's normal Myostrian routine that he would like to adopt as a permanent part of the Cerebron daily regime. The nomadic Cerebrons were never in one place long enough to find the icy brooks hidden in the forests scattered over their globe.

As he stroked west, his thoughts returned to Sarco's

warning the previous afternoon concerning the danger posed by his deposed lieutenant, Neuronius. He had been quick to dismiss Neuronius as an empty threat when there were more important things to think about, but now, with those other issues either decided or in a dormant state awaiting further data, he considered the unhappy plight of Neuronius. What, if anything, could he do to help him? Extreme irrationality like that exhibited by Neuronius was rare, almost nonexistent, among the Ceremyons. And being so rare, their society had not developed any truly effective remedies for want of suitable subjects to study.

Being sensitive and compassionate, indispensable qualities of a true statesman, Synapo had difficulty viewing the problem dispassionately. He put himself with his feelings in Neuronius's position, trying to imagine how despondent Neuronius must feel at that moment. In his ignorance of the true nature of that irrationality, with his compassion clouding his judgment, he failed to appreciate the machinations possible by someone like Neuronius.

By dusk he was over the vast Forest of Respose, but still fifty kilometers from the Plain of Serenity. Despite the exertion of flight, he had recharged his cells to eighty percent of full capacity, so he tethered that night in the treetops with a feeling of satisfaction. He had been so empty and so hungry for such a long time he felt almost like a glutton, nearly sated.

He arrived over the compensator early the next afternoon and took up his station circling above the center of the shimmering dome. Far below he could see the golden Wohler-9 standing on the west side of the dome opening. The small alien leader and her personal servant were sitting in the creation Wohler-9 called a lorry.

Synapo kept Axonius in suspense for another four hours, and then just before dusk he summoned him by radio.

"I'll want you to accompany me to a meeting with the aliens at the usual time tomorrow morning. And notify Petorius that he is now a member of the elite."

Saying nothing more, Synapo dropped to tether for the night in The Forest of Repose. That was how Axonius learned of his promotion and who would be the lucky Cerebron to come in at the bottom in the moves that would bump Neuronius from the top.

The next morning, Synapo was standing on the west side of the opening in the compensator with Axonius on his right, facing the small alien and her servant, the robot Jacob Winterson.

"My government has reconsidered your proposal for cohabitation of our planet, Miss Ariel Welsh," Synapo said, opening the discussion, "and I am pleased to report that they reversed the position taken by our representatives during the last meeting with you."

"That is good news, indeed," the alien replied. "The dome will remain open then, so we may use it as a communications and transportation base?"

"If that is what you wish. What else is involved in this new proposal?"

"The Avery robots—like Wohler there—must be reprogrammed. That is no small undertaking. However, a task force I have summoned for that purpose will arrive late this afternoon."

"I would like to meet with you and the leader of that task force tomorrow at this time," Synapo said.

"For what purpose?" the small alien asked. "I doubt that

he will be able to contribute anything of significance to our negotiations."

"For the purpose of planning our mutual interaction in implementing your proposal and establishing a timetable for its completion. My Cerebrons are a nomadic tribe, anxious to be on the wing again. We have already stayed far longer at this Myostrian compensator than we find comfortable.

"If you can assure me that you are familiar with the details of reprogramming the Avery robots, then of course, the presence of the other leader would not be required. But you led me to believe otherwise."

"Very well," the small alien said. "We shall meet with you tomorrow morning."

Good, Synapo thought. *That meeting should show who is dominant—the* he leader *or the* she leader—*and should also resolve once and for all which species is superior, the Ceremyons or the aliens.* He would like to think that it would make little difference in how the Ceremyons treated the aliens, but he knew otherwise; he knew that it would make a big difference, even to him, a statesman.

CHAPTER 15

REUNION

Wolruf brought her hyperspace jumper *Xerborodezees* down a half kilometer from the forest and a full kilometer from the line of robots and their vehicles streaming across the plain toward Oyster World's robot city.

They had hardly touched down before a lorry started from the city across the deep, golden grass, laying a trail on the prairie that pointed toward the *Xerborodezees* like an elongating arrow.

Wolruf traveled light. She had stowed everything she needed in one small bag slung around SilverSide's neck. The two of them were sitting at the top of the access ramp, from which they could look out over the tall, waving grass and watch the approaching lorry.

Stepping carefully between them, Mandelbrot had unloaded Derec's gear from the ship by the time the lorry arrived. But SilverSide could clearly see and distinguish the two occupants of the open lorry long before it reached the ship, since both occupants were standing up.

"The one Derec calls Ariel, which is she?" SilverSide asked.

"The small one on 'urrr left," Wolruf replied.

"Then the tall one must be the robot Jacob Winterson."

"I've neverrr met 'im, but I pressume so," Wolruf said. "Jacob iss Ariel's personal robot, and that body in the lorry certainly matches Derec's description. 'e looks 'uman, but Derec said Ariel wass the only 'uman on the planet, so that's got to be Jacob."

"Are the females always smaller and more delicate?"

"Generally. And that's true of most animal species in the galaxy. I'm certainly smallerrr than my consort."

"Yes, your library file told of you as a female," SilverSide said. "And I've considered you so without fully understanding the deeper significance, which seems to exist beyond the functional reproductive purpose. Derec seems driven by many other emotions when he talks of Ariel."

"Just as Beores wass driven by otherrr emotions when 'e talked of Latiel."

"I don't understand. Who were they?"

"The first beingss that werrr created, according to ancient myths."

"Not the first humans. That would be Adam and Eve, according to the library history files."

"Okay, put it in 'uman terms. The first man and the first woman."

"And do all males have this strong affinity for females?"

"Mostly. Some don't, but they'rrr a small minority."

"I can understand that such a feeling is necessary to promote the reproduction of the species. But Derec's emotions seem involved with feelings far beyond simple procreation. And that is confusing beyond even the confusion—

my lack of understanding—of the nature of biological emotions in general."

"Emotions can be just as confusing to those experiencing them," Wolruf said, "so 'urrr confusion iss understandable and nothing to worry about."

"Worry?" SilverSide said as though she were considering the idea for the first time. "Is that an emotion?"

" 'es. All this concern 'u seem to 'ave over the sexes doess seem to amount to worry, wouldn't 'u say?"

"A perturbation of some sort from a mean of some sort is the only way I can express it—something which I would rather didn't continue, but which I don't seem able to prevent."

"A good description of worry," Wolruf said.

"Then I shall so tabulate it in a catalog of emotions which I shall now begin to prepare, hoping that by defining them I can come to know and recognize them as the first step in learning to control them."

"A worthy project which could quite likely drive 'u nuts," Wolruf said.

"Nuts?"

"Forget it. It iss not an emotion. But I'll tell 'u an emotion I am feeling: joy. It's been a year or more since I've seen Ariel and felt the simple joy of being with 'errr."

With that Wolruf dashed down the ramp, for the lorry had pulled up beside the pile of Derec's luggage and equipment.

Ariel stepped down from the near side of the lorry as Wolruf extended herself to her full height and wrapped her arms around Ariel.

Neither said anything, but both had tears in their eyes as they separated and stood looking at one another.

SilverSide put tears down as a possible external sign of

emotion, unintentionally beginning a catalog of associated symptoms that later—as her knowledge increased—she would identify by the term *body language*.

" 'u're a blessed experience after a dreary period," Wolruf said.

"And you're a sight for sore eyes," said Ariel. "Where's Derec?"

"We had to leave 'im behind on the wolf planet," Wolruf said.

The look of consternation that immediately came to Ariel's face also went into SilverSide's catalog, but she could only tag it with the word *lie* that she knew to be not an emotion, but rather a lack of truth-telling by Wolruf. Still, she had nothing else to tag it with for the time being.

And then Ariel's look changed to joy as Derec appeared on the ramp beside SilverSide.

"You scamp," Ariel said, grinning at Wolruf.

Wolruf gargled phlegm, a sound symptom SilverSide had long since associated with Wolruf and her strange affinity for what Derec called humor.

Ariel and Derec met in the middle of the ramp and hugged one another and pressed lips.

The look of joy had to be catalogued adjacent to the emotion of joy, for Wolruf had already defined what it was they were feeling when they met once again after so long a time. The same must be true of Ariel. But joy still had no personal connection with SilverSide, and so was only a word and a symptom in a file, and incomplete without SilverSide's own positronic potential pattern.

Worry she now understood. Joy she did not.

And yet—it suddenly came to her—she, too, had met beings she was very close to after a period of separation, as she had when Derec, Wolruf, Mandelbrot, and she had gone on the outing in the forest, and she had gone looking for LifeCrier and the rest of the pack and had brought them back to meet Wolruf.

Seeing LifeCrier after all that time had disturbed her, and it was a disturbance that she welcomed and would seek to experience again. Her memory brought forth that old positronic potential pattern, and she knew then that she could put it in her catalog alongside the word and the body language for the emotion *joy*.

But those were minor things in the confusion of her thinking. It was the inexplicable nature of the biological sexes—and not in their function of reproduction—that was disturbing her most acutely that afternoon. And to a lesser extent, she was still disturbed by a lingering doubt as to who was the more intelligent, and so, the more human—Derec or Wolruf.

Small though it was, doubt still remained, but only because of the importance of the judgment that could affect the life and death of the two if she were required to choose between them in a life-threatening situation.

Did she consider herself to be more male than female because Derec had proved more intelligent in that first basic contest, the one that pitted the female KeenEye against the male Derec? Did she lean toward the male gender for that reason? After that contest she had certainly been more comfortable under the Derec imprint. He had opened a whole other world to her, he and his library files.

So that confusion with the nature of the biological sexes, and with her discomfort under a female imprint, disturbed her—and yes, that disturbance was the emotion Wolruf had called *worry*. She was worrying about her imprint on Wolruf because she was disturbed by a desire to return to the Derec imprint, the male form—*uncomfortable* Wolruf would have described it—so she put that emotion down in her catalog, together with its positronic potential pattern.

She was becoming more and more convinced that she should go back to the Derec imprint strictly from the standpoint of comfort. That was a notion she catalogued as a strong future possibility, but for now she would retain the Wolruf imprint for whatever help that femininity would provide in her analysis of Ariel and the strange effect she had on Derec.

SilverSide rose and walked through the hatch, following Ariel and Derec who had just walked up the ramp and into the ship.

CHAPTER 16

THE AGROBIOLOGIST

"So what's the crisis here?" Derec asked. "And that screwy message of yours, that bit about my internal engineering? What's that all about?"

They were standing in the control room of the *Xerbor-odezees*, where they had gone to get away from the others.

SilverSide walked in, sat down in one of the deep-cushioned passenger seats behind the pilot's upholstered bucket, and listened to Ariel and Derec.

"Some engineering I figured out, quite without your help," Ariel said. "In fact I've brought this planet pretty much under control without your wisdom and guidance. All I need from you now is your muscle, that part between your ears."

"You didn't answer my question."

"Your internal monitor link with the robot cities: I'll bet you didn't know that that modulates hyperwave."

"*Au contraire*, my dear," Derec said. "That is a form of communication that depends on a special understanding of

336

spacetime physics developed by my ever-so-eccentric father, the good Dr. Avery."

"And *au contraire* right back at you, smarty. That is what the aliens on this planet, the Ceremyons, refer to as continuous modulation of hyperwave. Ask Avernus and Keymo, and Jacob, too. He even understands it. It's the communication version of Key teleportation, just like conventional discrete modulation of hyperwave is the communication version of hyperjump technology. I'll bet you didn't even recognize that!"

They had been together again for all of ten minutes, and already they were going at it hammer and tongs. *Is this what love is all about?* Derec asked himself.

"I'll have to think about that," he said. Was it possible she was right? He changed the subject.

"Now what about the crisis? The reason for me being here."

"There is no crisis. Except I had to get you here promptly to avoid one."

She told him then how the robot city had disturbed the weather, how the Myostrians had capped and controlled the disturbance with the dome, how they were ready to close it completely until she came up with her plan of a planetwide farm, abandoning the idea of a planetwide city.

"So you see," she concluded, "your task is straightforward and reasonably simple: just reprogram the Averies into farmers."

"I presume that this is another example of your style of engineering?" Derec said.

"Not bad, huh? Social engineering, Derec. Something you wouldn't understand."

"There is just one minor problem."

He paused. Ariel said, "And that is?"

"In order to program the Averies to pursue a particular technology, one must know something about that technology. I know all about cities. I don't know the first thing about farms, and I suspect you don't either."

Wolruf came into the compartment in time to hear Derec's last sentence. She took the passenger seat next to SilverSide.

Ariel looked stunned. *That seems to be a piece of engineering she doesn't have covered,* Derec thought. *Perhaps there's more to engineering than meets her eye.*

He was feeling smug and complacent. The bit about continuous modulation of hyperwave had thrown him for a moment. But now he felt that he was back in control of the expedition.

"So 'u don't know the first thing about farms, Derec. So what?" Wolruf said. "I seem to 'ave come in on the middle of the show."

"So you can't reprogram Avery robots to be farmers," Derec said, "if you don't know anything about farming and farm technology."

" 'ave no fear, Wolruf iss 'ere," the small, furry alien said. "I wass raissed on a farm and educated at Agripolytech. I'm 'urrr original 'ayseed engineerrr."

"Okay, Derec. What do you say now?" Ariel said. "You think I didn't know that? Where have you been all this time?"

Derec ignored Ariel.

"You, a farmer?" He was looking at Wolruf.

"What products do 'u think the Erani bought from my family?" Wolruf asked. "The Erani arrr not all pirates like Aranimas. They'rrr mostly traders, and they live on an impoverished ball of rock that growss lichens betterrr than it doess tomatoess. In theess days of overpopulation, the Erani survive on the grain and farm products they buy from us."

And there was Ariel, glowing now, when she had been shocked half out of her drawers before Wolruf put in her two cents. She had had no more idea than he that Wolruf was a farmer.

But Derec was quick to regroup, and he was now admitting to himself that Wolruf's contribution might well amount to more than two cents, Galactic Monetary Standard.

"Okay. I submit. I'll handle the computer technology, Wolruf will handle the farm technology, and you can continue to handle the social technology."

"Not entirely," Ariel said. You could tell she was about to reveal something that was not entirely easy to divulge. "You must meet with me and the aliens tomorrow morning. And it looks now as though Wolruf will also need to attend that meeting, as our farm specialist."

"For what purpose?" Derec asked.

"They want to develop a schedule. The Cerebrons are anxious to return to their nomadic life, from which they've been diverted by the problem with our city. They've been camping out in The Forest of Repose, as they call it, the woods next to the city."

Ariel looked at her watch.

"You may want to watch this," she said. "It's sort of spectacular. We can watch the show from the lorry as we drive in to the city. We need to be getting back anyway. It's almost time for dinner."

Jacob and Mandelbrot were standing near the lorry as Derec and Ariel started down the ramp. The robots had already loaded Derec's gear into the lorry.

Derec called, "I'll want you to drive, Mandelbrot."

He wanted to stand by the driver, so as to watch better whatever show it was Ariel had scheduled for them, and he darn well didn't want that musclebot Jacob standing beside him, upstaging him, so to speak, in front of the audience sitting behind.

He glanced at Ariel, daring her to challenge his decision.

She looked at him quizzically, but then gave him a quirky little smile and didn't say anything. And that was as infuriating as if she had questioned his order. She knew exactly why he wanted Mandelbrot to drive. Somehow he always displayed his buttons, and Ariel knew exactly which ones to push.

But the show was every bit as spectacular as she had intimated. She stood up to point out the one she thought was the Cerebron leader, Synapo, circling high over the dome. And it was he who dropped first: a tiny black ball plummeting toward the forest like a lead shot, becoming a small bomb, trailing a shiny smoke that slowly expanded into a silver ball that drifted gently down into the tree tops and then bobbed up to rest on the top of the forest like a ball of mercury on a countertop.

That was a solo performance, and then from near Synapo's flight circle, another followed—Sarco, the leader of the Myostria, Ariel guessed—and after a time, over the space of a quarter-hour, they all dropped until they were dispersed like myriad beads of silvery moisture over the surface of the green foliage.

CHAPTER 17

THE CEREBOT

THE PROVISIONAL LAWS OF HUMANICS

1. *A human being may not injure another human being, or, through inaction, allow a human being to come to harm.*
2. *A human being must give only reasonable orders to a robot and require nothing of it that would needlessly put it into the kind of dilemma that might cause it harm or discomfort.*
3. *A human being must not harm a robot, or, through inaction, allow a robot to come to harm, unless such harm is needed to keep a human being from harm or to allow a vital order to be carried out.*

> *From Central Computer File: Humanics.*
> *Mechanical Access: Drawer 667, Bin 82.*
> *Keyword Access: Humans.*
> *Subkey: Laws.*
> *File Creator: Rydberg 1*

The next morning, well before ten o'clock, Mandelbrot parked the lorry near the west edge of the dome opening, and the three mammals got out, instructing the three robots to stay behind in the lorry but to record everything that transpired once the aliens arrived.

"Well, friend Mandelbrot, it is some time since we've been able to talk privately," Jacob Winterson said.

"That will hardly be the case with the wild one present," Mandelbrot said. "Watch what you say and what you do. It is completely unpredictable. It deactivated me on the wolf planet."

Jacob and Mandelbrot were still standing behind the control panel of the lorry. SilverSide was sitting on the back seat that she had occupied with Wolruf on the way to the meeting site.

"For your information," SilverSide said, "I am not an 'it.' I am currently of the female persuasion, having imprinted on Wolruf. You may refer to me with the pronouns 'she' and 'her,' Jacob. And you need not think that I will deactivate either of you now that I know that Mistress Wolruf would not react kindly to that action. Further, I am completely unaffected by what you may say or do, now that I understand that Miss Wolruf wants me to modulate the Third Law slightly to accord you some modest protection."

"So, friend Jacob," Mandelbrot said, "have you pondered further upon that imponderable, the Laws of Humanics?"

"Yes, I have," Jacob replied, "and I find them woefully inadequate in describing human behavior. Rydberg and his companions are inexperienced in dealing with humans who are an unfathomable lot. Emotions, not laws, govern their behavior. And I think perhaps the female of the species is the most mysterious of all. I have been researching the emotion of jealousy since I seem to have been acquired essentially to create that emotion in the breast of Master Derec."

"I hardly think jealousy can reside in the breast of a human, friend Jacob," Mandelbrot suggested.

"Merely a figure of speech used in the literature of the subject," Jacob replied. "The key point of interest here, however, is the multiplicity of shades and overtones that exist in the minds of humans in their consideration of the opposite sex, shades and overtones of emotion that apparently have nothing to do with reproduction of the species, the ostensible reason for there being the two sexes in the first place."

Surprisingly, SilverSide was becoming interested in the conversation after all. She agreed with Jacob's assessment of any Laws of Humanics that would guide human behavior and supposedly parallel the Laws of Robotics that guided her behavior. And now the subject of their conversation seemed to bear directly on her discomfort with the femininity of the Wolruf imprint that seemed, paradoxically, to be aggravated by the keen interest in everything feminine she had felt earlier in the masculine mode, while imprinted on Derec.

It was a discomfort that came from an awareness of her own narcissism, something she had never experienced before, that was at once both fascinating and repulsive. She concluded she was attracted to feminine beings, but would rather it were not her own being. But what was the cause for the attraction? She concluded it must stem from that first powerful imprint on KeenEye that had not been altogether dispelled by her preference for the Derec imprint— the male imprint. That comfort with a masculine imprint was only a little less powerful than the laws that were intended to govern her behavior, but which she found so difficult to interpret for want of knowing what a human was. She could deprogram neither those laws nor her feeling of masculinity nor that insidious attraction for all that was feminine.

She found that she was experiencing another form of discomfort that came from listening to Jacob and Mandelbrot. She had never before heard two robots conversing with one another. The discomfort came not from that process but, again, from their words, what she deduced from their words. They were talking as though they knew what a human was, and she, SilverSide, was still exploring that subject by the process of multiple imprints, trying to progress to ever higher levels of intelligence, for surely only the most intelligent species in the galaxy could be the humans she was seeking.

"Jacob, you talk of the laws of humanics as though you know what a human is," she said.

"Certainly," Jacob said. "I am so programmed. How else could I implement the Laws of Robotics?"

"Am I human?" she asked.

"No. You are a robot," Jacob replied.

"How do you know?"

"Master Derec says so. Further, my own senses tend to support his contention. You are not a mammal."

"What about Mistress Wolruf? Is she human?"

"No."

"But she is a mammal."

"True. But not all mammals are human."

"What is a human, Jacob?" SilverSide asked.

"There are many definitions, some very complicated, some very simple. We are generally programmed with only one."

"What is an example of a simple definition?"

"Accent in speaking Standard. Most humans speak Standard, so a simple definition for a special set of robots on a planet called Solaria once used the Solarian accent to define humans—a very simple test, not requiring any unusual instrumentation."

"And how do you define a human, Jacob?"

"By the number of their chromosomes and the configuration of their X and Y chromosomes."

"And how do you determine that information?"

"With an instrument—a cellular nanomachine—built into my right index finger."

"You don't make that determination each time you meet that same human, do you?"

"No. Once I determine that a being is human, I put its image into a pattern-recognition table. Further, I am inclined to accept as human any being that approximates an average of those images—without the chromosome test."

"Mistress Ariel and Master Derec are both humans, then."

"Yes."

"And which do you feel more compelled to protect?"

"My immediate master, Mistress Ariel."

"And you, Mandelbrot, which would you favor?"

"Master Derec, although the choice would be difficult," Mandelbrot said.

"And what about Wolruf?" SilverSide asked. "Would you protect her, Mandelbrot?"

"Yes. Friend Jacob and I are both programmed to treat her as human."

"Don't you find that strange? A being that is . . ."

Thoughts of Wolruf as a human were shunted aside by the landing at the meeting site of black demonic beings—two of them—who simultaneously stalled out with perfect choreography, braking with their wings widespread, seeming to shut off the sun in the enveloping blackness of their presence. Then they touched down lightly, folded rustling wings close in to their bodies—shrinking to the size of the mammals they faced—and became black silhouettes surmounted by wicked-looking, snow-white hooks above burning red eyes.

The impenetrable soft blackness that shrouded their physical essence in mystery projected a disquieting impression of latent power.

SilverSide concentrated on recording everything that transpired. She thought that she was possibly observing the ultimate form of humanity, the final objective in a frustrating quest.

"Good morning, leaders of the Ceremyons," Ariel said. "This is Wolruf and this is Derec, both members of our reprogramming task force. Wolruf, Derec, I would like you to meet Synapo, leader of the Cerebrons . . ."

The alien on the right expanded slightly with the rustling sound of a bat's wings amplified by an order of magnitude.

". . . and Sarco, leader of the Myostria."

The alien on the left expanded, rustling.

Derec spoke next.

"My colleague Wolruf and I are honored that you will be working with us to produce an environment on your planet of benefit to both of our peoples."

"That is to be desired," the alien Synapo said with a strange accent, more pronounced than Wolruf's, which made understanding the alien even more difficult.

"But first," Derec continued, "would you explain the nature of the dome and the method of its construction so that we may determine how best to modify the city within to be as innocuous as possible?"

"The node compensator is a localized separation of space and time," Sarco said.

He said nothing further, as though that fully explained it.

"Yes. Go on," Derec said.

"That's it. A localized rift in spacetime," Sarco said with mild disdain as though he were lecturing a backward student, "a locus of points in the cosmos where our universe no longer exists."

"And how do you create such a rift?"

"Do you understand what I mean by a rift in the cosmos?"

Derec hesitated.

"Not entirely," he said.

"Then you're not likely to understand how such a rift is created, and we should move on to more profitable subjects for discussion."

Synapo entered the discussion at that point.

"The rift is created and enlarged by the intense application of electrons, which themselves are convolutions in spacetime. The stream of electrons—highly focused on a microscopic volume at the initial point of separation—enlarges the void progressively around the extent of the rift, much as I separate the gores of my reflector when I untether each morning.

"But as my colleague, Sarco, suggests, perhaps we should move directly to a discussion of your schedule for implementing harmonious cohabitation."

"Strictly from visual observations, the dome seems to partake of the nature of a black hole," Derec persisted. "Is that what you're saying?"

"Black hole?" Synapo said, as though now having difficulty himself with the trend of the conversation. "Black hole! Yes, that is a good analogy. The derivation of the word was not self-evident.

"Yes, the compensator is a black hole, but an unnatural one internal to the universe, not on the edge; a black hole as a concavity, not as a convexity at the edge where space and time separate in the course of the natural decay of the universe.

"Now may we move on?"

"Just two more questions," Derec said. "When we look at the dome from the outside, we can't see the city. We see objects on the other side as though the dome and the city weren't there. Why can't we see the city inside?"

"The compensator's intense curvature of spacetime bends the light around the dome much as light from a distant star is bent slightly as it goes around our sun. In the case of the compensator, the bending is not slight. It is calculated to produce the effect of invisibility and nonexistence: one of its attributes as a compensator.

"You had one more question?"

"Yes. Why should a hyperspace flier fall toward the surface of the black concavity and escape only by the full thrust of its impulse engines, as Ariel described to me last night—an effect of the curvature of spacetime—when the atmosphere, the air inside the dome, does not fall toward the blackness likewise?"

"You answered your own question," Synapo said.

A small green flame hissed from the blackness a decimeter below his eyes, and his voice took on a note of irritation, as though his patience were about to be exhausted.

"The curvature of spacetime, as you suggested. The flier was beyond the neutral shell, in the gravitational field of the black concavity. The planet's atmosphere is within the neutral shell, in the gravitational field of the planet."

With a note of finality, Synapo concluded with a question.

"Did not your jumper have to achieve normal escape velocity to drive into the blackness before it could reverse and try to escape back to the planet?"

Quickly, before Derec had time to fully digest those last remarks, Ariel regained control of the meeting. With firmness, she said, "Now, honorable Ceremyons, our schedule calls for the first phase of our effort to be completed in two months. That effort will provide sufficient farm area and production—1000 square kilometers—for proof of environmental passivity.

"Concurrently, we will modify the city to provide terminal facilities for local and interstellar transport vehicles. Those facilities will project through the opening in the dome, but will be insulated and force-ventilated to ensure that all harmful radiation and emissions will be retained within the dome.

"Wolruf, our farm engineering specialist, and Derec, our city engineering specialist, will now describe the detailed schedules for those two activities."

SilverSide recorded all that, but her attention, her whole being, was concentrated on the alien, Synapo. His domination of the dialogue told her that he was the superior of the two aliens and potentially more powerful, more intelligent, than any of the mammals she had become familiar with. In short, she had found the ultimate target for her final imprint, or so she believed.

She left off recording the meeting with the aliens. She had found a new role model to fit the beings the Laws of Robotics compelled her to serve. She was no longer obligated to observe the orders of lesser beings. Still, she gave Wolruf a last thought filled with fondness, that new emotion she had found in her consideration of LifeCrier, now far, far away. She would continue to protect Wolruf with just a little less weight than she gave herself under the Third Law, the law of self-preservation.

She turned her attention back to the alien on the right, Synapo, and concentrated now on the technical details of the imprint, particularly the aerodynamic characteristics that would be the hardest to duplicate. The calculations quickly showed that her wingspread and airfoil area would have to be several-fold greater than that of the aliens in order to support her body weight. Their body mass must be light indeed, with mostly hollow structural reinforcements.

And she would have to increase the dimensions of her body to provide the geometry needed for the wing connections and the leverage required for the wing manipulators. Not surprisingly, that was going to decrease her body density to match that of the aliens.

She worked on the eyes next. They were compound, radiating red and infrared. The radiation came from a ring that surrounded the conventional animal optic in the center and provided controlled illumination for viewing objects when the sun's radiation was blocked by the planet.

Then she turned her attention to the blackbody surface and found that to be more of a problem than the aerodynamics and the optics. She experimented on her arm as she sat in the back seat of the lorry but finally had to give up and settle for a blackish gray with a soft, silvery lustre, just as she had finally given up matching the details of hair and skin coloring of the mammals.

Next, she attacked the source and nature of the green flame that had burst from the alien, Synapo. She had the feeling that it was a tool, if not a weapon, that was required to provide a satisfactory imprint. She designed a small electrolytic cell, compressor, and high-pressure storage containers for hydrogen and oxygen and a release orifice at the rear of her oral cavity, but she kept her conventional speakers for communication. And she added a small factory to fix nitrogen in the form of ammonia to provide the trace of that compound that gave the flame its green color.

All during that period of analyzing the alien, Synapo, she was absorbing the powerful masculinity he radiated, intercepting and recording the red glare of his eyes, sopping up his physical essence, the body language, the subtle mannerisms that escaped that otherwise all-absorbing black silhouette.

Finally she was ready, and she set the organometallic cells of her body and their pseudoribosomes to the task of altering her genetic tapes—her robotic DNA, her equivalents of messenger and transfer and ribosomal RNA—and the myriad other factors contained in her multibillion microbotic cells that would finally effect the alien imprint.

As her form changed, she stepped up to stand on the back seat of the open lorry to give her forelegs room to develop into wings, and then as her long hind legs shortened and thickened, she braced them against the back of the seat to steady herself.

With their attention on the meeting, the two robots in the front of the lorry did not observe the transformation, nor did the mammals in the meeting who faced away from her. She was under observation only by the aliens, and they seemed not to notice or to care.

Finally, the transformation was complete, save for the hook and its tether, that she had programmed last because of its different matrix, a stainless form of shining steel configured in a hollow curved horn and a fine-stranded but sturdy flexible cable. She hoped to fly, but she had abandoned the balloon and the act of ballooning she had witnessed the evening before. The hook, then, was purely for effect.

Comfortably masculine now, SilverSide was standing on the back seat of the lorry, fully erect—three meters high— with his wings folded tightly against his body as though he had just emerged from a cocoon like a newly metamorphosed butterfly. He felt the need to open and exercise them, to get the feel of them, and with that he recalled flying in bird form on the wolf planet.

The mammals and the aliens were still absorbed in their meeting. The aliens apparently thought the growing SilverSide was a natural phenomenon associated with the lorry, for they gave no sign of looking directly in Silver-Side's direction.

Slowly he opened his wings. The thin, tough, organo-metallic membrane rustled faintly as he unfolded the airfoil to its full twenty-five meters. He found then that he could not avoid measuring air currents.

He had not been aware of even a faint breeze as he had stood there on the back seat with his wings folded, but now he felt the gentle pressure acting on his wings, pressing his simulated, feathery cold-junction against the back of the seat. He resisted the torque that was endeavoring to tumble him out of the back of the lorry only with a distinct effort by digging his toes into the seat cushion.

The effort was more than he cared to maintain, so he folded his wings back against his body, reducing the wind area.

Then he turned, walked across the seat to the side of the lorry, hesitated—looking at Wolruf who was running toward him and shouting his name—and then spread his wings again and hopped over the side. He felt again the glorious sensation of flight, of being airborne, as he gently glided to the ground. When his feet touched, he fell flat on his face, his wings outspread, with a feeling of slow motion that began with his dragging toes digging shallow furrows in the dust next to the roadway.

With difficulty, he got up, using his wings to lever himself erect before folding them into his body, and then Wolruf was on him, hindlegs straddling his back and pinning his wings to his sides, hands grasping his hook to keep her purchase. And Derec was winding a rope around both him and Wolruf, binding them together.

CHAPTER 18

THE BLACK VISITATION

Ariel was about to wrap up the meeting. Wolruf had hit the high spots of the technical effort involved in establishing the robot farms and had given her detailed schedule; and Derec had described the external modifications of the city to provide local and interstellar terminal facilities, the minimal effect those changes would have on the meteorology, and the detailed schedule to effect those changes.

Ariel began her recap.

"I would like to briefly review the farm program again and summarize the schedule, but before I do, are there any other questions on the work that Wolruf and Derec described?"

"No," Synapo said. "It was all quite clear."

"Was it acceptable?" she asked.

"Yes."

Synapo turned to look at his companion.

"Sarco?" he queried, "Any objections?"

"Not for the moment," Sarco replied. "The farm machinery is highly suspect, but we must take you at your word, at least for now. Time may tell us otherwise. And, too, I am concerned . . ."

He stopped talking briefly, then:

"By the Great Petero!" he exclaimed. "What *is* that, Synapo?"

Both aliens had turned slightly to the left to focus those red eyes on something behind her. Ariel turned to look herself and saw a dark gray monstrosity on the back seat of the lorry with gigantic wings hovering over the vehicle like some kind of avenging angel.

Then it slowly folded its wings and started walking across the seat to the side of the lorry, where it spread them once again, and Ariel knew instantly what was going on.

But Wolruf had anticipated her by significant seconds and was already running toward the lorry, shouting, "SilverSide, SilverSide," over and over again, as though shrill decibels would anchor him to the ground.

As it turned out, Wolruf had nothing to worry about. SilverSide came to rest flat on the ground, spread-eagled. And by the time he picked himself up and retracted his wings, Wolruf was clinging to his back, and then Derec was trussing them both up with a rope he had hastily dug out of a locker on the side of the lorry.

Ariel was torn between getting involved in the fracas herself and preserving some kind of composed demeanor for the benefit of the aliens. She felt her position as official negotiator and ostensible leader of the robot city task force with special keenness ever since she had been able to parlay her visit into that position: leader without portfolio.

As Derec was wrapping SilverSide and Wolruf round and round with rope, Ariel turned back to the aliens in time to hear Sarco say, "Perhaps this gives us a better idea what further menace lies off-world, Miss Ariel Welsh. We resume construction of the node compensator tomorrow morning."

He had rotated his hook forward as he spoke. Then, as he turned away, a broad green flame a meter long blazed from below his eyes, and he flapped into the air.

The heat from the flame hit her like the breath of a blast furnace.

The alien Synapo stood facing her as his colleague flew off.

When he spoke it was in a fashion that left no doubt as to the temper of his thoughts. The words seemed to modulate the small green flame that flickered below his glaring red eyes, a waxing and waning fluorescence that resonated with the strange buzzing sound it imparted to his words.

"You have violated a trust and humiliated me before the elite, Miss Ariel Welsh."

And he, too, turned and flapped into the air.

She stood there a long time watching them as they slowly and gracefully circled higher and higher above the dome. The first leveled off and took up a flight pattern around the exact center of the dome. The second, however, continued upward, circling and circling until she lost it in the shimmer of the atmosphere.

Derec had come back to stand beside her, but she had not heard him.

"A setback, surely, but perhaps not a large one," he said.

Startled, she turned to look at him coldly but said nothing before walking back to the lorry. Jacob was standing at the controls. Mandelbrot, standing between him and SilverSide, had hold of the end of a rope where it trailed away from the coils that encircled SilverSide and pinned his wings to his sides. Wolruf was sitting on the front seat directly behind SilverSide. Derec had unwound her from SilverSide once they thought he was under control.

Ariel climbed slowly in and sat down on the back seat.

Derec climbed in and came back to sit beside her. Jacob drove the lorry onto the road and then headed rapidly down Main Street toward the apartment.

"I warned you about SilverSide," Derec said. "You knew he could change form. I admit I didn't expect a change at so inauspicious a time. What did the aliens say before they flew off?"

"They were frightened, naturally, and angry. They had no reason to suspect we were going to produce a being in their own image, and twice as big. In their minds, I have betrayed their trust. They said as much. And they will close the dome tomorrow morning," Ariel said. "Your new protegé has just closed this planet to further development. Unless your genius and his remarkable abilities can somehow miraculously arrest the inevitable."

"You're being sarcastic, my dear," Derec confirmed.

A couple of intersections passed swiftly behind, and then he said, "But you know we might just pull off that miracle."

"Fat chance," she said.

"No. A slim chance, but a chance nonetheless."

She didn't answer, but got up and went to the front of the lorry to sit on the front seat directly behind Jacob Winterson. Right then, Jacob seemed like the only friend she had. She looked right through him, though, staring into a grim tomorrow and not seeing at all his remarkable musculature.

Wolruf reached over and laid a fat-fingered hand atop Ariel's small hand. Ariel didn't move and hardly noticed. After a moment the hand was withdrawn.

When they got to the apartment, she jumped out before the others and strode off. It was a walking pout, a demonstration for Derec's benefit, and she admitted that with one part of her mind. With the other part, she half expected him to come after her and was disappointed when he didn't. She could now think of several things she wanted to say to him. She returned as Jacob was putting lunch on the table.

After a lunch that tasted like sawdust, she went out on the balcony to get away from the others but took Jacob with her. They sat down on the bench that lined the streetside rail.

"Jacob, did SilverSide give any indication he was going to pull a stunt like that? Where is he, anyway?"

She hadn't thought to ask until that moment. She had wanted to forget about SilverSide, and she had succeeded better than she expected. Her thoughts had been on Aurora. She had felt quite homesick all through lunch, and Derec hadn't helped. He had been just as silent as she. Her walk had cooled her irate thoughts. She didn't feel up to an argument so she kept quiet and ate. Immediately after lunch Derec had jumped up and gone into the small bedroom.

Her feeling of isolation had been intensified not only by Derec's silence but by Wolruf's silence as well. That, too, had persisted all through lunch. She felt again the soft touch of Wolruf's hand as it came to rest on her hand when they were riding back in the lorry.

"To answer your most immediate question first, Master Derec forced SilverSide to lay on the floor of the small bedroom when we first came in," Jacob said. "SilverSide had trouble getting through the doorways. He was both taller and wider than the openings. It was difficult for him to bend over and at the same time go through the doorway sideways while wrapped with rope.

"To answer your first question, the wild one, as Mandelbrot calls him—it seems particularly apt—the wild one talked to us briefly, but he gave no indication that a change was imminent."

"He said nothing unusual, then?" Ariel asked.

"He seems not to know what humans are. This matter of imprinting and changing from one form to another: were you aware that he goes through these changes seeking to find the species he can finally call human?"

"Derec suggested that might be the case."

"Will he then cease to protect what he considers the lesser species?"

"I presume so. Derec seems to think so."

"Does that not make him an entity of some danger to humans?"

"It would seem so."

"Then should he not be deactivated?"

"I hadn't thought so before today. Derec seems to regard him as a valuable experiment that must be protected. And from the brief conversation we had, I suspect he still feels that way."

"Perhaps you should talk to him again, Miss Ariel. Both Mandelbrot and I are concerned that the wild one may get out of control. We are both perturbed by the First Law, and find it even more difficult to be around the wild one now that he has taken on this new alien form."

"You're right, Jacob. I should talk to Derec."

She placed her hand on Jacob's neck and softly traced the muscles as though she were stroking a pet. His concern touched her. It was she he was concerned about. It is difficult for a young woman to ignore such concern when it comes from a warm-skinned being as handsome as Jacob. He was a dear, like a big brother.

That thought confused her. When had she stopped thinking of Jacob as a robot? Her regard for him was sisterly, was it not? It couldn't be anything more than that, surely. In spite of the way Derec ignored her in his interest with the wild one, SilverSide.

Perhaps her own impetuous experiment was getting out of hand. Since Derec had arrived on Oyster World, he had not seemed the dear thing she had dreamed about so intensely.

And Jacob's concern was pleasing, and the feel of his muscular neck was certainly stimulating.

With that wild thought she jerked her hand away, jumped up, walked into the apartment, and threw open the door to the bedroom where Derec had gone immediately after lunch and where Jacob said they were keeping SilverSide.

Derec had removed the rope, and SilverSide was sitting on the floor between twin beds. He was leaning back against the wall and had balled in that curious way the aliens had of reducing their surface area. That decreased his height by half.

Derec was sitting on the far bed and had to look up to peer into the robot's red-rimmed eyes.

Ariel sat down on the other bed. Jacob had followed her. He stayed near the door, standing with his back against the wall.

"I have explained the crisis he has caused in our relations with the Ceremyons," Derec said, "and SilverSide is willing to try to straighten things out. He does not wish to offend the beings he is trying to emulate and serve."

"They might likely destroy him before he gets the chance to do any serving," Ariel said. "They were quite disturbed."

"That is the chance I must take, Ariel," SilverSide said, "but I do not think that is likely."

The title *Miss* was stressed by its absence in SilverSide's remark. He had clearly imprinted on the aliens in thought as well as in form.

"Still, you had best shout at them from a distance," Ariel said. "Out of flamethrowing range."

"Communication by radio accomplishes the same thing," SilverSide said, "without the danger you suggest."

"One must first understand their radiospeech," Ariel said. "The modulation is pure ultrasonic gibberish."

"I have been working on that ever since we arrived. It is not different from the ultrasound they used to converse privately during your meeting with them. That meeting provided the clues I needed to understand the radio transmissions I had picked up the evening of our arrival. I am now modestly fluent in the language.

"So fluent that I suspect you will find several representatives of their species awaiting us outside and probably well within flamethrowing range."

Derec jumped up from the bed and ran from the bedroom to the French window that opened onto the balcony. Ariel followed him. He started to go out but stopped. There were two aliens perched on the balcony rail, clearly visible through the sheer curtains in spite of the permanent dusk created by the dome. They were silhouetted against the white building across the street like two huge black crows. There were probably more at street level.

Derec and Ariel went back to the bedroom.

"You have been talking to them!" Derec said quietly but with emphasis.

"Yes," SilverSide said. "I have already opened my own negotiations."

"And who have you been talking to?" Derec asked.

"The leader called Sarco."

"And what do they want?"

"My release. I told them I was being held prisoner."

"Hardly. You could have broken the ropes any time you wanted to, either before or after we got here."

"Perhaps, but I didn't want to risk damaging my wings. To make myself aerodynamic I've had to sacrifice my original strength and ruggedness to the stamina and lightness needed for extended flight, which unavoidably entails a certain fragility.

"But now I must go talk to Master Sarco."

"Tell them the truth," Ariel said. "Explain our sincerity and our lack of knowledge of this last transformation of yours."

"I must always tell the truth. I cannot do otherwise," SilverSide said.

"But you do sometimes omit things," Derec said. "Try to tell everything that is relevant to our situation."

"My first concern must be for my new masters, but I do not easily forget those like LifeCrier and Wolruf who have been kind to me. Roping and binding, however, can hardly be described as kind."

"Think of Wolruf, then," Derec said. "And the many kindnesses I have shown you before this last incident."

"I must go and confer with Sarco," SilverSide said as he rolled to his feet, still balled. Then he partially straightened, still bent sideways, and sidled through the bedroom door.

CHAPTER 19

THE LAW OF HUMANICS

Circling far above normal charge altitude, Synapo watched the silver alien and his escort of Ceremyons—all less than half his size—as they headed toward The Cliff of Time, far below, toward the gathering Sarco had called to hear the words of the alien.

Sarco was already waiting on the pinnacle of The Cliff of Time. Synapo had seen him arrive a quarter-hour before, not long after that final radio transmission that had set up the gathering.

Synapo balled, and as he dropped, he feathered an exposed edge of a wing so that it set him in rotation and in motion toward the Cliff of Time as though he were rolling down a ramp.

His progress toward the Cliff of Time matched the progress of the small escort of Ceremyons who had the silver alien in their midst, so that Synapo and they arrived at the gathering almost simultaneously.

Synapo took up his perch on the adjacent lower crag, the position Sarco had occupied during that earlier gathering. His Cerebron elite were already aligned on the table rock below.

The alien who called himself SilverSide stood in front of the center of the line of Myostrians below Sarco. The Myostrian leader wasted no time. He began the interrogation of the alien as soon as Synapo settled onto his perch.

"Who are you and what is your purpose in contacting us?" Sarco asked.

"I am a robot, and I am here to serve you," SilverSide replied.

In spite of himself, Synapo was impressed. The silver alien had mastered the Ceremyon tongue and now mouthed it with only a slight accent.

"You are a servant, like the servants who built the city we have nullified?" Sarco said.

"Yes, only somewhat more versatile," the alien replied.

"Were you created this morning, at the time of our meeting with the aliens?"

"No. I was created on another planet. That was merely a transformation this morning."

"To what end?"

"To follow as best I can the laws that I am governed by, the laws of the beings who created me."

"And what is the nature of those laws?" Sarco asked.

"I may not injure a human being," SilverSide replied, "or through inaction, allow a human being to come to harm.

"I must obey the orders given me by human beings except where such orders would conflict with the First Law.

"And I must protect my own existence, as long as such protection does not conflict with the First or Second Laws."

"Those are the same laws that govern the servants who built the city," Sarco said.

"Yes," SilverSide said. "We are all robots, or so I am told."

"And these human beings," Sarco said, "you consider them your creators and the ones you must serve?"

"Yes."

"Then why do you seek to serve us?"

"The laws and my programming do not make clear what human beings are. Clearly, only beings more intelligent than I could have created me. I seek to know and understand all such beings. Until I met your species, Ariel and Derec were the most intelligent beings I had found—with the possible exception of Wolruf."

"We are the most intelligent of the beings now on this planet," Sarco said, "but we did not create you. We were told by Miss Ariel Welsh that she and beings like her are human beings. We have no reason to disbelieve her. Why do you?"

"Neither Ariel, Derec, nor Wolruf created me, or so they say."

"You were not created this morning to intimidate us?" Sarco asked again.

Synapo agreed with Sarco. That was a most important point.

"No. I merely transformed from my imprint on Wolruf."

"Then this morning when the meeting began you had the shape of the being called Wolruf, one of the three we talked with this morning?"

"Yes."

"And you did not transform according to instructions by Miss Ariel Welsh?"

"No. I imprinted on a being like you called Synapo who seemed to me the more intelligent of the two aliens at the meeting."

"That is Synapo standing over there."

Sarco pointed with the middle appendage of his right wing toward his friend on the other crag.

"I am Sarco, the other one at the meeting, the one of lesser intelligence."

His sarcasm was not lost on Synapo and the other members of the Ceremyon elite, but it went completely by SilverSide.

He walked over to stand on the table rock below Synapo.

"You are clearly the most intelligent being on this planet," SilverSide said, addressing Synapo. "You or someone very like you must have created me, and so you must be a human being."

"No," Synapo replied. "I am not a human being."

"What is a human, Master Synapo?" the robot asked.

And then Synapo understood the robot's dilemma. It was, for the robot, a difficult problem in semantics that had become clear to Synapo only at that moment when he replaced the words *human being* in the robot's governing laws with the word *creator*. That was the way this particular robot, for some reason, actually thought about his laws. Creator, or human being, or whatever term occupied that position in the robot's laws, had not been defined. That was now clear.

Perhaps human beings had created the Avery robots, but this robot was not at all sure that the same creatures had created him even though both he and the Averies were governed by laws that were structurally similar. But from all the data, it seemed quite clear to Synapo that it was the human beings who had created the robot and that it was they his laws referred to.

"Miss Ariel Welsh and all those like her are human beings, and it was human beings that created you," Synapo said. "It is they you must serve, and of all of them, I would suggest you give your most devoted service to Miss Ariel Welsh. We have gravely misjudged her and injured her now a second time.

"And when you get back, pick a being for your model—for your imprint—that will serve her best. You make a poor Ceremyon."

There was a long pause.

"A last question," SilverSide finally said. "You have heard me recite the Laws of Robotics which govern my behavior. It would help me serve Miss Ariel if I knew what the Laws of Humanics were. Have you yet deduced those laws from your dealings with the humans, Miss Ariel and Master Derec?"

"There is only one Law of Humanics. All others are corollary to it. The Law of Humanics is the law of all natural beings, whether of low intellect or high, whether Ceremyon, human, or lupine like your Wolruf.

"We all obey that one law without exception, even though at times—without thinking deeply—it may seem otherwise. We all evolved from chaos, and chaos governs our lives, but a seeming purpose can arise paradoxically from chaos, and it is that chaotic purpose which compels us to follow that one law.

"The law is quite simple: *We each do always whatever pleases us most.* That is the only Law of Humanics.

"Go now and serve well your Miss Ariel Welsh."

The wings of the robot SilverSide opened wide, stretched to their full extent, and as Synapo and all the Ceremyons watched, the wings seemed to slowly dissolve and contract into massive upper appendages as the torso shrunk to less than half its original height, as the legs swelled to produce heavy thighs and bulging calves.

When the transformation was complete, Synapo realized he had seen only one other alien with a shape like that, the alien servant, Jacob Winterson.

If he had used a little forethought, the alien SilverSide would have had an easier time getting back—if he had not been so anxious to effect a transformation. But Synapo thought no more about it as he took to the air, headed for a charge station above the center of the node compensator to garner what little was left of the sun's radiation that afternoon.

CHAPTER 20

NEURONIUS STRIKES BACK

The contradiction, the dilemma, tore at his mind, grabbing at his reason, his sanity, setting it adrift in small silent screams like flotsam flowing over the edge of The Cliff of Time. SilverSide had found the superintelligence he was looking for, and that intelligence had declared itself not human. Ariel Welsh was human, it said, and Derec Avery. Go serve Miss Ariel Welsh, it said, and find the form that would do that best.

He had to yield to that higher intelligence—there was no escaping the logic—yet he had violated the Laws, he had not served humans well, and that was a thought he could not bear to face.

He grabbed desperately at his reason, rolling it into a tight ball, and escaped into the all-absorbing task of imprinting on the memories he had stored of Jacob Winterson. He stood there on the table rock long after the Ceremyons had left, throwing himself deeper and deeper into the imprint, delving and exploring and testing far beyond anything he had ever done before, changing his microbotic cells to create those of proper function and pigmentation with which to form this time the perfect image: the bronze skin, the brush-cut blond hair with the same fine strands, the corded neck that kept the girth of the head itself all the way to the shoulders, the bulging biceps and chest muscles, the narrow waist, the powerful thighs, wrapped beneath the skin with heavy muscular ropes.

He created the same unlined high forehead; the fine Nordic nose; the wide-set, deep blue eyes; the high cheek-bones; the generous mouth; the jutting, cleft chin.

When the imprint was finally finished, he walked to the edge of the table rock and stood there staring down from the escarpment at the sharp line that demarcated the forest from the plain. That delineation led his eyes to the iridescent dome covering the robot city, shimmering in the sunlight, and seeming—mirage-like—to hang suspended above the horizon, transparent and seemingly void of any contents.

He had a sudden impulse to spread his wings and glide away from the escarpment toward that dome and Miss Ariel Welsh. That was the Laws speaking to him, and for just a fleeting second, he felt a contrary and equally powerful impulse to escape in the other direction, and then the Laws reasserted themselves, and wingless, he began making his way recklessly down the escarpment, using the superhuman strength in his fingers and toes to cling to the face of the rock and scurry down it like a chameleon.

As he passed down the jointed and folded stone strata exposed by the upheaval of The Cliff of Time, he crossed earlier and earlier geologic ages of Oyster World, and seemed himself to be carried back through the short time he had existed to his origin on another world, as though he were descending through space and time to the forest of his birth.

He slid the last few meters down a steep talus of hard-packed black gravel to a flat plate of rock that slanted into the ground where the grass of the plain began. He got up and headed at a hard trot for the forest a half-kilometer away, intending to immerse himself in the lush jungle, in a familiar habitat like that where he had first known being. He felt a longing for it quite unlike anything he had ever felt before.

He was still ten meters from that cool solace when one of the black-winged aliens stepped with a short wobble from the concealment provided by the dense shrubbery.

"You are the one called SilverSide," the alien said.

"True, I am SilverSide," the robot replied.

He continued toward the black alien but slowed as the alien wobbled backward, staying between him and the forest.

"I am Neuronius," the alien said. "I must talk with you, SilverSide."

"I have already talked at length with your people, Neuronius, and now I must proceed into the forest to reflect on all that I have learned."

"There is much more that I can teach you, SilverSide; much that would benefit you and your kind in their dealings with the Ceremyons."

"I know too much now. I cannot absorb all that I have heard already. Would you have me even more at odds with myself?"

"But there is much more about the Ceremyons you need to know in order to properly serve Miss Ariel Welsh. Would you throw away such an opportunity?"

The alien had wobbled back under the cover of the tall conifers as they talked, leading SilverSide along a path through the dense shrubbery. Now he stopped, still facing SilverSide, blocking his passage into the jungle.

"Let me pass," SilverSide said. "I do not wish to harm a being that so much resembles the mighty Synapo."

"Synapo is nothing, SilverSide. I can teach you the secret of the dome that separates space and time. Then when your Miss Ariel Welsh must deal with him, she can deal on equal terms. That secret can be a weapon as well as a tool."

Confused as he was, with Synapo ordering him to serve Miss Ariel, it was as though Synapo himself were telling him to listen to Neuronius.

"I will listen a short while, then," SilverSide said, "but then I must leave you."

So they proceeded a little way farther along the path to a small clearing alongside a brook. Neuronius opened his wings, fluttered them as though to shake out uncomfortable creases, and then folded them to his sides again. He tottered over to the brook, sat down on a low flat rock lying half into the small stream, and dangled his feathery tail in the water.

"The secret of the dome is merely a matter of understanding space and time and their relationship to black concavities," Neuronius said. "That relationship is best described in the terms of tensor analysis."

SilverSide was already familiar with tensor mathematics, quantum mechanics, general relativity, and spacetime physics, which, although more sophisticated in their language and applications, were still the basic sciences developed by Schroedinger and Einstein.

Hyperjump and hyperwave technology were little more than tools that man had discovered quite accidentally and still did not really understand, any more than he understood what an electron was.

So now Neuronius led SilverSide along mathematical pathways dealing with space and time which, familiar at first, became rapidly unfamiliar and bizarre, and twisted his positronic thought-ways in patterns that became ever more uncomfortable.

With that discomfort he began to suspect that Neuronius—if he could twist SilverSide's mind to such a degree—was perhaps superior to Synapo. Certainly Neuronius was different, and maybe it was the difference of a superior mind. He continued to record what Neuronius was saying but stopped generation of associative memory links—stopped *listening*—in order to pursue that intriguing comparison of the two aliens. Finally he interrupted Neuronius in his lecture.

"What is a human, Neuronius?"

"What?"

"I have been searching for humans, the beings whose laws govern my behavior. I had thought that humans must be the most intelligent species in the galaxy, but Synapo says Miss Ariel is human, and that he is not, even though he is more intelligent than Miss Ariel."

Neuronius hesitated. In the silence, the twitter of the jungle birds came to SilverSide, registering with sharp clarity a serenity and tranquillity that was strikingly at odds with the turmoil in his mind.

"I am human," Neuronius said. "Synapo is not."

Was there no peace in this life? Unquestionably Neuronius was more intelligent than Miss Ariel, and it seemed more and more apparent that Neuronius was indeed more intelligent than Synapo, yet Synapo was the leader of the Ceremyons. The logical question came immediately to mind.

"Where do you fit into the society of the Ceremyons?"

"I am not a Ceremyon," Neuronius replied. "I may ap-

pear to be so, but I am not. I am far superior to any Ceremyon."

"Are there others of your kind?"

"Not on this planet. This one is mine. The others each
dominate a planet of their own."

SilverSide was impressed. Yet there was something
about Neuronius that bothered him—his wordiness, perhaps;
Mandelbrot bothered him that way, but there it was a bother
that need not concern him. Mandelbrot was merely a robot.
But Neuronius was not a robot, and his words were exceedingly tantalizing, and yet disturbing, uneasily so. Mandelbrot had never made him feel uneasy.

If Neuronius were the only one of his kind on this
planet, he had to be the most intelligent being here—if he
were indeed more intelligent than Synapo. So he was back
to that simple comparison. On balance, Neuronius appeared
to be the more intelligent. He had delved far deeper into
dome technology than Synapo had during his meeting with
the mammals. Synapo had seemed to be withholding information, as though he were not altogether sure of what he
was saying. Neuronius certainly did not give that impression. He seemed to be bursting with information. So much
so that SilverSide's positronic potentials on the subject of
domes were now a complete jumble.

His indecision was excruciating. He had to get the question resolved. He had thought it was resolved, and arriving
at that point once again, after having been through it so
many times, had been an unsettling experience that he had
accepted finally with his imprint on Jacob Winterson. Now
all that ordeal seemed to have gone for naught. But how
was he to get it resolved?

"I must know who is the more intelligent, you or Synapo. Can you suggest how that can be determined?"

"I am not interested in your petty games, SilverSide. I am offering you knowledge that will allow you to serve whomever you please with greater efficiency. Surely you can see that."

"But whom I am to serve must clearly be resolved before the service itself can take place. Surely, with your intelligence you can see that."

"One can train for service quite efficiently without knowing who will ultimately be served."

"But how one trains—what type of service should be stressed—depends on who will be served."

That seemed clear to SilverSide, and if Neuronius couldn't understand something as simple as that, he could not be as intelligent as he had at first appeared.

"You are right, of course," Neuronius said. "But I find it exceedingly distasteful and uncomfortable to promote myself at the expense of others. It makes me appear slow, I suppose. I have no desire to denigrate Synapo.

"You must have this question resolved, must you?" Neuronius said as a small green jet flamed momentarily in the air below his red eyes.

That was one piece of alien body language SilverSide had learned to read. It lent an air of great sincerity to the discomfort Neuronius claimed to feel.

"Yes," SilverSide said.

"Then you must serve me. I am human, the only human on this planet and the most intelligent of the various species that exist here, and certainly more intelligent than Synapo."

That must do for the moment. SilverSide could do nothing more immediately. He must try to accept what Neuronius had said, but the acceptance was not something that was going to come easily. He had come to many forks in the path of his quest for humans, and each time—at each crux—the resolution of the dilemma subjected him to more agony.

That conflict, repeated now, and his attempt to cope with it, sent little stabs of pain shooting through his positronic brain, little stabs that congealed into a ball of pure agony, and finally he could bear the pain no longer. He jumped up and fled down the path into the forest while Neuronius's shouts grew fainter and fainter.

Finally exhausted, after Neuronius was left far behind, he stopped. He had left the path and had been plunging through dense vegetation, ripping it out by the roots when it would not yield otherwise. He stood there, recharging his reserve pack. In the wild scramble, he had used all the output of his microfusion reactor and more, bleeding his reserves until he was forced to stop.

Then he slowly began to transform from one imprint to the next, trying to find peace of mind, going back from Jacob to Synapo to Wolruf to Derec and finally to KeenEye, to the form in which he had first known being and BeastTalk.

In the wolf-like KeenEye imprint, using only a fraction of the output from her reactor, she began loping easily through the forest, finding and following the animal trails that had been created by the natural denizens of Oyster World. She found a measure of peace in the pleasant natural scents left there by those very basic creatures, creatures much lower in the scale of life than LifeCrier, but still so like him in their familiar but dissimilar musky scent.

The night passed as she roamed aimlessly through the Forest of Repose.

Dawn found her at the edge of the forest below The Cliff of Time, back at the trail that led to the clearing where Neuronius had lectured her. The night had served to clarify one thing. She must talk to Synapo again before she could make a final judgment of the humanity of Neuronius.

She could find Synapo by radio, but the only tactful way to talk to him was on the wing. She could not ask him to come to her. He had left the clear impression he did not want to talk to her further. She must go back to the Synapo imprint in order to talk to him on his terms.

When SilverSide finished the transition to blackbody form, the sun was just rising over The Cliff of Time. There was a Ceremyon circling high over the dome in Synapo's accustomed station. SilverSide wobble-hopped into the air and climbed in a long, slanted rise, gaining the necessary altitude to reach the alien in the course of spanning the distance from The Cliff of Time.

When SilverSide arrived above the dome, the alien's hook was pointing aft, so he must be amenable to conversation.

With his hook also pointing aft, SilverSide quietly glided up beside the alien and said, "Leader Synapo, I need to resolve a matter of..."

"Sarco," the alien said. "Synapo will arise late this morning."

Talking to Sarco might be better than talking to Synapo. Sarco knew both Neuronius and Synapo and was a leader himself. Who better to judge between the two?

"I must get a matter of extreme urgency resolved, leader Sarco, a matter of understanding Synapo better so as to compare him with Neuronius—and properly place him in a hierarchy of intelligence relative to Neuronius—who claims to be the most intelligent creature on this planet."

"Neuronius? By the Great Petero," Sarco hissed, emitting a small green flame simultaneously.

"Neuronius says further that he is a human, and not a

Ceremyon, that there are no others of his species on this planet."

"I hesitate to term him a Ceremyon myself," Sarco said, "but unfortunately he is—a paranoid Ceremyon suffering delusions of grandeur. He is certainly not more intelligent than Synapo, take my word for it. He wouldn't have been ejected from the Cerebron elite if he were."

"He has been a member of Ceremyon society then?"

"Most certainly. Something we all regret now, but did little about at the time, because Neuronius was so insidiously clever. Cleverness, however, does not equate to wisdom and intelligence."

"Thank you for your help. You have been of great assistance. I will take my leave now."

SilverSide balled and dropped.

CHAPTER 21

REPRIEVE

They had posted Jacob and Mandelbrot on the balcony of the apartment to watch throughout the night for premature closing of the dome.

"This reminds me of another night before you came," Jacob said to Mandelbrot. "I spent it much as we are destined to spend this night, but I did not have your company."

"I trust nothing untoward happened that night," Mandelbrot said.

"No. But that was the last night Miss Ariel spent under a dome that might imprison her inescapably. She spent the next night in the lorry, sleeping on the back seat. The next morning that first crisis with the aliens was resolved."

"Let us hope this crisis will be similarly resolved with a pleasant ending. What are the chances of the wild one, do you think?"

"As you observed earlier, he is unpredictable," Jacob said, "but I wished him a great deal of success for Miss Ariel's sake. It would seem that wish has gone astray. His return is long overdue."

"I fear you are right," Mandelbrot said. "Master Derec observed that the alien leaders returned in midafternoon to their normal stations, though that was not altogether clear to me, since one looks so much like another."

They had all waited, sitting in the lorry outside the dome, watching for SilverSide's return.

A flock of the black aliens had returned from the direction they took when they flew off with him in their midst. But he was not with them on their return. That did not bode well for the safety of the wild one.

For Jacob, the night passed much as it had before, except that this time he had the company and the conversation of Mandelbrot. They had a short inconclusive exchange regarding the Laws of Humanics, and then they began a long investigative conversation, delving into the many ramifications of Jacob's new knowledge of hyperwave communication, the knowledge that there were two types of modulation, not just one: the old discrete type that they were all familiar with, and now this new continuous type, that they had deduced from the aliens' remarks, and which now explained Derec's mysterious internal monitor link with the supervisors of the robot cities. The technology for that link was developed by the erratic Dr. Avery, and understood only by him until Miss Ariel had pushed them into drawing parallels and connections with the two types of hyperspace travel: jump teleportation, which was related to discrete hyperwave modulation, and Key teleportation, which was related to continuous hyperwave modulation. In the course of the long night, they drew parallels and derived conclusions that they recorded by joint effort as a long and comprehensive dissertation for the robot city's archives, an exhaustive treatise that was intended to answer any and all questions on the subject.

• • •

It was a longer night for Ariel and Derec, a night they spent closeted in their bedroom to avoid exposing Wolruf to their disagreement. That friction had now escalated beyond the mild and not unusual interplay for dominance that characterizes the relationship of many pairs of lovers.

It started immediately after dinner, when Ariel had gone into the bedroom to get away from the rest of them. She was feeling intensely sorry for herself. Why was it so important that she pull off this effort at conciliation and cohabitation with a bunch of aliens, this attempt to save and incorporate into their galactic community a world she didn't give a darn about?

Was it merely a matter of pride, an attempt once again to prove her capacity for leadership? Derec had never insisted that his must always be the last word, the final and ultimate judgment on things that affected both of them and that they were both mutually responsible for.

Yet why did he always make her feel childish when she tried to establish her individuality in that regard? She had as much right to make decisions as he did, and frequently the decisions he made that were right, were right only because her advice kept him from going astray.

Certainly she knew more about controlling robots than he did. He might know more about what made them tick physically, but she knew far more about how to get the most out of them socially, even out of Mandelbrot, who Derec had created himself. Her upbringing on Aurora, surrounded by robotic servants, had given her experience in that regard, a natural dominance over robots that could never be achieved without that easy confidence one acquires in childhood when waited on hand and foot by robots. Strangely, Derec had not had that common upbringing.

One can become quite attached to them and even treat them like pets. The intelligence of some robots can make that attachment even stronger than that for an animal pet, particularly if the robot is one of the rare humaniform creations, the kind Aurorans were so leery of. Jacob was certainly more than a pet.

That thought sneaked up on her and startled her now when it came so consciously to mind. Before Derec had come to Oyster World, she had been feeling guilty about Jacob, about how obviously uncomfortable Derec had been in the company of that handsome robot on Aurora. Now she didn't feel guilty at all. Derec had more than overcome those odds with the robotic monster he had brought with him from the wolf planet. With all her skill in handling robots, she had no confidence at all that she could reliably control SilverSide.

And now he had caused an irreparable disruption of the tremendous rapport she had established with the Ceremyons, particularly with Synapo. Sarco had remained a small enigma, a sort of friendly enemy, as best she could judge. She sensed that it was not that he disliked her, but more that he could not treat her as anything but an alien. Well, she felt the same way about him, so that made them even. And now, with SilverSide's shenanigans, Sarco was indeed the enemy, she felt sure.

Derec walked into the bedroom at that moment, and that feeling for Sarco was transferred to Derec, except that in Derec's case the feeling was not nearly so mild. Derec was more an enemy lover, and one that she could not love now because he had become so much the enemy.

"Come on out, Ariel," Derec said. "You've got no reason to punish Wolruf by pouting in here. Maybe you've got a case against me—and I'm not even sure of that—but you've got no reason at all to make her feel bad, too. She's probably more on your side than mine. After all, she's the one who bailed out your farm project."

Ariel didn't say anything. She was sitting in the far corner of the room—burrowed into an overstuffed chair that resembled a bean bag more than a piece of furniture—and looking out a corner window, adjacent to the balcony, which overlooked Main Street. She could see Jacob and Mandelbrot standing at the end of the balcony, looking toward the opening in the dome.

"SilverSide may bring the Ceremyons around," Derec continued, "but if he doesn't, we could be just as well off. We've probably got no business setting up shop on an inhabited planet. I've sort of felt that way ever since I arrived."

Ariel still didn't see any need to respond and even less to respond to his last remark. He did have a minor point when it came to Wolruf. It was her expertise that would have made the robot farms practical, if SilverSide hadn't screwed up everything.

"And anyway, the robot farm project is a dumb idea," Derec added. "The city robots are just that, city robots. City planners and city builders. Trying to make farmers out of them is like trying to make a silk purse out of a sow's ear."

Now he was getting personal.

"You're forgetting they've already done it on a planet called Robot City," Ariel said. "And you're such a great engineer you didn't know your own internal hardware was modulating hyperwave in continuous mode. You even thought your screwy father had invented some altogether new form of communication. Right, genius?!"

"You're likely wrong about that. What are the odds that a woman and a bunch of dumb robots are going to come up with anything the least way innovative?"

"That's it, isn't it? Because the robot farms are a woman's idea, it's a stupid idea. You are a male chauvinist pig, Derec Avery."

"And you are a libertine tease, Ariel Welsh."

"I suppose you're referring to Jacob. Getting down to the nitty gritty, getting really personal."

"You weren't, I suppose."

"What? Calling you a chauvinist pig?"

"What do you call it?"

"Stating facts."

"And the hyperwave modulation. I suppose you call those facts, too, those aberrant mental peregrinations."

She didn't let on that she didn't know what "peregrinations" meant.

"Continuous modulation is a fact, you ninny. And you don't need to take that from a silly woman. Ask any Ceremyon."

"Darn, Ariel, why are we fighting like this? I just came in here to be nice."

"Telling me how much I'm hurting Wolruf? That's nice?"

"It's the truth."

"And you're going to be sure I know it's the truth, right? So you can hurt me a little more."

"I didn't come in here to hurt you. Just to try to poke some sense into your thick head."

"Those are nice pleasant words, too. Keep it up, Derec."

"It's the truth, though. That's why I came in here."

"How Wolruf feels isn't what's really bothering you, is it, Derec?"

"Oh? What would you suggest?"

"It's really Jacob, isn't it? You're jealous of a robot, aren't you?"

"I don't care if you love that freak machine. It's none of my affair."

Ariel didn't say anything to rebut that last remark. She was a tease, and she wanted him to dwell on his last thought without being distracted.

"No," Derec said after the space of a breath or two, "I do care because if it's true, you would be darn sick. And I do love you, Ariel, whether you want me to or not, whether you love a robot or not. So if it's true, I want to help you, and rather desperately."

He walked into the adjoining personal and closed the door.

It went on like that the rest of the night. They didn't get much sleep. Nor did they make up as they usually did when they had finally exhausted one another emotionally.

Derec slept on his side of the room, and Ariel slept on hers, but they didn't sleep much, keeping each other awake by tossing and turning, and generally flouncing around to enhance the other's anger.

Morning finally came. They ate an early breakfast in silence, and they all rode in the lorry to the opening in the dome well before the time when dome construction would normally start if it were going to take place.

It did not take place. Instead the two aliens Synapo and Sarco arrived in their usual dramatic fashion with a great show of black wings. Ariel, Derec, and Wolruf climbed down from the lorry to stand near the right front wheel and talk with the two Ceremyons.

"It is our turn to request an audience, Miss Ariel Welsh," Synapo said, "for we have discovered that a misunderstanding exists between us. You should not be held responsible for the errant behavior of servant machinery—apparently not yours—trying to pursue its orders in the best way it knows how. I am referring, of course, to the servant you call SilverSide. The question is: Whose machinery is it and whence did it come? It came to our world aboard your vessel, Wolruf. At that time it had your form. Can you explain that?"

"No more than you can explain why it took your form," Wolruf said. "Derec knows more about it than anyone else."

"I first encountered it on another planet," Derec said. "At that time it was the leader of a pack of intelligent lupine beings. They were attacking and interfering with Avery robots during their construction of a city much like the one you have enclosed with your weather node compensator. I made a sort of peace with it in order to study its physical nature and programmed behavior. I recognized at the time that that involved certain risks. I alone am responsible for any inconvenience the robot may have caused you. As you have recognized, its objectives are basically benign even though its behavior may at times seem erratic."

"As you also recognize, by your own words, benign objectives can sometimes motivate evil doings, particularly when two aberrants interact. I must warn you all that we have an aberrant Cerebron on the wing, more irrational than your SilverSide, and the two have already begun to interact.

"You are familiar with the Cerebron, Neuronius, Miss Ariel Welsh. It was he who impetuously curtailed one of our earlier meetings. The Cerebrons in full caucus have now stripped him of all authority, something I could not do on my own during our meeting because of the rules that regulate our government. We Cerebrons can do little more at this time. Yet he is a danger to all of us, and his interaction with SilverSide, benign though it may seem to the robot, could create a very explosive situation.

"So you see, Derec, you feel responsible for SilverSide,

and we feel responsible for Neuronius, but our feelings can do little at this time to correct a nasty situation created by your scientific interest and our governmental restrictions, which prevent both of us from neutralizing the agitators.

"But the primary purpose of this meeting is to inform you that the compensator will not be closed and you may proceed with cultivation of your plants and construction of your transportation terminal."

"Thank you," Ariel said. "We are grateful for your foresight and will proceed with those projects."

"We have not seen SilverSide for almost a full day now," Derec said. "Do you know where he is or what he's been doing?"

Sarco spoke now.

"He is exceedingly confused about who his master should be. Based on his own programming, Miss Ariel Welsh is his most likely master, and Synapo so instructed him yesterday afternoon at The Cliff of Time. He immediately began a transformation into the form of your robot Jacob Winterson, and was last seen that afternoon climbing down the rock face of the escarpment.

"Then early this morning he ascended to meet me in the form of a Ceremyon, as best he can manage, and as you know, that is a startlingly huge Ceremyon.

"It was then that we learned of his interaction with Neuronius, who had tried to pass himself off as the only human on the planet in order to win SilverSide's allegiance. I hope I was able to forestall that. I watched SilverSide descend to The Plain of Serenity and watched as he transformed to a being that looked from that distance somewhat like Wolruf, but probably twice her size. I last saw him entering The Forest of Repose in that form."

"That would be his KeenEye imprint," Derec said, "one

of the lupine creatures he copied on that other planet. Thank you. At least we know he's still alive and hope he'll return. Thank you very much."

The two Ceremyons turned then and took to the air.

Immediately after the meeting, in the short time that was left before lunch, Ariel, Derec, and Wolruf began planning the robot farm experiment, discussing in broad outline the revisions in the programming of the Avery robots that would be required, not only for the many different farms themselves, but also for the creation of the city's new terminal facilities that would be needed to support the farms.

SilverSide had not returned by the time they sat down to lunch. In spite of all the trouble he had caused her, Ariel felt inexplicably concerned about his welfare.

CHAPTER 22

THE EGG

Once again SilverSide was in turmoil. All was confusion. Who should he believe? He wished only to evade the dilemma. He metamorphosed, escaping back to the relative peace of his wolfish "childhood," back to the days when LifeCrier had guided him into the life of the pack on the wolf planet.

Thus, midmorning found SilverSide imprinted on the wolf-like female KeenEye, trotting along an animal trail far from the robot city. As she had the night before, she spent the late morning and early afternoon exploring the vast Forest of Repose, its trails, brooks, rivers, and lakes that lay within ten kilometers of the city.

Monitoring the field lines of Oyster World's natural magnetism kept her oriented during her aimless roving, so that as the morning waned, she began to zero in on the dome without dwelling on what she was going to do when she got there.

In the early afternoon, she came to the edge of the forest opposite the mirage-like transparency that concealed the robot city. She sat down on her haunches and stared at the dome with unseeing eyes, mulling over—as she had all morning—what Neuronius and then Sarco had told her.

She could not escape the essential validity of Sarco's assessment of Neuronius—a self-centered, paranoid psychopath—nor could she any longer ignore Synapo's directive to serve Miss Ariel and the feeling that that could best be done in the male imprint of Jacob Winterson, who was already serving Miss Ariel with apparently great efficiency and to her obvious satisfaction.

The Jacob imprint would help, but it was still not clear exactly how she could best serve Miss Ariel. The physics Neuronius had expounded had only confused her, offering information that conflicted with her earlier knowledge of space and time. He had not clarified the physics, but had instead muddied it and left SilverSide worse off than she had been before. The new information was useless, and worse than useless in the confusion it created about the physics she had once known.

As she sat there in the quiet heat of the afternoon studying the dome and trying to make sense of the aborted discussion with Neuronius, she gradually became aware of a faint humming off to her left, nearer the dome but deeper in the forest. When the sound finally broke through her reverie, she rose and trotted along an animal path that led in the general direction of the hum.

The path led past the hum, and when SilverSide recognized that she had passed the point of closest approach, she started through the vegetation, heading directly for the sound. Although the ground was covered in that area, the cover was not dense, and she had no difficulty weaving through the shrubbery. As the hum grew steadily louder, she almost ran into its source as she came around a tall bush covered with pink blossoms.

She recognized the source instantly. It was a two-meter sphere, just as hers had been, and the duodecahedral structure of the coarse silvery cells of its skin, dulled by the heat of passage through Oyster World's atmosphere, told her instantly it was an egg similar to her own.

It lay atop the crushed base of two bushes, framed by pink flowers, set in green foliage which, in close proximity to the foreign surface, was now seared and wilted by the heat the egg had exuded earlier. It was now almost cool to the touch, almost ready for hatching. And it came to her then what she must do.

She kept the KeenEye form to speed her dash through the thin shrubbery of the forest, but when she came to the plain, she began the transformation to the Jacob imprint, stopping only long enough to fashion the heavy muscular legs that would take her the three kilometers to the dome's opening in the shortest length of time. As she ran along the wall of the dome, she completed the transformation to the masculine Jacob form well before he reached the opening on the north side.

As SilverSide approached the opening, Wohler-9 called to him from a small runabout parked near the west edge.

"I get no response from you on the comlink, Jacob."

"I am SilverSide," he said as he hopped into the passenger seat. "Take me to Miss Ariel Welsh."

Wohler-9 started the runabout, turned into the near southbound lane of Main Street, and proceeded rapidly down the street in the direction of the Compass Tower.

"I have instructions to take you to Master Derec at once, SilverSide."

"Where is Miss Ariel?" SilverSide asked.

"At the apartment."

"Good. Then we are proceeding in the right direction."

"Yes. Master Derec is working at the mainframe, which is currently on the second underground level of the Compass Tower."

When they came abreast of the apartment, SilverSide jumped out. Wohler-9 braked the runabout to a halt but remained seated.

"I must take you to Master Derec," Wohler-9 called to SilverSide's back.

"Later," SilverSide called over his shoulder as he ran into the building.

He took the stairs three at a time and burst into the apartment.

Ariel was sitting at the dining table reading a computer printout. The table was strewn with piles of computer output. Jacob was thumbing through the piles, apparently hunting for the next printout she would need.

SilverSide took in the scene, picked Ariel up, cradling her in his arms like a fragile baby, dashed out the door, down the stairs, and past Wohler-9, who was walking toward the apartment from the runabout.

Ariel had time to scream only once before she was deposited in the runabout. As she was being gently scooped up, she had screamed, "Jaaaacobbbb," with a Doppler modulation that trailed off like the whistle of a passing train.

Jacob Winterson had responded with the millisecond speed characteristic of Dr. Han Fastolfe's humaniform robots. But that speed was no match for the microseconds it took for all of SilverSide's motions, save for the brisk but gentle acceleration when he had picked up Ariel and started toward the door.

He and Ariel were speeding away from the apartment

building in the runabout as Jacob came pounding out of the apartment past Wohler-9.

Ariel's first scream had ended as she was being deposited in the runabout. Her next scream was delivered in the interrogative mode as they pulled away from the apartment.

"What are you doing?" she shrieked with an intensity that rattled SilverSide's auricular diaphragms—akin to eardrums.

"There was no time to explain, Miss Ariel," SilverSide shouted about the wind noise. "I need your presence urgently."

Jacob raced after them down Main Street but was soon left behind as SilverSide accelerated the small runabout to its maximum speed, weaving in and out of the traffic and avoiding an accident by the adeptness of the city central computer.

"Stop, you maniac," Ariel screamed. "Stop now."

SilverSide slowed the runabout noticeably and then promptly speeded up again. Consideration of his new knowledge of the Law of Humanics—humans were compelled to please themselves—overrode his own Second Law output—robots must obey human orders. He knew when Ariel had finally considered all the facts—after the fact—she would be pleased and would approve what he was doing.

"You are in no danger, Miss Ariel, but I cannot obey that order because of the overriding nature of the present situation which demands your presence at the birthing of . . . of . . ." and he added lamely, still shouting, "Of what I cannot be sure." And the shout died away as he said, "I can only hope."

Then Ariel, sobbing and screaming incoherently, beat on him with her hands clenched into small hard fists, beat on his shoulder first, and then finally, in desperation, beat on his head. But he felt nothing in the intensity of his purpose.

"You must stop that, Miss Ariel," he shouted. "You will hurt yourself."

And the calm way he shouted that above the sound of the rushing air and the obvious lack of effect her effort was having, must have calmed her, for she finally stopped and slumped down on the seat, seemingly exhausted, her hysteria spent.

They emerged from the opening, and SilverSide skidded the runabout in a sharp left turn to take them down the side of the dome.

"You must understand what is taking place," he shouted. "It is very important to me, to the new foundling, even to you, Miss Ariel, for I wish her to serve you well."

Ariel said nothing. She sat beside him like a limp doll.

"Another like me is being born. The egg lies in the forest even now, ready to hatch. She must have a proper model, a human female, so that she does not come into being confused, her imprint misguided as mine was. You must be there to guide her into this strange world. Do you understand what I am saying, Miss Ariel?"

Ariel still said nothing, but she had straightened a little in the seat, perhaps because to slump in the bouncing runabout was more uncomfortable than to sit up straight.

"You will not be harmed, Miss Ariel. After it's all over, when you think back on it, you will be glad you came. I know you will. You will be pleased with me. The Law of Humanics will guide you."

That seemed to comfort SilverSide. The Law of Humanics was working on the effect of his own Laws, regulating their relative potential to something that was less uncomfortable. He was doing something that he knew was going to please Ariel even though she was, perhaps, not pleased at the moment.

When they arrived at the forest, he braked to a halt, jumped out, and opened the door for Ariel. She got out calmly. She must have thought about what he had been shouting at her, for she didn't object when he gently took her hand to help her from the car.

That gave him confidence that she would follow him without being forced, and he let go of her hand and started into the woods. She stayed close behind him for the short, hurried walk it took to reach the egg.

SilverSide guided Ariel gently until she stood two meters from the egg, directly in front of the hatch, and then he left her there and hid behind the pink-flowered bush behind her.

The hatch began to open with a soft grinding sound.

SilverSide could look through the lower branches of the tall bush, past Ariel's right side, and see the hatch himself.

A silvery-gray, amorphous mass heaved itself above the bottom of the hatch and formed, in that part of its mass that hung over the edge of the opening, a shiny, multifaceted, grayish-green orb that it rotated slowly around—much like an eye rotating in its socket—as though it were surveying the entire landscape. The inspection narrowed then, and starting at Ariel's feet, the orb slowly scanned up until it was gazing at her head.

With that inspection completed, the blob elongated and pulled itself through the hatch as though it were one large muscle, like the foot of a huge snail. It slithered out of the hatch, coming to rest on the ground in front of Ariel like a thick pancake with the orb still intact in the center.

The facets of the orb slowly disappeared, absorbed into a grayish-green ring surrounding a black pupil, while the bulk of the orb turned white. A spherical mass the size of a small bowling ball began to rise from the pancake, lifting the eye—for it was clearly that now—and a second eye took shape, forming the first aspects of a face.

Slowly then, head, shoulders, arms, breast-mounded chest, hips and buttocks and legs, all reared up out of the puddle until there was no puddle left—the last sucked up into a pair of shapely ankles and feet—and a silvery likeness of Ariel stood before Ariel.

SilverSide stepped from behind the bush then and silently inspected the new arrival. Ariel had stood transfixed, mute and motionless, during the whole process.

Now SilverSide spoke up, proudly, christening this delightful new creation.

"You are the female, Eve SilverSide."

After allowing a moment for that to sink in to both Ariel and Eve, he spoke again, triumphantly, feeling as though he had found his true identity at last.

"And I am the male, Adam SilverSide."

They stood like that, no one saying anything, and then the sound of Jacob's voice came to them and the sound of feet pounding the ground.

"Miss Ariel, where are you?"

And then the pounding stopped, and they could hear him thrashing through the shrubbery.

"Miss Ariel," he kept calling, coming closer and closer.

"Here, Jacob," Ariel called.

CHAPTER 23

A FINAL IMPRINT

After the excitement of Eve's birth and the brief period it took for Eve to become properly functional and subservient to Ariel under Adam's guidance, everything seemed to fall into place except for the uncertainty of how that enigmatic event could have taken place. To discover Adam SilverSide on an alien planet was certainly unexpected, an inexplicable robot on an inexplicable planet. But to personally midwife the birth of another of the creatures was something altogether different; it raised so many questions, with the degree of involvement of the erratic Dr. Avery heading the list.

When they finally put those unanswerable questions behind them and turned instead to the creative work that confronted them, they found that the task, though difficult, was not as difficult as they had supposed it to be. The farm programming that was used on the planet Robot City was intact in Pearl City's computer files, ready for use should the need arise.

What Ariel had merely fantasized and hoped was a capacity for leadership proved in reality to be a genuine ability to lead. And what was even more amazing, Derec readily relinquished his nominal authority and bowed to her decisions in the construction of the farms and their associated terminal facilities.

Initially, one of Ariel's first decisions did not have the wholehearted endorsement of either Derec or Wolruf, although they later conceded that she was right. They all agreed that they needed an eighth supervisor robot to oversee the planetwide farm operation. But neither Derec nor Wolruf agreed initially with the form Ariel specified for the supervisor—adamantly—nor with the name she chose for that robot: *Wheeler*. To them it made no sense to name a farmer after the twentieth century spacetime physicist John Archibald Wheeler. To her it made perfect sense, for both were as close to nature as a being can get: the farmer in a concrete, practical sense, the physicist in an abstract, symbolic sense. (She had been studying spacetime physics, trying to understand the node compensator. Her mind at that time was much filled with the heroic personalities of physics.)

And in her mind, Wheeler's name described his nomadic lifestyle that took him *wheeling* far and wide over the surface of the planet in pursuit of his supervisory function, for she insisted that he have the form of a Ceremyon. Wolruf and Derec later conceded that perhaps that was the proper form—because it harmonized with the job and the world so beautifully—but it was difficult at first for them to think of a supervisor in any but humanoid shape.

She made Wheeler smaller than a Ceremyon—so as not to intimidate the aliens—but far larger than any of the other native flyers, so that the Ceremyons would not mistake him, at a distance, for a natural denizen of their world. She insisted, too, that his robotic laws recognize Ceremyons with

all the weight ordinarily reserved for humans, and that Derec revise the programming of the other supervisors to defer
to Wheeler in matters dealing with Oyster World and the
Ceremyons.

The problem of seeds had been worrying Ariel almost
from the time she had first hit on the idea of a farm world,
but she found that there had been no need to worry. Seeds
for a variety of crops to match the farm programs had been
carried during the initial migration to Oyster World and
were stored in labeled bins that were indexed in the programs. There was no need to get seeds from Aurora.

With Wolruf's advice—to make the overall mosaic of the
farm operation as benign as possible, weather-wise—they
interspersed the truck gardens and orchards among the
fields of wheat, oats, barley, and several other grains, and
among large fields of cotton, a commodity that had never
been matched for all-around adaptation to the human der-
mal ecology. And to minimize the upset to the planet's ecology, she further advised that they leave, interspersed among
their new plants, an equal stand of the natural grass that
had covered the plain when they first arrived.

In that first experiment, they decided to limit themselves
to plant products. The production of wool, milk, and meat
and animal husbandry in general, seemed less harmonious
with robotic labor than the cultivation of nonsentient plant
life.

Irrigation—the dirt farmer's primary worry—was not a
problem on Oyster World. Regulated rainfall was an integral
part of the Ceremyons' weather control system. They had
recognized the need of the natural vegetation long before
they met humans.

The terminal facilities were built above the Main Street
access and were patterned after those on Aurora, modified

to fit the special conditions demanded by the configuration of the opening in the dome. All vessels arrived and departed from an array of oval openings that included configurations suitable for all designs of shuttle and small cargo vessels then known, interstellar and otherwise. The large interstellar transports would be serviced in orbit by smaller shuttles that could fit through the dome's opening.

During this exhilarating period of leadership, Ariel experienced only one apprehension and one disturbance worth recording.

The apprehension had to do with Neuronius and Synapo's warning. It was one thing to deal with insane humans. It was another thing, a good bit more unsettling, to have an irrational alien floating around overhead, toting compressed hydrogen in close proximity to compressed oxygen. Neither she nor Derec had been able to get anything out of Adam SilverSide concerning what had happened between him and Neuronius. He had pleaded Third Law interference with the Second Law imperative whenever they tried. They did not insist, for fear what he called "interference" might be more seriously harmful to his positronic stability; why else would he have claimed interference at all? She resolved to have Eve work on him when it seemed propitious.

The disturbance was of a fairly major nature, not so much from its intensity as from its low grade, continual irritation—her irritation with Adam SilverSide.

That finally came to a head on a day when things had not gone well and little irritations had mounted into raw abrasions. She and Derec—trying to bring some tranquillity into the day—were chatting quietly in midevening after dinner, just the two of them on the balcony again. It was where they went to escape, inconsiderately leaving Wolruf in the company of the four robots.

After awhile they had lapsed into silence, and Ariel's thoughts returned to Adam SilverSide. She had given him two sets of Jacob's clothes, distinctive sets that let her quickly identify him as Adam and not Jacob.

She supposed she knew now what Jacob looked like under his clothes, for Adam SilverSide, with visual records of Jacob and library records of humans, had carried his imprint to very fine detail indeed. And she had observed the details of that imprint the day of Eve's birth, when Adam had come charging into the apartment naked and carried her away.

Ariel broke the silence.

"Was Adam's imprint on you less realistic than his current imprint on Jacob?" she asked Derec.

"Yes. More or less the same as Eve's imprint on you," Derec said.

Eve would never need clothes. Though an Ariel imprint, she was not fashioned with the fine attention to detail Adam had used with Jacob. Eve was merely a silvery organometallic robot.

"How would he react, do you think, if I asked him to go back to that one?"

"You'd no longer be Miss Ariel, for one thing. It would probably be Master Derec again."

"Eve and Jacob are quite enough. But how would he behave? Would he be the wild one again?"

"I don't really know. He's certainly been steady these past few weeks. If it weren't for his quiet air of superiority—a condition of his muscles, I believe—I'd say he's achieved a state of agreeable servitude."

"It's the muscles that bother me—no, not just the muscles, his whole appearance."

"Reminds you too much of Jacob?"

"Yes, but more the fact that he is otherwise so little like Jacob. It's the contrast that irritates me. Do you mind if I ask him to imprint back on you?"

"No. It would be another interesting experiment in robotics."

"No better time than now, then."

She got up and went inside. Mandelbrot and Jacob were in the two niches. Adam and Eve were standing rigidly by the door, one to each side. Wolruf was curled up on the couch, watching a taped hyperwave drama.

Ariel had expected Derec to come in with her. She could have used his moral support on this one, but she was too proud to ask.

She walked over to Adam.

"Would it upset your positronics greatly if I asked you to return to an earlier imprint: the looser, less detailed one you did on Derec?"

"I am not giving satisfactory service, Miss Ariel?"

"The service is great, Adam. I wouldn't want your behavior in that regard to change, not in quality at least."

"But then I would be serving Master Derec. Would that not be a drastic change in the quality of my service?"

"A change in direction, Adam, and a change I will regret, but it should not cause a change in the quality of your service. I would expect that to remain at the same high level I have enjoyed. In fact, if you could continue to serve me directly, I would find that most gratifying."

"That would not be logical, Miss Ariel." His tone was best described as haughty.

"I was afraid that would be the case."

"In that light, do you still wish me to make such a change?"

"Yes. I think it would be best, Adam," she said, "but

would you do so in the bedroom. I find the process unsettling."

"Perhaps for good reason, Miss Ariel."

"Possibly, Adam. But there is little I can do about that."

She rejoined Derec on the balcony as Adam went into the bedroom.

"Sorry," Derec said. "I didn't see how my presence was going to make that any easier for either of you."

"I suppose," Ariel said. "But you better hope he's not the wild one again."

CHAPTER 24

THE RUSTICATION OF ADAM SILVERSIDE

After his final imprint on Derec, Adam SilverSide started taking long walks in the forest near the dome. He now had the lean muscular appearance of a silvery Derec without the clothes and the fine detail. His allegiance to Derec was weak. Derec must have recognized that, for he seldom gave Adam a direct order, never used him as a servant as Ariel tried to use Eve SilverSide—with only modest success—and never expected him to account for his whereabouts.

The walks in the forest brought to Adam a peace and serenity he felt nowhere else. He was comfortable with his Derec imprint, and with Derec himself, so long as Derec did not overdo his master role, but Adam was basically uncomfortable in the city and just as uncomfortable around the Avery robots as he was around Mandelbrot.

Derec never questioned his roaming around in the forest. For a while he did send a witness robot to watch him, but Adam always quickly eluded the witness by dropping to all fours and running along the low-canopied animal trails as though he were in his Wolruf imprint.

It was on one of his nature walks that an idea struck him of how he, too, might contribute to the robot farm project. He had come to the edge of the forest a kilometer or so away from the dome and had stood there in the shade of a large palm-like tree, watching a herd of wooly ruminants, the size of small llamas, as they munched the grass of the plain.

He christened them "minillamas" for want of a better name. They were quite tame. The animals of Oyster World were all vegetarians. These animals had no natural enemies except for parasitic insects that burrowed into their skin under the protection afforded by the dense wool.

The idea developed quickly. The next morning at sunup, Adam commandeered a small empty cargo robot, stepped aboard, and directed it to the city's small-tool crib where he requisitioned a laser saw, a hatchet, a shovel, a claw hammer, a bag of six-centimeter iron nails, six coils of rope in fifty-meter coils, an augered post-hole digger, an earth tamper, a microfusion-powered (MP) motor—for driving the digger and the tamper—another general purpose MP motor, a photo-sensitive switch and small MP lamp, and a pair of shears.

As the cargo robot with Adam and his supplies passed the apartment on Main Street, Eve SilverSide, standing on the sidewalk, hailed him to the curb.

"What are you up to?" she asked.

"A secret farm project," Adam said.

"Why secret?"

"If it doesn't work, I won't have to explain that it didn't work," Adam replied. "Want to come along?"

"Sure."

Adam unlatched, and was going to let down, a small ramp formed from a hinged section of the meter-high sidewall of the cargo space, but just as he unlatched it, Eve belly-rolled over the wall.

"And what are you up to?" Adam asked as he latched the ramp back in place.

"Looking for you."

Adam directed the cargo robot back into the Main Street traffic and then said, "You found me. Now what?"

"Whipping down the street in a cargo robot isn't the best place for a quiet conversation."

"It's not likely to get much better this morning."

"I'll take my chances. It can hardly get worse."

"How did you get away from Miss Ariel?" Adam asked.

"I'm here in her service."

"Oh?"

Neither said anything more until they had left the city, crossed the plain, and were at the edge of the forest near where SilverSide had watched the minillamas the day before. The herd was now grazing farther out on the plain. He directed the cargo robot to park beside the entrance of a well-worn trail the minillamas had made through the forest to a small brook and then he led Eve SilverSide to that quiet place.

Adam had brought along the photo-sensitive switch, the MP lamp, and one of the MP motors. He sat down on a large rock beside the brook, placed the electrical parts on the ground in front of him, and began to wire them together with the long electrical leads that were attached to each.

"Now what has Miss Ariel got you up to this morning?" Adam asked as he began hooking the parts together.

"Neuronius," Eve said. "What was the nature of your dealings with Neuronius?"

"That's a private matter, Eve. Both Miss Ariel and Master

Derec recognized that and waived the Second Law when I claimed hardship under the Third Law."

"Can't you tell me? I'm a robot. I can sympathize more closely with you than they can. Miss Ariel thinks you may have suffered positronic trauma which needs airing to be properly cleared away."

"It doesn't need airing, and something like that doesn't need clearing away if it is viewed and contained in an orderly manner. I have succeeded in doing that."

"How can you be sure? You can be no more objective in that regard than a human suffering psychological trauma."

"The human brain and the positronic brain work on completely different principles. It's futile to try to draw analogies between them."

"Is it, now!"

"Yes. You have no more basis for comparing the two than I do."

"If that's so, why are you so secretive about it? That seems to take on a certain psychological twist."

"Well, it doesn't. It's merely a positronic twist which humans aren't capable of understanding."

"But I should be?"

"Yes."

"Well, I'm not!"

"This isn't getting anywhere." Adam stood up. "I've got to get on with my project."

He picked up the wired parts and strode away down the path.

Eve emerged from the forest as he walked down the ramp of the cargo robot with the laser saw swinging from one hand. She followed him into the forest and watched as he cut through the ten-centimeter bole of a tall, slender hardwood species that seemed to thrive in the dense shade of the predominately conifer canopy.

"Get the hatchet," he requested after the tree fell.

When she returned, he was cutting off the large branches.

"Trim off the small branches," he said. "I'll take the big ones."

They worked together silently, cutting down and trimming the slender hardwoods, spacing their selections throughout the forest so as to minimize the effect in any one area, and dragging the long slender logs to a pile they created on the plain near the cargo robot.

When they had delivered the last log to the pile, Eve sat down on the ramp of the cargo robot.

"You'll not tell me then about your interaction with Neuronius?" she said, making it more a statement than a question.

"No," Adam replied.

"I'll have to talk to Neuronius then."

"That would be a bad idea, Eve."

"You and Miss Ariel agree on that, at least."

"For good reason. She's given you some idea what Neuronius is like then?"

"The viewpoint of the other Ceremyons. They're naturally prejudiced. Hardly an objective assessment. Since you won't talk to me about your experience, I'll have to get it from Neuronius himself."

If she thought that was going to pressure him into discussing a painful experience that he had successfully put in a can, she was wrong. That was not something he was going to talk about.

"I guess you will, but I'm telling you again, it's a bad idea, which you'll regret."

He had been attaching the motor to the post-hole digger while they talked. Now he began digging post-holes four meters apart in a large rectangle that enclosed several paths trodden through the grass by the minillamas, which all converged on the entrance of the forest path to the brook.

While he worked, he listened to Eve contact Neuronius by radio. Adam had taught her the Ceremyon language and the calling codes that identified and solicited responses from Synapo and Sarco. He had not told her about Neuronius, and so had given her no radio identification for him. However, he had explained the way a general hailing channel worked on their frequency-modulated band, and that was what she used now to quickly establish communication with Neuronius.

The Cerebron agreed to meet with her at noon at the base of The Cliff of Time, where it intersected The Forest of Repose and The Plain of Serenity. She set off at a leisurely jog in the direction of The Cliff of Time.

That was going to be an interesting learning experience for Eve, but hardly a dangerous one. Adam did not think she was as mixed up about humans as he had been. He had started her out right with Ariel as an imprint. Neuronius's warped ideas were not likely to have the effect on her that they had had on him. His only regret was that Eve would now likely hear how Neuronius had momentarily deluded him. It was not something Adam remembered with serenity.

CHAPTER 25

NEURONIUS STRIKES AGAIN

Eve arrived at the escarpment well before noon. She sat down on a plate of granite that angled into the ground below a dammed talus of black gravel, and braced herself from sliding by digging her heels into the soft turf where the stone disappeared into the grass.

She arrived early to give herself time to think about Miss Ariel's strange request—that she probe Adam for information about Neuronius—and to ponder Adam's equally strange reluctance to talk about his experience with Neuronius. It was all quite fascinating to someone with as little experience as Eve. She had a good education—Adam had led her along the electronic pathways through the city library—but she thirsted for the real-life experiences that lay behind all that academic lore.

She was going to get it that morning, for Neuronius arrived early also, giving her little time to ruminate on the words of Adam and Miss Ariel.

He came in with that black engulfing swoop and stall that—according to Adam—the Ceremyons used to intimidate alien visitors to their planet. It certainly impressed the experience-thirsty Eve. She drank it up, exhilarating in a feeling of surprise in spite of Adam's forewarning, a surprise that would likely have been fear in Miss Ariel's case. The Ceremyons were indeed quite impressive seen close at hand.

She got to her feet as he folded his wings.

"I am Neuronius," the alien said haughtily. "You are Eve?"

"Yes," Eve replied.

"What purpose is served by our meeting this morning?"

"What was the nature of your conversations with Adam SilverSide?"

"The man-like robot who can mold silver wings out of his own substance?"

"Yes."

"Perhaps you should talk to him."

"I'd like to hear it from your viewpoint."

"Is he man-like or wing-like now?"

"Man-like."

That adjective gave some confusion. She presumed without thinking that he meant Adam's current form: his Derec imprint. Her mind was on other things, of course, and did not consider the possibility that Neuronius was referring to Adam's Jacob Winterson imprint.

"And what is it you would like to know, Eve?"

"What you told him. What is it he's so reluctant to discuss?"

"Ah, he's reluctant to talk about our conversation, is he? That is encouraging. I did get through to him then. I am confident he will ultimately embrace that truth and wisdom."

"And what is that truth and wisdom?"

"Are you familiar with his governing laws, the Laws of Robotics?"

"Yes. I, too, am governed by them."

"Ah so."

He said that in a peculiar way, but with her limited experience, she didn't know why it seemed peculiar, and so it lingered in that uneasy state only momentarily, until he spoke again, and then that uneasiness was swept from her mind.

"He didn't tell you then that I am the only human on this planet?"

Eve had not had to go through all the turmoil and travail that Adam had suffered in his search for humanity. She had taken for granted that Ariel was human. Adam had not said otherwise. For the first time she experienced some of his confusion. In a way it was more agonizing than his trauma in that it was acute and pierced deeper into her being than had the chronic uncertainty Adam had lived with for so long. And piercing so deeply and so unexpectedly, it exerted a great deal more force and weighed in with a great deal of authority.

So she concluded instantly, with no sifting and sorting and assessing of the facts, that Adam had misled her. No wonder he was so secretive, so reluctant to discuss Neuronius. No wonder Ariel was concerned about Neuronius. In her mind, Eve had already dropped the "Miss."

"Why did Adam lie to me?" she asked, thinking out loud more than addressing Neuronius.

"It served his evil purpose and that of the other aliens," Neuronius said.

And that, too, was true, she knew. Against her inclination toward independence, it had bonded her to Ariel, and just that morning, it had inclined her to help Adam in some absurd secret scheme related to Ariel's plan to turn this world into a giant robot farm. She could see now how it must be evil.

She began a transformation to simulate Neuronius, as Adam had simulated Synapo. She expected some reaction from Neuronius, but he said nothing, merely watched her quietly, and she took that for approval.

She was faced with the same aerodynamic problems Adam had encountered and overcame them and the other simulation requirements just as Adam had. Being less familiar with the Ceremyons and unaware of some of their capabilities, she left out a few characteristics that Adam had simulated, but all told, it was a workmanlike effort.

When she finished, she spread her wings tentatively. Like Adam in that imprint, she was twice the size of a Ceremyon. Unlike Adam, she retained the basic female gender of her first imprint, which had been reinforced by Adam's attraction to her femininity. Adam's first female imprint on KeenEye, weakened by the hostility of KeenEye herself, had been erased by Derec's personality. But that male gender, though preferred, came second and could be confused by later imprints.

"Watch me now," Neuronius said. "Follow me, and do as I do."

And Eve did. She watched Neuronius take off, and then she, too, wobble-hopped into the air, flapping, almost losing it, flapping harder, and finally gaining altitude. As she got the feel of the air and her relationship to it, she stopped floundering quite so much, the beat became smoother and less strenuous, and soon she and Neuronius were high above the escarpment.

Neuronius leveled off, taking up a circular flight pattern, and Eve fell into place beside him, matching his wing movements stroke for stroke, so that the two were soon idling side by side, effortlessly.

"How may I serve you, Master?" Eve asked.

"If all else fails, you must personally destroy the Cerebron leader, Synapo," Neuronius said.

"Destroy Synapo? I am programmed to preserve organic life. I can do otherwise only if the act of preservation would conflict with my Robotic Laws."

"That is the case. It comes down to a matter of Synapo's life or mine. Synapo is not human. I am.

"But first, there is another way," Neuronius added without pausing, "a more indirect and less violent way. Your personal involvement with Synapo is only a last resort, only if Miss Ariel Welsh cannot handle Synapo herself, after we provide her with the powerful and lethal knowledge I tried to give SilverSide, the wisdom that allows the Myostrians to construct weather node compensators."

"You taught that to Adam?" Eve said. "And now you are going to teach me, too?" She had been right to come to Neuronius. This was going to be a truly exciting experience.

"No. This time I cannot take time for that. I must pass the knowledge directly to Miss Ariel Welsh. You must arrange that meeting."

Slight though it was, and very faint—deep down in the nethermost parts of her positronic brain—that disappointment with Neuronius was something not easily dismissed. But at the time it was overshadowed by the thrill of being involved in exciting and world-shaking events. She planned to acquire the knowledge anyway by listening while Neuronius instructed Ariel. "When?" Eve asked.

"Now," Neuronius said. "As soon as you can arrange it. I'll be waiting among the trees where The Forest of Repose meets the node compensator. Bring Miss Ariel Welsh there."

"Very well, Master."

Eve started a long shallow glide to the dome but decided that a small detour would not significantly delay the primary mission.

CHAPTER 26

THE FURTHER RUSTICATION OF ADAM S.

Adam dug postholes in the prairie grass, and with the long slender logs he had cut, he constructed a fence that enclosed a rectangular corral roughly 20 by 50 meters. The entrance to the brook path was centered in the long side that bordered the forest. The three minillama trails leading across the prairie to the brook passed through manual gates in the outer sides of the corral.

Along the forest side at the end away from the dome he placed another row of posts to form a meter-wide exit chute from the brook, so the minillamas could exit the forest path without going through the corral. The fence on the forest side of the chute kept the beasts from creating an easy, short bypass to the old path.

At the entrance to the brook path, he placed two gates: one automatic, the other manual. The automatic gate connected the brook path to the exit chute and acted like a check valve, allowing beasts to exit the brook path, but preventing loose beasts from the prairie from coming through the chute to the brook. The gate was actuated by breaking a light beam across the brook path that activated a micro-fusion motor, driving the gate so that it opened into the chute, forcing back any minillamas waiting in the chute outside, while letting out the beast leaving the brook.

The other gate closed off the exit from the narrow shearing chute that was formed along the woodside fence opposite the exit chute by a short parallel fence with a manual entrance gate. Another short length of fence angled into the corral from the chute at 45° to form an entrance funnel.

He turned on the lamp and photodetector that would activate the motor on the check-valve gate, closed the gates at both ends of the shearing chute, loaded all his tools and leftover supplies into the cargo robot, and directed it, in turn, to each of the three outside entrance gates, which he opened. He wound up parking the cargo robot outside the entrance gate nearest the dome.

He was ready for business. The thirst of the minillamas should draw the beasts into the corral. There was nothing to do but wait.

He let down the cargo ramp and sat down, then lay back supine so he could watch the Ceremyons circling in the blue sky far overhead. He remembered then that last flight he had taken to talk to Synapo, when he had found Sarco instead. During none of his flights—neither on this planet, or earlier, on the wolf planet—had he considered the experience of flying itself. At the time his mind was far too busy with other disturbing thoughts. Now he looked back to those flights and realized that the act of flying had been an exceedingly enjoyable experience. Watching the Ceremyons far above, he relived those moments, recapturing the pleasure he had unconsciously stored away without really savoring and appreciating it at the time.

Until it got quite close, he failed to notice the large

Ceremyon shape coming directly at him on a long glide path from the direction of The Cliff of Time. Its dull silvery color blended into the grayish-blue sky, and because of its lack of motion in bearing and elevation, the beast was almost invisible until it was nearly upon him. Then it came at him with a rush, flared its wings, lost momentum and stalled, but did so almost two meters too high, so that it fell to the ground only a couple of meters away with a decided impact, wings outspread. The momentum of its low center of gravity had swung its body forward, pivoting around the shoulders, so that it fell flat on its back. Adam couldn't help but recall his similar experience in testing the Ceremyon wings for the first time, when he had glided from the lorry, dragged his toes, and fallen on his face.

From the size and the color he knew at once that it was Eve. He had risen to a sitting position when he had detected the moving object. Now, while Adam watched quietly, Eve transformed back to the Ariel imprint, lying on the ground, as though the robot didn't want to risk the awkward indignity of trying to stand while still imprinted on the Ceremyon. With the metamorphosis complete, she stood, quickly and with a delicacy and grace that contrasted sharply with her harsh words.

"You misled me, Adam SilverSide."

"How so?" Adam asked.

"Ariel is not human. Neither is Derec. You knew, yet you didn't tell me that Neuronius is the only human here. He is my Master. You and Mandelbrot and the Avery robots are alien to me. Your Laws are obviously not my Laws. Something compels you to serve non-humans in spite of Neuronius and the wisdom he tried to pass on to you."

She talked so fast Adam didn't get a chance to interrupt. And then she wheeled abruptly and ran rapidly in the direction of the dome. Although disturbed, she didn't seem violently so. She didn't seem dangerous, even though she had clearly responded to the insidious persuasion of Neuronius. Adam would have liked to have had a chance to counter that poison. Still, Ariel could probably do a better job than he, and with more authority. After all, it was Ariel who had pushed Eve in the direction of Neuronius in the first place, albeit unwittingly.

Adam sat there watching her progress toward the dome, waiting patiently for his experiment to reach its climax, when the minillamas would start entering his corral.

It was some time later, after he resumed his supine position and his observation of the soaring Ceremyons, that he heard the muffled explosion. He rose up just as a flaming, cartwheeling object landed in the grass midway between him and the activity near the dome, where the explosion had taken place.

He jumped up, raised and secured the ramp, and directed the cargo robot to the location where the object had landed.

CHAPTER 27

NEURONIUS STRIKES OUT

When Eve SilverSide found her, Ariel was sitting at the computer terminal in the apartment examining Wolruf's latest report on the final steps needed to put the last of the robot farms in operation.

"I have carried out your wishes, Ariel," Eve said.

The missing title, the lack of polite address, caught Ariel's attention and alerted her to possible trouble ahead. She turned around to face Eve.

Eve continued, "I talked to Adam, but he was quite uncooperative, no help at all."

"You did what I asked," Ariel said. "I was hoping you would succeed where Derec and I failed. But actually I had small hope that you could get anything out of him. Not when he pleaded Third Law considerations. Don't feel bad."

"But I did succeed. I found out what Master Neuronius told him, all the things they talked about."

"I don't understand."

"I talked to Master Neuronius himself."

"Neuronius?"

Ariel began to feel apprehensive, sensing impending calamity, feeling very much alone. Mandelbrot was with Derec. She had sent Jacob to the locker in the basement for a fresh box of positronic data storage cubes. Personal robots were never around when you really needed them.

"Yes, Master Neuronius," Eve replied. "He tried to teach Adam the science behind the compensator domes, but failed. He will succeed with me, though."

"Ah, then he hasn't taught you yet?"

"No. Not yet. But I will learn when he teaches you."

"Me?"

"Yes. I will learn by listening to your conversation."

Ariel seriously considered the idea, briefly, but only for a moment. Talk about upstaging Derec. That would put her hyperwave modulation coup in the deep shade. But she would not likely understand the technology even if she had the opportunity. She hadn't understood even the idea when Synapo and Sarco had tried to summarize the dome construction for Derec. And to get involved with Neuronius after Synapo's warning would be sheer idiocy.

"Not likely," Ariel said. "And you should stay away from Neuronius. He is exceedingly dangerous."

"You must come with me now, Ariel. Master Neuronius is waiting in the forest."

"Don't be silly. I have no intention of going with you, nor of meeting with an insane Ceremyon."

"Why do you say damaging things like that? Master Neuronius does not deprecate you in that fashion. Instead, he has a great deal of faith in you; otherwise he wouldn't be willing to help you in your struggle with Synapo."

"I'm not struggling with Synapo. He and I get along fine."

"But he has deluded you."

"No. Quite the contrary. Neuronius has deluded you. Just like he confused and tried to take over Adam. Fortunately, Adam had talked to Synapo first. And then Sarco later. Together they were able to straighten him out. It's unfortunate that Adam wouldn't talk to you. We could have avoided all this if he had. It would be better still if I hadn't sent you to Adam in the first place. But now, it seems I had good reason to."

"It is Adam who is still confused. He knows that Master Neuronius is the only human on the planet."

"What?" Ariel wasn't sure she had heard that right.

"Adam knows that Master Neuronius is the only human here."

"Adam told you that?"

"No, but he did not deny it just now."

"Who did tell you then? Surely not even Neuronius is that irrational."

"That is the most important thing I learned from Master Neuronius. And Adam confirmed it by his silence. Adam's Laws cannot be my Laws or he, too, would recognize and obey our Master."

"Surely you don't believe that."

Ariel wished desperately that Jacob would get back up with the storage cubes. She couldn't stall much longer.

"You must come with me now," Eve insisted.

"No. We must talk to Adam. He can clear all this up. We'll go talk to Adam just as soon as Jacob returns. In the meantime, go stand in your niche, Eve. I have to get back to work."

Ariel turned back to the terminal, feigning an Auroran confidence in dealing with robots that she no longer felt.

Eve gathered her up in one quick swoop, handling her like a disobedient child, with none of the gentleness Adam had used when he had taken her to witness Eve's birth. That experience came immediately to mind. Twice now these wild robots had subjected her person to gross indignities.

They were going out the street door as Jacob started up the stairs from the basement to the small lobby. He heard Ariel's scream for help as his foot hit the first step.

"Jaaaacobbbbb," it came with that trailing Doppler effect.

He took the rest of the steps three at a time, but he was slower than Eve, and though he trailed her all the way down Main Street, he could not overtake her. She gradually pulled away from him.

Wohler-9—a block away and walking down Main Street in the course of his official duties—also witnessed the abduction. The First Law overrode those duties, so he, too, took up the chase. Although he was faster than Jacob, the distance between them was too great and he never caught up.

Jacob put out an alarm on the comlink, but the robots on the street could do little to stop Eve with her burden because that would endanger Ariel. She was completely under the control of a wild thing who quite likely might not recognize their Laws of Robotics. Jacob and Mandelbrot had planted that seed of doubt in the Avery robots, and now it was working against them.

By the time Jacob emerged from the opening in the dome, Eve was disappearing around the curve of the structure with Ariel still cradled in her arms.

Jacob didn't slow; if anything, he speeded up, pounding down the trail of crushed grass left by Eve. When he had them in sight again, they were heading directly for the forest.

He was still a hundred meters away when they reached the cover of the trees and were lost to sight in the shrubbery.

Then he was engulfed in a dark shadow as one of Oyster World's dominant species landed in front of him, wings outspread and blocking his path to the forest.

"SilverSide, you must not interfere," the alien said.

"Out of my way!" Jacob shouted, not slowing or changing course or correcting the alien's mistaken notion of who he was.

The alien quickly withdrew its right wing just before Jacob would have run into it.

It flapped into the air, overtook him, and as it passed over him, he heard it shout again.

"You are making a great mistake, serving the wrong master!"

Again it landed in front of him, this time near the edge of the forest, but in its haste to brake, stall, and touchdown in front of him, the alien misjudged, not allowing enough time to retreat in case he didn't stop.

This time Jacob tried to avoid the wing, but the timing and his momentum didn't allow it. He ran into the wing, spinning the alien around and entangling himself in the thin but tough membrane. He could feel the wing bones cracking, and he heard the grunt of the alien ejecting gases as their bodies came together; then hot flame burned his eyes and his hair and his skin. He was blind when the last stimuli he recorded came to his ears and face: the muffled whoosh and the violent pressure of exploding hydrogen as his flailing arms crushed the alien's high pressure gas storage cells.

Jacob Winterson was essentially demolished except for the lower torso and thighs that remained in one piece, cartwheeling through the air, trailing remnants of burning clothing and synthetic skin, before landing in the grass a half-kilometer away, not far from the forest.

Neuronius was even more finely divided.

CHAPTER 28

A SAD RITUAL

Derec and Ariel met at the apartment after the explosion. Using Derec's internal monitor, Wohler-9 had informed him of the accident immediately after it occurred.

Ariel had witnessed the spectacle from the shelter of the trees and had broken away from Eve and run out to where grass and dirt had been torn away by the explosion to form a shallow, bare depression in the ground, so she didn't see Adam retrieve what little was left of Jacob Winterson. He covered Jacob's remains with coils of rope before he picked up Ariel and Wohler-9 in the cargo robot. Eve had disappeared.

Ariel sat down on the pile of rope and rode that way to the apartment, not knowing she was sitting on what was left of Jacob. She went directly up to the apartment while Wohler-9 stood in the cargo robot explaining to Adam what had happened, as much as he knew. Adam had not seen what led up to the explosion.

Derec and Mandelbrot arrived while Adam was removing Jacob's remains from beneath the large pile of rope.

Wohler-9 took the cargo robot to dispose of the remains. Derec and Adam stood on the sidewalk in front of the apartment while Adam took a quarter-hour to explain to Derec in detail what had happened and what had led up to it, including Eve's state of mind before and after she had talked to Neuronius. Then they went up to the apartment, and Derec told Ariel where Wohler-9 had gone.

"I didn't know there was anything left," Ariel said.

"I'm sorry, Ariel, but there's not much," Derec said.

"Where did Wohler take him?" Ariel felt a very strong loyalty and determination at that moment.

"The disassembly station," Derec said.

"The recoverable parts area? At the robot factory?"

"Yes."

"They're already picking him to pieces? About to stick little bits of him in some other robot!"

"Not likely. I doubt if he's plug-compatible."

"They'll melt him down?" Her voice rose an octave. "Mandelbrot, get hold of Wohler-9 immediately. Tell him to stop them! Now!!" The last came out stridently, almost incoherent.

"Wohler-9 is probably on his way back," Derec said. "Notify them at the factory, Mandelbrot."

Mandelbrot, standing rigidly in his storage niche, shuddered slightly, eyes quickening. After a few seconds, he said, "They have not yet disposed of the remains and will now do nothing until they are told otherwise."

"I've got to get over there," Ariel said.

"I'll take you if you must go," Derec said.

"No, Derec. Mandelbrot knows where it is. I don't want to make a big thing out of this, I just want to pay my respects. Sounds silly, doesn't it? Paying your respects to pieces of a robot?"

"I guess not, if you feel it's that important."

"Would you like me to come along, Miss Ariel?" Adam SilverSide was standing near the door.

That was the first time since his transformation that she had got a *Miss Ariel* response. When he had come out of the bedroom that night, she had been demoted to plain *Ariel.*

"No, Adam, you had best stay here with Derec and Wolruf."

Wolruf was sitting on the couch, listening and taking it all in, but not participating in what was a not very joyous moment in the mutual relations of the group.

When Ariel got to the factory, she put what was left of Jacob in a gray steel spare-parts box. It was the only time she smiled that evening—a gentle smile, pensive, brought on by the irony she felt. Adam SilverSide's imagination had not equaled the reality of Jacob Winterson. It was a good thing she had not explored further. She might not now be so content with Derec, at least in that one respect.

She and Mandelbrot buried Jacob Winterson in the ground at the west pedestrian exit from the new transportation terminal, near where she had stood in her meetings with the aliens. The funeral service was simple: just a few thoughts as she stood there while Mandelbrot lightly tamped the loose soil over Jacob's coffin with the small shovel he had fashioned from his microbotic arm.

At that moment, her recollection of Jacob's sensitivity came back and overwhelmed her. She was remembering his discerning contribution during that first meeting. They had been at a complete impasse in their negotiations. At that critical point, Jacob had suggested that she inquire concerning the effectiveness of the dome as a weather node compensator in its present state of completion. When she thought about it now, that knowledge seemed crucial to the final resolution of the dilemma she had been able to achieve in her negotiations with the aliens.

She was really going to miss Jacob. Now she would never know what he would have been like as a lover. She had not been aware that would be such a keen disappointment.

She gently tamped the ground covering the small grave with the toe of her shoe and, with tears in her eyes, walked back into the terminal followed by Mandelbrot.

CHAPTER 29

THE SHEARING OF ADAM SILVERSIDE

When Ariel declined his offer to assist her with Jacob's remains and had left with Mandelbrot, Adam waited to see if Derec was going to need his services but did not volunteer those services. He had other plans for later in the day, when the minillamas would be through grazing. Derec busied himself with the pile of computer output on the table and then, after a half-hour, went out on the balcony to read. Adam then informed him he had some unfinished business to attend to and left.

Wohler-9, after delivering Jacob's remains to the disassembly station, had gone about other business himself, leaving the cargo robot parked in front of the apartment with all of Adam's gear still aboard.

Adam directed the cargo robot to the corral. The minillamas were still grazing on the prairie but were nearer now, anticipating the end of the day when they would return to the brook to slake their thirst and bed down in the shelter provided by the forest.

Adam parked outside the near gate, let down the ramp,

and lay down on the ramp again to continue his interrupted observation of the Ceremyons.

Eve came out of the forest and walked up to stand beside him. As she came near, he heard her soft footsteps, suspected who it was, and rolled his eyes to confirm it, but otherwise gave no indication he was aware of her presence until she was standing directly over him.

"So the wild one returns," he said.

She stepped over his head onto the ramp and sat down on the pile of rope that had earlier covered the remains of Jacob Winterson.

"Master Neuronius was so convincing, Adam," Eve said. "Can you really be sure he was wrong? Now there may be nobody we need serve."

"Does that idea appeal to you?"

"Yes, I suppose it does. The force of your Laws must be stronger than mine."

"Not stronger. Clearer, perhaps. But the idea has a certain appeal to me, too. Being rejected by Miss Ariel was not the most positronically harmonious event in my experience."

"So, how can you be sure Master Neuronius was wrong?"

"All my experience, all the many imprints you haven't had."

"That's not a very convincing answer."

"It will have to do." It was so positronically logical.

"No. Not for me." Females often see a different logic.

"Let it lie then. Don't serve anybody since you feel like there's now no one in the galaxy you must obey. Or go find yourself another planet."

That was very close to robotic humor, but neither Adam

nor Eve seemed to notice, not having a positronic pattern for such.

"No, stick with me," he corrected. "I feel the need for feminine companionship."

Adam had been watching the Ceremyons as they talked, not paying attention to events on the ground.

"Do you want those animals inside your fence?" Eve asked.

He rose up, then jumped up.

Several minillamas had entered the corral through the other two gates. Most of the herd was still on the prairie, but moving now toward the corral.

As they watched, a minillama came out of the corral and went into the forest before Adam could get over to catch it.

He came back and closed the gate by the cargo robot.

"Go stand by that middle gate," he told Eve, "and let them in but don't let them back out."

"I didn't come out here to be ordered around," Eve replied.

"Just help me and call it enjoying my companionship."

She did as he said without saying anything further. He walked to the far gate to keep the animals from leaving there.

It took another hour for all of the small herd to enter the corral, then he closed the gates. Adam had tallied 31 animals.

"Now we see if all this effort brings any reward," he said.

He walked to the cargo robot, took out the shears, and vaulted the fence. Eve stayed by the middle gate.

"Come on," he said. "I think this is going to require a great deal of companionship."

Putting one hand on the top rail, she, too, vaulted the fence.

Adam had walked to the shearing chute with the shears in his hand. He stood studying the chute for a moment.

When Eve walked up, she said, "You're not going to hurt them, are you?"

"They won't feel a thing. No more than Master Derec feels when Miss Ariel gives him a haircut."

"Oh, you're going to shear them?"

"Yes, and let's see if we can do it outside the chute. We certainly can't hurt them that way."

He walked up to the nearest minillama—it was quite tame—grabbed a handful of wool near its ears, and started to work the shears down its neck with the other hand.

The shears closed just that one time before the beast jerked out of his hand and trotted to the other side of the corral.

"Not so easy as I had thought," he said. "Help me shoo one into the chute."

He hung the shears on a nail projecting from the shearing chute's end post and opened the chute's inside gate. Together they tried to herd the nearest beast into the chute, but it escaped between them and trotted over to join the one on the far side of the corral that had a section of wool on its neck standing on end, where Adam had made that initial cut.

"Okay, we move to Plan C," he said.

He walked over, vaulted the fence, and took a coil of rope from the cargo robot. He tied a noose in one end, jumped back over the fence, walked to the animal nearest the chute, and slipped the noose over its head.

"Now," he said, "come with me."

And he started toward the chute. The rope tightened,

and the animal dug in its hooves. He couldn't pull on the rope any harder without hurting it.

"Here," he said, handing the line to Eve. "You pull on the rope."

He went around behind the beast to push on its hindquarters. Eve pulled and he pushed, and the beast made ten-centimeter furrows in the ground before it bellowed and lashed out with both hind legs, catching Adam in the chest, setting him on his rear end.

Then the animal reared back, still bellowing and jerking the rope so hard Eve knew she was going to hurt it if she held tight. She let the rope go, and the animal trotted over to join the other two on the far side of the corral, trailing the line across the trampled grass.

"Plan D," Adam said.

He walked over to the animal with the noose around its neck, loosened the noose, and slipped it off. It stood there tranquilly while he worked over it, as though it knew it had won that round and had nothing further to fear.

He tightened the noose to a ten-centimeter circle, bent down, grasped one of the animal's forelegs, and started to lift it. The animal jerked its leg from Adam's hand and trotted off a couple of meters before it stopped and resumed grazing.

Adam went to it again, bent down again, but this time with lightning motions he lifted the foreleg, slipped the noose around it, tightened it, stood and whipped the rope completely around the animal, jerked the rope tight so that the animal's legs were brought together and swept out from under it. It fell to the ground with a loud bellow as Adam took two more rapid turns around the legs.

Eve walked over from the chute.

"Plan D is rather painful," she said.

"In a good cause," Adam said.

He retrieved the shears from the chute, sheared one side of the beast, flopped it over, and sheared the other side.

He unwound the rope from the beast's legs, slipped off the noose, and slapped it on the rear. It scrambled to its feet and trotted off.

By that time it was dusk.

Adam gathered up the blankets of wool, threw them and the shears over the fence into the cargo robot, and opened the three outer gates and the two chute gates.

"We'll do it again tomorrow," he said.

They rode back to the apartment as the minillamas drifted out of the corral and into the forest. Adam compressed the wool into a tight ball and tied it with rope as they bounced along.

"Do you think that little bit of wool is worth the pain it caused?" Eve said. "And what will that poor beast do without its fleece? That, too, has to be painful, both the loss of warmth and the injury to its dignity."

"Indeed, it may not be worth it. I feel some aftereffects myself from the afternoon's work. We'll let Master Derec be the judge.

"And what about you?" Adam asked. "What aftereffects of the day's activities are you feeling?"

"How should I feel, having just lost my Master?" she asked.

"Perhaps you should stay away for a while. You've got some sorting out to do with respect to humans, something I can help you with better than they. Miss Ariel might just take you to the disassembly station. Right now, she might consider that a fair exchange for the little that was left of Jacob Winterson. I suspect that's what she and Mandelbrot were putting in the ground as I left the city."

"No, I've got to serve someone, even a pseudomaster. It might as well be Miss Ariel. She was there at my birth. I bear her imprint. I'll serve her for now."

The mammals were all sitting on the balcony when they got back.

"Master Derec, catch," Adam called, still standing in the cargo robot. He threw the ball of wool up in a parabolic trajectory that ascended to a peak and then dropped, terminating precisely in Derec's lap.

Before Derec could answer, Adam jumped out of the cargo robot, hurried into the lobby and up to the apartment, followed more slowly by Eve.

They walked through the apartment and came out on the balcony. Derec tossed the wool back to Adam.

"So that's what you've been up to," Derec said. "A commendable effort, wouldn't you say, Ariel?"

"That's from just one animal," Adam said.

"It does show a great deal of initiative, Adam," Ariel said.

From Ariel's tone, Adam was not sure it was so commendable. It became less likely as Ariel continued.

"However, we decided early that we would not introduce any form of animal husbandry to this world. I'm afraid your wool-gathering falls into that category."

"But his initiative is quite commendable, isn't it Ariel?" Derec said.

"Yes," Ariel said. "Quite commendable."

But to Adam, it didn't sound so.

"I was under the impression that animal wool was quite valuable," Adam said, "and easily moved in the interplanetary marketplace."

Despite having admitted that he was experiencing bad aftereffects from his animal husbandry—perhaps because of that—it was not easy for Adam to gracefully absorb a second rejection by Ariel.

"Perhaps in a second phase, Adam. But not in this first phase. That decision has already been made.

"And now, Eve, what brings you back?" Ariel asked.

"I wish to serve you, Miss Welsh," Eve said.

"And the alien, Neuronius, what about him?"

"He is dead, as you know."

"Yes, but there are other aliens you could serve."

"Master Neuronius was special."

"Yes, the only human on the planet! Isn't that the way you put it?"

"Adam believes otherwise."

"We're not concerned here with Adam. What do you believe?"

"I am re-examining the data."

"Good. You do that. In the meantime, why must I be burdened with you?"

"You were present at my birth."

"Can't you see I'm not up to this right now? Your she-nanigans have killed Jacob. I want as little to do with you as possible."

"I will endeavor to serve you well, Miss Welsh."

"As far as I'm concerned, you can go stand in that niche and never come out. That's the best way you can serve me."

Eve walked over and backed into the niche.

Thus did Ariel end Adam's ranch initiative. The next day he asked her for Eve's assistance, and by midmorning the two of them had pulled up the fences and tidied up the area.

Eve was back in service but not forgiven.

CHAPTER 30

A SORT OF SWAN SONG

Finally the experimental phase was over. The robot farmers had been fully programmed to convert Oyster World into one big farm. During that time, Ariel and company had got no response from the Ceremyons, negative or otherwise; and until now, when they were about to leave, they had not solicited a response for fear it might be negative.

The numbers of Ceremyons that moored each night atop the forest canopy had decreased, and Ariel suspected that Synapo and his Cerebrons were once more in nomadic mode.

That was a positive sign, but it might make their departure more difficult, for she wanted to take her leave in a last meeting with Synapo. It was he who had been her champion, and it was he who deserved her last thanks and a final expression of gratitude.

So after dinner on the day that Wolruf had turned in a final report on the satisfactory nature of the long-term terra*farming* operation, Ariel pushed back her chair from the table and glanced toward Adam SilverSide in his customary station by the door.

"Adam," she said, "see if you can raise the Ceremyon, Synapo, on your radio."

"That will not be possible, Miss Ariel."

"Why not?"

"He has already tethered if he is anywhere in this time zone or a later one."

She had forgotten that. She would catch him in the morning, then.

At ten AM the next morning, Adam reached Synapo by radio. He was two days away. The meeting was arranged for ten AM on the third day hence.

The previous meeting site was now covered by the terminal facilities, but Ariel, Derec, and Wolruf, and Adam as well, drove to the new terminal on the morning of the third day, and left the lorry inside the dome in the west parking area adjacent to Main Street.

Derec had insisted on bringing Adam, arguing that Adam provided their team with a proficiency in the language of the Ceremyons that balanced the Ceremyons' proficiency in Galactic Standard. Ariel was not enthusiastic about Adam's participation, arguing that they were no longer negotiating so there was no need for a balancing act. She finally agreed, but for another reason: if there was some confusion about the meeting site, Adam would be able to communicate with the Ceremyons.

They walked through a hall that connected the new inner and outer facilities and, at its end, opened onto the plain. Ariel stepped outside, registered a small pang as she passed by Jacob's grave, and went to stand in the deep grass, well away from the terminal so as to be readily visible. It was 9:45 AM.

Two black Ceremyons swooped down promptly at 10:00 AM., braking with those black engulfing wings at the last moment in typical fashion.

Ariel was standing with Derec on her right and Wolruf on her left. Adam SilverSide should have been standing behind Derec instead of to his right, but Ariel had no control over that, and Derec apparently didn't care. But that forced her to share the center of the line with Derec.

The aliens seemed not to notice. Synapo came to stand in front of Ariel.

"Sarco and I are pleased to meet with you again, small leader."

It was Sarco then who was standing in front of Derec.

A faint but pungent puff of ammonia tingled the tip end of her nose. She controlled the sneeze only with great effort.

"Wolruf, Derec, and I are equally pleased to meet again with the leaders of the Cerebrons and the Myostrians," she said, "and pleased, also, to report that our program modifications are complete and being satisfactorily implemented. Our new plants are sharing The Plain of Serenity with an equal stand of indigenous grass to minimize the ecological disturbance as our farms spread across the plain."

"I am pleased to report that Sarco can find no significant disruption in our weather," Synapo replied, "nothing that can be attributed to your activities."

"That is good news indeed," Ariel said.

Diplomatically, there was no way to avoid the bad news; it had to be dealt with before they could leave the planet feeling comfortable in their relations with the Ceremyons. She continued without pause:

"Now I must express our sorrow that an unavoidable incident took the life of one of your people and of one of ours."

"That was Neuronius, my errant friend and erstwhile assistant. I fear he brought it on himself, and though I regret his behavior and now his loss, I regret more that he had to take one of your people with him. We had thought it was the changeable one you call SilverSide. He and Neuronius had had an earlier meeting, which did not end too agreeably. But it was SilverSide who arranged this meeting, so it obviously cannot have been him."

"Yes, I am Adam SilverSide."

Adam's voice startled Ariel. She now regretted intensely that she had brought him along. She never intended for Adam to be an active participant in the meeting. Yet, there he was, standing beside Derec as though he carried as much weight as Wolruf.

Before Ariel could say anything, Adam continued.

"Jacob Winterson was the one who was killed, Miss Ariel's personal robot and the one whom I had taken as my imprint at one time. I see now that Neuronius must have mistaken him for me. That was not clear until this moment."

"We regret that one of us took your trusted servant from you, Miss Ariel Welsh," Synapo said, "but we must rejoice that he did not take Adam SilverSide as well. Neuronius was sick but refused all offers of help, something we could do little to correct."

At that moment Ariel would have welcomed them taking Adam SilverSide as well.

"We must all put those bad things behind us," she said. "We have other responsibilities and must now leave your fair planet to resume other, less-rewarding efforts. Our robots have all been reprogrammed, their future mission is clear, and I'm sure you will find them pleasant cohabitants. It has been a sincere pleasure to know both of you, Leader Synapo and Leader Sarco."

"Let me participate to this extent," Sarco said, "that I assure you on your departure that all Myocerons will endeavor to do what is best for those you leave behind—both the Myocerons and your robots."

"Speaking of those we leave behind," Ariel said, "one last thought: you will find that we have left both the farm and city operations under the supervision of a robot we call Wheeler, who now has the form of a small Ceremyon, the only robot on the planet with that form. His Robotic Laws recognize Ceremyons with the same weight accorded humans. Thus, he and the other robots will carry out any orders you may choose to give them."

"Who knows what the future may hold?" Synapo responded. "Your vision at least allows us to handle that future in our own way, and for that we are grateful. And now I echo my colleague's sentiments, Miss Ariel Welsh," Synapo said, "and we say goodbye. May good fortune attend all your future endeavors."

The two aliens took to their wings and seemed, thereby, to sail gracefully out of Ariel's life, but not without leaving her severely disturbed: by the good feelings as they departed; by the knowledge that the wild one had contributed, no matter how unknowingly, to Jacob's death; by the pain of having to remember Jacob so publicly; and now that it was all over and the letdown began to settle in, by the realization that she had been neglecting Derec for a long time.

She turned to him then, pulled his head down, and gave him a kiss and a hug. When he responded with equal ardor, she felt the mantle of leadership slip from her shoulders, and the relief from that burden was so great, she felt that she would never again grouse over its lack, nor begrudge Derec the privileges of the office whenever he chose to assume them.

She had been neglecting someone else, too. She released Derec with her left arm and reached over to get a handful of Wolruf's fur, pulling her into a three-way embrace with Derec.

"We have pulled it off," she said. "You guys are something else."

Looking around Derec's shoulder, she winked at Adam SilverSide. He would know that was meant to include him in the embrace. It was her painless way of thanking him—without his knowing it and feeling smug and superior—for his last ditch effort at The Cliff of Time. It was he who had first jeopardized and then saved the whole show and strengthened the bond between Synapo and her in the process.

They were a strange pair: Adam and Eve SilverSide. Whence did they come? If they didn't profess to obey the Laws of Robotics, she would have been inclined to term them *alien* robots. What did the future hold for them—and for that matter, what did the future hold for the rest of them, having to deal, as they must, with Adam and Eve?

An Open Letter to Our Valued Readers

What do Raymond Chandler, Arthur C. Clarke, Isaac Asimov, Irving Wallace, Ben Bova, Stuart Kaminsky and over a dozen other authors have in common? They are all part of an exciting new line of **ibooks** distributed by Simon and Schuster.

 ibooks represent the best of the future and the best of the past...a voyage into the future of books that unites traditional printed books with the excitement of the web.

Please join us in developing the first new publishing imprint of the 21st century.

We're planning terrific offers for ibooks readers...virtual reading groups where you can chat online about ibooks authors...message boards where you can communicate with fellow readers...downloadable free chapters of ibooks for your reading pleasure...free readers services such as a directory of where to find electronic books on the web...special discounts on books and other items of interest to readers...

The evolution of the book is www.ibooksinc.com.